GREED

Chris Ryan was born near Newcastle in 1961. He joined the SAS in 1984. During his ten years there he was involved in overt and covert operations and was also Sniper team commander of the anti-terrorist team. During the Gulf War, Chris was the only member of an eight-man team to escape from Iraq, of which three colleagues were killed and four captured. It was the longest escape and evasion in the history of the SAS. For his last two years he has been selecting and training potential recruits for the SAS.

He wrote about his experiences in the bestseller *The One That Got Away* which was also adapted for screen. He is also the author of the bestsellers *Stand By, Stand By, Zero Option, The Kremlin Device, Tenth Man Down, The Hit List, The Watchman, Land of Fire, Greed, The Increment, Blackout, Ultimate Weapon* and *Strike Back. Chris Ryan's SAS Fitness Book* and *Chris Ryan's Ultimate Survival Guide* are also published by Century.

He lectures in business motivation and security and is currently working as a bodyguard in America.

CHRIS RYAN

GREED

arrow books

Reissued in the United Kingdom by Arrow Books in 2008

20 19

Copyright © Chris Ryan, 2003

Chris Ryan has asserted his right under the Copyright, Designs and Patents
Act, 1988 to be identified as the author of this work.

This novel is a work of fiction. Names and characters are the product of the
author's imagination and any resemblance to actual persons,
living or dead, is entirely coincidental

First published in the United Kingdom in 2003 by Century
First published in paperback in 2004 by Arrow Books

Arrow Books
The Random House Group Limited
20 Vauxhall Bridge Road, London, SW1V 2SA

Addresses for companies within The Random House Group Limited can be
found at: www.randomhouse.co.uk/offices.htm

The Random House Group Limited Reg. No. 954009

www.randomhouse.co.uk

A CIP catalogue record for this book
is available from the British Library

Penguin Random House is committed to a sustainable future for
our business, our readers and our planet. This book is made from
Forest Stewardship Council® certified paper.

Printed and bound in Great Britain by Clays Ltd, Elcograf S.p.A.

Typeset by SX Composing DTP, Rayleigh, Essex

ACKNOWLEDGEMENTS

To my agent Barbara Levy, editor Mark Booth, Hannah Black, Charlotte Bush and all the rest of the team at Century.

PROLOGUE

A smear of blood was still visible around the edge of the hand, where it had been severed cleanly from the rest of the arm. The flesh around the fingers had started to tighten and decay. On the second finger there was a twisted gold ring, but the metal had been streaked and discoloured, as if exposed to a sudden, searing heat.

The Labrador dropped the hand on to the ground, shaking it free from its mouth.

Jack Turner looked up. It was early morning, the dew still fresh on the fields. The dog had bounded back from a small patch of woodland, on a hill that looked across the Kent countryside and out to Ashford beyond. Turner took this walk with the dog every morning. Never before had he come across anything more interesting than an empty beer can.

He bent down, examining the hand more closely. The skin retained a soft, creamy colour. Whoever it once belonged to, it was certainly a woman. 'Dodger,' Turner shouted to the Labrador. 'Follow, boy.'

He marched quickly in the direction of the woods. The wind was whistling through the trees and there was a distinct chill in the air. In the background, Turner could hear a pair of blackbirds fluttering away. The dog bounded ahead of him, panting as it ran across the wet ground.

The earth lay open and fresh, like a wound cut into the surface of the ground. Turner could feel his pulse quickening as he approached. At the centre of a clearing between the trees there was an open pit, stretching ten feet across and five or six feet deep, the size of a mass grave.

Turner slowed his pace as he approached. Whatever sights might await him there, he sensed his stomach was going to heave.

Only a few parts of the body could be seen as he peered gently across the lip of the trench. He could see a foot, a part of what might once have been an elbow, the fragments of a spinal chord, a tuft of what could have been blonde hair. The blood had all long since seeped into the ground and disappeared. Next to the body lay two yellow canvas travel bags, singed but still intact.

Holding his breath, Turner leapt into the trench, took the first bag between his hands and unzipped its chord. He looked briefly inside, closed his eyes, then looked again. Bank notes. Thousands of bank notes, packed into neat, tidy wedges.

Reaching inside, he took out a sheaf of euros, dollars and pounds and held it in his hands. The notes were high denominations – fifties mostly, with a few hundreds thrown in as well. Turner had never seen so much money in his life, nowhere near. Without counting it he had no way of knowing, but he guessed there must have been a million, maybe much more, in the one bag he had opened. He reckoned he had at least two grand in his fist alone.

Turner reached for the second bag. Already he could sense what he might find there. He pulled back its zipper, reaching inside. Another pile of notes, packed tightly together.

The wad of notes in his hand he stuffed into the pocket of his jacket. Then he re-zipped the bags, making sure he left them exactly as he found them.

Scrambling against the mud, Turner pulled himself up from the ditch and shook the dirt free from his hands. The Labrador nuzzled up close to his leg. 'I'll tell you what, Dodger old boy,' Turner said gruffly, 'a dead woman and several million pounds in a ditch – there must be quite a story behind that.' He reached into a pocket, took out his mobile phone and dialled 999.

ONE

The woman sat perfectly still, examining her face in the mirror, and her expression revealed disappointment with the person looking back. Her hand moved slowly across the dressing table. She took a brush and applied a thin dusting of make-up to her face, carefully painting away the traces of a tear on her cheek. Behind her, a black robe and veil lay draped across the bed.

Nasir bin Sallum closed his mouth and clenched his stomach muscles tight so that not even the sound of his breath would escape. He let his eyes rest upon her for a moment, admiring the delicate upwards slope of her neck and the polished smoothness of her skin.

It is important for an assassin to appreciate his victim before he kills her.

With her right hand she started running a brush through her long black hair. Sallum remained silent, gripping the length of thin, taut climbing cord between his hands. Outside the apartment block – situated in the Al Mansorah district of Riyadh – he had already removed his shoes, replacing them with a pair of socks thick enough to make almost no sound as he moved swiftly across the carpet.

Suddenly, he sprang forwards and ran towards her chair. He could see her ears twitch as she heard the first stride. He could see her eyes move up as she caught sight of movement in the mirror. And he could see her fist tighten the grip on her hairbrush as she felt the floor vibrate under the weight of her assailant. But her reactions were slow. She knew something was happening but in the few seconds available to her she was unable to react.

It's like strangling chickens on the farm. Sallum slipped the rope around her neck in one swift movement. He pulled sharply, tugging her neck backwards, and could hear the breath escaping from her lips, the stretching of the muscles running through her neck. He leant forward, bending towards the mirror, and their eyes met in the glass. He could read the thoughts written in her expression. Who is this man? Why is he killing me?

Sallum pulled harder, twisting the rope into her skin. *It's not her fault I am here this afternoon. There is no need to hurt her unnecessarily.*

Her eyes were bulging from her head now, the pupils enlarged. The pressure from the rope prevented any air travelling through her throat and her breathing had stopped, diminishing the flow of oxygen into her heart. Her grip on the hairbrush tightened and her arm tried to lift itself to strike her assailant, but the strength was already fading from her. Then her grip suddenly collapsed and the brush tumbled on to the dressing table before bouncing on to the floor.

Sallum worked the muscles in his forearms, steadily increasing the pressure of the rope on her neck. In the mirror he could see her eyelids blink and then slowly close. She was dead.

Sallum released the rope and let her body curl gently forwards until her head was resting amid the make-up on the dressing table, next to a picture of herself with her family, all of them having a picnic somewhere among green fields and tall trees. He reached down to check her pulse. It was as he expected.

Sallum relaxed, stretching his muscles. It was important to exercise after an execution. You had to stop the tension building up in your back. He glanced through the tiny flat. It consisted of just this small bedroom, a shower room, a kitchen you could hardly stand up in, and a sitting room furnished with a single sofa, a television and a DVD player. The place was shabby, poor and impersonal: the furniture all looked as if it had been picked up second-hand.

Well, what could an English woman who divorced her Saudi husband expect?

Her handbag was lying at the foot of the bed. Sallum took it in his hands and examined the contents. The usual junk women carry around with them – lipsticks, mirror, address book and some old photographs – but it also held her passport, her driving licence, her Saudi identity card and a letter detailing her appointment with the minister.

She had changed since the passport photograph had been taken four years previously. She was older, but also sadder – at a glance Sallum could tell that those four years had not been kind to her. Asiya al-Kazim, according to her passport, was 26, born in Wolverhampton of Muslim parents, but married to a Saudi man for three years, and subsequently divorced. Nobody would miss her for days.

Sallum moved to the dressing table, picked up a jar of nail varnish, and began to coat his fingernails with the pink liquid. Five manicures over the past two weeks had worked – his nails looked just like a woman's. Taking the mascara next, he dabbed make-up carefully on to his eyelashes. Then he picked up a stick of red lipstick, and peering close to the mirror, applied a thin layer to his lips. Get it right, he reminded himself: enough to make him look like a woman, but not so much that it made him look tarty.

Lips, eyes, and nails. That should be enough to fool anyone.

Sallum picked up the black robe from the bed and fitted it over his shoulders. Then he lifted the black veil over his face, adjusting the cloth so it draped over his shoulders, completely obscuring his face. He looked across at the mirror: only his dark eyes and red lips were discernible through the veil. The rest of his face was completely masked.

From his bag he slipped out a pair of plain black women's shoes with a half-inch raised heel. He pulled on a pair of nylon pop socks then slipped on the shoes and took a few unsteady paces across the floor. He had practised several times, but walking precisely like a woman seemed like one of the hardest skills for a man to acquire.

So long as I don't speak or lift my veil I will pass for her.

He walked back through the door and shut it carefully behind him. The corridor was empty as he made his way back down to street level.

Sallum stepped out into the baking heat of the Riyadh afternoon, the veil and the robes already causing him to sweat.

I must not dawdle. The day's killing is not yet complete.

Matt Browning let his finger rest on the second button of Gill's blouse. He slipped his right hand inside the soft white cotton, gripping the taut, lively breast hidden behind her bra. He could feel it stiffen beneath his palm. His left hand gripped her side then worked its way along her back, rubbing the skin and stimulating the nerve endings beneath. They had been together nearly two years now, and Matt knew the spots, and how to work them.

He could hear her breath quickening. Outside, a hundred feet below her twelfth-storey apartment, waves were crashing against the rocks of the Marbella shore-line. An early evening wind was starting to whip in from the Mediterranean, rustling through the curtains. Matt could feel Gill's sharp, red fingernails clawing through the hairs on his chest.

His hands moved faster across her skin, unclasping her bra, plunging inside her jeans, and their lips collided. Matt could feel her hands unbuckling the belt of his trousers. He tore the jeans from her, flung them on to the cold, limestone floor, and suddenly he was on top of her, his face nuzzling into the soft skin of her neck, his body thrusting into her. 'Do it to me,' she muttered. 'Do it to me now.'

Half an hour later, Matt lay back on the sofa, spent. A ripple of quiet sensory satisfaction ran through every muscle of his body. He was tired yet invigorated. Christ, he thought. Gill has the shortest fuse of any woman I have met. She could kill a man who turns up ten minutes late for a date.

How do I possibly tell her?

He looked into mellow, green eyes and flicked a lock of long auburn hair away from her face. Gill looked good just about anyway you could imagine: in jeans and a T-shirt, dressed up for a formal party, in her swimsuit down on the beach, or covered with kids' paint after working down at the nursery. But she looked best of all naked. She was completely comfortable in her own skin, treating it the way some women treated an expensive new outfit: as something she was proud of, and wanted to show off to the man she was with. The demure, quietly spoken girl was unpeeled whenever he undressed her, revealing the powerful, passionate woman hidden underneath.

Christ, thought Matt, the thought running through his brain like a tape stuck in a loop. How do I possibly tell her?

'I think we'll have a live band rather than a disco,' said Gill. 'That would be nicer, don't you think?'

Matt nuzzled his face into her back, aware of the thin layer of post-coital sweat coating her body. He flicked his tongue against her earlobe distractedly.

Gill pushed him away. 'And we need to decide what the readings are going to be. I don't suppose you have some special poem.' She looked at him and smiled indulgently. 'No, I didn't think so.'

Standing up, Matt reached for his boxer shorts and pulled them up around his waist.

'There are just so many choices to make.'

Matt took a deep breath. That temper – that was what worried him. 'There isn't going to be any wedding,' he said at last.

'What do you mean there isn't going to be a wedding?'

'There isn't going to be a wedding because I'm a loser and a fuck-up,' said Matt. 'I don't deserve a princess like you.'

Geoff Burton looked down at the passport, then up into the eyes of the woman standing in front of him. Light brown, with a trace of make-up around them.

Sallum could read what he was thinking: they all look the same under those bloody veils.

I might as well be a camel for all he cares.

Burton was a rugged man, six feet tall. He looked hot in his uniform, even though the Riyadh Hilton was air-conditioned. Asiya al-Kazim was due to see the minister at three. She had half an hour. 'You're Asiya al-Kazim?' Burton said.

Behind his veil, Sallum nodded. He handed across the letter of appointment. It was written on Ministry of Defence headed notepaper, an invitation sent three weeks ago. This soldier will have heard of her, Sallum decided. Her name had been splashed across the British papers a few months ago. A Wolverhampton girl, a Muslim, Asiya had married a Saudi who charmed her off her feet, then moved out to Riyadh. She'd soon realised she wasn't allowed to drive, couldn't shop, couldn't work, and her husband beat her senseless every night. So she'd decided she'd rather be back in Wolverhampton. She divorced the Saudi, then discovered the catch. Under Saudi law, she couldn't leave the country without her ex-husband's permission, so she was trapped here. A couple of backbench MPs had been making a fuss about why British soldiers were helping defend a country in which a British woman was effectively held prisoner. Sallum had researched her story, and chosen her because she had an appointment with the minister. And because he knew a British soldier would not try to search a Saudi woman. She was the perfect cover.

'Got your ID card?'

Sallum fished in the handbag, pulling out the card and handed it across. Behind the veil he lowered his eyes demurely. He could see the solider glancing at his nails, noticing how neatly trimmed and varnished they were. Just like a woman.

'And a driving licence?' said Burton.

Sallum handed it across. Burton scanned the documents then looked back up into Sallum's eyes.

Sallum could tell the man wanted to frisk him, but the latest briefings from the embassy said the Saudis objected to their women being searched by non-Muslim soldiers. Anyway, he would have been told she had already been searched by the Saudi officials outside the hotel. The British had insisted on that condition when they'd agreed to stop searching Saudi women. It was so rare for a woman to have any official business in a country where they weren't allowed to work, the restriction hardly seemed worth arguing about.

'The minister is in that room down there,' said Burton, pointing.

Beneath his veil, Sallum permitted himself a thin smile.

The salty smell of the sea kicked through the evening air. Matt took a deep breath, filling his lungs, and looked out across the wide expanse of the Mediterranean. The insults and abuse Gill had flung at him in the last few hours were still stinging his ears.

He started to run, his feet hitting a steady rhythm against the sand. Running had always been his way of relaxing. The pounding of his muscles, the straining of his calves and the thump of his feet against the ground combined to send the blood rushing through his veins, sharpening his reactions and clearing his mind. It was running that had first taken him into the Army, and then the SAS. And it was quickness and agility that had qualified him for the special forces: he wasn't the toughest soldier they had ever seen, but he was one of the fastest.

Whatever my troubles might be, at least the sun is on my back and the sand beneath my feet.

He looked up towards the Last Trumpet. It was a perfect location for a restaurant. Perched on a scenic hilltop, a kilometre west of Puerto Banus, it was a short drive from Marbella and within easy striking distance of the smart hotels and plush villas that lined this part of the coast. The balcony overlooked the jagged hills tumbling into the ocean, and into the sand-lined coves below. On a clear day you could see the north-African coastline twenty miles away. On a bad day you could watch the thunderclouds looming over the sea. It was the kind of view that made people want to linger and order another cocktail.

But selling a few cocktails and a few hamburgers are never going to make enough money to get me out of this jam.

It hurts now, he told himself, but I have done the right thing. Maybe it's old-fashioned, but a man shouldn't marry unless he is able to offer his wife a decent and secure life. Instead of debts and death-threats. Gill deserves better than that. It might hurt her now. But if we married she'd be hurt much worse. If I love her – and I do – then it's better this way. It will hurt me more and her less – and that's the way it should be.

Matt started to consider what life without Gill might be like. He had known her most of his life. Her older brother Damien had been his best friend when they were all growing up together in south London. For years she had just been Damien's funny little sister, but when she'd moved to Marbella after her family started the bar, he had realised that she'd blossomed into a poised and graceful young woman.

Our lives have been woven together. Hard to unravel them now.

Matt pushed himself faster, picking up speed.

Whatever else I might lose, I won't lose my strength or my fitness. It might be the only thing I can rely on.

The bar was already starting to come to life as Matt stepped on to the balcony, still gasping for breath after sprinting the last few hundred yards. The maid was on her hands and knees scrubbing the floors, and at the back Pablo was making the evening delivery from the village: a couple of sackloads of potatoes for the chips, some steaks, hamburgers and chicken breasts, and plenty of peas and carrots. The diners at the Last Trumpet were not great gourmets, but they knew what they liked, and the servings were always huge.

Matt picked up some of the post that was lying on the bar: brown envelopes, with names and addresses printed by computer. Bills and bank statements – he didn't need to open them to know that the news would be bad.

If I'd realised that life outside was quite as difficult as this, I might have stuck it out in the Regiment.

Sallum stepped away from the soldier and walked swiftly down the length of the hotel's corridor. Fools, he reflected. They should have known better than to trust the Saudi guards to search me. Surely they know the

14

Saudi army is riddled with supporters of the Holy Cause.

He knocked lightly on the door. Richard Brent, the minister's assistant, opened the door and guided Sallum to the sofa in the centre of the room. 'Some tea, Mrs al-Kazim?' he said politely. 'Or maybe some water?'

Sallum shook his head. Only delay is dangerous, he reminded himself. His eyes quickly scanned the room. Two men, both middle-aged and weak. No cameras, no security guards. The window was open, but they were on the seventh floor of the hotel and there was no building overlooking them. Everything was exactly as he had been told it would be.

'Pleased to meet you, Mrs al-Kazim,' said David Landau, standing up and offering his hand. Beneath his black robe Sallum eased his hand to the front of his jeans and pulled out the Heckler & Koch P7 pistol, equipped with a silencer. He chose the P7 because its unique firing system made it the perfect concealed weapon. It could be carried safely while fully loaded – Sallum knew of assassins who'd shot their own genitals off – but as soon as you gripped the handle it was unlocked and ready to fire. It weighed less than two pounds, and yet its four-inch barrel made it an effective deadly weapon at close range. It was the fastest gun he knew of.

Sallum steadied himself, switching from the posture of a woman to a man. Leaning slightly forward on his left foot, he thrust the pistol upwards, his hands and the gun breaking through the robes.

Very few men are perfect shots with both their left

and right hands. Sallum was not one of them: he reckoned he was a ten per cent better shot with the right hand than with the left. At this range it didn't matter. He could hit both men – and the P7 was designed to be fired with either hand. He levelled the pistol on Landau, loosening off three rounds in close succession. Then he turned the pistol towards Brent, who was starting to flee towards the door. He had covered only two steps before Sallum stabbed the trigger three times in quick succession. Each of the six shots was effectively muzzled by the silencer, the noise no louder than a cork being pulled from a wine bottle.

Landau fell backwards, hitting the sofa with the side of his head. The first shot had blown through his skull, the second ripped into his heart, and the third cut open his neck. Blood flowed swiftly on to the fabric, staining the surface of the seat.

Brent crumpled into a heap on the floor. The first bullet had shattered his forehead, the second took out his left eye. The third bullet had hit him in the centre of the chest. Oxygenated blood started to gurgle from his mouth and a deathly moan escaped from his sagging lips.

One more bullet for each man, just to make sure.

Sallum knelt down next to Brent, clipped a fresh magazine into the P7, wedged the barrel of the pistol into the man's ear and squeezed the trigger. The bullet tore open the opposite side of Brent's head. Sallum walked three paces to where Landau lay sprawled across the sofa. He rammed the pistol into his open mouth, fired, and stood back. Brain tissue was now spattered across the cream fabric. Sallum dipped a finger into the gooey mess and lifted it to his nose.

The smell of infidel decadence.

His work completed, Sallum sat, placing himself opposite the door, the gun in his hand, ready to react if anyone came in. The meeting was scheduled to last half an hour, and he had another seven minutes to wait. To leave early would be suspicious. He would take the time to adjust the robes and the veil, to get his breath and his pulse-rate back under control.

He started to stretch. Always exercise after an execution, he reminded himself.

He checked the pistol, then placed it back inside the belt of the jeans he was wearing beneath his robes.

I still have four bullets in the gun. Enough if I have to fight my way out of here.

He stood up and walked calmly towards the door. If I die, what of it? he reflected, glancing down the length of the corridor. I have killed three infidels today. The sacrifice of my own blood would be an honour.

The chatter and buzz of the early-evening cocktail hour had started, and Matt glanced through the restaurant. Janey, the manageress, was holding court at the bar, regaling an elderly couple with some of the more salacious local gossip. Out on the balcony a group of muscled men were sitting at a table covered with open beer bottles and empty crisp packets. Three of them Matt recognised. Local gangsters, they worked the informal, underworld trade routes between Essex and

Marbella, shipping stolen cars, guns, drugs, anything that turned a quick and easy profit. The other three he hadn't seen before, but judging by the whiteness of their complexions they were fresh off the plane. Looking for work, probably. Or making a delivery. As long as they kept to themselves, and paid for the beer and the food, nobody at the Last Trumpet would bother them. Along the Marbella coastline, that was the only way you stayed in business.

'You OK, Matt?' said David, a former paratrooper now doing security work for some of the Arab bankers who kept houses along the coast.

They can see it in my eyes, Matt thought, and in the way my shoulders are sagging. 'Keeping my chin up,' he answered. 'You?'

'Touch of bother up at the big house,' said David. 'One of the lady sheiks went a bit crazy, slapped one of the cleaning girls around a bit. You know what those Arabs are like, they treat the servants like scum. Anyway, this girl's brother goes crazy, starts coming up to the house looking to defend the honour of their family. Usual Spanish macho bullshit – a lot of lip and not much action.'

'Let me know if you need some help,' said Matt. 'The way I'm feeling I could use a good scrap.'

'Need extra money, Matt?' David took a sip on his glass of beer. 'I'd have thought you'd be doing OK with your share of this place. I spend enough money in here to pay off Victoria Beckham's credit-card bills.'

Matt grinned. 'I can always use a bit more.'

On the TV screen Sky Sports was playing, showing a Newcastle-Sunderland game, but apart from Keith, the local Geordie, nobody was very interested. It was mostly a Southern crowd along this stretch of the Marbella coast. Boys from Essex and Kent and London with their Barbie-doll girlfriends, at home among their own kind. The Northerners tended to settle further along towards Torremolinos. To Matt, they were even more foreign than the Spanish.

Matt swung open the door to the back office. He only owned a fifth of the bar, and Janey was the manageress, but he always looked after the back office – the main reason, he sometimes suspected, that Damien had wanted him to come in as an investor. Damien had been looking for a man he could rely on to add up the night's takings and get the cash into the bank the following morning without getting robbed. Matt also made sure there was no trouble at the bar.

Maybe Damien wanted me to keep an eye on Gill as well, Matt considered as he sat down in front of the computer. The three of us were like one big family, always running in and out of each other's houses. Gill just didn't like her family much, not when she grew up and realised what it was her Dad and her brother actually did for a living. She came out here to get away from that – and then she was stupid enough to fall in love with me.

Matt rubbed his eyes, trying to focus on the numbers. The bar was a living. If only I had been a bit more sensible, he thought. I might still have Gill, and we might be going on our honeymoon in Marrakech in a couple of weeks' time.

The light was flickering on the computer screen. Matt took another sip of the Coke he'd poured at the bar and switched on to the internet, waiting patiently while the modem searched for the connection. The software took an age to load, but Matt didn't mind waiting. He suspected the news was not going to be good.

He had learnt about trading shares just after getting out of the SAS and picking up a job bodyguarding Harry Stroller, an American internet entrepreneur who had made five hundred million dollars from floating his company during the dotcom boom – and then seen the value of the business double in the next year. Despite their different paths through life, Matt and Harry were men chiselled from the same stone: they were the same age, 35, they were both physically fit and mentally alert, they both liked to drink beer and chase girls, and neither of them minded taking a risk. The only real difference, Matt sometimes reflected as he sat for hours outside board meetings, was that Harry could programme a computer and work a spreadsheet, and Matt could throw a knife and fire a gun. Harry's skills paid millions, and Matt's just a few thousand. And when you get that close to the big cake, you want a slice of it for yourself.

After three months the two men had become solid friends, disappearing to bars together after Harry was through with his work. He'd started giving Matt share tips, and at the height of the dotcom bubble that was a valuable commodity. Harry knew from the bankers and brokers he talked to each day exactly which stocks were about to fly and when, and he passed the information on to Matt. Whether it was exactly legal or not, Matt wasn't sure. But he wasn't about to shut down a goldmine by asking anyone.

Soon, the tips became a lot more valuable than the job. Harry was paying a thousand dollars a day to protect him, but Matt was making five or ten times that just by trading shares. At the end of the job he had made enough to buy him his share in the Last Trumpet, to invest in a flat in London, to get a new silver Porsche Boxster, and to leave over enough to keep trading. The restaurant gave him a stake in a real business, something he could work at, and be proud of.

But by the time Matt stopped working for Harry he was addicted to trading. And he made the biggest mistake of all. He thought he was clever. He carried on trading shares, but without Harry to tell him what to buy and sell, every share he bought went down instead of up. The money quickly evaporated, and then the debts started to mount up.

It wasn't greed. I was just trying to make the money for you, Gill. To give us a decent life together.

Matt looked at the computer screen, where the shares in his portfolio were displayed in neat tables. Ten different stocks, all of them purchased in the last six months. All of them with borrowed money. And all of them trading heavily down.

Greed

At a rough calculation, Matt reckoned he owed a half-million. And the people he owed it to didn't just charge interest. They didn't just downgrade your credit rating. They killed you.

TWO

Matt glanced towards Alison once, looked away, then found his eyes moving back towards her. A seven, maybe. No, make that an eight. Borderline nine, even.

Bad thought, Matt. You've got enough problems without eying up other women.

She was tall, with blonde hair that tumbled down the back of her neck, and a strong athletic build: a woman, Matt judged, who knew her way around the gym as well as the bedroom. She was wearing tight leather trousers and a pink silk blouse with the top two buttons undone. A single string of pearls was wrapped round her neck, there was a one-diamond earring glittering on either side of her face, and just enough cleavage on display to hook your interest.

What's a girl like that doing in a bar known locally as the Last Strumpet?

'A British minister killed in Saudi Arabia,' said Keith, holding up a newspaper. 'They must have had some inside help from the rag-heads. Otherwise I don't see how they could have got to the man. Not with the security he would have had around him.'

Matt stole another glance at Alison. Definitely a nine.

She had a way of growing on you. 'Not necessarily,' he said, looking back towards Keith. 'There's always a way of getting to a man.'

She was standing by herself, he noticed, but didn't seem lost or nervous or insecure, the way a lot of women might when stranded by themselves in a bar. They either looked too eager, as if they were almost inviting one of the guys to come and try their luck, or they looked too sour, as if they were warning all the men in the bar to keep well away. But this one looked as if she was just enjoying the gin and lime in her glass, the night air, and the breeze blowing in from the sea, the same way a man would if he was having a drink by himself.

'You reckon?' said Keith. 'How then?' Keith claimed to be a former policeman, but Matt wasn't sure he believed him. He had neither the strength nor the character Matt would expect from someone professionally trained. He was too loud, too cocky: his muscles were strong, but his mind was flabby. The closest Matt reckoned he'd been to any real danger was a late-night brawl in a pub or a ruckus at a football match. Men who had seen real action didn't joke about it and didn't talk tough: they knew it was ugly, raw and violent, and that even the strongest men were frightened in the face of death. A traffic cop, maybe – or a parking warden. If it wasn't for the fact that he spent most of the little money he earned at the bar of the Last Trumpet, Matt wouldn't have taken the time to talk to him.

That's the trouble with life after the Regiment. You have to talk to wankers all the time.

'I'm not telling you, mate,' said Matt. 'I might want to kill you one of these days. No point in telling you in advance how I'm going to do it.'

'If you were going to kill me,' said the woman, 'how would you do that?'

Matt turned round to see Alison standing just a few inches behind him. Her eyes were looking straight at his, her glass held slightly to one side, her lips were poised on the cusp of a smile. Classy, he reflected, having noted her voice's pure, round vowel sounds. A lot classier than most of the women who hang around at the Last Trumpet.

'Meticulous preparation, that would be the key,' said Matt. 'I'd have to get to know everything about you.'

'And where would you start?'

Matt saw the way her finger was curling around the edge of her glass. There were no rings, he noticed. She was acting tough, but she still seemed slightly nervous. Her skin looked soft and was lightly tanned, but had none of the wrinkles women quickly collect when they move to the Spanish sun. On holiday, he decided. Maybe she was just divorced and looking to catch up on some lost time. Or maybe she was one of those London career harpies who suddenly find all their girlfriends have got married and had kids and they don't have anyone to go on holiday with except themselves. Either way it didn't matter. She was definitely interested.

'I'd start by finding out all about you, where you live

and what you do, then I'd want to find out what interests you and excites you. I'd want to know what your passions are.'

'My passions?'

'Sure,' said Matt. 'A woman's passions are her main weakness.'

'I reckon the only killing you know about,' Alison said, her lips drawing back into a smile, 'is lady-killing.'

'That's probably the most dangerous sort,' said Matt, laughing.

Deciding to get rid of Keith, Matt took a bottle of Moet & Chandon from behind the bar – one of the privileges of being a shareholder – and cracked it open. The beach, he suggested to the woman, was the perfect place to drink champagne on a warm evening. Somewhere they could hear the waves in their ears and feel the sand beneath their feet.

One of the best things about basing yourself in Spain, Matt reflected as he took her arm and guided her gently down the steep metal staircase that led from the terrace to the beach, was the constant parade of girls on holiday with tight skirts and loose morals. Easyjetters, some of the guys at the bar called them. They came in by jet. They were easy. They were cheap. And after a couple of days by the pool some of them were even orange as well.

But this woman wasn't like that. She might be easy – he would find out soon – but there was nothing cheap about her.

'I don't even know your name,' said Matt, sitting

down on one of the rocks that jutted out from the sand.

'Alison.'

'I heard you let that little friend of mine take off your party dress.'

'I know the song, thanks.'

Matt fell silent. It was only two days since he had split up with Gill. The pain was still there, weighing on his mind. Her parting words were still echoing through his thoughts, and the image of her tears still burned his memory. A hundred times he had thought about calling her: a thousand times he had told himself he mustn't. He had made his choice, he must learn to live with it.

Maybe I need something to help me get over Gill. Maybe I'll never sort out the mess I'm in and just need to move on. Forget about the past, and everything in it.

'You're quiet.'

'Just thinking.'

'Oh.'

Alison leant forward and brushed her lips against his. Matt moved his face towards her and their lips collided, the kiss turning into a long, passionate embrace. She tasted different, and felt different. It was two years since Matt had slept with any woman other than Gill, and he had started to forget how each had her own unique flavour, her own way of touching you, her own noises and movements. Gill and he had got together when he'd left the Regiment, and they'd gone back to the crowd of people they'd known before he'd become a soldier. There had always been plenty of temptation at the bar, but he'd never so much as looked at another woman.

Alison's hands were moving quickly over his chest and shoulders, her fingers pressing through his blue denim shirt. Through her bra and her blouse he could feel her nipples starting to harden. 'Not here,' she whispered into his ear. 'I want to fuck you all night, and we can't do that on the beach.'

He stood up, holding her hand, and they started walking. It was ten minutes to his apartment, a one-bedroom place overlooking the sea, just down from the main coastal road.

Matt pushed open the door of the flat, hoping it wasn't too much of a mess. It was a standard guy's place – a few pieces of furniture, none of them bought with any great thought. A big hi-fi, and a row of CDs filed away on the bookshelf in alphabetical order. A wide-screen TV, with a PlayStation 2 underneath it and a collection of games. A small kitchen, with a big fridge containing beer, some orange juice and six frozen double pepperoni and sausage pizzas. The only individual touch was the framed pictures on top of the hi-fi, one of his mum, the rest of himself in uniform with some of his mates from the Regiment.

Matt picked a CD from the shelf – Sonny Rollins, in his opinion the greatest jazz saxophone player of the 1950s. He fed the disc into the player then turned around to look at her, noticing the way the light caught her hair, emphasising the fact that she was a near platinum blonde. A sad, soulful tune slowly filled the room, the lines of the melody straying in different directions, and Matt gripped Alison around the waist, feeling the tight leather of her trousers firm against his hand. Already he was wondering how she would look naked, what would be the contours of her body, how her shape would fit against his. She wasn't saying anything, but it suited him that way. He kissed her lips, his mouth moving quickly down the length of her neck, his hands wrestling with her belt buckle. 'Undress,' he said. 'Undress for me now.'

She took off her clothes with the same relaxed grace she'd displayed in the bar, like a woman who was perfectly comfortable with herself and her surroundings. She unpeeled her trousers first, uncovering slender, finely sculpted legs. Then she dropped her blouse to the floor, revealing slim, elegant shoulders and breasts that seemed larger than they'd looked when she was clothed. Her bra and knickers were red lace La Perla, designed more to provoke than to protect. She must have known she was going home with a guy tonight, decided Matt. A woman doesn't wear underwear like that unless she is on the prowl. I just happened to be standing in the right place.

Alison dropped to her knees before him, unbuttoned the fly of his jeans. Her tongue moved slowly, teasingly against his groin, and Matt could feel his muscles relaxing as the pleasure flooded through his body. He ran his fingers slowly through her long hair, admiring the skill with which she seemed to be working every nerve-ending in his body. He waited until he could stand it no more, then scooped her up in his arms and carried her towards the bedroom. Her hair broke free, trailing across his shoulder. He rolled her on to the bed and lay on top of her, his movements swift, urgent and uncontrolled. He could feel her yielding beneath him, and could feel her excitement mounting as he pushed into her. Within minutes, her screams were ringing in his ears.

Forty minutes later Matt leant back on the bed. Every muscle in his body felt stretched, each nerve taut. At his side, Alison rolled over, reaching out for her bag and retrieving a packet of Dunhill. She lit one, blowing a plume of smoke high into the air. Then she lit one for him and moved to place it between his lips, but Matt shook his head.

'I've given up,' he said, breathing in the smoky air. 'Did I approach you in the bar, or did you approach me?' he continued.

The trace of a smile flashed across Alison's lips. 'You mean, are you the hunter or are you the prey?'

'Exactly,' said Matt.

She reached across the bed to rest her head on his chest, her tongue flicking across his nipple.

Matt reached out across the bed to find her. His hand moved through the sheet. Nothing. Drowsily he opened his eyes, looking around the tiny room. Nothing. Light was streaming in through the window and the sky was bright blue. He stood up, walking towards the bathroom. 'Alison,' he shouted. He could hear his voice bouncing off the walls. Then silence. Nothing. She was gone.

Matt shrugged and walked towards the kitchen. He threw some coffee into the percolator, and took a flask of orange juice from the fridge, drinking it straight from the bottle. The smell of her still lingered on his body. Strange, he reflected. Last night she was all over me, this morning she wakes up and buggers off without so much as saying goodbye.

That's a guy's job, isn't it?

Matt glanced at his watch. It was already half past nine. He needed a shower, and he needed to get on with his life. Last night was fun, but that was all. She was right to take off.

'You're a stupid boy, Matt Browning.'

The sound of the voice rattled through his ears, catching him off-guard. Matt looked up. The man sitting on the sofa was called Harry Pointer. Matt had met him a couple of times before. A fat, ugly brute of an Englishman with a nasty rash on the top of his balding head, Harry ran errands for Gennady Kazanov, local landlord and an investor in the Last Trumpet. Harry wasn't the heavy muscle, although he knew how to throw a punch and fire a gun when he had to. But mainly he did the talking and the translating: the muscle that travelled with Kazanov spoke Russian or Ukrainian or Georgian, not English.

'How the fuck did you get in?' demanded Matt.

'Mr Kazanov owns the block, remember,' said Harry. 'He has keys to all the apartments.'

'And that gives you the right to barge in here whenever you like?'

Pointer shook his head. 'No,' he replied slowly. 'The fact you owe us half a million gives us the right.'

'I've told you,' said Matt, 'I'm doing everything I can think of to get you your money back.'

'Thinking isn't what you do best.'

Pointer stood up. He was wearing cream chinos and a bright blue shirt, and the tattoos were visible all the way up his arm.

'Tell Kazanov he's just going to have to wait,' said Matt.

'He's waited already, Matt. He's tired of waiting. Mr Kazanov is a patient man; he knows that sometimes it takes time to make money, but even his patience will be exhausted eventually. You know what troubles him: he doesn't see you working. He watches, and he sees some guy too busy knocking off the tourist honeys in the bar to spend his time worrying about how he's going to pay Mr Kazanov back.' Harry paused, moving closer to Matt. 'And Mr Kazanov doesn't like that.'

Matt shrugged, walking towards the balcony. He looked to the beach below. A pair of girls were sunning themselves, one in a pink bikini, the other in blue. He looked more closely. No, neither of them was Alison.

'We know where she works, Matt. We know all her movements.'

'That's more than I do.'

'No.' Pointer laughed. 'We know where *Gill* works, Matt. The Dandelion Playschool, Puerto Banus. The kids get out at two-thirty every afternoon. She walks home to her apartment. Takes her about fifteen minutes. Plenty of good spots along the way where a couple of men could pick her up, take her away to somewhere quiet.'

Matt turned slowly away from the window. His eyes narrowed and he could feel the muscles in his chest tightening. He had few expectations of Kazanov. He knew better than to believe the man had made his money in the Russian oil business. He knew he was a hard, ruthless thug who had worked for the KGB before looting a fortune when the system in his country started to come apart. And he knew that if he didn't get his money back to him sometime, he was likely to come after him. But Gill . . .

'Don't even think about it,' Matt snapped.

A thin smile started to spread over Pointer's lips. 'A primary school teacher. I reckon she uses her hands a lot,' he said, drawing out each word. 'All that painting and building things with the kids. If some guys snatched her and chopped off her right hand, I reckon that would be pretty bad for her.'

Matt squared up to Pointer, close enough to smell the coffee on his breath. 'I'd kill any man who laid a finger on her,' he said, his voice rising. 'I'd kill the man, then I'd kill Kazanov. Then I'd kill you. Slowly.'

Pointer backed away. 'Calm, Matt, calm,' he said quickly. 'We're just having a hypothetical conversation.'

'Let's keep it that way.'

'You've got a month, Matt,' said Pointer. 'Then we

come after you. And you can shout and scream and threaten all you like, but remember this: we don't give a fuck if you've been in the Regiment or not. To me you're all just a bunch of pussies. And anyway, there is no back-up. You are just one man, and we're an organisation. We'll kill you, and then we'll cut her up, and there's nothing you can do to stop us.'

Matt looked straight into Pointer's eyes: it was like gazing into the face of a statue, he thought. 'Where the hell am I going to get half a million pounds in a month?'

THREE

The look in the man's eyes told Matt everything he needed to know. There wasn't any money. There never would be any money.

I'm just an embarrassment. They want to get rid of me.

Eddie Addler shifted his pen from one side of his desk to the other. His eyes darted up to the window, then to the door, then to one of the oil paintings hanging on the wall. Anything, Matt thought, to avoid looking me in the eye.

'I'm sorry, but I don't think there is anything we can do,' said Addler. 'With the state of your portfolio, there's just no chance of giving you any more credit.'

Tatton & Friedland was a private bank set up only seven years previously, but its St James's Place offices had been decorated to make it look far older. There was wood panelling on the walls, which were adorned with stuffed fish in cases and a collection of oil paintings of dogs and huntsmen. Matt had felt instinctively uncomfortable the first time he had set foot in the place. He should have trusted his instincts.

'If I could get some collateral, I was thinking maybe I could trade my way out of trouble.'

Harry Stroller had introduced Matt to Addler, back when he was still working for him full-time. At first Matt had dabbled in just a few shares, dealing through his usual bank account. As Stroller's tips had made him wealthier, he'd suggested Matt get himself a proper banker. Tatton & Friedland dealt with a small group of rich clients, mostly technology entrepreneurs or City bankers. You needed a quarter of a million to invest to get through the door. Matt had only just qualified.

'In these markets, Mr Browning, I can't help feeling you'd just be trading yourself into more trouble.' Matt could hear the pained tone in Addler's voice: polite still, but on the brink of rudeness.

'I made money before, I can make it again,' said Matt.

'From these records, I see you made a lot of money trading while you were working for Mr Stroller,' said Addler, looking at the computer screen on his desk. 'Spotting which internet and technology shares were moving up. Maybe Mr Stroller was discussing his own thoughts with you – I can't judge. Since you stopped working for him, you have made a series of investments on your own. You had a half-million in your portfolio, now you are down half a million.' He paused, looking directly at Matt for the first time. 'Let me give you some advice. You're a soldier by training. You're good at it, I'm sure. Trading shares is different. Even the best City operators are losing money this year. Do yourself a favour. Stay out of the game.'

Matt swallowed hard. 'I'm in a jam,' he said. 'I need

to make that money back, and I need to make it quickly.'

Addler's eyes moved back to his computer screen. His expression closed. 'I'm sorry,' he said coldly. 'We're a bank. We can't help you. We'd like to help you – we'd like to help lots of people – but we can't. That's business.'

The offices were almost empty compared to the last time he had been there. Ark Technology Systems occupied a refurbished warehouse in Clerkenwell, its insides gutted and rebuilt with stainless steel floors, frosted glass partitions and plasma screens covering every wall. Each desk had once been home to at least two computers, and there'd been so many girls running around in short black skirts and tight T-shirts that Matt had found it impossible to concentrate on the work. Not that there had been much to do. As Harry Stroller had admitted after a few beers one night, bodyguards were mostly there for show, part of convincing the investors they had a big business worth protecting. Bill Gates had a bodyguard, so Ark had one too. Like the plasma screens, and the immaculately groomed receptionists, Matt was there mainly for decoration.

The decorations were all gone now. It was like walking through a house that had been left empty for a few years. A chilled emptiness had descended on the building, and dust was gathering in the corners. There was still a receptionist, and maybe two dozen people occupying a few of the hundred or more desks. But Ark was a pale, waning shadow of what it once had been.

Stroller shook Matt warmly by the hand. A broad grin was playing on his face. He was a short man, just over five foot five, with broad shoulders and black hair that was thinning on top, but sporting a thick, neatly trimmed goatee beard. 'I don't need a bodyguard, Matt,' he said. 'The only people likely to kill me are my shareholders.'

'That bad?'

Stroller turned on his heels and walked back towards his own desk in the centre of the main floor. He'd always refused to have his own office – very 'old economy', he used to point out – even though Matt had argued that it was impossible to protect anyone adequately who worked in an open-place space. Now it didn't matter any more. There were so few people around, the third floor was a private office.

'Look at this place,' said Harry. 'Hardly recognise it, do you? The good times have gone. The orders have dried up, and the venture capitalists aren't taking my calls any more. Heck, I can't even get a date.' Stroller leant back in his chair and swung his right foot on to the desk. 'Internet billionaire had a kind of ring to it. Chicks went for that. Close-to-bankrupt computer nerd doesn't work the same kind of magic.' He paused. 'But, hey, when's the wedding?'

'There isn't going to be a wedding,' said Matt. 'I can't afford to look after myself, never mind Gill.'

'You're in a mess?'

'The worst mess I've ever been in,' Matt confessed.

'I lost all the money I made when I was working for you, and I lost a whole lot more as well. The people I owe it to want it back.'

'And you were wondering if any of my friends might need a guard,' said Stroller. 'Somebody who might share a few stock tips with you?'

Matt paused. Once you got used to the taste, he reasoned, swallowing your pride wasn't so hard. 'If there was anyone on the circuit who needed a reliable man, I could use a break.'

'I like you, Matt – but let me tell you something,' said Stroller, standing up from his desk, his expression suggesting he was fast losing interest in the conversation. 'You know what I've learned about life over the last few months. When you're down, you're down, and nobody wants to help you. I can't even help myself.'

The words were still echoing through Matt's mind as he stepped back on to the street. A year before, he had bought himself a one-bedroom flat close to Holborn. The plan had been to use it on his trips to London – back when he thought he was still a big shot who had to fly home to see his banker. It might have been a good investment, but the place now was mortgaged to the hilt, and the bank was already threatening to repossess it. Four months had passed since Matt last made a mortgage payment, and right now there was no chance of making one.

The walk took about twenty minutes. Matt could have hopped on a bus or taken a cab, but he reckoned he needed the time to clear his mind. When he'd flown to London he hadn't been sure what he was looking for. A way out. Another loan, or a new job . . .

Harry's right, Matt thought. Nobody is going to help me. Why should they? I'm a thirty-five-year-old guy. I know how to fight – but out here in the real world, away from the Regiment, who cares about that? I don't have anything to offer.

There was something about making all that money, so quickly and so easily – it does something to your head. It stops you from thinking straight. And when that happens, you're as good as finished.

A tramp was sitting in the doorway of the office building next to his flat. A man of maybe forty-five or fifty, his skin was pitted with spots and a black beard was starting to crawl down his chin. His hair was matted with sweat and grease. A can of beer was held in one hand, a piece of brown cardboard in the other: 'EX-FORCES. SERVED IN THE FALKLANDS. PLEASE GIVE GENEROUSLY.'

Matt fished around in his pocket and took out the fiver he would have spent on a taxi. He knelt down, handing the money across. 'How does this happen?' he asked.

The man looked at him suspiciously, taking the money and folding it into his fist. 'I'll thank you for the money,' he said in a Birmingham accent slurred by alcohol, 'but my story is my story, and it's about the only thing I still own. So I'll not be sharing it with you.'

The smell of the man hit Matt hard in the chest: a

stale odour of dead fish, cheap spirits and damp cloth. 'Where's your dignity?' Matt said, his eyes suddenly intense and full of anger. 'You were a soldier, man.'

'Fuck off,' spat the tramp.

Christ, thought Matt. I threw away *my* dignity today. *I'm just inches away*.

Maybe I should just get out of the country, he thought. Go to Moscow, Hong Kong, Nigeria – anywhere. Change my name. Change my face, even. Get some security work and become another person. It's not so hard. I've been Matt Browning all my life, and where did it ever get me? Why not try on some other identity. I could hardly make a worse mess of things.

No. That might save me, but it won't save Gill. And if anything happened to her because of me, I couldn't live with it. My dignity would have been stripped from me for ever.

'Pleased to see me?' Alison looked up towards Matt as he walked into his flat, a lipsticked smile spreading across her lips.

Matt looked at her suspiciously, his eyes moving across the slender curves of her body. 'What are you doing in my flat?'

'We need to talk,' said Alison.

Matt laughed. 'Don't tell me – you're pregnant. That's all I need right now.'

Alison stood up, moving away from the sofa. 'I'm here to help you.'

'You're the only person who's said that recently.'

'I know, Matt. I know everything about you.'

Matt stood closer to her, looking directly into her eyes. 'Who are you?'

'Like I said, we should talk.'

'Then start talking,' said Matt. 'I've got all day.'

Alison walked towards the kitchen. She took a glass from the shelf, blew away a thin layer of dust that had settled on its surface, filled it with water and raised it to her lips. 'My name is Alison Hammond,' she said slowly. 'I work for MI5.'

The silence lasted several seconds as her words hung in the air. Matt looked at her closely, wondering if she would suddenly change shape: he had met her as a pick-up in the bar, and now, suddenly, she was a spy who had broken into his flat. 'Go on,' he said quietly.

'I have a proposition for you. Whether you choose to accept it or not is up to you. It could solve all your problems.'

'I'm out of that game,' Matt snapped. 'I left the Regiment two years ago. I've done all that misguided shit about risking my life for my country several times already, and I don't need it. These days I'm just interested in chilling out and looking after myself.'

'And making a right screw-up of it too.'

'What do you know about me?' said Matt angrily.

'As I said, everything,' Alison said coldly, swilling the remains of the water into her throat. 'Matt, we know you better than you know yourself.' She paused, looking away from him and walking back towards the window. 'After I left you in Spain, you were visited by a man looking to collect some money. You are half a million pounds in debt, and because the money is owed to Gennady Kazanov, if you don't pay it back soon you're a dead man. I have some pictures of people who didn't keep up with their debts to Gennady. I can show them to you if you like, but you might need a stiff drink first. He usually severs a couple of limbs before he finishes you off. Even the KGB thought he was a bit rough when he used to work for them. We have files on him going back a long time. You're in pretty deep there.' She hesitated, walked back to the kitchen and refilled her glass with water. 'But I think you know that. Two days ago you split up with your fiancée, Gill. Yesterday afternoon you took a Go flight from Malaga to Stansted – budget airlines, Matt. A year ago you were going business class on BA. You spent the night here, ordered in a pizza and two beers. Today you went to see your banker, then your old friend Harry Stroller. You were looking for help. But you were stupid, Matt. The rich only help themselves. That's what makes them rich.'

Alison walked back towards Matt, her lips turned in an engaging smile. 'You see, Matt, we've been watching. We know everything. But most of all we know of a way to help you.'

'Help me?' said Matt. 'I know about Five – you don't help people.'

Alison ran a hand through her hair, messing its neatly brushed appearance. 'We do deals sometimes,' she said, her tone hardening. 'Win-win deals, where both sides

come out ahead. That's what we'd like to do with you.'
She stretched out an arm and Matt felt her fingers
brushing against the skin on the back of his neck. A
tingle ran down his spine, a sensation that mixed
anticipation and excitement in the same delicate
movement. She has class, he reflected. Social class, sure,
but also poise and brains – and she's playing me like a
cheap guitar.

He felt Alison's breath on his skin as she asked him,
'What more do you have to lose?'

FOUR

The traffic was backing up behind the roundabout that led down to Wandsworth bridge. Thick clouds were lying low over the Thames, shrouding the city in a dark, heavy gloom. A way out of my troubles, Matt was thinking – that's what Alison had said. Right now, I'm not in any position to turn offers down.

There was no choice. He had to see what she had to say. But it wouldn't be a simple way out, of that he felt certain. It wouldn't be safe either.

He pumped the accelerator on his Porsche Boxster and pulled out into the roundabout. He could see Alison's metal-blue Audi TT just ahead. The Holiday Inn sign was plastered against the skyline, sitting next to a B&Q superstore, a BP garage, and a McDonald's. Matt swerved the car around the bend moments before an orange light turned red.

I might as well get some fun out of this car. I won't have it much longer.

He pulled up in the car park of the hotel. Very Five, reflected Matt, taking the Porsche down a gear. The spooks generally met in anonymous, corporate locations, as if they were just computer salesmen. It was part of the routine, a way of throwing their targets off the scent, keeping every operation at a safe distance from the organisation itself. If they invited you to the Thames House headquarters, you knew the conversation didn't matter.

I thought I was through with these kind of games.

When he'd left the Regiment after ten years of active service, Matt had vowed to himself that he would never go back. He'd seen enough violence and risked his life enough times. His appetite for danger was sated. Lots of his mates had become bodyguards or mercenaries, but after a spell working for Stroller, Matt hadn't wanted to do that.

If you were going to kill people it had to be for a cause, not just for money.

'Nice car,' said Alison, suddenly appearing next to him, a playful smile spreading across her lips.

Matt noticed the way the wind caught her hair, blowing it away from her face. Beautiful, he reflected, in the same way a leopard is beautiful: sleek and slender and perfectly groomed. 'Thanks,' he muttered.

'Shame it's going to be repossessed by the finance company next week.' Alison turned smartly towards the entrance of the hotel.

Keep swallowing, man.

He followed her into the Holiday Inn. The lobby was nondescript, with pale blue carpets and a standard wooden desk, the kind of space you might see in a thousand different hotels around the world. 'Room 262,' Alison said to the girl at reception. 'They're expecting us.'

They remained silent in the lift. Then Matt followed Alison down a corridor and they stepped into the room without knocking. The bed had been pushed to one side, and the desk had been placed next to the window. The curtains were drawn, and only a desk lamp was illuminating the faces of two men sitting either side of the desk.

Matt looked into their eyes. The first man was about fifty, with greying hair combed across his head to disguise a bald patch. He wore a charcoal grey suit, with a pink silk tie and a checked shirt with silver cufflinks. The second man was maybe forty-five, with brown hair that looked as if it could use a trim and ears that stuck out too far from his head. He wore a blue suit and a striped tie, probably from a school. Neither of them smiled or even looked at him.

Let's call them Pinky and Perky, thought Matt: Pinky for the guy with the tie, Perky for the younger guy with the scruffy hair. He knew enough about Five and the way it operated to know that he wasn't going to be given their names. Never mind. It wasn't as if he was ever going to add them to his Christmas card list.

I'm back. I'd better start getting used to it.

'These two men are going to ask you a few questions,' said Alison, her tone cold and businesslike. 'I'll be down the corridor. You'll see me again when they've finished.'

Matt looked for somewhere to sit down but they seemed to have forgotten to provide him with a chair. Forgotten? No. If there wasn't a chair, that was because they wanted it like that. They didn't want him relaxed.

They want to see whether I can still handle pressure.

'Your name is Matt Browning,' said Pinky, looking down at the notes on his desk. 'Thirty-five years old, two years out of the Regiment, served with distinction for ten years. Saw action in the Gulf, Ulster, Bosnia and a couple of other places that seem to have been mysteriously deleted from the files because the British Army wasn't officially supposed to be involved. Chechnya, Indonesia.' He paused, shifting to another sheet of paper. 'A tough soldier, exceptionally steady under fire, fantastic endurance, but takes things personally. Short-tempered. Sometimes prone to excessive violence, even by SAS standards.'

Matt looked at the man closely, but could read nothing in his expression. 'I know my record, thanks,' he said curtly. 'I've no apologies. Sometimes violence is the only language people understand.'

'Not officer material,' said Perky, looking down at the notes on his desk. 'Good sense of leadership, popular with the men and decisive in combat, but not easy to control. He doesn't always see the bigger picture, nor always understand about putting the interest of the campaign above the interests of his own men. Doesn't always listen to advice from his superiors. Doesn't learn from his mistakes.' He paused, looking up at Matt. 'Would you say that was a fair assessment?'

Matt shrugged. 'I'm out of the Regiment,' he replied. 'I assess myself these days.'

'We're going to read out a list of words,' said Pinky.

'I want you to give us your first reaction to each one. OK?'

'Fine,' said Matt, shifting his weight from one leg to another. 'Shrink school. I know the drill.' He glanced down towards the small stack of flash-cards that Perky was pulling from his briefcase. At about the time he had left the Regiment a bunch of moronic management consultants had been hired to start testing the men's aptitudes and ambitions. It was all rubbish, according to most of the men, and Matt agreed with them – their main ambition was not to get killed, and you didn't need some consultant examining you to tell you that.

This stuff is fine for regional sales managers at Vodafone. Fighting men don't need it.

'Money,' said Perky.

'Control.'

'Hope,' said Pinky.

'Children.'

'Blood,' said Perky.

'Food.'

'Anger,' said Pinky.

'Fools.'

'Desire,' said Perky.

'Safety.'

'Greed,' said Pinky.

'Stupid,' said Matt.

Both men looked down at their notes, and made a series of marks on the papers spread out in front of them. Then Perky picked up his mobile and called up a pre-recorded number. 'You can come back in now,' he said. 'We're finished.'

Matt relaxed. 'Did I pass?'

'We're here to ask questions,' snapped Perky, 'not answer them.'

Matt briefly imagined meeting the man in a dark alley, thinking about the marks his fist would leave on his jaw.

'Our assessment is that you're psychologically impaired,' Perky continued. 'Maybe that's why you never got the promotions you wanted in the Regiment.'

Matt shrugged. 'Impaired?' he said sharply. 'I've noticed that you two couldn't find your way out of a dark room without someone coming to rescue you. I'd call that thinking pretty straight.'

'As we were saying,' Pinky leant forward on the desk, 'lacks respect for authority. No direction in life. No moral compass. Lacks socialisation.'

'Right,' said Matt, grinning. 'I thought moral flexibility was what Five was looking for these days.'

Behind him he heard Alison at the door, and he turned to watch her as she walked back into the room. She glanced towards the two men, nodded, then looked towards Matt. 'We're about to explain a mission to you,' she said. 'You might be interested, you might not be. Either way, I want you to understand that everything we are about to tell you is confidential. If you walk away, forget everything we say. Understood?'

Matt nodded. 'Agreed,' he said. 'I might be out of the services, but I'm still a loyal citizen.'

Alison returned one of her old smiles, the type Matt had seen in Spain but hadn't seen here in London: a smile that spoke of warmth and interest, not simply manipulation and control. 'OK,' she said softly. 'Great.'

Pinky took a Toshiba notebook computer from his case and set it out on the desk. 'You probably already know that the greatest security threat we face, indeed all the developed nations face, is al-Qaeda,' he began. 'We are fighting them in lots of different ways, shutting down training centres, rounding up sympathisers, stopping the flow of weapons. But one of the ways we are fighting them is financial.'

'Al-Qaeda has a lot of money,' said Perky, picking up the flow of the conversation where his colleague had left it. 'Its roots are in Saudi Arabia, and that's a rich place. But it has a lot of support right across that region. There are contributions coming from everywhere – Jordan, Egypt, Pakistan, Malaysia. That's what makes them so deadly. Fanatics we can handle. Fanatics with cash are a different story. Overall, we estimate the organisation has at least five billion dollars at its disposal. They hide their money, and they are good at it. So it could be a lot more.'

Matt could feel his heart sinking. They hadn't told him what the deal was yet. But they had started talking about al-Qaeda. Whatever it was, it was going to be dangerous.

'Before September the eleventh, al-Qaeda kept its

money hidden in offshore centres around the world.' Pinky glanced towards Alison as he spoke. 'The usual places – Gibraltar, the Isle of Man, the Cayman Islands, Luxembourg, Switzerland. Mainly Switzerland. It's got the best banks in the world, and the Arabs like Zurich and Geneva. The place is swarming with them.'

'But after September the eleventh it started getting too hot,' Perky continued. 'The Americans started clamping down hard, particularly on the Swiss. They told them they didn't mind the usual drugs dealers, Russian mafiosi, and tax dodgers who use their banks. They could all stay secret. But they wanted to know about the al-Qaeda accounts, and they wanted to shut them down. The Swiss didn't have any choice. Either they played along, or Credit Suisse and UBS and the rest of them were going to get kicked out of Wall Street. They couldn't afford that, so they had no choice. They had to start shutting al-Qaeda accounts down and seizing the money.'

Matt leant forward. 'And the Americans decided to share all of this information with you because they love MI5 so much?'

'No, they needed our help as well,' said Alison. 'A lot of al-Qaeda money was passing through the City of London as well. It's a big money-laundering market, everyone knows that. We froze out what we could, but it's in Zurich that most of its money is stored.'

Pinky looked towards Matt, a frown creasing his brow. 'Al-Qaeda saw what was happening in Switzerland. They could see the heat being turned up, and they could see their accounts being frozen. The Swiss authorities tracked and seized about one billion dollars. Ever since then, al-Qaeda have been slowly moving it out.'

'You're saying even the Swiss don't know where the money is?' said Matt.

'Al-Qaeda are smart,' Alison interjected. 'They hide it well. It's all stored away in accounts nominally belonging to Kuwaiti or Pakistani or Jordanian business-men. Nobody knows whether they exist or not. And not asking questions is the first principle of Swiss banking.'

'Now they are clearing the money out,' said Perky. 'It works like this. An al-Qaeda Arab turns up in Zurich. He goes to the bank and withdraws say $25,000 in cash. Euros or dollars or Swiss francs, it doesn't matter. He walks down the street to a jewellery store or a goldsmith and he buys diamonds or gold, pays cash, and stashes the goods away. Next day, another $25,000 from another bank, more gold and diamonds. The next day, the same again. By the end of the week that's $125,000 turned into commodities. If there's eight of them, that's a million dollars. They spread it around as well, just so no one gets too suspicious or starts recognising them. Sometimes they get a train up to Munich or down to Milan and buy the gold and diamonds there.'

Matt listened closely. Five wouldn't be sharing this information with him unless they wanted something very badly.

'The CIA calculates that about a million dollars

might have been taken out of the Swiss banks so far, and just about all of it has been turned into gold and diamonds,' Pinky said. 'You can see it in the prices. Both gold and diamonds are up this year. That amount of money going into a market has an impact.'

'So what's the point?' said Matt. 'What do they want the stuff for?'

'To hide,' said Perky. 'They've realised that money kept in a bank is never going to be safe. Not when you are fighting a war against the United States. Eventually it's going to get tracked down and seized. They'll keep small amounts, carefully laundered. But not the big stuff. They want that somewhere they can keep their eye on it.'

'The diamonds and gold are being hoarded for a few days, then taken in vans down to the north Italian or the French coasts,' Pinky continued. 'They are loaded on to boats, then taken out across the Mediterranean to the Middle East. The stuff is picked up by al-Qaeda and driven out to safe locations. It could be anywhere – the Saudi desert, the Atlas mountains in Morocco, along the Nile delta, somewhere in Iraq or Iran. The point is, nobody is going to see it again. The Americans aren't going to track it down, and nobody's going to freeze the account. It's safe.'

'And the beauty of gold and diamonds is that they are both the world's oldest, most internationally accepted currency,' Perky interrupted. 'You can walk into any jewellery shop in the world and get cash for either. Instantly. No questions asked.'

'Al-Qaeda can keep their money safe for when they really need it,' Perky continued. 'And there's nothing we or the CIA or anyone else can do to touch it. The Moroccans or the Iranians aren't exactly going to let us go in and start searching around for it.'

'Thanks for the lesson in global economics and financing terrorism,' said Matt. 'But where do I come in?'

Somewhere in the pit of his stomach, Matt knew the answer. Alison turned to look at him, brushing away a lock of blonde hair that had fallen across her face. 'We want you to steal their money.'

The coffee tasted good. Matt swilled it down quickly, keen for the caffeine to kick into his bloodstream. He looked towards the window. In the distance he could see the Thames winding eastwards, a barge chugging slowly through the fading light of the afternoon. Across the road he watched a young couple emerging from B&Q with tins of paint under their arms. Ordinary suburban life. Just what he'd been planning.

There must be lots of honest, safe ways of making a living. It's just that none of them seem to suit me.

Alison had suggested they take a ten-minute break. Matt had walked back down to the lobby and bought himself a coffee from the bar. He needed a few minutes to himself. What he thought of the proposition, he couldn't yet say.

Whatever I decide, one thing is for sure – this time is the last time. The pay-off will have to be good enough that I'm out of this game for ever.

He swilled back the last of the coffee and took the lift back up to the second floor. Alison was already waiting in the room with Pinky and Perky. Matt looked directly towards her. 'So what's in it for me?' he said.

'We want to cut off the money to al-Qaeda,' she replied. 'It's the most effective way to hurt them. They can plot all they like, but any really big terrorist spectacles are always going to be expensive. Without money they are nothing, just angry Arabs waving placards.'

Pinky looked up and scrutinised Matt's face, perhaps searching for signs of weakness or indecision. 'We have flows of intelligence reports coming through,' he said. 'We could identify one of the boats shipping the gold and the diamonds across the Med. Our proposition is this: we put together a small group of men, highly trained men like yourself. We give them the information, the practice and the equipment. They go out and hit the boat.'

'Our sources tell us that each boat contains at least thirty million dollars,' Perky said. 'They travel across the Med from Italy, usually with a crew of about six al-Qaeda men on board. They are always armed, but they aren't trained to special forces standard. Nothing you couldn't handle. Five would give the team all the technical training necessary to take out the boat, and all the specialist equipment. You'd get all the logistical help you needed.'

'When the job is done, you'd get to keep the money.' Pinky cleared his throat. 'No questions asked. Our interest is not in collecting al-Qaeda's money, and we don't care what happens to it. We just want to make sure it's not under their control any more. The thirty million is your pay-off for the mission. Even after it's fenced, that's got to be worth ten million or so. Ten million dollars between five men. You can do the maths yourself. Not bad for a week's work.'

'Think about it.' Alison took a step closer to where Matt was sitting. Her eyes locked on to his, peering down at him, the expression hovering between sympathy and a challenge. 'It's the perfect crime. Lucrative *and* patriotic.'

FIVE

Matt slammed the door shut on the Boxster and dropped the keys in his pocket. He walked swiftly towards the doors of the Novotel Hammersmith. Another day, another anonymous hotel – those Five boys should think of a new trick sometime.

Matt's head was bowed as he walked, the lines of his forehead creased. Before stepping inside he glanced up towards the sky. Sunshine was breaking through the clouds, sending a shaft of light down on to the traffic snarling its way across the flyover. 'Room 662,' he told the receptionist. 'They're expecting me.'

'Sixth floor,' she said. 'The lifts are over there.'

Matt walked purposefully. The decision had been easier than he might have imagined. After the meeting with Alison and her two stooges he had gone back to the flat by himself. She had suggested coming with him but that hadn't felt right: this was a decision he needed to make by himself. There were plenty of friends in London he could have gone to see – his parents, schoolmates, even Gill's brother Damien – but it was a conversation he needed to have with himself. It was his choice. Nobody else could make it for him.

He went out for a curry and a beer. One thing the Regiment had taught him was that you shouldn't fight on an empty stomach – and you can't think straight if you're hungry. After a chicken jalfrezi and two bottles of Cobra, Matt reckoned the calculations had been made and the odds stacked neatly into place.

He could say no. Nobody was forcing him, he could just walk away. From somewhere, somehow, he'd then have to find a lot of money very quickly. Either that, or disappear somewhere where Kazanov and his thugs would never find him. Tempting, but there were two problems. What would happen to Gill? And how much of a life would that be? You can hide for a while, if you have to. But for the rest of your life? Never see your mates or your family again? Never walk through the streets you played football in as a kid? Never admit who you really were? That wasn't any kind of life worth living.

Or he could say yes. The mission would take a month at most. It was a lot of money, enough to pay off all his debts and set up himself and Gill with a new life. It was the fresh start he needed. It would be dangerous, sure, but he didn't mind that. He had risked death before. One more trip around that carousel wouldn't make any difference. He'd take his chances, the same way he always had in the past. One boat raid, then they'd be home. They would have surprise on their side, they would have the right gear, and they would be trained. Al-Qaeda were good, hardy fighters, and he would never underestimate them. But he fancied the odds, they were plenty good enough to roll with. There was just one problem: he had to trust Alison, and he had to trust the people he was working for. His fate was going to be in their hands.

Trouble was, the Regiment had been full of stories of missions for Five going wrong. They looked after their own people, but when it came to soldiers they were reckless, they took chances. They reckoned that's what soldiers were there for. Spies were for thinking. Soldiers for dying.

Matt added that up as two problems with saying no, and one with saying yes. When you laid it out like that, it wasn't much of a choice at all. He'd do it. Whatever the risks.

The door of the lift shut as Matt pressed the button for the sixth floor. A door closes, a door opens, he reflected to himself. If I take these next few steps I'm committed, for better or worse, for richer or poorer, in sickness and in health.

Just like the marriage I backed out of.

Alison was sitting in the bedroom, her legs neatly crossed. She was wearing a black skirt that stopped just short of her knee, over a pair of black, patterned tights. Her shoes were black and pointed like daggers, and her blue jumper clung tightly to her breasts and her waist. A professional smile was drawn across her lips.

She knows, thought Matt, looking into her eyes. This is a woman who knows plenty about men, and how they react. She already knows what I'm going to say. Probably even knows the tone of voice in which I'll say it.

'Where are Pinky and Perky?'

'Who?' she asked.

'You know, the two squeaky pigs.'

'They're waiting down the corridor,' said Alison. 'I wanted to talk to you first. To hear your decision.'

'One question first,' said Matt. 'Why me?'

'You're a good man, with a good record of service. You might not have been officer material, but that's no mark of disrespect. A lot of the best soldiers aren't. For this mission we need someone trained to SAS standards. And we need someone who needs cash.'

Matt moved across the room; he didn't want to feel her eyes upon him. 'I was a screw-up as a share trader,' he said. 'I thought I could make money, and I couldn't. I probably didn't have the brains, and I certainly didn't have the training. But one piece of advice from that has stayed with me. Whenever you were looking at a company or a trade, if it looks too good to be true, then it probably is.' He turned around, looking right at her. 'That's my problem. This looks too good to be true.'

'Cynicism is OK, Matt,' Alison replied sharply. 'We don't want you to be too trusting. But I don't understand what you mean. In what way is it too good, exactly?'

Matt spread his arms in front of him. 'Here I am, a washed up SAS man, hardly employable, then this good-looking blonde comes along and says I can make two million dollars for a few weeks' work,' said Matt, his tone hardening. He paused, looking towards the window. 'So I'm just wondering, aren't there some rats scurrying around somewhere, and shouldn't I start smelling them? Why an *ex*-SAS man, for example? Why not just give the details of the boats to the Regiment, let them take them out. Even better, tell our American friends about it. Delta Force would love to have a crack at those guys. I don't see why you want someone like me to do it. It complicates the mission. What don't I know?'

Alison stood up and stepped closer to Matt. 'Listen,' she said. 'I like you, I think you can tell that. I'm not going to try and smart-talk you into anything. You're too clever. The reason we're not using the Regiment, or Delta Force, or anyone like that, is very simple. The mission is off the books, Matt. Unofficial. Anything goes wrong, we have complete deniability. Think of the possible consequences if this was an official Regiment mission. British soldiers storming a boat in another country's territorial waters? Killing some men our enemies would claim were just innocent Arab business-men – stealing from them?' She brushed a hand across his cheek, her skin delicate against the stubble on his face. 'So, I'm sorry, if anything goes wrong, then the view of the British government is this: it's just a bunch of former soldiers who've turned themselves into gangsters. Nothing to do with us.'

Matt pushed her hand aside, but not roughly. There would be plenty of time for touching later. Her story was good enough. In the twisted world of Five it was convenient for them to use men who were completely expendable. Back in the Regiment bar, MI5 was an organisation known mainly for its arse-covering and back-stabbing.

But Matt's mind was already made up, and he had heard nothing to make him change it. He needed a second chance, and this was the only one on offer.

You make your decision and you go with it. You hang up your doubts with your coat at the door.

'OK, I'll do it,' he said firmly. 'Where do we start?'

Alison drew away, the hint of a laugh in her eyes. She was, Matt judged, a woman who was used to getting what she wanted from men – and he was no exception. He was doing what she wanted. She'd known he would.

'I'll get Pinky and Perky,' she said.

Matt could have used a beer, but mineral water was all there was. He took a sip and looked across the desk. Pinky and Perky were sitting on chairs on either side, their ties straight and their legs crossed. Alison perched on the side of the bed. It feels right to get back to work, Matt decided. This is what I'm good at.

'Five men,' Pinky said. 'That's the number we'll need for the mission.'

'Why five?' Matt asked.

'Pirates,' said Pinky. 'That's basically what you'll be. You'll be raiding a boat and stealing everything on board. Our calculations are that you'll need a small dinghy to approach the boat, and one man to steer that, and you'll need four men to hit the boat. That makes five.'

Matt nodded. 'All ex-SAS?'

'Maybe, maybe not,' said Alison. 'We've got some guys in mind already.'

'Who are they?'

Perky turned towards the laptop on his desk and pulled up a file. 'MI5 keeps records of all you SAS boys, as you may know,' he said. 'The taxpayer went to a lot of trouble to turn you into killers. We like to know where you all are, and what you're up to.'

'We know,' said Matt. 'And don't think we like it either. We've served our time; we're free to do whatever we like.'

'Within the law,' Pinky said archly.

No point in arguing now, thought Matt. 'So who have you got?'

'When you look at the qualifications,' Pinky said, 'the field starts to narrow down. We want men only recently out of the Regiment. Much more than three years as civilians and they'll be too flabby. We want men who need money and need it badly. But at the same time, we don't want complete drunks, cokeheads or psychopaths. That rules out a few as well.'

'There's always Regiment guys who need money,' said Matt. 'It's not like we get big pay-offs when we leave.'

'Exactly. Here are two names,' said Perky. 'We'd like you to approach both men.'

Alison moved closer to where Matt was standing. 'With the SAS men, it would be better if you make the approach,' she said. 'It'll come better from you.'

Matt looked down at the piece of paper. Two names were printed in small black lettering: Joe Cooksley and Alan Reid. He knew both men quite well but they had not been close friends. He had served alongside them both in Bosnia in the 1990s. They hadn't been in the same squadron, but they had worked together on the assassination of Janos Biktier, one of the local warlords who'd thrived under Milosevic's patronage, and whose men had been raping and killing their way through Kosovo. An evil bastard. Matt had enjoyed that mission: Biktier richly deserved the bullet he'd left in his skull. Cooksley and Reid had been in a team that had proved itself under fire, providing Matt with the cover he needed as he moved in for the final kill. He had been happy to trust them with his life then. He would be happy enough to do so again now.

Poor bastards. I wonder what kind of messes they're in to qualify them to make it on to this list?

'Any particular reason for these two?'

'We've asked around,' said Pinky. 'We hear they're good men, and for different reasons they might need money. We think you should talk to them. If they don't want to, there are more names we can give you.'

'There's a regimental get-together tomorrow night in Hereford,' said Perky. 'You should go. Get talking to them.'

Matt nodded. 'That makes three, if they agree. Who else?'

'You'll need some specialist help,' said Alison. 'This is stealing. The gold and the diamonds in the boat will almost certainly be in a safe, so we'll need someone who knows about cracking those open. I've got someone in mind. And once you've got the stuff, you'll need someone to fence it. You can't just walk into Ratner's and offer them thirty million dollars' worth of gold and jewels. I know someone who can help you with that too.'

'So do I,' said Matt.

Damien. Damien will know the right people to deal with.

Alison, Pinky and Perky exchanged glances. They are saying something, Matt realised. But not out loud. Not so I can hear it.

'It would be better if I chose the gang members,' said Alison.

'Better for you, maybe,' Matt said swiftly. He could see her face turning to stone and some words starting to form on her lips, and he could tell they were likely to be harsh. He relaxed, flashing her a grin – he could be manipulative too. 'Listen,' he said. 'The guy I have in mind is good, and I can trust him for reasons of my own. But if you don't like him, he's not in. OK?'

'Maybe,' said Alison.

'Meanwhile, I'll start talking to these guys.'

'It has to be secret,' said Perky. 'Any leaks will cost lives.'

'Hey,' said Matt, 'anything goes wrong, I'm the one who's getting his balls blown off.'

Alison looked towards Matt, her eyelashes dropping coyly, and her red, painted fingernails brushed the edge of his wrist. 'Mr Browning,' she said softly, 'thanks for accepting the mission. I'm sure it will be a pleasure for us to work together.'

The bar was hot and crowded, the smell of beer already thick in the air. Matt stood in the doorway for a moment, letting the scent of the place fill his nostrils. It wasn't a scent you could put in a shop. Nobody was ever going to bottle it and sell it as aftershave, but to him, it was as sweet as any cologne. It smelt like home.

He walked slowly through the room. The sergeants' mess was open every evening, and although it usually catered for only serving members, it was the venue for every reunion. Tonight, the class of 1990 – the year Matt had joined up – was meeting. That was one of the things Matt admired most: the spirit and camaraderie of the Regiment. You could leave it, but it never left you.

On the walls were photographs, paintings and captured weapons from past campaigns. Matt glanced to the left. Up there was a Barrett .50 sniper rifle, the model used by the IRA for the bulk of its assassinations of British soldiers. Matt had been on the team that captured that weapon from a Provo sniper in 1993, and the sight of it now stirred proud memories. Next to it was an AK-47 captured during the battle of Mirbat in Oman in 1972.

He caught the eye of one of a group of lads standing close to the bar. Young men, maybe twenty-six to twenty-eight. There was a look of hunger in their eyes. Like looking in a mirror, thought Matt, but one that returns a reflection of how you looked a decade ago.

They might look like boys to him, but they were already battle-hardened sergeants. It reminded Matt of how he had aged over the past decade.

The Regiment teaches us how to do amazing things, he realised as he took his first sip of beer. Fantastic feats of endurance, physical stamina and bravery. But they don't teach us the lesson we most need: how to survive on the outside.

He heard a voice calling his name: a raucous Geordie accent he would have recognised anywhere. Steve Watts had been one of his great pals in the Regiment. They had been on the same training courses together. Matt always remembered a rain-sodden night hiking across the Brecon Beacons with a heavily laden bergen on his back, when it seemed as if every muscle was about to explode and his spirit was already past breaking point. It had only been Wattsie's jokes that had pulled him through. Another time they had been holed up together in the bleak, dark hills of County Antrim, ambushed by a group of Provos, heavily outnumbered and under withering fire. One of them had to make a break across open country to call in some back-up. Matt offered to flip a coin, but Wattsie had said no. He had a good feeling about it, and he'd take the chance.

Matt had met plenty of people since leaving the Regiment, and made lots of new friends, but none of them were brothers like Wattsie.

Playing with life and death. It forms bonds between men that are impossible in the ordinary run of civilian life.

'Look at that tan, man. That's the life,' said Wattsie, his thick, muscled hand slapping hard against Matt's back. 'I look at you and I think, What the hell are you doing back in Newcastle, Wattsie, you daft bugger? The lasses aren't in bikinis because it's too bloody cold, the beer costs two bloody quid a pint, and the football team still hasn't won anything. I'm telling you, I'm on the next plane out.'

Matt grinned. Whatever your problems, they could melt away in the company of men such as this. 'How's it going?'

'Not so bad, mate, not so bad,' said Wattsie. 'Those al-Qaeda boys, we've got a lot to thank them for. Put a few blokes like me back in business. I started doing a bit of security work, then nothing. After six months, things were so bad I did a few nights as a bouncer down at Quayside. The lasses are the worst. The lads, you just give them a bit of a slap, let them sleep it off out the back. But the lasses, you don't want to start roughing them up, but some of them are so drunk, there's nothing else you can do.'

'But it's got better?'

Wattsie took a swig on his beer, nodding to the barman for a fresh glass. 'After September the eleventh, all the Yanks and Japs started pissing themselves,' he said. 'They want protection. Bodyguards for executives, advice on how to search their factories. Now, that assassination of David Landau out in Saudi has made them all even more nervous. Business has never been so good. So I'm back on my feet. Can't complain.'

The world has become a tense, edgy place, but that is good for men like us. We thrive in nervous times.

'But a bar in Marbella – that's the life, though,' said Wattsie. 'I'll bring the wife and kids out in the summer, we can afford it this year, not like the last two years. We could use a holiday.'

'There's always a beer waiting for you at the Last Trumpet.'

The next hour drifted past in a series of drink-fuelled recollections. Old fights, old officers, accidents with girls, engagements with the enemy – anecdotes it was good to share with men who had lived through the same traumas. Matt bought a pint for Danny Sparsen and Rhys Davids – two men he had fought with in a nasty search-and-rescue mission in Chechnya, getting out some British businessmen who had been selling arms there, and who seemed to have enough pull for a Regiment squad to be sent over to rescue them. He owed his life to Rhys, and Danny owed his life to Matt. More bonds, none of which could be untied by the passage of a few years. Rhys was working for his brother's building company in Newport: Danny had been guarding some oilfields out in Kuwait. They were getting on with their lives.

Will Darton wandered by to say hello. He was a Rupert, but one of the better ones. Matt had fought with him in Sierra Leone, and found him straight and honest and willing to listen to his men. A cut above the usual Sandhurst crap. Maybe that was why he hadn't made it above Major, and was now out in civilian life along with the rest of them. Will was retraining as a surveyor near Chippenham, and had just had his first kid: after the second beer, he confessed that he was bored. The grey, narrow repetitiveness of office life got to him.

After ten years in the SAS, everyone found it hard to find something else to do with their lives, something that held the same promise of danger, purpose and excitement. They were all searching, but only a few of them would find it.

Matt had been getting worried that Cooksley and Reid might not show up. By the time they arrived at 11.30 they'd already had a few beers in town. Matt got in a fresh round of drinks. Both men had changed little since the last time he had seen them: a few more hairs missing, and a few more lines etched into the skin. Cooksley was a slim, wiry man. At first sight you might think he was nervous: he stumbled over his words, and could seldom find the phrase he was looking for. But Matt knew he was only socially shy. In any other setting he had the heart of a lion. Reid was shorter, around five foot eight, with black hair and stocky shoulders. His eyes were almost black, his skin was drawn tight over the bone of his face, and his muscles were taut and lean. Cooksley was working in marketing for a company that made mobile phone accessories, and Reid said he was doing some bodyguarding for a rich American. Both men said they were doing fine. Glad to be free and finally making some money, said Reid flippantly, but behind the bar-room bravado Matt knew the truth was very different. They would not have been on Alison's list otherwise. Neither man would admit to it, but as the evening wore on Matt could tell it was there somewhere. Behind the broad smiles, the old war stories, the rounds of beer and the dirty jokes, there was a shadow: he could hear it in the tone of their voices. Some hidden trouble was eating away at each of them.

I can see it in them – and they can probably see it in me.

'To fallen comrades,' said Wattsie, raising his pint high.

Matt raised his glass and poured beer down his neck. There were days when you couldn't help wondering if the fallen were the lucky ones. 'To the survivors,' he said. They knew what he was talking about. Life in the Regiment was tough, but at least you had your comrades around you. On the outside, you walk alone.

'To the survivors,' echoed a dozen voices around the room.

SIX

The house was a 1950s semi, its white paint starting to fade. An Astra van was parked on the short gravel driveway. It stood on the outskirts of Pembridge, a village of five hundred people about ten miles north of Hereford, close to Shobdon private airfield. From the seat of his Porsche, Matt could see the kids' clothes on the washing line, fluttering in the wind blowing down from the Welsh hillsides. Judging by the size of the two romper suits, he'd guess they were about four and two.

Suburban family life, thought Matt. It suits some men, but not me. After I collect the two million, Gill and I are going to live somewhere hot and glamorous.

He stepped out of the Boxster, stretching his legs as he walked around the vehicle. In the distance he could see Cooksley walking down the lane, a newspaper and a pint of milk under his arm. A dog was with him, a Collie, barking and running ahead. The man's head was bowed, looking at the ground, following the curves of the pavement. His shoulders were sagging, and his eyes looked weary.

'Good to see you last night,' called Matt.

Cooksley looked up. 'You too, mate.'

Matt followed him into the house and accepted the offer of a cup of coffee. Sarah was spooning some milky porridge into the mouth of Danny, the younger of the two boys. Callum was running around waving a Monsters Inc toy. 'You a man,' he said, thrusting a green one-eyed Mikey into Matt's hands.

A smell of nappies and food filled the kitchen and the floor was covered with brightly coloured lumps of plastic. Sarah Cooksley looked tired and hassled, her eyes drooped and lines of exhaustion collected around her face. She had been a beauty when he had first seen her one night in a bar in Hereford. Matt had tried to chat her up himself, but she had thinned him out. It was a surprise when she started going out with Cooksley – she was obviously drawn to the silent, brooding type. Two years had passed since Matt had seen Sarah, but it could have been ten: her long brown hair had been cut into a short bob, her eyes had lost their sparkle and her skin its shine. She was still a beauty, Matt decided, but a troubled one. He knew nothing of her life, but he could tell it was a struggle. Daily existence was grinding her down.

'You haven't changed a bit,' she said, kissing Matt on the cheek. 'How's Gill?'

'She's fine,' Matt replied with a stab of guilt. 'Still in Marbella.'

Matt took the coffee Sarah made him, spent a few minutes play-fighting with Callum, then looked up towards Cooksley. 'Let's go for a walk,' he said. 'I need to talk to you.'

A path led away from the back of the house into the hills. The border between England and Wales lay somewhere close to here, stretching across the peaceful contours of the landscape. A few sheep were grazing in the fields. A light rain was falling, and Matt pulled the collar of his overcoat high up around his neck. The two men walked in silence. Matt wanted to put a safe distance between himself and the house before he began.

The things we are going to discuss are not for the wife and kids to hear.

He climbed over a stone wall, glad to have the chance to flex his muscles. He had drunk a skinful of beer the night before, and he had felt it when he'd woken up. The air would do him good, and so would the exercise.

'Things aren't OK, are they, Joe?' he said.

Cooksley, he knew, was a man of few words, and most of those had only one syllable. He looked up at Matt, the surprise written on to his face. 'Who told you?'

'Five,' Matt answered.

Cooksley walked on, staring at the ground. 'We're out of that game, Matt,' he said. 'Our time is served.'

Matt shook his head. 'I'm back.' He turned to look at his friend. In Cooksley's eyes he could see something he had never seen before, not even in the treacherous, bandit-infested mountains of Kosovo: fear. 'They've told me to recruit four men,' he continued. 'Men who need money, who'll take a chance if they have to.'

'Bastards,' muttered Cooksley. 'I knew Five kept tabs on us all, but I didn't realise they had access to our medical records.'

'What is it, Joe? Are you ill?'

Cooksley walked on, striding across the open field. 'It's Callum and Danny, they have cystic fibrosis.'

Matt stopped in his tracks. 'Christ, I'm sorry. Is there anything you can do?'

'The doctors don't reckon so,' said Cooksley. 'It's incurable. Both of them are going to die.' He paused, looking down into the mud. 'Sarah's cracking up, I don't know how much longer she can stand it.' He looked around. 'You don't know what it's like, Matt. Think of the worst torture you can imagine, then multiply it by ten. And you still wouldn't even be close.'

Matt started walking again, pushing on through the field. 'If there was any treatment you'd get it on the National Health, wouldn't you? You wouldn't need extra money?'

He could hear Cooksley taking a deep breath, turning something over in his mind. 'There's a doctor in California called Peter Beelah. He's working on a gene therapy. It's completely experimental, and unregulated. Some people think you shouldn't even mess around with genetics. But if it's our only chance, we'll take it. The boys would have to be there for a year, getting treatment every day.'

'How much does it cost?'

'Half a million dollars,' he replied. 'Bugger it, Matt,

76

I'm just an ex-soldier. I sell mobile phone accessories for some crappy little firm in Hereford. I'm making eighteen bloody grand a year, plus commission. But there never is any commission, because the product's rubbish and I'm a rubbish salesman. Where the hell am I ever supposed to get that kind of money?'

'I'm not here to sell you anything,' said Matt. 'You are your own man, and you make your own choices.' He started climbing over the wall they had reached, holding out an arm to help his friend across. He could tell from the way Joe held himself that he was desperate to hear more.

'It's one mission,' he continued. 'It will be illegal, and off the books, but we'll have help from Five, and there will never be any charges. It will take about a month. At the end, the pay-off will be more than enough to take care of both kids.'

Cooksley laughed bitterly. 'Where do I sign?'

Matt rested his hand on his friend's shoulder.

'If it would save my boys, I'd walk through hell,' said Cooksley sharply. 'With a smile on my face.'

Matt stepped into the dark room. A chink of light was shining through a half broken pane of glass, but there was nothing else to illuminate his path. He walked over a beer bottle, and an empty pizza carton. Kneeling down, he shook Reid on the shoulder. 'Wake up, man,' he said. 'We need to talk.'

Reid sat bolt upright, his expression angry, his fists clenched as if he were about to throw a punch.

Instinctively Matt ducked away: he'd felt one of Reid's blows on his jaw before – they'd fallen out over a girl – and he'd promised himself never to take another one. He had a punch that would rock Mike Tyson.

Reid looked at Matt, blinked, then grinned. 'What the hell are you doing here?'

'Cooksley told me where to find you,' Matt replied. 'He said you'd be kipping down here for a couple of nights. Clean yourself up and let's go get some food. I want to talk to you.'

Reid struggled up from the mattress and walked towards the bathroom. He was still wearing the jeans and the sweatshirt he'd had on the night before, and Matt could still smell the beer on his breath. Matt looked around the room. He'd known some guys to doss down in some rough looking places for a few nights when they needed to and not let it get to them. But this was a hovel. A small house about five miles from the village, set amid a group of three agricultural buildings, it belonged to a farmer who owned apple estates along the Welsh borders. At harvest time, farmers like that bring in cheap labour to pick the fruit. This was where the labourers would sleep. There was one sofa, two mattresses on the floor, and what only the most optimistic estate agent could call a kitchen – a sink, a kettle and an electric ring encrusted with old baked beans. Paper was hanging loose from the walls, the single uncovered bulb hanging from the ceiling was broken, and a bucket in the corner was collecting the water that dripped through the roof. What Reid was doing here, Matt had no idea. But he could see why he was on Alison's list.

Dressed in a fresh pair of chinos, with his chin shaved and his hair combed, Reid didn't look particularly successful or prosperous, but at least he didn't look like a tramp. They drove in silence back to Hereford, parked the car, and headed towards Ascari's Café on West Street. Reid had hand-rolled a pair of cigarettes in the car and now he lit one, putting the other in his pocket. It was already nearly noon, but Ascari's served breakfast all day and it was the best fry-up in town. Greasy, protein-rich food was what they both needed. It would settle their minds, and then they could talk.

What's happened? Matt asked himself as they walked through the street. She'd been working as a waitress by night and studying to be a beautician during the day when Reid met her, and Matt had first met her at a squadron Christmas party. Way out of your league, they'd told Reid. This was a woman who didn't need to study beauty, she was already there. But, Matt admitted later, they were jealous as well. Jane was the best-looking woman any of them had ever been out with. Tall, with dark hair and strong cheekbones, she held herself like a princess. Reid had fallen hard, and never so much as looked at another girl after that. So what's happened? Matt wondered. Reid and Jane lived just down the road from Cooksley in Pembridge. They had a lovely house, two kids, Eddie and Chloe. Matt had been with him in Bosnia when Eddie was born, and he'd never seen anyone so happy. When he got the camcorder film from Jane of Eddie taking his first steps, he risked being RTUd by breaking into a UN warehouse to steal the batteries to get the camcorder working. He risked his career just to watch a baby waddling across the floor.

So what's he doing sleeping in a farm labourers' barn five miles from his family? How do our lives get so tangled up?

A plate of eggs, bacon, sausages, beans, black pudding and chips landed in front of him. Matt pitched some ketchup on the side of the plate, and loaded the first forkful of sausage into his mouth. 'You've got a lovely wife, and two nice kids,' he said. 'What are you doing kipping down in a place like that?'

'Sometimes the breaks go with you, sometimes against you.'

'But Jane, the kids – you haven't split with them have you?'

Reid put down the fork, a piece of bacon still hanging from it. 'Leave Jane? Are you joking?' He paused, put the food into his mouth and chewed slowly. 'Sometimes I think I love her too much.'

For a moment Matt found himself thinking about Gill, wondering what she might be doing.

'So, this loving her too much,' he said, 'you express it by walking a couple of miles down the road and sleeping in a hovel? Christ, we should have let the Kosovans finish you off when they had the chance.'

'You don't understand.'

'Tell me then.'

'I lost my job,' said Reid. 'I had some work body-guarding a French guy, paid quite well. I lost that, and we ran up some debts. Then I got some work for some South Africans, but they buggered off without paying me, so that was even worse. We were getting more and more behind with the mortgage, taking out loans just to pay for the kids' shoes. Then I get a job looking after a Columbian guy in London, but it fell through after two days. I haven't worked for a month, and I haven't earned any proper money for six months.'

We're all the same, thought Matt. Trying to keep some woman happy. We just have different ways of going about it.

'You told Jane you still had the job, and you were dossing down in the barn, right?'

'You know the kind of woman Jane is,' Reid said. He turned to his cup of tea, stirring in two sugars. 'She's a princess. She expects a man to be able to go out and earn a living and support her and the kids. I can't go home and look her in the eye and say that I'm not able to do that.'

Matt didn't know what to say. 'Sooner or later, you've got to level with her.'

Reid shrugged. 'Maybe something will turn up,' he said sourly.

Matt paused. 'It just did,' he said.

Reid looked up towards him, a question-mark in his eyes.

'There's a job,' said Matt, lowering his tone. 'For

Five. Off the books, unofficial, but we get training and gear. At the end, a big pay-off.'

Matt watched him closely. He had seen Reid in many different situations: under fire, showing incredible bravery and determination; in a funk of cold fear when he lost his nerve; drunk out of his brain on cheap beer; sighing over pictures of his children on a cold, lonely and distant battlefield. But he had never seen the look he saw in his eyes now: hope, mixed with relief. 'How much?'

We listen in different ways. Some of us want to know who we hit. Some of us how dangerous it is. And some of us just want to know how much.

'Enough,' said Matt. 'You could get your princess a new tiara, yourself a new car, and still never have to work again.'

'And you're in charge?'

Matt shook his head. 'Five are in charge,' he replied. 'They just started with me.'

Reid took his hand-rolled cigarette from his pocket, slipped it between his lips, and searched around for a light. 'One question,' he said. 'Who handles the money? I don't mind doing a job for Five, but I wouldn't want their thieving hands on my cash.'

Matt nodded. 'A friend of mine,' he said. 'Five don't know it yet, but we bring along our own boy for that end of the deal.'

Reid drained the last of his mug of tea, glanced towards the window, then looked back at Matt. 'Well, if it's good enough for you . . . I can't face going back to Jane and telling her we might lose the house. Christ, we might have to go and live at her mum's.'

You look at people you grew up with, the first thing you notice is how they've aged, Matt realised as he shook Damien by the hand. Then it hits you. If they've aged, so have you. 'You're looking good,' said Matt.

'You too,' said Damien.

Matt glanced along the length of the bar. The Two Foxes was an average boozer, in a side street around the back of Camberwell High Street in south London. To anyone dropping in for a pint it looked like one of thousands of pubs tucked into every street of the city: faded Victorian coach lamps on the walls, thick, stained wood around the bar, beer mats on every table, and the same pair of old geezers nursing their glasses of stout and rolling their own. But to anyone in the know, it was an office – a place where the Walters family, and a few of the other south-London crime dynasties, came to carve up the spoils. Two men sipping on pints might well be arranging who could and couldn't sell dope on the Brixton streets. Two guys at the bar sinking whiskies and sodas could well be arranging protection for the Albanians who shipped eastern European hookers into the massage parlours of south London. To the innocent, it was just another pub. To the regulars, it was as busy with deals as the trading floor of any City bank.

The SAS had been Matt's escape from this part of town, and this kind of life. Crime had been Damien's. The Army had given Matt respect and dignity, and the gangs had made Damien richer and better dressed than he would have been. He looked different to Gill – his hair was black, he was six inches taller, and his eyes were darker – but there was similarity in some of their gestures and mannerisms. You could tell instantly they were moulded from the same materials.

'How's business?' said Matt.

'Too much competition,' said Damien. 'Can't keep the margins up. People think it's a soft option, but it's bloody hard graft.'

There had never been any secrets between Matt and Damien: there were no pretences about what Damien and his family did for a living. They had grown up together. Maybe when Matt was five or six he'd started noticing that Damien's parents had a lot more money than his. Certainly after Matt's father injured himself at the factory and couldn't work again, somehow Damien always had the cash for new trainers, new records, and a new car when he was eighteen. But that had never been a barrier between them. All through their teenage years they had run through the streets together, getting into the same fights and chasing the same girls. The night before Matt left to join the Army he went round to Damien's house, and his father spoke to him, told him he could have a better life and make more money working for one of his gangs. 'That's the life for a man who wants to fight,' he could remember the old guy saying to him. 'We look after our boys a lot better than the Army looks after theirs.' And maybe, looking back on it fifteen years later, he was right.

'And you?' said Damien.

'OK,' replied Matt. 'Gill sends her love.'

'Tell her to ring mum,' said Damien.

Inside, Matt was squirming. On the drive back from Hereford he had called Damien, telling him he was in town and suggesting they get a beer. He still hadn't spoken to Gill since the split. She obviously hadn't told her family. If she had, he suspected Damien would be furious with him. Gill may have moved to Spain because she wanted to put some distance between herself and her family – she didn't approve of the way they made their money – but she was still blood.

'I'm swapping trades,' said Matt. 'Mine for yours.'

Damien looked up at him. Even though he was the same age as Matt, he looked younger. Most people would guess he was twenty-nine, thirty. He spent half his life at sea, and sailed his own small dinghy every weekend off the Essex coast, which gave his skin a thick, weatherbeaten appearance. His teens and his twenties he had spent on the smuggling runs between Holland and the Essex marshes. He'd take a boat over to Rotterdam, pick up some gear, and be back by dawn. That made him both an expert sailor, and a man who knew all that could be known about navigating at night.

Damien had thick black hair, swept back over his head, clear blue eyes, and strong shoulders that sloped away from his neck. It was in the way he laughed that Matt could see bits of Gill in him: he always started giggling right at the start of one of his own jokes, and Gill did the same thing.

'Aren't things OK at the Last Trumpet? Last time anyone looked at the books it seemed to be making a bit of money.'

Matt shrugged. 'The bar is fine,' he replied. 'It's just not making the kind of money I need to get myself out of the jam I'm in.' He paused, letting the alcohol fill his veins. 'I've lost a bundle dabbling in shares, and I need to get it back quickly.'

'And you want to rob it?'

'Listen, between you and me, I've been tapped up by Five for a job,' said Matt. 'It's just parting some money from some very nasty boys so they can't do anything bad with it. The twist is, we get to keep the loot at the end. It's a private job, not Regiment.' He looked at Damien. 'Listen, at the end of the job we might have a lot of valuable stuff. But hot. What's your advice?'

Damien whistled, running a hand through his hair. 'The trick with robbing is to make sure you're nicking from the right people,' he said. 'That's why people rob banks, insurance companies. You just get a few middle management types riled up, and they don't scare anybody. It's like having some bunny rabbits chasing after you. But who are you nicking from, Matt, and what are they going to think?'

'I can't say, not yet,' Matt replied. 'I can look after myself. The money is worth it.'

'OK, so long as you know what you're getting into, that's all.'

'I know,' said Matt. 'It's how I fence the money that bothers me.'

'How much?'

'I can't say yet,' answered Matt. 'But unless it was the Bank of England, more than you'd find in any bank.'

'Then you want to make sure you keep hold of the money yourself,' said Damien. 'Don't let Five go near it. Any job you do, it's not getting the money that's the problem. It's getting rid of it, and splitting it up.'

'Could you help?'

'Since Dad died business hasn't been so great,' said Damien. 'The gangs, they're like a corporation. You have to prove yourself a coming man. You have to bring in some big deals.' He glanced through the pub, his voice dropping to a whisper. 'I could use something big. In this line of work, you're only as tough as your last hit.'

Matt nodded to the barman for a refill. 'You are my oldest and best friend,' he said. 'If anything happened to you I'd never forgive myself.'

'Dangerous?' said Damien, his face cracking into a laugh. 'You know that Camberwell breeds the hardest villains in the world.'

The flat was on the twelfth floor of Chelsea Harbour, a luxurious development of apartments, shops, restaurants and a hotel overlooking the Thames on a curve of the river where Chelsea starts to turn into Fulham. Matt stood in the lift and glanced down at his watch. Eleven-fifteen. Late.

Maybe I should have bought her some flowers.

He felt uncomfortable walking through the lobby.

He could see some of the high-class Chelsea girls and their banker boyfriends looking at him suspiciously. Who let the security guard in? they were thinking. The Porsche fitted in with the other hundred-grand vehicles in the car park, but Matt was wearing jeans, sweatshirt and a waxed green jacket – fine for a Regimental reunion but out of place amid the marble and gilt of this lobby.

Who cares? Another month, maybe I'll buy a flat here myself.

He pressed the buzzer. Alison was wearing a red silk kimono when she opened the door. In the background he could hear a George Michael CD playing on the hi-fi. Those thirtysomething birds, they love old Georgie, Matt reflected as he stepped into the apartment. He hits all the right notes.

An elegant expanse of leg was exposed as Alison walked across the polished pine floorboards towards the kitchen. 'I thought you might be hungry,' she said, looking back at him. 'So I made you something.'

Matt slung his jacket over the sofa. The apartment was plusher than he would have expected. It had polished wood floors, spotlights inset into a white ceiling, and black wooden Oriental furniture – stuff Matt had last seen in the antique shops of Hong Kong. On the back wall was a huge 1950s modernist painting, covering twenty feet by ten.

The civil service is paying better these days.

'I'm starving,' he shouted towards the kitchen.

A huge window made up one wall, and Matt looked

out over the snarling traffic and noise of south London, its lights twinkling back at him. If I look closely, Matt thought, I can probably see the council tower where Mum and Dad lived. That was on the twelfth floor as well.

'It's ready,' she called back.

The kitchen was made out of polished granite and stainless steel. The units and appliances looked like the kind of machines girls drool over, but they meant nothing to Matt: he preferred cooking over an open camp fire. She was leaning over the hob, a flame turned up high underneath a wok. Matt could smell prawns, garlic, chillis, ginger and noodles. 'Get some wine,' she said, pointing towards the fridge.

Matt pulled a Chablis from the rack of bottles, uncorked it, and placed two glasses on the table. 'It went well,' he said. 'Reid and Cooksley have signed up. They don't know what the mission is yet, so maybe they'll back out. But they're brave men, and by Christ they need the money.'

Alison put the steaming wok down on the table, laying two plates and some chopsticks at its side. 'I knew you could do it,' she said, running her fingers through his hair. 'That's why I chose you.'

'There's another guy as well,' said Matt. 'Damien Walters. His family runs with the gangs in south London. He'll come on the job, and take care of the fencing for us.'

Alison swallowed the food in her mouth, looking directly at Matt. 'Your future brother-in-law?'

'You know about him?'

'I work for MI5, Matt,' she replied. 'Walters. Went to school with you, old pals. He's gay, but discreet about it. It doesn't stop him being a hard man when he needs to be. His father Eddie Walters was a big-time gangster, controlled a lot of the money in south London. Damien is struggling to play in the same league. I'm told he's not quite cutting it, not yet. I hope you haven't told him what we're planning?'

'Everybody needs a motive,' Matt said quietly. 'If they didn't need the cash, they wouldn't be up for this job. We need someone we can trust on the team, and he has the right skills. He can steer the boat for us, and he knows how to fence the money after we've taken it. I say he's in.'

'I don't like it – it's a conflict. You and he are going to be loyal to each other, not to the team. It could cause splits.' Alison took a sip on her wine. 'We won't fence the money ourselves, but we can find a reliable person who can. You don't need to be suspicious, Matt. Five will look after everything.'

'Right, and nice girls don't stay for breakfast,' said Matt. 'I've talked about it with Reid and Cooksley and they agree with me. If we don't get control of the money, then we don't want to do it.'

'I was planning our own man,' said Alison. 'Ex-Special Boat Squad. Needs cash in a hurry. I think you should go and talk to him.'

Matt shook his head. 'We want our own people.'

A smile flicked over Alison's lips. 'I've no

objections,' she replied carefully. 'Like I said, once you get the money, it's yours. We just want to make sure al-Qaeda don't get it.'

Matt nodded. He noticed the way her kimono was slipping aside as she crossed her legs, revealing the soft tanned skin of her thigh. 'Damien's in, so that makes four,' he said. 'He knows about boats as well, so he covers that angle as well. But who's the fifth guy?'

'Ivan Rowe.'

'Tell me about him.'

'In the morning,' said Alison, putting her wine glass down on the table. 'You are staying the night, aren't you?'

Matt glanced again at her thigh, his gaze moving down her slender legs, down to her ankles and her feet. He looked back up slowly, his eyes roving across her body until he met hers. 'Of course.'

A low double-bed with crisp white sheets and a black duvet sat in the centre of the bedroom. The side table was cluttered with make-up and hairbrushes, a couple of chick-lit novels and a thick, hardback biography of Field Marshal Montgomery. The wooden blinds were shut, hiding the lights beaming across the river.

Matt ran his hand up the inside of her leg. The silk of the kimono was charged with static. He kissed her hard on the lips, feeling her tongue jab back at him, as he pushed her down on to the bed. She yielded, softly at first, then with mounting urgency. He could feel her turning him over, surprised by the strength of her shoulder and arm muscles as she pushed him roughly down into the mattress. Her red fingernails were clawing into his chest, her lips brushing against the skin of his neck.

A woman who likes to take control.

Half an hour later he lay back on the pillow, the smooth skin of Alison's cheek resting on his chest. He had noticed something in her eyes as they made love: passion, certainly, but an edge of anger, as if she were fighting him at the same time. He ran his hand along the curve of her spine, enjoying the way her flesh moved beneath his grip. Better than the first time, he reflected. Like a new gun, a woman always took time to get to know. You had to unlock her, find out which muscles to squeeze and what words to mutter in her ear.

'I was glancing through your file,' she said, her voice lazy and sleepy.

'Old war stories,' answered Matt. 'They don't mean much any more.'

'I was reading about Janos Biktier. That was some mission.'

The Kosovan warlord, thought Matt. The guy Cooksley, Reid and I finished off. 'Just work,' he said.

'His gang is still in business, though,' said Alison. 'And his son's in charge now. Nikolai Biktier. Nasty piece of work.'

'So what?' said Matt.

'Nothing worries you, does it? Not even the thought that one of those guys might come after you one day.'

Matt laughed. 'Right now, a few crazy Serbs are the

least of my worries,' he said. 'I owe half a million to a psychotic Russian gangster, and I'm out to steal thirty million from al-Qaeda. Why worry about a Serb?'

Alison buried her face into his skin, her eyes closing. 'No fear,' she said softly. 'I like that in a man.'

SEVEN

It's in the morning that you can tell what a woman really looks like, Matt decided, dragging the razor across the stubble of his cheek. At night, their faces are painted, their bodies are decorated with jewellery and clothes, and their moods are lightened by wine.

Alison remained completely still while she slept, her hand lying across his chest. When she woke her face was as fresh and lively as it had been the moment she drifted off to sleep. She walked quickly from the bed on the first ring of the alarm at seven precisely, as if there was not a minute to be lost.

A woman who enjoys her work.

He dried his face. Matt hated shaving without foam, and with a woman's razor – but these came with staying overnight at a woman's place. Pulling his jeans back on, he stepped out into the sitting room. Light was streaming through the plate glass window. Alison was already dressed, wearing black linen trousers with a dark blue silk shirt, and a cream jacket was slung over her shoulder.

'Off to work?' He poured a cup of coffee from the pot on the table.

'This is work,' she said. 'I'm taking you to meet Ivan.'

He followed her towards the basement. Take the Porsche, she instructed him. She could get a taxi home later on. He steered the car out on to the King's Road. Victoria, she told him. They would meet Ivan close to the station.

On the car radio, there was a story about the assassination of David Landau. The Prime Minister was due to make a statement about the killing in the House of Commons this afternoon. There was speculation of new powers for the security forces to counter the threat from al-Qaeda.

'Is that what this is about?' said Matt, steering the car into Sloane Square. 'Landau's killing?'

In the car's mirror, Alison was applying some lipstick. 'It's about defeating al-Qaeda,' she answered.

'But getting to Landau – that was a blow for Five, wasn't it?'

Alison shrugged.

'You need some kind of public relations coup to make up for it, don't you?' Matt persisted. 'To make up for the fact none of you knew anything about that murder, or about September the eleventh either.'

'Just keep your eyes on the road,' she said. 'You worry about your job, I'll worry about mine.'

The Easy Everything café was right next to the railway station. At 8.15 in the morning, Matt was surprised by how full it was. There could have been fifty people there – mostly students, backpackers and travellers, all of them sitting by themselves, huddled over computer screens, cups of coffee at their sides. Alison walked swiftly towards the back of the room.

The man was sitting alone, his eyes peering at a web page.

'Ivan,' said Alison. 'This is Matt.'

The man raised a hand as if to silence her. Matt judged he was around thirty-two, thirty-three. He had short black hair, cropped close to his head, and he was wearing a white T-shirt and black jeans. A black leather jacket was slung over his chair. Tall and thin, his muscles tucked neatly into his arms. Probably a lot tougher than he looks, decided Matt. 'Give me two seconds,' he said.

The accent was Ulster, but the soft Ulster of the coast, not the harsh, grating Ulster of Belfast. Matt had learned to tell the difference when he had been in the Province with the Regiment. He glanced towards the screen, noticing how intently the man was staring at it, and the way his fingers were drumming against the desk.

Ivan moved and clicked the mouse, then looked up towards Alison, a mischievous grin playing on his face. He pushed the chair back, stood up and offered Matt his hand. His grip was warm, decisive. 'Bridge,' he said, looking towards Matt. 'The sport of princes. Do you play?'

'Princes?' said Matt. 'Why not kings?'

Ivan laughed. 'No, that's the horses,' he replied. 'And kings can afford to lose. Princes can't.' He paused, his eyes shifting towards Alison. 'There are only two games that require pure skill and brain power and are nothing to do with luck. Chess and bridge. But bridge you can play for money.'

'What about robbery?' said Alison.

'Ah, yes, robbery – that would be a third,' said Ivan, the smile remaining on his lips. 'Shall we find somewhere we can talk?'

Matt followed them towards a small café around the corner. He ordered a plate of bacon, eggs and beans. Ivan asked for the same, Alison for a slice of toast. Some workmen were sitting opposite them, discussing last night's football results. A couple of backpackers were looking at a map of London. Apart from that, it was empty. 'Which part of the Province are you from?' said Matt.

'Portrush,' said Ivan. 'Up on the north coast.'

'I know it,' said Matt. He assumed Ivan was another soldier, and immediately began wondering what regiment he might have been in. 'I did some work around there in the nineties. Lovely coastline. Windy, though. That air comes straight in from the North Pole. Gets into your bones.'

'It's lucky I never killed you then,' said Ivan, a gentle smile on his lips.

The food arrived on the table, the steam from the beans rising up into Matt's face. He paused. The words took a moment to turn through his mind. 'You're a Provo?' he said.

'Was,' said Ivan. 'Let's get our tenses straight.'

Matt looked towards Alison, but she was eating her

toast, not looking at him. 'Maybe she didn't tell you, but I was SAS,' he said sharply. 'Past tense, too. But when it comes to a fight, I still know which side I'm on.'

'For this mission you'll be on the same side,' said Alison. 'You can both leave your history behind. This is a fresh start for both of you.'

'What did you do?' asked Matt. 'For the IRA.'

Ivan started eating his food. 'I broke safes,' he replied. 'The IRA does a lot of bank robberies, in the Province and on the mainland. That means cracking safes. That's my skill.' He paused. 'It's a bit like bridge, you see. A safe needs to be finessed.'

'The gear you're taking will be in a safe, Matt,' said Alison. 'None of your guys knows about that.' She smiled. 'So Ivan's on the team.'

'Why?' said Matt bluntly. 'What's your story? If you're a Provo safe-cracker, why aren't you round the corner casing the local Barclay's?'

'Tenses, tenses,' said Ivan. 'I *was* with the Provos, I'm not any more.'

'Nobody quits,' said Matt. 'It's against the rules. You resign, they kill you.'

'Ivan was turned by Five, Matt,' said Alison. 'He spent three years as an informer. Now he wants out. His cover could break any day. Five will help with a new identity and some money, but you know how it is. Ivan has a wife and two children. He needs *a lot* of money to disappear for ever. Five doesn't pay like that, it's not in our budgets.' She looked straight at him. 'You need a safecracker, he needs the work.'

'And Five's just bringing us all together,' said Matt sourly. 'Like one big happy family.'

Ivan pushed the remnants of his food away from him. 'Listen, you don't want me along, I'm not coming,' he said, his tone hardening. 'Frankly, I'm not crazy about working with a bunch of SAS tossers either. I might have been disillusioned with the Republican cause, man, but I've no time for the psychopaths, racists and bigots the British Army sent over to shoot *our* people either.' His face was starting to redden with anger. 'So, you want to blow your bollocks off trying to crack a safe? Go right ahead. Fine by me.'

'One question,' said Matt. 'Did you ever kill a British soldier?'

Ivan looked straight back at him. 'No,' he answered, his tone clear and direct. 'Did you ever kill a Republican soldier?'

'Three. All armed, all on active service.' He paused, looking directly at Ivan. 'I got paid for it, but I'd have done it for free.'

'Cool it, Matt,' Alison snapped. 'That war is over. We're fighting a new one now.'

What does she know about war? Matt asked himself. *She can start them, but she can't fight them.*

He shook his head. 'There is no way I'm working with a Provo,' he snapped. 'You can just forget it.'

Matt walked silently down the street. His head was bowed, his muscles tightening. He was about to push a couple of million dollars off the table for a principle, but it was a good principle.

You never compromise with the enemy.

'You should have told me,' he said, not looking at Alison.

She said nothing.

'A Provo scumbag,' Matt continued. 'He's a traitor. He's betrayed one cause, he'll betray another. And Christ knows how I'll sell it to Reid and Cooksley.'

Alison stopped. 'For God's sake, grow up,' she said, swivelling around to face him. 'You need this job. This isn't some bloody pleasure cruise. You're going up against the toughest, best-organised terrorist group in the world. If there was one thing the Regiment should have taught you, it's that perfect planning makes for perfect missions, and fucked-up planning makes for fucked-up missions. And dead soldiers.'

Matt turned away from her.

'I'm planning the perfect mission,' he heard her say. 'Don't think for a moment that I give a damn for your feelings.'

'Feelings don't come into it,' Matt said, leaning into her face. 'What would you know? All you've ever done is sit behind a desk all day, sending men out to die. When you're in the field, you have to trust the men you're with absolutely. You have to be willing to die for them, and know they'd die for you.'

'You sound like a junior officer struggling to give his first pep talk and falling flat on his face,' she snapped. 'I've heard enough about duty and comradeship. In case you hadn't noticed, you're not in the Army any more.'

Matt looked away. A dark cloud was looming in the sky above them, threatening rain. 'When Reid was in the Paras, he was a corporal in a patrol that got hit with a pipe bomb by the IRA. Three of his friends died. I can't see Reid and your man Ivan getting on too well together.'

'We're professionals, Matt. We get the job done, no matter what it takes,' replied Alison. 'At Five we don't enjoy paying Provo informers. We don't like building a network of informers at every mosque in the country to keep tabs on al-Qaeda either. We do what we have to do.'

Matt turned to walk away. 'If Reid and Cooksley won't buy it, then neither will I. Your Irishman's out.'

'Then you're out as well, Matt,' replied Alison swiftly. 'This is my mission, don't forget that.'

Always level with the rest of the guys on the team, thought Matt. Whatever other rules you might have to break, that one must always be obeyed.

He looked across at Cooksley and Reid. They were sitting in a café just around the corner from his flat, finishing off some tea and sandwiches. Both men had travelled up from Hereford this morning, and although neither of them yet knew what the mission was, Matt could tell they were committed. They needed the money desperately. They would take whatever risks were necessary to get it.

'There's a problem,' he said simply.

'Already,' said Reid, fiddling with some Rizla papers. 'We haven't even started yet.'

Matt nodded. 'The woman running this is a Five officer called Alison,' he said. 'She wants us to bring along a guy called Ivan. He's a safecracker. The job is going to involve some explosives. That's his bit.'

'So,' said Cooksley. 'Sounds fair enough. Blowing a safe is a specialist job. None of us have training in it.'

'He's a Provo,' said Matt. 'Turned by Five, so he's a traitor as well.'

Around him, Matt could hear the clatter of plates and cups, the waitress shouting at the chef for more sandwiches. But on his table it was completely silent. Reid was holding his coffee halfway between the table and his mouth, but his hand had stopped moving. 'A Provo,' he said, lighting the cigarette he had just rolled, and taking a sharp intake of breath. 'I tell you what, Matt, I'll kill him, then we get on with the mission.'

'I don't like it, Matt,' Cooksley chipped in. 'A team has to have men who can trust each other.'

Matt shrugged. 'I've told her we don't want him,' he said. 'It's up to you guys. You don't want him, the mission's off.'

'Do the mission and then kill him,' said Reid, stubbing out his cigarette in the ashtray. 'That's my plan.'

Reid and Cooksley sat quietly in the corner of the room. Matt recognised their expressions from a hundred different briefings when they'd all been in the Regiment together. Their faces said: What kind of crap are the Ruperts going to throw at us now?

'When do we hear about the dough, Matt?' said Cooksley, looking up from the sofa.

'When we're all together,' replied Matt firmly.

He went to answer the door. Ivan was standing outside. Matt showed him through to the sitting room, handing him a coffee. He checked his watch. Four minutes to three.

'Nice to meet you boys,' said Ivan, stepping into the room and nodding in the direction of Cooksley and Reid.

They looked back, nodded, but remained silent. Their expressions were suspicious, hostile. You didn't need to be an expert in body language, noticed Matt, to tell what was going on.

'How'd your game go?' said Matt.

'Won the game, but lost the rubber,' said Ivan. 'I play on the internet because that's where all the best games are now.' He took a sip of coffee. 'I'll teach you to play if you like. You have the look of a useful bridge player to me.'

'And what do they look like?' asked Matt.

'Two things about bridge,' said Ivan. 'You've got to count the cards, and you've got to judge the man. Counting, anyone can learn that. But judgement, you've either got it or you haven't. Nobody can teach you.'

Matt noticed Cooksley shaking his head in despair.

'Nobody can teach how to be a wanker, either,' said Reid.

'OK, drop it,' said Matt, anxious to calm everyone down. 'There'll be some hanging around on this job, there always is. Maybe we'll learn. We can make it a foursome. Very civilised.'

'There's nothing civilised about bridge,' said Ivan. 'People think it's just for little old ladies, but it's the roughest game there is.'

Matt walked back to the door to let Alison in. 'Everything OK?' he asked.

Alison walked past him. 'If you want Damien on the team, then you have to take Ivan as well,' she said briskly. 'That's the deal. Take it or leave it.'

'Don't give me orders,' Matt retorted. 'I make my own choices.'

Alison turned around to face him, her eyes alight with indignation. 'You were an inch away from being a dosser. You make crap choices.'

Matt turned away. Inside, he was fighting down the desire to snap back at her. Stay calm, he reminded himself. Turning quickly, he walked back to the door, glancing at Damien. He had known him since they were in primary school, and he reckoned he could read his friend's face like a tabloid newspaper: whatever he was thinking was right there in a 72-point black headline. Right now Damien could see a prize a few inches away from him, but feared it was about to be snatched away.

I'll lay out the facts, and let the team take the decision. What else can I do?

He walked through to the main room. 'If we're

doing this, I want proper Regiment rules to apply,' said Matt, standing next to the window. 'Everyone's equal. We take decisions as a group. Everyone pulls his weight. No flapping, no panicking – and if you fuck-up you say sorry and move on. OK?'

Around the room, he could see four men nodding back. Two of them were SAS and two weren't, but whatever their background, they were all warriors.

'We've all agreed to take part in this mission,' he continued. 'But I'm about to give you the details. If you don't like the sound of it, you are still free to go. Nobody's forcing you to do anything. But after this discussion, if you're still up for it, you're committed. There's no backing out. OK?'

He looked through the room again. No dissent.

Matt nodded towards Alison. 'This is Alison. She's a senior MI5 officer. It's her plan, and Five are going to be helping us with logistics, materials and planning.

'We're hitting a boat on the Mediterranean,' Matt continued. 'It's running gold and diamonds for al-Qaeda. There will be at least thirty million dollars in gear on board. Fenced, it should be worth ten million.' Damien cast him a look of confirmation. 'We get to keep the money, no questions asked.'

He looked into their eyes. It was more than they had expected. Unbelievably more. Behind the expressions he could see the calculations being made: two million translated into treatment for the children, a new house and car for the wife, escape from the Provos, or respect among the gangs in Camberwell. Fear and desire and escape. *Those were the currencies being traded.*

'Two million each?' said Cooksley.

'In cash?' added Reid.

'You heard it right,' said Matt. 'The mission should take a month, from today to pay-day. We'll take a day to tell our families, whoever. After that, silence. We're out of contact until it's over. We're all here for our different skills. Cooksley, Reid, and I are all ex-SAS. We know about fighting. Damien is an old pal of mine, and he knows everything about boats. He's also going to help us fence the goods. And Ivan . . .' Matt paused, looking across at the Irishman. 'Well, I've told you about Ivan.'

Matt looked towards Reid. The calculations again: working with a Provo against the money he desperately needed. Swallow some pride, Matt thought. Get used to it.

'How dangerous is it going to be?' said Ivan.

Matt glanced towards Alison.

'Usual risk, high but acceptable,' she said. 'They'll be armed, and they'll do their best to kill you. Against that, you'll have training, numbers and equipment on your side.'

'I meant afterwards,' said Ivan. 'You steal from al-Qaeda, they're going to come after you.'

Another good question, thought Matt. He might be a Provo, but he's sharp. He glanced back towards Alison, noting the hesitation in her eyes. It was the first time he'd seen that: every other question pitched at her she had batted straight back with total self-belief. Not this time.

'There's no such thing as a safe mission,' she said slowly. 'From your different backgrounds, all of you know that. Five can't make any guarantees. But think about it. A boat in the middle of the Med. No one can see or hear you. You kill all the al-Qaeda men on board, then you disappear into the night. How are they ever going to trace you?'

Matt looked around the room. He could see the men nodding, satisfied with the reply. They're hungry for the deal.

They don't want to hear about the risks, and, in truth, neither do I.

'We need to speak among ourselves,' said Matt. 'About Ivan.'

Alison nodded. 'We'll take a walk around the block,' she replied. 'But remember, I think it would be safer for Five to organise fencing the goods. I'll trade you Damien for Ivan.'

'It's not a game of swapsies, it's our lives,' said Matt sharply.

Ivan stood up and looked at each man in turn, his expression dignified, polite, but also questioning. 'I don't want to work with you boys any more than you want to work with me,' he said. 'But I reckon on our different battlefields we've all learnt some of the same lessons. In a crisis, you take your allies where you find them, and you deal with life as it is, not how you'd like it to be.' He turned towards the door, not looking back.

'And remember, a proud man is sometimes also a poor man.'

The door slammed shut. Matt stood silent. Somewhere in the back of his mind, he could see two million dollars slipping away from him. A proud man is sometimes also a poor man, he reflected.

I've been both, and I know which one I prefer.

'Tosser,' said Reid, his expression darkening. 'Stupid Provo tosser.'

'I reckon that's your vote then,' said Matt, trying to smile.

'Maybe she's bluffing,' said Reid. He bent down to pick up a packet of tobacco from the floor. 'I didn't like the look of her much either. Stuck-up, posh totty. I might shag her, but I don't want to take orders from her.'

'He's a bit smart, isn't he?' said Cooksley. 'It's not just that he's a Provo, there's something sly about him.'

'Tell her we'll do it ourselves,' said Reid. 'Four guys is plenty to take a boat if it's the right four men. That's us. We can learn how to blow a safe. There's plenty of Regiment guys can give us some lessons in explosives.'

'Your vote, mate,' said Matt, looking towards Cooksley.

Cooksley hesitated, his eyes rooted to the ground. 'It's the kids,' he said. 'I need this money. I'd team up with Saddam Hussein if I had to.'

'And you, Damien?'

'I'm the trade, aren't I?' said Damien

'We still listen to what you have to say,' said Matt. 'Everyone's voice counts.'

'No trust, no deal, that's my view. He's too different from the rest of us. That makes him a threat.'

'And where else does anyone suggest we're going to get this kind of money,' said Cooksley. 'We're all here for the same reason, we need this job. She knows it, and so does he.'

'No, we bluff her,' shouted Reid. 'She needs us as well.'

'OK,' said Matt. 'We'll bluff her, but in the end, we'll all make our own decisions.'

He made a round of teas, and waited in silence for Alison and Ivan to return. Nobody was saying anything.

They're all thinking. Thinking and making their choices. That's something a man has to do in silence.

'Well,' said Alison, standing in front of them, Ivan at her side. 'Have you made a decision?'

There was no hint of compromise in her voice, Matt noticed. Nothing to suggest she might bend to anyone else's will. 'It's no good,' he said, looking towards Ivan. 'It's not personal, but we don't think we can work with you. The trust won't be there.'

Alison stepped forward. 'You're an idiot, Matt,' she said softly. She glanced around the room. 'You are all idiots. Why? Because there are lots of men like you, I just have to keep working my way down the list. But there's only one of me. None of you is going to get another offer like this one.'

Matt glanced towards Reid. He reckoned he could see him wavering. He was thinking about going back to his hovel, about moving in with his mother-in-law when the house got repossessed. 'That's our decision,' Matt said, looking back towards Alison. 'It's final.'

'Fine,' said Alison briskly. 'It was nice meeting you, gentlemen. I'm sorry it hasn't worked out.' She looked up towards Ivan. 'Let's go.'

Matt could hear them walking back down the hallway then the sound of the latch opening. He looked down towards Reid. He could see him wrestling with something. 'OK,' he whispered. 'We'll do it.'

Matt looked towards Cooksley, then Damien. Each of them nodded in turn.

'Stop,' he shouted down the hallway. 'We'll take him.'

We do what we have to do. What other choices do we have?

A smile was playing on her lips as Alison walked back down the hallway. 'I'm going to forget this ever happened, and we'll pick up where we left off,' she said. 'Ivan's in, and Damien's in. That's the compromise.'

'You're tough,' said Matt.

'Hey,' said Alison, combing a lock of blonde hair away from her forehead. 'If you want to play softball go to the park.'

I'll remember that.

Matt looked back towards the gang. 'Right, we were talking about whether it's dangerous. So long as none of us ever start mouthing off, the people we nick the stuff from won't ever know. And that's not going to happen, so I reckon we're OK. Al-Qaeda will suspect a lot of people. They're hardly short of enemies. But I don't think they'll suspect a gang of British mercenaries.' He looked towards Ivan. 'Sorry, British and Irish.'

Alison reached into her bag. 'I'm going to give each of you five thousand pounds in cash,' she said. 'That's an advance on expenses. Inside each envelope, there is an address. We will all assemble there tomorrow evening. You'll get a detailed briefing on the mission then.'

She walked to each man in turn, smiling briefly as she handed across the envelopes. Her fingers lingered as she placed the money in Matt's hand, brushing against his palm. He could feel the weight of the notes, and the crisp smell of the freshly minted money.

He raised his coffee cup into the air. 'Here's to the mission,' he said, looking around. 'Just as soon as the work is done, we'll drink to it with something stronger.'

He could see Reid looking in the direction of Ivan. The anger was still in there, festering, eating away at his nerves. That spelt trouble. We'll deal with that later, Matt decided. In the kind of mess he was in, he had to take each day as it came.

Planning ahead is for people who can afford it.

EIGHT

The sand felt cold and damp against the soles of Matt's feet. He had abandoned his trainers, opting to run barefoot along the edge of the water, letting the waves lap up against his ankles. The Atlantic was cold compared to the Mediterranean, chilling the blood in his veins. But the air smelt fresher and cleaner, the salt and the brine filling his lungs each time he took a breath.

The beach was two miles from Bideford, on the North Devon coast. The sand curved in a long arc and was framed by black rocks and with mellow green hills. A few sheep were gently grazing the hillside, but otherwise there was not another soul in view. Matt had been here once before, and the contours of the landscape had remained imprinted on his memory. A family holiday, maybe when he was nine or ten, in a caravan park with his mum and dad. Looking back, he realised it can't have been much fun for his parents. The caravan was cramped – it was impossible for Mum to cook anything – and it rained half the week. But for the ten-year-old Matt it had been the wildest adventure ever. A week away from the council estate, away from the dirt, the fumes and the noise of south London. And the chance to run free on the sand, play in the waves, explore the hills and the countryside.

It was then that I learnt two things about myself – I don't ever want a boring office job, and I don't ever want to be poor.

He picked up his pace, pushing himself to run faster, taking deep breaths of salty air. What would Dad say about what I am doing now, Matt wondered, looking up into the sky.

He'd say, take your chance, boy, like I should have taken mine.

Matt had arrived in Bideford the night before, and had met up with the rest of the gang. The location was obvious enough. Bideford was an old naval town, and it made sense that there would be some training facilities tucked away there. They were based in a disused naval barracks, which, from the state of the place, Matt guessed hadn't been used since the Second World War. About three miles east of Bideford, it was a corrugated iron shack next to a series of crumbling gun embankments. There were seven iron cots to sleep in, a pair of electric rings to cook on, and a loo you had to walk across fifteen yards of frozen mud to reach. Not luxury, Alison had explained as she showed them around, but it was only for three nights, and they would survive.

And she's staying at a hotel in town.

Matt had risen earlier than the others and got out on to the beach for a run. He checked his watch – eight-thirty. He turned and started jogging back towards the base. They were due to start work at nine, and he needed something to eat first.

Up ahead, he could see Damien walking by himself, chucking stones into the sea.

'Keeping fit?' Damien said as Matt started jogging alongside him.

'We'll need to be,' said Matt. 'You sure you're in good enough shape?'

Damien nodded. 'Two hours in the gym every day,' he said. 'The gangs are tougher than they've ever been. It's not just a bunch of boozy south London robbers like it was in Dad's day.'

'With two million you could get out,' said Matt. 'Do something different with your life.'

'Maybe,' said Damien, looking out into the sea. 'If I had someone like Gill to settle down with. You're a lucky man having a girl like that, Matt, luckier than you know. It's harder for gay men. We don't settle.'

Alison was dressed in dark blue cords, green wellies, a green Barbour jacket, and a Hermès scarf holding her hair in place. A Chelsea girl up in the country for the weekend, Matt thought. Gill would have been down on the beach with him at dawn, going for a run, exploring the rock pools, getting her hair wet in the sea and her feet dirty in the sand.

'What are you always running away from?' said Alison, looking up at the sweat dripping from his brow as he arrived at the base.

'Maybe I'm running *towards* something,' he said,

grabbing a towel from his kit bag. 'Did that ever occur to you?'

Reid and Cooksley had brewed some coffee, and fried up some bacon, beans and eggs. Matt grabbed a plateful, wolfed down the food hungrily, then put his jeans and sweatshirt back on.

Ivan was sitting on his bed, connecting his mobile phone to a Palm Pilot. He concentrated on the tiny screen, lines on his brow, ignoring the noise around him.

Matt waited until he had pressed a button on the screen. 'How's the bridge going?'

'I got the contract – three no trumps, the greatest of all bids,' said Ivan softly.

'So who do you play against?' said Cooksley, looking across. It was the first time that either Cooksley or Reid had spoken to him.

'Other enthusiasts,' said Ivan. 'You don't need to know who they are. Just that they can play, and they pay their debts.' He paused. 'Those are the only two questions worth asking about a man.'

Pinky and Perky walked into the room, nodding to Alison. Great, thought Matt. The Comedy Club has arrived. Both men were wearing chinos, sweaters, and long thick grey overcoats. They stood at the front of the room, unpacking laptops from their cases. Alison looked around the room. 'These are two colleagues of mine from Five,' said Alison. 'They will take you through the basics of the mission, and explain the moves you need to train for.'

Pinky took off his coat and hung it on the back of a chair. 'Al-Qaeda are shipping gold and diamonds back to the Middle East,' he started. 'The mission is to intercept one of their boats, and take its contents.' He paused, pointing to a map on the screen of his computer. 'The boats generally leave from here, Portofino, on the North Italian coast. They sail through the Med, towards the Middle East Coast. It's a five-day trip. The landing points vary but it's always somewhere in Jordan or the Lebanon. The best place to base you is right here.' He jabbed his thumb at the screen. 'Cyprus.' Perky looked around the room. 'On Cyprus you'll be just a few nautical miles from the interception. Our intelligence sources will tell us when the boat is leaving and where it's going. Satellites will track it from there, so we'll be able to give you a precise location of the target.'

'Your task is to find the boat, raid it, take the goods, then sink it, and get out as fast as possible,' Pinky continued. 'For obvious reasons, we don't want anyone left alive. Except, of course, you lot.' He smiled, but was met only by stony stares on the faces of the men in front of him. 'Tony Bulmer, formerly of the Special Boat Squadron, is going to spend the next three days with you. He'll give you training on how to board the boat.'

Great, thought Matt. That's just what we need. Some animal from Shaky Boat roughing us up.

'Bulmer doesn't know what the mission is, and he isn't meant to know,' continued Pinky. 'He doesn't know who you are either, so don't start shooting your mouths off. He's been told you have to hit a boat, and that's it.'

Just then Bulmer walked smartly into the room, looking more like someone who had stepped out of a student union bar than a parade ground. Matt paused. The man was nothing close to what he had expected. He must have been in his late twenties, and was dressed in baggy blue trousers and a bright-red T-shirt. His hair had a green streak in it, and was spiked up with gel. He looked more like a sales assistant at a surfing shop than a soldier.

He looked down at the five men sitting in front of him, his face immobile. 'You lot look like you could use some licking into shape,' he said.

'Piss off,' said Reid.

'Let the man do his job,' Ivan said warily. 'We all need training if we're to stay alive.'

'Hey, who asked you, bogtrotter?' said Cooksley.

'Good to see we're all getting along so well,' said Bulmer. 'Perhaps we'll start with some team-building exercises.'

Matt could feel the water biting into his naked skin. It was as if blocks of ice were being dropped on to his body, freezing up his nerve endings and chilling the blood so it could hardly flow through his veins.

A wave rolled over the top of him, pushing him below the surface of the sea, filling his mouth with salty water. He struggled to open his eyes, kicking his legs to push himself back to the surface. His head broke above the waves, and he rolled into a crawl to drag himself forward. To the next bay, he reckoned, it was about a mile, past some evil rocks jutting away from the beach. If he swam hard, he should be there in half an hour.

A few yards ahead he could see Cooksley and Reid: Cooksley he knew was a strong swimmer, Reid less so. Ivan was some way ahead of them, Damien a few yards behind. Ten minutes earlier Bulmer had marched them down to the beach, told them all to strip off and start swimming. 'See you at the next bay,' he'd shouted. 'If the fish don't get you.'

Matt could feel another wave crashing over his head, and a gust of cold wind whipping around his ears. 'You OK?' he shouted across to Damien.

'Apart from the hypothermia.'

By the time Matt pulled himself on to the beach he reckoned he'd swallowed at least two pints. He swam every day in Marbella, but there it was warmer, gentler water, and he only went out when the sun was shining. It wasn't Bideford in March, with the temperature close to zero. He grabbed a towel from the pile Pinky and Perky had left on the beach, and started drying himself off, unfreezing his limbs. Ivan, Cooksley and Reid were already ashore, Damien was just swimming up to the beach.

'Fancy a dip?' said Matt, looking directly at Pinky.

Pinky shook his head.

'It might do you some good,' Matt continued, shaking his head so that the man got sprayed with droplets of sea water. 'You look a bit flabby to me.'

Perky stepped forwards. 'Don't get lippy, sonny,' he said. 'I can break you any time I want to.'

From behind, Matt could see Bulmer striding across the beach. 'OK, you lot,' he shouted. 'That was just a warm-up, get your blood flowing a bit. Next time, we'll do it at night.'

Matt wiped the sweat from his face. The run had taken them five miles across country, over the rugged hills that led away from Bideford. It was open countryside, but vicious winds gusted in from the sea and it had started to rain, a torrential downpour that soaked right through his track suit. Matt struggled to control his breathing. He was a better runner than he was a swimmer, but the pace was punishing, pushing him to limits of endurance he hadn't tested since he had left the Regiment.

I thought I'd put all that behind me.

'OK,' shouted Bulmer as they jogged their way back into the base. 'Fifty press-ups.'

He paced up and down as the five men fell to the ground, pushing their bodies up and down. 'There are squid down on the beach stronger than you layabouts,' he shouted. 'Get inside and we'll see if your minds are in better shape than your bodies.'

A ripple of pain ran through Matt's shoulder as he used his forearms to heave himself up and down. He'd lost shape, he reflected, since he had left the Regiment. He was a fit man, but not yet back to his peak. Looking around at the others, he could see Reid struggling to keep up. Damien was fine on the press-ups because he worked out in the gym every day and sailed at the weekends, but he was struggling with the running. Ivan, for an ex-Provo safecracker, was perhaps the fittest of them. Odd, thought Matt. Nothing with that man was quite how he'd expected it.

'You want to cut down on those fags, mate,' said Bulmer, shouting in Reid's ear.

Lucky this job is just a few days. I'm not sure we'd last a whole campaign.

The coals from the brazier emitted a soft glow, spreading its heat throughout the shack. Matt sat close to the fire, soaking up the warmth. His skin was slowly starting to defrost, his blood to unthaw. 'Christ,' he said, looking towards Reid. 'I haven't been that cold since I spent a couple of months on training on the northern flank in Norway.'

Reid nodded. 'Say what you like about the Regiment. At least they never chucked you in the water. Not on purpose anyway.'

Bulmer tapped a metal cane against the desk at the front of the room. 'Listen up,' he said sternly. 'Tonight I'll run through the basic principles of a seaborne assault. Tomorrow night, we try the real thing. We'll keep trying until we get it right.' He smiled. 'Given the state of you, we'll probably be spending Christmas together.'

He pointed towards a picture on the laptop. 'I've been told you'll be hitting a standard, small cargo ship much like this one,' he said. 'You see these all over the Med. This one is a hundred and five feet long, with a beam of thirty feet, and a draught of thirteen feet. It's got two engines on it, with a combined power of six thousand brake horsepower. That's enough to do about fourteen knots at full tilt.'

Bulmer walked round to the front of the desk. The light from the ceiling glinted off the gold stud pinned into his ear. For an assault, you use the wake,' he said. 'It's going to be dark, you'll be blacked out and using night-vision goggles, so they aren't going to be able to see you. The problem is they might hear you coming. Then you transfer to a light, plastic dinghy. Their engines will be churning up the water, creating plenty of noise. You steer your dinghy directly into their wake. That way they shouldn't hear you.' He held up a fifteen-foot aluminium pole with a hook on its end. 'Then you use a grappling hook like this. Cast it to the stern, and pull your dinghy right up into the boat. You'll have a few seconds to jump on board. Then you move swiftly through the vessel, killing everyone on board.' He stopped, sitting back down on the edge of the desk. 'Any questions?'

'There might be a lookout,' said Reid.

'You'll have to shoot them,' said Bulmer. 'It's going to be rocky on the dinghy, because the water will be all churned up. We'll practise shooting on a dinghy that's bobbing around like a yo-yo, so you'll have a chance to get used to it.'

'What happens if we go in the water?' said Damien.

'Then you're fish food, that's what,' answered Bulmer. 'That's why we're going to keep practising boarding the enemy craft until we get it right. Fall into the drink and the engines will slice you like a turnip in a blender. A quick if messy death. And at least you'll be buried at sea like proper sailors.'

Bulmer looked round the room, checking to see whether there were more questions.

There were none. No one wanted to make the lesson last any longer. They were all dog tired and freezing cold, and all they wanted to do was get some sleep next to the fire.

'Right, you lot,' said Bulmer, standing up from his desk. 'Now it's dark, we'll go for a quick swim around the bay. Then we'll knock off for the night.' He paused, pointing towards the door. 'Get your kit off. We'll have some towels ready for you on the beach.'

Reid looked towards Matt. 'It's bloody fishy the way he keeps making us take our kit off. He does that once more, I'm going to let the crabs have a taste of him.'

Alison's skin felt soft and smooth, as he buried his face into her hair. Her touch was soothing his sore and aching muscles, relieving some of the stresses that had built up during the hardest day's training since he'd left the Regiment. He could smell the salt on his own skin, contrasting harshly with the perfume and soaps on hers. And he could feel the hardness of his own muscles against the softness of hers.

'Where the hell did you find that Bulmer bastard?' he said, lying back on the bed after they had finished making love.

Alison laughed. 'I thought you'd be tougher than Navy boys.'

'We are,' Matt said sharply. 'Still, I thought the Navy was just for poofs. But there's nothing soft about him.'

'Tougher than the IRA guy as well?'

'Of course,' said Matt. 'But he's never had the training. Damien's the same. They're street fighters.'

'Who could keep up with you?' said Alison, pulling him closer towards her, her fingers running through the hairs on his chest.

'You want these al-Qaeda bastards pretty badly, don't you?' said Matt. 'To go to this much trouble.'

'Believe it,' said Alison. 'Since Landau got hit, you can't imagine the pressure Five is under to get some results.'

'Is there more in the pipeline?'

'In Britain, yes,' said Alison, her expression turning serious. 'Sometime in the next month there's going to be an al-Qaeda spectacular in Britain. We don't know what it is – if we did, we'd stop it – but we know it's coming.'

'You're that certain?'

'We had a tip-off about Landau,' said Alison. 'Low-level, no one paid much attention to it. But now the same source is telling us al-Qaeda is planning something massive in Britain in the next month.' She ran a hand through Matt's hair. 'We're pretty sure it's right.'

'I better get back to the shack, then,' he said, climbing out of her bed and pulling on his clothes. 'The others might be wondering where I have got to.'

'You don't want them thinking you're the teacher's pet,' Alison said playfully.

'Aren't I?'

Alison shook her head. 'I treat you boys all the same.'

Matt hung on tightly to the side of the dark green dinghy. It skimmed like a Frisbee across the surface of the waves, lurching from left to right in sudden violent movements. It was dark, and a low-lying mist was hanging over the surface of the sea. That, combined with the spray from the waves, was keeping their visibility down to just a few yards.

All five were on board, with Bulmer at the back barking instructions. They were wearing thick black wetsuits and had blacked-up faces to make certain they were invisible against the night sky. Damien, the best seaman among them, and, Matt judged, probably the bravest, was sitting at the prow, taking the full impact of the waves as they splashed into the boat. Ivan sat next to him, crouched down low, Matt and Reid behind them. Reid had his hand on the outboard motor, steering the boat. Matt was charting their course. It was tougher than he expected. He had a GPS fix on their target – a tub that Bulmer had rented for the evening – plus a Garmin eTrex Vista handheld GPS receiver. The device processed the GPS co-ordinates of their target, and displayed a constantly shifting coastal map and compass reading to guide them towards their destination. Even so, in total darkness, with no lights and with the boat heaving through the waves, it was going to take all his concentration to get anywhere close.

'Right,' he shouted to Reid. 'Keep banking right.'

A wave sloshed over the dinghy, filling Matt's mouth with water. He spat into the sea but the salt was still on his lips. The craft started turning, rolling with the swell of the water. At least the Mediterranean won't be as rough as this, thought Matt. Or quite so cold.

'Steady her – couple of degrees left,' said Matt. He looked down at the Garmin to get a fix on his position. The target was less than a mile away, straight ahead of them. They were one nautical mile from the coast, heading down towards Bude. The wind was starting to drop, and through a break in the clouds a beam of moonlight was breaking through. 'Increase the power,' said Matt. 'We're approaching.'

He leant forward, squinting, trying to pierce through the darkness. He could make out the outline of a shape, but whether it was the boat, rocks or seagulls, he couldn't yet say. 'Goggles on, men,' he barked.

MI5 had equipped each of them with a pair of Rigel 3200 night-vision goggles. Each set looked like a set of miniature black binoculars, with fibre webbing to strap them on to the head. The Rigel weighed just over a pound, and gave good crisp vision of two hundred metres in clear starlight, and one hundred metres in thick darkness. Tonight, realised Matt, a hundred metres was all they were going to get.

He strapped his into place. The Rigel worked with thermal imaging. Instead of looking for light signals, as your eyes do, it searched for heat, looking at the upper end of the infra-red spectrum. Anything hotter than its surroundings – like a boat or a man – would be displayed on the screen in front of the eyes. Looming up ahead he could see two shapes, both defined in a pale, luminous green light. The hull of a ship. And a man standing on its deck.

'Ignore the man,' shouted Bulmer from the back of the dinghy. 'We're practising a zero-resistance contact.'

Reid steered the dinghy closer to the ship. Spray hit Matt in the face again, drenching his goggles, making it almost impossible for him to see anything. The dinghy moved slowly forward, the engine churning up the water. Matt could feel the hard plastic of the craft vibrating as it skimmed into the wake of the boat. His balance was getting harder to hold. 'Steady her,' he could hear Bulmer shouting behind him. 'The men on the left and right need to shift their weight to keep her steady.'

Matt moved out to the edge of the dinghy and Reid did the same. The dinghy tossed, then flattened out. They were drawing closer to the ship, the waters beneath them heaving, the spray spitting into their faces. 'Get the hook ready,' shouted Bulmer. 'We're ten feet from the target.'

Matt watched as Cooksley slung the hook forward. He had watched him throwing it fifty times during the day, each time getting closer to perfection. Cooksley had been one of the best marksmen in the Regiment. But that was on dry land, when you could steady your arm and line up your eye. Now he was aiming from the prow of a dinghy, kicked around in the waves. He gripped the hook, leaning forward. Ivan was holding his waist to steady him. The hook hit the stern of the boat, and Cooksley started pulling. Matt could feel the dinghy bouncing along the surface of the sea. 'Get ready to move up,' he shouted as the dinghy was pulled closer to the boat.

The four men stood up in one movement. A wave rolled on to the side of the boat, catching Matt by surprise. He could see foam swelling around his feet. He was slipping. Reid crashed into his side, and suddenly Matt was submerged beneath the water. Blackness engulfed him, a mouthful of icy water disappearing down his throat. Kicking his legs, he broke back on to the surface before another wave crashed over him, pushing him under, and he could feel the engines of the ship dragging him towards their blades. He was just six feet away from the blade slicing through the water.

Christ. Fish food.

He gave his legs a powerful kick to steer himself back to the dinghy. He grabbed its side, holding it tight. With the other hand, he tore the goggles from his face, slinging them inside the vessel. He looked around. Ivan, Cooksley, Reid and Damien were all in the water. The target was sailing away.

'Jesus,' shouted Bulmer, looking down at the men bobbing about in the water. 'I hope the fate of the world doesn't depend on you lot.'

★

Matt kissed Alison full on the lips, aware of her breasts pushing back at him. Her hair fell across his chest, and her hands were starting to run down his back, teasing his flesh, and gently rubbing his muscles. They had made love once already, and Matt wanted to get back to the shack. He'd been away for two hours – spend too long and some of the other men might start getting suspicious.

Alison's good, but she's not the woman I love.

'How's the training?' Alison's voice sounded lazy and tired.

'Hard,' said Matt. 'We're not as fit as we were when we quit the Regiment. It's amazing how quickly you lose it. We're making progress, though. It took Cooksley a few tries, but he's getting the knack of the hook. We'll be OK on the day.'

'Just one more night, then you'll be off.'

Matt shrugged. 'Why the rush?'

'A boat will be crossing the Med in the next few days,' said Alison. 'You need to be ready.'

'It's better to be properly trained,' said Matt. 'If al-Qaeda are sending boats out all the time, there'll be another one in a week or two. It's dangerous to go too early.'

Alison sat up, drawing the sheet up to cover her breasts. 'You've heard of a man called Charles Booth.'

'The head of Five,' Matt said, caressing her exposed ankle. 'Sent in to shake the agency up, get some results after September the eleventh.'

'My boss,' said Alison. 'He needs a break on this Landau case. The PM and Home Secretary are all over him.'

Matt's hand stopped half-way up her thigh. 'Did Booth authorise this mission?' he asked. 'Personally?'

'That's need-to-know information.'

'And I don't need to know?' Matt raised his eyebrows.

Alison laughed, pulling him towards her, the sheet falling away to reveal her breasts. 'All you need to know is how to fuck me,' she said.

Matt steadied himself on the prow of the dinghy. His legs were swaying from the combined force of the waves and the wind, and he had to keep adjusting his position to hold his balance. He raised the Bushmaster Leupuld high-precision rifle to his right eye, lining up the night-vision goggles with its telescopic sights. The Bushmaster was a light semi-automatic weapon, precision manufactured from aircraft-quality aluminium. The rifle weighed just seven-and-a-half pounds, and the twenty-round magazine added another pound. American-made, Matt had noted when they were given the guns. The kind of weapon you could buy in any American hunting shop. If anything went wrong, Five didn't want the gang to be carrying anything that could link them back to the British government.

He steadied his shoulder. The target was standing on the deck of the boat: three old tires roped together, with a life jacket slung on top. He levelled his sights. The boat swayed, knocking him off balance for a moment. He recovered, put the gun back to his eye, took aim and fired.

The bullet missed.

'Wanker,' growled Bulmer behind him. 'Listen, if there's a lookout, you're going to get one shot. No second chances. They'll have depth charges, machine-guns, the fucking works. They start chucking charges into the sea it will blow this dinghy apart. Then they'll rake the water with the machine-guns. You boys will be finished.'

Damn, thought Matt. He steaded himself again, waited for the wave to pass, tensed his shoulder, and pressed the trigger. Through the telescopic sights, he could see a tear ripping open in the life jacket. He smiled to himself.

'Reckon you got lucky,' growled Bulmer. 'Now do it again.'

Damien and Ivan had cooked up a round of steak sandwiches, and were passing them around the team. Matt squirted some ketchup on to his, and took a thick bite, swallowing quickly. Neither of them would be the next Jamie Oliver, but this was just the kind of food needed after a hard day at sea.

'We could train and train for this mission,' said Perky, standing at the front of the room. 'But there isn't time. An al-Qaeda boat will set sail in the next couple of days. That's the one we want to hit. Bulmer's going to take you out again tonight, to run through tactics one last time. There's a BA flight from Heathrow to Cyprus tomorrow at two. We've booked tickets for you.'

'You'll be staying at the Amathus Beach Hotel in Limassol,' said Pinky. 'It's a standard package holiday place next to the beach. As far as the rest of the world is concerned you're just a bunch of Brits on a stag week.' A grin flashed on to his face as he looked around the room. 'Drink plenty, and chase the girls round the pool. That'll be your cover.'

Nobody laughed, Matt noticed.

Don't ever retrain as a comedian, Pinky. You haven't got it.

'We'll be tracking the boat by satellite,' said Perky. 'When it's within five hours' sailing of Cyprus, Matt will get a text message saying: "Don't forget Mum's birthday. Ring her on this number." The last four digits of that number will be the expected time of arrival off the Cyprus coast.

'A ship has been hired for you in Mongari, a fishing village close to Limassol. Matt will be given the details. Your guns and explosives will be shipped out to the British embassy in Cyprus in diplomatic bags. They'll be delivered to the boatman and he'll stash them on board. After that, there won't be any more contact with the embassy.'

Matt took another bite on his sandwich.

Keeping us at a distance again. In case it goes wrong.

'When you get the signal,' said Pinky, 'get down to Mongari, and set out to sea. There will be a radio receiver on board the boat. When we have it, we'll patch through the precise co-ordinates of the al-Qaeda boat. After that you're on your own. Any questions?'

'What's the plan for the gear once we've taken it?' said Damien.

'That's for you to decide,' said Alison. 'It's all yours. Ship it anywhere you like, anyhow you like.'

Matt handed out the cups of tea. His hands were numb from the day's training on the water, and he held the cup tightly to try and get the circulation moving again. Each of the men sitting around the fire looked just as tired and cold; they were fit and strong, but they were still mortal, and the day had been tougher than any of them expected.

Behind him, Alison spooned some sugar into a cup but remained silent. Matt checked that Bulmer had left the room, and so had Pinky and Perky. This was a discussion he wanted to keep private.

'Listen up,' said Matt, 'there's something we need to discuss.' He paused, taking a sip of his tea. 'We're going to be off soon. I just wanted to make sure everyone is straight on a few things before we start. That way we make sure there aren't any arguments later.'

He sat down next to the fire. 'After we get the money, Damien will organise fencing it. We ship the stuff from Cyprus to Rotterdam, then we bring the money back to England.'

'We all go and collect it together, right?' said Ivan.

'If you like,' answered Matt.

'The money comes off the boat, right?' said Damien.

'We put it on to a cargo boat to Rotterdam. None of us will be able to touch it while it's in transit. We all go together to the port in Rotterdam, and get the stuff off the boat, then we'll deliver the stash to the fence, and split up the cash. OK?'

'How do we know the boat's going to Rotterdam?' Reid asked.

'You'll have to trust me,' Damien said.

'We'll decide who to trust, thanks,' snapped Cooksley.

'I'm glad we finally agree on something,' Ivan chipped in.

'OK, OK,' said Matt, raising his hands into the air. 'Like Damien says, we'll all go get the money together. The point I was trying to make was this – if anything goes wrong after the hit and we get split up, we all meet up in ten days' time. The money will be buried at a spot in Kent, and I'm going to give each one of you the GPS co-ordinates. Like I said, it's just a back-up plan. But if we need to, we'll split up the money then. March the thirty-first at 11.00 a.m. Be there.'

'And what exactly are you planning to go wrong?' said Ivan.

Matt rolled over on his side, spent and exhausted. Alison's legs were still wrapped around him, her hair still draped across his neck, and her fingernails still digging into his back. He could feel her sweat on his skin, and the sweet smell of her perfume lingered on the rumpled sheets of the hotel room.

'Next time I see you, you'll be a rich man,' she said.

'You like your men rich?'

Alison shrugged. 'It doesn't matter. I don't expect men to look after me.'

'Do you always sleep with the men you send out on missions?'

Alison smiled coyly. 'Only the ones who please me.'

'And after the mission?'

She shrugged again, pulling the sheet back over her silky breasts.

'We're expendable, right?' said Matt.

'You want me to describe you as collateral damage?'

Matt pulled on his jeans and started doing up the buttons on his shirt. 'It makes no difference what you call me.'

He stepped out alone into the darkness of the street. Bideford at one in the morning in March was an empty place. The few pubs and restaurants were closed, and most of the lights in the houses were out. A quarter of a moon was hanging in the night sky, its light shimmering in the long inlet that stretched through the centre of the town. Ahead, Matt could hear the sound of the waves breaking on the shoreline.

As he walked, he thought of Gill. He had called Janey, the manager at the Last Trumpet, earlier in the day. He knew he'd defied Alison's instructions that none of the gang should contact their family or friends until the mission was over. But he wanted to know where Gill was, what she was doing, and how she was taking the separation.

I still think about her all the time. Even when I'm with Alison.

Especially then.

Janey hadn't seen Gill, but she'd run into one of the other girls from the Dandelion nursery, who'd commented that Gill had seemed down, and asked where Matt had gone. 'I don't think she's told anyone you've split,' Janey added. 'That's probably a good sign. Like she doesn't want it to be permanent.'

Matt pulled his collar around his neck to protect himself from the chill wind blowing in from the sea.

If I sort myself out, will Gill take me back?

'You cheating, miserable bastard,' shouted a voice from the darkness. 'You sick, sodding slag.' The punch felled Matt. A fist collided with his jaw, the bone crunching into his flesh with the force of a hammer. If he'd seen it coming he might have been able to steady himself, recover his balance and return the blow. But it came straight out of the darkness. His foot slipped and he could feel himself falling to the pavement. He jabbed out an arm to break his fall and caught his elbow on the kerb, sending a jolt of pain through his arm. 'What the fuck,' he muttered.

A boot crashed into the side of his chest, blasting the air from his lungs. Matt coughed violently, gasping for breath. His hand swung around, reaching for the leg to pull the man down, but he missed. The boot swung back, then forwards, this time hitting him on the side of the neck. The flesh started to swell instantly. Matt reached out, his reactions quicker this time, and his hand clamped on the boot. He yanked at it, hard. The man swayed, his balance thrown, and another yank brought him crashing to the pavement. Matt pulled back a fist high into the air, preparing to deliver a powerful blow directly to the man's teeth.

The least you deserve is an expensive trip to the dentist, you bastard.

'Damien,' he said, looking down into the face of his assailant. He stopped himself just in time. 'Christ, man, what the hell are you doing?'

'What the hell are *you* doing,' Damien spat, his face purple with rage and sweat. 'You're screwing her, aren't you?'

Matt rubbed his jaw with his hand. It was bruised, but there was no blood. 'Yes,' he said quietly.

'You're meant to be getting married in a few weeks,' said Damien. 'How could you do that to Gill?'

'We split.'

'Split? From Gill? You didn't tell me.'

Matt pulled himself up from the pavement. 'I broke it off,' he said. 'I'm in too much trouble to marry anyone, let alone Gill. I do love her, but I can't have her around me right now. She could get killed as well.' He helped Damien back on to his feet. 'I need this mission to get my life back together. When I do, I'll go back and marry her – if she'll still have me.' He paused, looking down at the water. 'I'm more certain of that now than I have ever been.'

NINE

Mongari was a few miles from Limassol, but it might as well have been on a different planet. Matt checked his watch as he walked with Ivan down the quiet street. It was just after ten at night, and whereas the holiday resort would be noisy with drunken clubbers staggering their way through the streets, here there was just the sound of the few fish restaurants that lined the bay being shut up, and the screeching of a couple of cats being put out for the night.

The two of them had come alone. The flight from London had landed mid-afternoon, and they'd transferred straight to the hotel. The rest, it was agreed, would stay behind in the bar while Matt and Ivan went to check the boat and the gear were all lined up.

We could get the call at any minute. We have to be ready twenty-four hours a day.

The houses in the village were all painted white. Half a moon was hanging in the sky, gently illuminating the curve of the dock and the fishing boats moored along the wooden jetty. The moon was rising, Matt noted. That meant that on the night of the raid it would be relatively light, unless there was cloud cover. That would make it easier for them to see the target. But it would also make it easier for the target to see them.

Given the choice, I'd rather take them by surprise.

Glafacos Hasikos was prowling along the edge of the jetty, his face illuminated by the orange stub of a cigarette glowing in the corner of his mouth. Matt walked up to him. 'Do you know the way back to Limassol?' he said.

'It's too far to walk, you'll have to go by bike,' Hasikos replied, chucking his cigarette into the water behind him.

That was the phrase arranged as a password. This was their man.

'Is this the vessel?' said Matt briskly.

The ship behind him was a tug boat, about eighty feet long, with a black metal hull and a pair of white cranes on its deck. At a quick glance it looked at least ten years old, but it was still in good shape. This was just what Matt wanted. He didn't need a new, untested boat, and he didn't want an old cranky one either. This raid would be dangerous enough without the equipment cracking up on them.

'I'll take you aboard,' said Hasikos.

Matt followed him on to the ship. Hasikos was a small, overweight man, with fingernails stained from nicotine and two days of stubble on his chin. The boat was moored to the jetty, but still swaying from the swell washing in from the open sea. 'Show us the electronics, and then where the gear is stashed,' said Matt.

The bridge was towards the front of the boat. Matt

was not an expert sailor, but he felt comfortable about handling this. The ship was equipped with radars, giving position and depth of water. And there was a GPS locator. No nonsense about using the stars to guide you. If you could drive a car, you could drive this.

A green inflatable dinghy, identical to the one they had trained on in Bideford, was strapped to the side of the boat. Next to it was a long hook.

'Where's the packages?' Ivan asked.

Hasikos led them down into the hold. A single battery-powered electrical light was burning in the corner, its pale light struggling to illuminate the metal interior of the vessel. Four crates were resting to the side of the stairway. Ivan told Hasikos to leave the hold for a few minutes. Matt opened the first of the boxes up. Two Bushmaster rifles and two Beretta 92 pistols. There were ten magazine cartridges for the rifles, each one holding thirty bullets. He checked the rest of the crates. Six more rifles, six more pistols, and another thirty magazine cartridges.

That made twelve hundred bullets, Matt calculated, not counting the pistols.

Should be enough to deal with six men. Two hundred each.

'How's your gear?' he said, looking across at Ivan.

Ivan had opened the first of a set of three smaller crates. Inside each one were three two-pound blocks of Semtex. He unpacked the first one, holding it in his hand. The explosive had no smell, and the consistency of children's modelling dough, but evidently Ivan had handled enough Semtex in his life to tell that in this batch the cyclonite and penaerythrite tetranitrate – the two main chemical ingredients in the explosive – had been mixed to perfection.

'It'll be fine,' he said.

Matt climbed back on to the deck. Hasikos was leaning against the railing, ash from his cigarette dropping into the sea. 'Everything is as it should be,' he said. 'I can't say for sure when we'll be taking her out. Just make sure she's ready at all times, and the tanks are full of oil.'

Hasikos nodded. Matt had no idea how much Five had already paid him, but it had to be a lot.

'She's a good craft,' Hasikos said. 'I've worked her for ten years. Try to bring her back in one piece.'

Matt grinned. 'The boat's not going down unless we do. And I'm not planning to let that happen.'

Waiting around. That was always the part of any mission that Matt hated the most. The hours dragged slowly by, the nerves gradually building in all of your muscles and the tension rising in the pit of your stomach. It preyed on your mind and grated on your nerves.

You just want to get out there and get into the thick of it.

Matt glanced out across the pool. There were a few young couples, some families with toddlers in tow, but mostly singles. There was a wet T-shirt contest down on the beach and Cooksley and Reid had gone down to take a look. Matt couldn't be bothered. He'd had his fill of women for this month. There were more important things to do than watch some podgy slapper from

Sheffield tip a bucket of water over her head.

The sooner I can get out of here and get back to Gill the better.

It was four o'clock in the afternoon and the heat of the sun was starting to ebb when Matt called the group together in a quiet corner of the poolside. 'I want to make sure we're all agreed about what happens to stuff when we've taken it, and when we split up the money. We agree a plan, and we stick to it. That way, there's no room for disagreements later.'

'We need to get it to Rotterdam,' said Damien. 'That's the best place in the world for fencing gold and jewels. About half the illegal trade goes through there – gold smuggled out of Russia, diamonds from South Africa, the works. I've got a guy who'll take the lot, and give us at least a third of full market value. He pays laundered money, cash. A mixture of pounds, euros and dollars. All of it untraceable.'

'Can't we do it somewhere closer and get the cash quicker?' said Reid, tapping his cigarette lighter against the table.

Damien shook his head. 'The point is that al-Qaeda are going to be looking for us. Try fencing this stuff in any city on the Med and word will get around. A bunch of white guys trading big quantities of gold and jewels a few days after their boat got hit. They aren't stupid; they'll be on to us like a flash.' He paused, opening a can of Diet Coke. 'The market in stolen jewels in Rotterdam is so big, no one is going to notice.'

'So how do we get it to Rotterdam?' said Ivan.

'We've bought two Land Rovers,' said Damien. 'Cooksley has stripped them down, taken out the engines and the undercarriages. We're going to stash the stuff inside those, then put them on a boat to Rotterdam. There's a cargo ship that leaves in three days – we should be able to get them on that. The trip takes seven days, but it's much safer than putting it on a plane. Customs almost never bother to check an imported second-hand car, but anything of that weight on a plane will automatically make them suspicious.'

'So the gear is out of our sight for a week?' said Reid. 'I'd rather watch my stash.'

'This is the best way,' said Matt. 'We stop here for a week, drink some beer, then get on a plane to Rotterdam the night before the cargo ship arrives. We collect the stuff together, and take it together to Damien's man. We get the cash, split it up there and then, and go our separate ways. Job done.'

Reid nodded. 'Wouldn't it be better if we all went on the boat?' he said. 'I don't want it out of my sight.'

Damien shook his head. 'It's a cargo boat. It'll be perfectly safe,' he said. 'We'll all watch it go on to the ship, and we'll all watch it come off. Anyway, you can't ask for five blokes to come aboard a cargo vessel to watch their stuff. It would just create suspicion.'

Reid looked away. 'It's my gear, I want to look after it myself.' He looked to Matt. 'Maybe we should split the gear up here, and then go our separate ways.'

Matt looked around the table. 'We need to trust each

other,' he said, a note of impatience in his voice. 'That's the only way this is going to work.'

The bar was heaving with bodies. It was quarter to twelve at night and the main strip running through Limassol was brightly lit, full of people streaming up and down, standing outside every doorway, all of them drunk. The boys were wearing tight T-shirts, baggy jeans and baseball caps, and the girls were in mini-skirts and high-heels, with studs sticking out of their belly-buttons.

'Get me out on the ocean,' Matt said to himself.

Somewhere I can hear myself think.

The noise of the disco next door and the people at the bar crashed against his eardrums, making it almost impossible to hold a conversation. Matt reckoned they were the oldest men in the bar by at least a decade.

'The point about bridge is you have to plan several moves ahead,' Ivan was saying in his ear. 'That's what distinguishes the great players from the ordinary players. You have to see the whole game before anyone else can see it.'

Across the bar, Matt could see Cooksley and Reid chatting to a pair of girls. No chance, boys, he decided. Way too young. They looked nineteen or twenty, sisters maybe, with brown hair and green eyes, and bodies that were pressing hard against their clothes. Both of them had Bacardi Breezers in their hands and smiles on their faces. I know that sort, thought Matt. Right now, they are cuddly and sexy. At thirty, they'll be fat.

'So how many moves do you plan ahead, Ivan?' said Matt. 'In life, not in cards.'

'Three,' replied Ivan. 'More than that, you can't see what's happening. Less, you're just being stupid.'

In the distance, Matt could see two men approaching Cooksley and Reid. Brothers, boyfriends – it was impossible to tell. They looked pissed up. Their faces were red, and their eyes were woozy, and it was written all over their body language that they were ready to kick it off. One of the girls put her hand on to Reid's back, rubbing it provocatively.

You're trying to start something.

'How many moves do *you* plan?'

Matt laughed, looking back towards Ivan and taking a swig from his beer bottle. 'Frankly, I think two is my limit,' he answered. 'And that's on a good day.'

The first punch had been thrown quicker than he'd expected. One of the boys had put a fist into Reid's face, knocking him sideways. The boy didn't look like a trained fighter, Matt judged, but he was young and fit – and he had several pints of beer sloshing around inside him, and that always makes a man braver. Reid staggered two paces backwards, about to regain his footing, when his foot caught some spilt beer. He slipped and crashed to the floor, pulling a few bottles and glasses with him. When he lifted his head, Matt saw a deep-looking cut in his ear. Immediately there was blood on the side of his face, and the crowd around them seemed to freeze.

Mistake, thought Matt. That's a man whose punch

was legendary even in the Regiment.

The girls were backing away now. It had started as a bit of fun, making their boyfriends jealous, but now the situation was escalating into something violent and ugly. The fun had shut down.

You girls can start it but you can't finish it.

Reid rose to his feet, the boy taunting him with a drunken grin. Matt watched as Reid pulled his fist back, the shoulder muscles powering up. He threw a left straight into the boy's face. Then, as a right crashed into his nose, the boy's knees buckled beneath him.

The second boy had smashed a beer bottle and was now advancing with it towards Reid and Cooksley, waving the jagged glass edge.

'Police,' shouted one of the men behind the bar. 'Someone call the police.'

This has gone far enough.

Matt signalled to Ivan and Damien, and the three men moved swiftly across the floor, pushing aside the crowd of people gathered to witness the action. One boy was out cold on the floor, Reid was circling the other, waiting for his moment to strike. Two of their mates had walked up and were starting to confront Cooksley, and the two girls stood behind them, their expressions terrified. Cooksley was trying to calm them down. 'That's enough, lads,' he said. 'Let's not all spend the night in a Cypriot police cell.'

In the distance, Matt could hear the wailing of a police siren. He marched into the centre of the crowd, shoving one of the boys aside, and grabbing Reid by the

shoulders. From past experience he knew that once
Reid had too much juice inside him he could turn into
a dangerous animal. Reid was resisting, but with the
help of Damien and Ivan, Matt was strong enough to
wrestle him towards the door, blood dripping on to his
shirt.

'You fucking tossers,' shouted one of the boys from
the bar in a scouse accent. Reid turned around and
attempted to lunge back into the crowd. Matt struggled
to hold him – the man had the shoulders of an ox – and
signalled to Ivan and Damien to give him a hand.

Reid snarled as they hauled him off towards the
door. 'A bloody Irishman and a bloody bender!' he
roared. 'Get your stinking hands off me and let me finish
this fight!'

'You're a fucking idiot,' Matt shouted back, steering
him out into the street. 'Just leave it. You get yourself
arrested, the whole job goes to bloody pieces.'

After the trouble in the bar, Matt wasn't about to let the
gang out of his sight. The next morning they were
sitting around the hotel, none of them drinking anything harder than orange juice or coke. Reid had a
plaster stuck over his ear and a bruise on his face, but
otherwise was in good enough nick. 'You don't look
any uglier than usual,' Matt remarked, after he patched
him up. Reid had apologised to Ivan and Damien and
although they had laughed it off Matt suspected it still
rankled. Insults, he knew from long experience, are
seldom forgotten quickly.

It's going to be hard work to keep this team together.

Ivan was trying to teach them the basics of bridge. He and Cooksley made up one team, Matt and Damien the other. They had played a few rounds already, and Matt could see that Ivan was wondering whether Cooksley and Reid weren't more suited to snap. He was clearly struggling to hold back from making any condescending remarks.

The game was not so different from soldiering, Matt decided, laying down an ace of trumps and collecting the trick from the table. *You save your big gun for when you really need it.*

'OK,' said Damien. 'After I get this money I can see I'm going to piss it away playing cards.'

'I'll have it off you in no time once we're playing for money,' said Ivan, glancing upwards. 'I'm already working out how to spend four – my two and your two.'

Matt glanced at both men, aware of the tension in both sets of eyes, then gave himself a break by collecting a new round of drinks from the bar. Two Cokes, two orange juices and a large bottle of still mineral water. 'Great looking stag party we make,' he said, putting the tray down on the table. 'I feel sorry for the bride if this is the most fun we know how to have.'

He glanced at his cards. One ace, a couple of queens, and a pile of fives or sixes. Rubbish, he decided. A beep from his mobile broke his concentration. Matt fished the phone from his pocket. A text message. He pressed the button, glanced at the words displayed on the tiny screen, then looked up at the men seated around the table.

'Time to go.'

'Finish the round?' said Ivan.

'Who do you think you are?' Matt said, standing up. 'Sir Francis fucking Drake?'

TEN

The boat ploughed steadily through the night water. Damien stood on the bridge, his hands steady on the wheel. It was one o'clock in the morning and a bank of clouds had drifted across the night sky, dimming the light of the moon. As the darkness descended upon them, their faces were illuminated only by the green glow of the radar screen.

Towards the back of the boat Matt could hear a pair of gulls squawking and the insistent monotonous hum of the engines. But the men had all quietened down – and so had the wind.

There is always a moment of stillness before a mission begins.

'How far?' Cooksley asked, standing next to Matt on the bridge.

'About three nautical miles,' said Matt. 'Maybe another twenty minutes' sailing.'

The radar screen showed their position as a small green dot. Ahead there was another dot, marking the position of the target. It was moving, but they were moving faster. To keep on its track, Damien just had to steer the boat into its slipstream.

Matt looked into the sky, watching the last of the moon slip behind the clouds. The darker it gets, the better, he decided. They can't see us, but we can see them.

Damien steered the boat in silence, keeping his eyes fixed on the radar. Their training was completed, and each of them had practised their moves a hundred times over. Each man knew exactly what he had to do and when. If everything went according to plan, they would be back on the boat in an hour, and safely tucked up in their hotel bedrooms in three hours.

But when did it ever work out the way the plan said it should?

Damien killed the engines on the boat. It was one forty-five. The level of noise suddenly reduced, a stillness descended upon them.

Matt could hear the waves lapping against the vessel – it seemed to be getting rougher as the wind started to pick up again. 'Get the dinghy ready,' he said. 'The target is a mile due west of here.'

Reid and Cooksley lowered the dinghy into the water, steadying it as it started to sway. Matt checked his Bushmaster rifle, made sure his pistol was securely fastened to the belt of his wetsuit, and that his night-vision goggles were strapped into place. 'All systems go?' he said, looking around.

Reid, Cooksley and Ivan nodded. Their faces were all blackened up, and they were wearing black wetsuits with lightweight body armour strapped around their chest. Through the pale light, only their eyes could be seen clearly.

'Your explosives in place?' Matt asked Ivan.

'Ready,' said Ivan.

Matt turned towards Damien. 'OK, we're off,' he said. 'When we've cleared their boat, we'll radio you. You need to get your foot on the accelerator of this thing as fast as possible and bring it across to join us. OK?'

Damien nodded. 'Let's just fucking do it.'

Matt jumped down into the dinghy and sat next to Reid at the back. Ivan and Cooksley were ahead of them. The outboard was already fired up and its engines sliced through the water. 'Due west,' said Matt, leaning back as the dinghy powered away from the boat. 'At least we haven't got that bastard Bulmer shouting at us.'

He could see only darkness ahead. The dinghy was bouncing across the surface of the water, crashing through the waves that assaulted its hull. Matt held the Garmin navigator firmly, checking their progress against the co-ordinates of the target. He still couldn't see it, even through the night-vision goggles, but at the rate they were travelling he reckoned they would be there in nine minutes.

'Two degrees left,' he muttered.

Matt could feel the dinghy changing direction. He checked their position again. The target was straight ahead of them now. The al-Qaeda boat was moving at a steady pace of eight or nine knots, but the dinghy was going much faster, rapidly closing the distance between them. They were now just one nautical mile from the target.

'Goggles on,' he shouted across the boat.

He pulled his Rigel down over his eyes, checking the rest of them had done the same. The frames felt heavy around his face, cutting into his skin. But Matt had fought in goggles before, and knew that the pain was irrelevant. In pitch blackness, the ability to see was the greatest weapon of all.

If you can see your enemy before he can see you then he's already a dead man.

Matt looked up. Cooksley and Ivan were marked out as green blobs. He scanned across the ocean. Right now, there was nothing except for a small flock of birds drifting through the sky to the east. 'One degree right,' he told Reid.

Where are you?

The target appeared as a tiny pale-green dot, floating on the edge of the horizon. Matt's eyes locked on to it, watching as it grew steadily larger.

'You see it?' he whispered to Reid.

'Clear as daylight,' said Reid. 'That's our boy.'

Matt checked the Garmin. The instructions from Bulmer were that the noise of their engine would travel no more than a thousand metres at sea – sound travels poorly across water because of the noise of the waves and because the curve of the earth deflects it away from the surface. But Matt wasn't planning on taking any chances.

His stomach was heaving. The dinghy was rocking

wildly with every wave, and it seemed rougher now than on any of their training exercises. He could see that Cooksley had already thrown up – some of it was now running down the side of Reid's wetsuit. The vomit was mixing with the water splashing over the side of the boat and swilling around Matt's feet. Ivan was making retching sounds, leaning over the side of the vessel. From the state of his own stomach, Matt thought he was about to join him.

They were drawing closer now, the engine growling at a steady pace. The noise of the ship and the hissing of the wind drowned out the sound of their dinghy. They didn't need any electronics to guide them towards the target. They could see it looming towards them, illuminated in vivid green on the screens of their goggles.

Matt scanned the surface of the vessel. From this distance it looked like a rough cargo ship, about eighty feet long, the sort you could see in any docks. There were a couple of winches at the back for loading and unloading, and a bridge at the front. Not much on deck. He could see the outlines of the stern, and the heat from the engine beneath it. He searched for signs of a lookout but could see nothing. It was now one-thirty in the morning, local time. There should certainly be one man on the bridge, maybe two, but it didn't look as if they had posted a lookout on the stern.

This might turn out easier than expected.

Matt's stomach heaved once more and he put his face low over the water, trying to keep as quiet as possible as he vomited burger and chips into the sea. He looked up and saw vomit smeared across Reid's face: the man was concentrating so hard on the target he had forgotten to wipe it away.

'Steady her,' he muttered to Reid.

They were approaching the tail-end of the wake, five hundred metres from the boat. 'There's someone there,' muttered Ivan from the front of the boat.

Matt looked up towards the target. There was the faint trace of a green object towards the stern. He steadied his head, letting the goggles get a lock on to the object – a round, green blob with things that looked like arms. No question – it was a lookout. The man was pacing up and down, and, as they got closer, Matt could see that he was smoking.

Stupid. He should know that night-vision goggles work on heat. You might as well wave a placard above your head saying COME AND SHOOT ME.

'Wait till we're down to fifty feet,' Matt muttered. 'Cooksley . . .'

The plan was that they'd fire simultaneously. Matt picked up the Bushmaster rifle and held it tightly in his right hand. 'Move her up,' he muttered.

Now they were positioned right in the centre of the wake: the turbulence of the water would smother the noise as effectively as the silencer on a pistol. The prow of the dinghy jumped up as the engine roared forwards, the thick white water of the wake breaking over the top. Matt could feel the waves bouncing off the surface of his wetsuit but clinging to his hair and face. The glass of his goggles was constantly soaked, and he had to keep wiping them. They were within three hundred metres. 'Forwards,' he muttered to Reid.

He looked again to the surface of the ship. The green blob was pacing back and forth, the cigarette still dangling from its lips. Ahead, Cooksley was holding his rod, gripping it firmly between his fists. Ivan was at his side, both hands gripping the sides of the dinghy, his body swaying as the vessel rolled through the waves and the swell.

Two hundred metres. They're so close I can practically smell them.

Matt knelt forwards, struggling to find the perfect balance as the boat rocked through the wake. He took his goggles off, letting them hang freely around his neck. His forearms rested on the sides of the dinghy, and he raised the rifle to his shoulder, putting his eye to the kite-sight. Two yards ahead he could see Cooksley doing the same. He trained the sights on to the green blob, aiming precisely two inches above the cigarette. That, he calculated, should lodge the bullet directly into the man's brain.

He looked towards Cooksley. 'Now,' he muttered. If they both shot at the same time there was a greater chance of hitting the target, and no extra risk of alerting the rest of the crew.

Matt squeezed the trigger. The rifle kicked back against his shoulder as the bullet flashed through the night sky. A wave hit the dinghy, and Matt struggled to stay upright. He kept his eyes locked on to the stern of the target. The blob was down – but whether he was dead or just wounded Matt had no way of knowing.

Piss off to meet Allah, you bastard.

Matt could hear the roar of the propellers as they drew closer: two massive blades of steel, cutting through the water. Another hundred metres to go. The smell of diesel and oil caught on the wind, filling Matt's lungs.

Reid turned the dinghy left then right, steering through the narrow channel of water dead in the centre of the wake. On either side of them, banks of white water were starting to rise, reaching six or seven feet into the sky. The water poured down on them, covering Matt's face in spray. 'Keep her steady,' he muttered.

The stern was looming above them now. It rose twenty feet, a solid wall of black steel, its surface pitted with rust. The tips of the prop blades could just be seen slicing through the churning surface of the water. They were twenty metres away. Matt could feel the engine starting to drag them towards it, the dinghy gliding across the surface of the water as if it were being sucked up by a vacuum. 'Turn it around,' he said.

Reid spun the engine into reverse. At this point in the approach, the suction from the ship's engine was enough to drag them forward: they needed the outboard to stop them moving too quickly towards it. If they collided with the propellers it would slice up the boat.

'Got it,' Reid said, looking back at Matt.

The dinghy was moving more steadily towards the

stern now – forty, thirty, then twenty feet. Cooksley stood up, Ivan gripping him at the sides, and slung the hook forwards. It clanked against the metal of the stern, bounced, and started falling backwards.

Christ, man, don't drop it.

Cooksley gripped tighter to the pole, slinging it forwards again. This time the hook settled into the stern, the metal catching on metal. Cooksley tugged once. It was secure.

Ivan grabbed a thin aluminium caving ladder, holding it steady as Cooksley used the hook to pull them closer to the ship. Ivan slipped the ladder on to the stern, holding it steady, a ramp between the dinghy and the boat. 'She's ready,' he said.

Matt moved swiftly forwards. His feet bounced off the surface of the dinghy, his hands gripping on to the sides of the ladder. He steadied his balance, then yanked himself forwards.

The first man over the top faces maximum danger. That's my job.

He started hauling himself upwards. Three rungs up, a wave crashed over the side of his body. The force of the water knocked him sideways, his left hand breaking free from the ladder. His left foot was bashed out, leaving all the weight on his right foot, and a bolt of pain ran up to his knee. He could feel himself starting to be washed down towards the propeller. His right hand gripped tighter to the ladder, desperately hanging on. The salt of the water was stinging his eyes. When he managed to get himself squarely back on to the ladder he moved swiftly up five more rungs. Christ, he thought. That was close.

Using his forearms he pulled himself up on to the deck, then crouched down low, ripping the Bushmaster from his back. He held the gun to his eyes, looking out over the deck. For forty feet it was empty metal, with two cranes at the side and a lifeboat. To his right he could see a body lying crumpled on the deck, a pool of blood seeping out of the hole in the head just above the ear, and a cigarette still smouldering at its side. Matt glanced back down to the men behind, giving them the thumbs-up sign. Reid was already on the ladder pulling himself upwards.

Ahead, Matt could see the back bridge. One light was illuminating the deck, and he could hear the tinny sound of radio music being carried on the wind.

Behind him, Reid landed on the deck, then Cooksley, then Ivan. Matt checked the dinghy was secured to the stern with a rope. All four men then lay flat on the cold, wet metal: blacked-up, out of sight of the bridge.

'There's two up there, I reckon,' Matt whispered. 'Move up to twenty feet, then we'll drop them.'

Matt rose slowly and started walking stealthily across the deck, holding his breath, taking care not to make a sound on the metal surface. Right now, surprise was the best weapon. A single sound and they would lose it. Reid walked two paces behind him, ready to give him covering fire if any shooting started.

When they were twenty paces from the bridge, Ivan

and Cooksley moved up ahead to attack from the front. Ivan was following standard operating procedures as if he'd been in the Regiment all his life.

No wonder those bastards were so hard to kill when we crossed the water.

Matt paused until they were in position, and watched as Cooksley glanced through the front windows of the bridge. Cooksley waved two fingers in the air, indicating that there were two targets on the bridge. Matt pointed to the ladder that linked the bridge to the main surface of the boat, then with Reid at his side walked up the metal stairs.

Matt stood by the metal door of the bridge and waited until Ivan and Cooksley were in position by the front windows of the bridge.

'Fire!' Matt barked, putting a thumb up.

Matt heard four shots firing in unison, the tracer fire lightening their faces. He watched as the man on the wheel spun round then collapsed, his body colliding with the deck. The sound echoed down the length of the boat. The second man reeled back on his heels, staggering towards the hold. He was clutching his shoulder, his face clenched in agony. Wounded, Matt judged – but not yet fatally.

'Forward!' he shouted. 'Let's get in there.'

Matt sprinted the last few feet, Reid right behind him. He swung open the door and burst on to the bridge, running forwards, his rifle held out before him. Immediately a hail of bullets filled the tiny metal room. Matt could see the wounded man leaning down towards the hold, blood streaming down the side of his neck. His ear had been shot clean from his face. '*Hajaba!*' he shouted. '*Hajaba!*'

Matt didn't know much Arabic, but he knew that word.

The bastard is telling them to hide.

Cooksley and Ivan's initial burst of fire must have been deflected by the strengthened glass. That was the only way the men could have survived the initial attack. The man now held up a pistol. He tried to steady himself but blood was pouring from his ear, dripping over his eyes and obscuring his vision. One shot rang out as he fired. Matt heard the metal somewhere behind him cracking as the bullet hit it. Another shot. This time it seemed to have winged Reid, as his arm dropped in agony.

Matt levelled his Bushmaster to his eye, steadied his arm and pulled the trigger. The shot was true. The bullet exploded between the man's eyes, sending him reeling backwards, his mouth wide open and blood trickling down the side of his face.

Matt rushed forwards, put his rifle to the head of the first man, and fired a double-tap into his skull. He looked dead, but there was no point taking any chances.

'You OK?'

'Just grazed my arm,' said Reid.

'So the rest are in the hold,' said Matt.

They had no way of knowing for sure how many men were on board. MI5 had reckoned six, meaning there could be three below, but it could be more. A metal stairway led down from the bridge into the hold, but it was pitch black. Matt knelt down, level with the stairs, swivelling his eyes through the space. Even with the goggles, he could see nothing.

'Torch!' he shouted.

Reid collected a torch from his belt and shone it down the stairwell. A bullet broke through the silence, striking the wheel and ricocheting into the window of the bridge. It had flown through the three-yard opening to the stairwell, but it was impossible to tell exactly where in the hold it had come from, or who had fired it. The sheet of glass shattered into fragments, tumbling on to the floor. Matt ducked. If they were in the hold, and this was the only entrance, they were well dug in.

This could be a nasty fight.

Behind him, Ivan and Cooksley had entered the bridge. The boat was rocking from side to side as it steamed forwards with nobody at the wheel. 'See if you can shut this bloody thing down, Ivan,' Matt snapped. He looked towards Cooksley. 'See if there's another way down,' he said.

Cooksley ran down the length of the boat, inspecting the cranes, the lifeboat and the engine hatch. 'Just the engines,' he said, returning to the bridge. 'We can get down to that, but I don't know if it leads anywhere.'

Reid shook his head. 'Unlikely,' he said. 'The engine room is usually sealed off from the rest of the boat. Even if it's not, any man going down there will get fucked.'

'We got some stuff to blow away the bastards in the hold?' said Matt.

'We have Semtex,' said Ivan.

'Reckon you can make a small bomb that's not going to sink the ship?' said Matt.

Another bullet rattled out of the stairwell, followed by three more. All four men instinctively moved out of range. 'Give me two minutes,' answered Ivan.

Matt, Reid and Cooksley approached the edge of the stairwell, pointing their rifles down, loosening off a few rounds of ammunition: if there was anyone down there waiting for them, they needed to clear them out of the way. The sound of gunfire echoed through the hold. Matt could hear the metal bullets hitting metal walls and listened out for the familiar sound of bullet ripping into flesh, the cry of a wounded man. But he could hear nothing. This was useless, he decided. They were just shooting into thin air. The men down there had taken cover and were just waiting for them to come down the stairs.

Then they'll pick us off one by one.

It was almost two o'clock, Matt realised, glancing at his watch.

If we hang about, they'll radio someone for help. We need to get this finished off now.

Ivan returned holding a small round ball of Semtex wrapped up with black tape, no bigger than his fist. A detonator cap was fitted to it, with two long pieces of wire stretching out. 'This thing scares the crap out of me,' he said. 'So I hate to think what it will do to them.'

Despite himself, Matt smiled back. The wind was

starting to pick up, and the waves were smashing into the side of the vessel.

Ivan motioned to Matt to stand well back. Reid and Cooksley followed, and the three men stood at the back of the bridge, moving out of range of the blast. Ivan joined the two wires together, then dropped the bomb down the length of the stairwell. He turned swiftly on his heels, running to the back of the bridge, and placed the wires on to the battery pack.

The explosion rocked through the vessel. Matt could feel its steel frame shuddering under the force, the bolts and rivets shaking loose. A pale cloud of smoke started to emerge from the hold.

'Nice fireworks,' said Cooksley.

'It's still early days,' said Ivan grimly.

'Let's get down there.' Matt stepped towards the hold. 'Reid, Cooksley, you cover me.'

He held the Bushmaster in his right hand, approaching the edge of the hold. He scanned the stairs, but could still see nothing. Cooksley and Reid stood behind him, their rifles raised to their shoulders ready to fire. Matt lowered his foot on to the first rung.

If one of them gets me, at least he'll go down in a hail of bullets.

He jumped the three feet on to the floor in one swift movement, his knees breaking the fall. The last two rungs had been mashed up by the explosion. He rolled over, using his goggles to scan the room. The smell of the explosion and of melting steel was thick in the air, and smoke still filled the room. He could make out a shape that looked like a man. Correct that, he told himself. Three shapes that each looked like a third of a man.

He walked on through the hold. About ten yards from the staircase lay the head of a man. A couple of yards away, his torso, and on the other side of the room his legs. Blood, guts and intestines had spewed from him, spilling out on to the metal floor.

'That's one,' said Reid suddenly, standing behind Matt. 'Where's the rest of the buggers?'

'Over there, I reckon,' said Matt.

The hold was narrow and dark. At the side there was a small kitchen area and a stock of food. A TV and DVD player was on a chest, but the screen was now blown out. At the back there were six bunk beds and a few travel bags.

'Seven beds,' said Ivan. 'I count four bodies – three upstairs including the lookout, and one down here. That means there are three men left.'

Matt moved further forwards. At the front of the hold there were two thick steel doors. The steel bolts on the outside were open, but the doors were firmly shut. 'They're in here,' he said. 'They've locked themselves into the walk-in safes – the gold and the diamonds will be in there as well.'

Ivan thumped his fist against the door. 'Christ, about eight to nine inches thick,' he said. 'Solid steel. Reinforced. That's not what we planned for.'

'I don't give a fuck what it's made of,' snapped Matt. 'Can you blow it or not?'

Ivan ran his hands across the door, his finger running over its steel skin as if he were giving it a massage. He paused, focusing on the joint where the open outside lock was. 'This is the weakest part,' he said. 'I reckon a strip of Semtex will create enough force to crack this thing open. But it could blow a hole in the hull.'

'What are the odds?' said Matt.

'I'm not a fucking bookmaker.'

'Just give us the bloody answer,' said Cooksley.

'About sixty–forty in our favour,' said Ivan. 'Position the Semtex in the right way, and most of the force of the explosion travels on a horizontal axis. It goes into the door and punches a hole in it. But you can't stop some of the energy the blast releases from travelling downwards as well. And that could put the loot at the bottom of the sea. And us with it, if we don't get out damned sharpish.'

Matt looked towards Reid and Cooksley. 'Shall we take a vote?'

'What are the options?' said Reid.

Matt shrugged. 'They can't have much to eat or drink in there. At some point, they're going to come out, take a chance on whether we shoot them or let them go.'

'They'll call for help,' said Reid. 'They could easily have a radio or a satellite phone in there.'

'And they are fanatics,' added Ivan. 'They might just decide to die in there rather than let us nick their stuff.'

'I say we blow them now,' said Reid.

'Me too,' said Cooksley.

'Go to work,' said Matt, looking towards Ivan.

'I'll need a couple of minutes.'

Matt climbed back on to the deck, followed by Cooksley and Reid. Ivan had explained that when the blast went up, the over-pressures created by the explosion would kill anything within twenty yards. They needed to be out of range. Matt switched on his radio, patching through a connection to Damien. 'Start sailing to meet us,' he said. 'There are four men down here. Ivan's about to blow them, but there's a chance he might sink the ship. So I want you nearby.'

Matt tucked the radio back into its holder and leant over the side of the ship. The waves were beating against the hull and the wind seemed to have gathered yet more strength, sending the clouds swirling through the sky. Inside his wet-suit it was suddenly starting to feel very cold. It had been more than two years since he had killed a man: the last mission before he left the Regiment had been the hostage rescue in Chechnya, and two men had gone down. Over his career, he calculated there had been twenty-eight to thirty-six kills, depending on which bullet had hit whom. He remembered each one of them, and would carry the memories to his grave.

Ivan was back on the deck now, alongside Cooksley and Reid. 'The charger is ready,' he said. 'Take cover.'

Matt turned his back to the bridge, leaning on the railing at the stern. He crouched down, preparing for the impact of the explosion.

If the Irishman hasn't got it right, Cooksley and Reid will be sending him to the bottom of the sea to get our stuff.

The blast shook through the vessel. It felt as if the explosion heaved the boat several feet above the water. The hull shook furiously as the boat caught a wave and started to lurch to the left. Water started to splash across the deck, washing over each of them. Matt could hear the sound of creaking metal, the noise of joints and girders being wrenched out of position. The smell of charred and melting steel drifted through the air.

Matt walked unsteadily back towards the stairway. The boat was rocking still, tossed around by the waves. As he looked down, he could see the stairs had collapsed. He slung his rifle aside and took out his pistol. Using his arms, he levered himself down into the hold. The smoke was intense, making him choke as soon as the fumes hit his lungs. Matt released the safety catch on the pistol, looking into the darkness. The door had collapsed inwards, a hole punched clean through the metal. Matt levelled his pistol and fired six shots in quick succession.

If anyone is alive in there, that should draw some return fire.

He waited five seconds, reloaded the pistol with a fresh magazine, then started walking slowly forwards. Cooksley, Reid and Ivan were at his side, their pistols cocked, ready to fire. The door had been turned into a mess of twisted and burnt metal, scraps littered across the floor. Matt pushed it aside, shining a torch into the strongroom. His eyes locked on to the figure of a man sprawled across the floor. His leg was severed clean from his body, and blood was pouring from him. His gun was lying several feet from where he had fallen.

'*Rahmet,*' he was muttering. '*Rahmet.*'

Sorry, pal, thought Matt. You can beg for mercy in any language you like but you're not going to get it. He knelt down, pressed the nozzle of the Beretta 92 to the man's head and squeezed the trigger. The bullet exploded into his skull, sending his brains spilling out on to the floor. His eyes closed and blood started to pour out of his still open mouth.

Matt looked around. There were two other men in the hold. One was already dead, his head blown clean away from his body. The other was slowly dying. A gaping hole had opened up his chest where a chunk of steel blown out of the door had cut straight through him. Now his ribcage was sticking out of his torso. His clothes had turned into shreds. Reid jammed his pistol into his mouth, finishing him off with one shot.

Somewhere I can hear water. Gushing.

'Is she holed?' Matt shouted to Ivan.

Ivan looked up from the doorway, his expression tense. 'Afraid so,' he said. 'It's torn a strip of metal the size of a man from the bottom of the boat. We're shipping water.'

'It's going to sink?' said Cooksley.

'You stupid Irish twat,' shouted Reid. 'I knew we shouldn't trust you.'

'Shut it!' Matt snapped. 'Damien is on his way with the mother ship. I reckon we've got twenty minutes to get this gear transferred before she goes down.'

He looked towards the back of the hold. The boxes were stacked one on top of the other, maybe fifty of them in all. Opening the first one, Matt looked inside. Diamonds. Tray upon tray of them, stacked in neat rows like chocolates. He opened another box. Gold. Ten bars, five on each side of the crate. For a moment he was transfixed by the display of wealth laid out before him.

More money than any of us ever dreamt of.

'Let's get this stuff on deck,' he barked.

He took the first crate and walked back to the broken stairway. Reid positioned himself at the top, a bandage now strapped over his arm wound, Ivan stood beneath, ready to pass the crates up. Matt passed the boxes from the hold to Ivan – and once they were on deck, Cooksley stacked them close to the dinghy. It was back-breaking work, the water spitting up from the hull all the time, soaking their feet. The diamonds were light enough, a few pounds of glass and tissue paper, but the gold was like carrying sacks of coal. Sweat was starting to pour from Matt's brow as he lugged box after box. But there was a lightness in his step. They had faced the risks and overcome them. This was just grunt work.

'We should go,' said Matt, the water swirling around his knees and rising fast. 'There's only a few crates left.'

'No,' snapped Reid. 'We've risked our lives. We take it all.'

'Don't be an idiot,' said Ivan. 'There's no point if everything goes down to the bottom of the ocean.'

Reid jumped into the hold and jabbed his finger into Ivan's face. 'You got us into this mess.'

Matt looked at both men, exasperated. 'Shut the fuck up and get up the top, we've only got another five minutes, man.'

Matt waded through the rising swell of water, and started lifting the last few crates four at a time on his shoulder. He passed one load up to Cooksley, then the next. 'That's it,' he said, passing the last of the crates to Ivan. The boat was filling rapidly. Somewhere beneath him, he could hear the sound of metal tearing, as waves beat against the hole ripped open in the hull.

Christ, the sooner we're out of here the better.

Matt levered himself on to the deck. The boat was starting to list as water filled the hull. They were drifting helplessly, tossed about on the waves. 'Any sign of our ship?' Matt asked.

Cooksley and Ivan took the corpse of the first man they had killed and tossed it down into the hold. Then they heaved the two bodies from the bridge down the stairs. It was important to make sure all the men went down with the ship, leaving no traces on the surface of the sea. By the time they had finished their hands were smeared with blood.

Reid shook his head. 'He can't be far.'

'About two miles,' said Ivan. 'It could take him fifteen minutes to get here. That's if the bugger knows how to steer in a straight line.'

'I thought you said he knew about boats,' said Cooksley. 'That's why we brought him along.'

'He does, and he'll be here,' said Matt. 'Just get this stuff on the dinghy.'

They started loading, each crate carefully placed in the craft. They stacked the boxes one on top of another, using the straps from the life jackets to belt them into place. All the time, the water was filling the boat at a faster pace. It was leaning badly to one side, making walking difficult without slipping, and the waves were climbing closer and closer to the rim of the deck. Come on, Damien, thought Matt. She won't hold for more than a couple of minutes.

Matt scoured the horizon, looking for some sign of the boat. Nothing. He knew Damien would be steering without lights, so he might well not see him in the pitch dark. He tried the radio again, but the device was struggling to locate the frequency. Either that or Damien wasn't answering.

You'll have to be here soon. We can't swim from here, and we're not abandoning the gear.

He could see from their faces that the gang was losing its patience. Damien should have been there at least five minutes ago. Cooksley and Reid's eyes kept squinting towards the horizon. Ivan's face was tense and uncertain. 'What the hell is keeping him?' said Matt, his words almost drowned out by the wind and spray hitting his face.

A wave rolled over the surface of the deck; the boat was struggling to stay above the surface.

I can feel her slipping beneath my feet.

Matt worked with Reid and Cooksley to lash the

crates to the dinghy, each crate packed tightly to the next one. As they worked, the boat was starting to sway and heave as the waves broke closer to its deck. Matt looked out into the horizon. Total darkness. The boat was wobbling like a jelly beneath his feet. He slashed at the ropes securing the dinghy. Behind him he could hear a giant sucking sound, like water disappearing from a bath but amplified a hundred times.

I've never heard a boat sinking before, he thought. But I bet it sounds something like that.

The crates took up the entire dinghy. 'Pull on life jackets,' shouted Matt. 'We might have to swim for it.'

He tightened one of the jackets around his waist and dived into the water. Two ropes were dangling from the dinghy. He grabbed one, holding on to it, and kicked his legs to keep his head above water. Wave after wave broke over his head, pushing him below the surface of the ocean.

I can survive out here, but not for long. If the dinghy goes down then we are all fucked. And it's dangerously low because of the weight it is carrying.

Matt glanced around. Ivan was holding on to another rope. Reid and Cooksley were bobbing about in the water, taking huge gulps of air every time their heads broke free of the waves.

Now I know why Bulmer wanted us to practise our swimming.

Struggling to keep his head above water, Matt realised he could hear it before he could see anything – the noise of an engine, the sound broken up by the waves, but growing steadily louder. Behind him, he could hear the hull of the boat cracking, and saw one half disappear into the sea. Another hour, and all trace of it would be gone.

A light shone in the distance. Damien, thought Matt. He watched as the searchlight moved rapidly towards them, beaming out across the sea. Matt raised his hand into the air, waving it frantically, before remembering that they had blacked up faces and had worn black wetsuits to make sure no one could see them. That worked both ways. Damien wasn't going to see a hand in the water.

'There should be a flare,' shouted Ivan. 'See if you can reach it.'

Matt levered himself up to the side of the dinghy and peered over the rim. At the back, there was a small box with a red cross marked on it. Medical supplies, thought Matt. And maybe flares.

Pulling himself into the boat, he reached into the box. Bandages, disinfectants, antibiotics, aspirin.

For fuck's sake, who needs this rubbish?

Flares, he noticed, grabbing them. He held the gun high over his head, firing the flare into the sky, watching as it hung like a firework over the ocean. Beneath its fierce light he could see the boat vanishing underneath the waves. And he could see their own ship, maybe four hundred metres away.

Matt perched on the edge of the dinghy, watching while Damien steered his craft closer towards them.

It pulled up alongside, and Damien killed the

engines. His searchlight was turned on to the water, picking out the crates and the four men.

'You blokes look like you could use a cup of tea,' he said.

ELEVEN

The clouds had cleared, revealing a sky of bright stars whose light settled on the pure sand and the dark blue water. Matt paced along the shoreline, the waves lapping at his feet. There could be few better spots, he reflected, in which to collect your fortune. It reminded him of how much he loved the Mediterranean.

Wherever Gill and I decide to make our home, it will be somewhere looking over this sea. The water is in my veins.

'That's it!' said Reid at his side.

Matt followed the line of Reid's finger, pointing out to sea. The cargo ship was steaming slowly into the bay. 'Get the dinghy and trucks ready,' he said.

Matt felt tired but invigorated. After the last night the adrenaline was still pumping through his veins. Damien had fished them all out of the water and they had loaded the crates on to their own boat. They had waited for an hour, watching as the last remnants of the al-Qaeda ship disappeared beneath the waves. They wanted to make sure it was safely at the bottom of the sea, since a floating wreck would be discovered within a few hours. Then they sailed back to Cyprus, cleaning themselves up on the boat. Damien laid anchor a kilometre from the coast, while the rest of them went ashore in the dinghy. The plan had been for Damien to stay with the loot overnight: it would be safer to keep it at sea than on dry land. He would meet them at the bay at two o'clock the following night to transfer the crates into the Land Rovers and then on to the cargo boat bound for Rotterdam.

Reid had insisted on staying with Damien – both he and Cooksley were suspicious about letting the money out of their sight, and wanted at least one of them to stay on the boat. Matt had to work hard to make sure Ivan didn't stay as well: it might create suspicions, he told them, if none of them made it back to the hotel.

The team finally stumbled back into the hotel at five in the morning, exhausted but in high spirits. As far as the receptionist was concerned, it was just a stag party returning after an all-night bender. They went to their rooms, but it took Matt a couple of hours before he could get off to sleep. Too many thoughts were racing through his mind: how quickly can we get the money, how soon can I pay off my debts, how long before I see Gill again?

All of them woke late, and spent the day lounging around the pool. The team now looked tired and haggard; none of them had slept for more than a couple of hours. But they were also happy and relaxed, noticed Matt. They were all coming together. There was, he decided, nothing like the combination of danger and success to create camaraderie between men.

And now, here's the pay-off.

The ship was within sight. Damien was at anchor two hundred metres from the shore, with Reid at his side. Matt pushed out the dinghy to meet him, Cooksley and Ivan remaining on the secluded beach preparing the two Land Rovers. The dinghy bounced through the waves and pulled up alongside. Matt cast up a rope for Damien to catch and clambered up on to the ship.

'We've made it,' he said, thumping Damien on the back.

'Well, Reid and I thought about turning around and sailing straight for Argentina,' said Damien. 'But then I thought – nah, I'd miss Camberwell.'

Matt laughed. 'And we'd have to track you down and kill you as well.'

'I believe you would too,' grinned Damien.

The work was slow and hot, but none of them minded. Their spirits were high. Each crate had to be loaded on to the dinghy and steered back to shore. That took three trips. Then they opened up each case, wrapped the trays of diamonds and the bars of gold in tissue paper, and stowed them away inside the hulls of the Land Rovers. Both cars were already loaded on to the back of a truck, their engines removed, ready to be taken down to the docks. They had been parked behind a high sandbank to keep them out of sight of any passing traffic. There was not much chance of anyone seeing them: the beach was at the end of a dirt road leading nowhere, and Ivan had cased the location two mornings running to be sure it had no visitors.

Unpacking the crates and transferring the gear, Reid and Cooksley struck up a chorus of the Good Ship Venus: 'We sailed to the Canaries, to screw the local fairies, we got the syph in Tenerife and the clap in Buenos Aires,' they sang in a deep, rolling baritone. By the next verse, Matt, Ivan and Damien had all joined in: 'We sailed to the Bahamas, where the girls all wear pyjamas, they wouldn't screw our motley crew, they much preferred bananas.'

The song completed, all five men stood around laughing. Matt put the last of the gold bars into the Land Rover, then stood back from the truck. 'There's one more thing I want to do,' he said.

In his hand, Matt held one tray with six diamonds in it. He took them out one by one, holding them in his hand, admiring the way they caught and reflected the light from the stars, then handed one to each man. 'Let's keep one of these each as a souvenir,' he said. 'Give them to our wives or girlfriends.'

'You could give one to that cute waiter in the hotel,' said Reid.

'That mouth of yours is going to get you into trouble,' Damien said.

They all took one diamond, slipping them into their pockets. 'One left,' said Cooksley.

'Why don't we give it to that barmaid at the hotel,' said Reid, laughing. 'I reckon she'd shag all five of us for one of these sparklers.'

'Or Alison,' said Ivan. 'She gave us this job. I reckon one of these would look good around her neck.'

'Alison, yes,' said Matt. 'Let's keep one for her.'

Matt turned the diamond over between his fingers, letting the sunshine from the window catch its light. 'Alison?' he said into the phone.

'Matt,' she answered quickly. 'You OK?'

'Never better,' he answered. 'The mission went like clockwork.'

'Good work, Matt. When are you coming back?'

Matt hesitated before answering. 'It will be a few days before we can get the goods fenced. We'll be in Rotterdam, then back in London.'

'I'll plan a celebration,' said Alison. 'Maybe even cook you something.'

Matt put down the phone and walked back into the sunshine. There was easiness to his mood he hadn't known for months. A burden had been lifted from his shoulders – the burden of debt and failure. He could walk more freely now.

At a table next to the pool, the rest of the gang were collecting bottles of Keo, the local Cypriot beer. It wasn't the best Matt had ever tasted; nothing could beat the Filipino San Miguel he'd sampled when he'd spent two months fighting some communist insurgents in that country. But when the sun was shining and you were about to fold two million into your pocket, all the beer tasted sweet and all the girls looked good. Or was that the other way around?

He collected a round from the bar and slammed the bottles down on the table. 'Get these down your necks, boys,' he said.

'You're paying for a round, Matt,' laughed Damien. 'Now we *know* you've made a lot of money.'

Ivan was shuffling a deck of cards, but Reid had already told him to forget it. They had better things to do than sit around playing games. Such as, Ivan had asked quizzically?

'Drink beer, and work on my tan.'

'And you?' Matt looked across at Ivan. 'What do you think you might do when we collect the money?'

'I suspect I'm going to suffer from too many choices,' answered Ivan, putting his cards down on the table. 'I must become a different man, yet I will still be who I am, with the same wife, and the same children.'

'Translate that into English for us,' said Reid

'I can go anywhere, and be anyone,' said Ivan. 'So I reckon I'll go to Boston, somewhere around there. There's a good Irish community, the air is clean, and it's not too hot. But I don't know. I might feel differently tomorrow. How about you?'

'Use the money to make more money, that's my plan,' said Reid. 'I'm through with working for other people. Building, that's what I want to do. Buy some land with planning permission, put up some new houses, sell them on. Try some barn conversions as well. There's always money in that game. You just need some capital to get started. Well, now I've got it.'

'And what about you?' Ivan said, looking towards Cooksley.

'California,' he replied. 'That's where Jane and I are going for a year. The kids are getting booked in for gene therapy. We'll spend the next year with them, doing everything we can to make sure they pull through.'

'And when they recover?' said Matt. 'What then?'

'I can't even think about that, Matt. Until I know whether the children are going to be OK, I can't focus on anything else.' He paused, sipping on his beer, lost in his own thoughts. 'And how about you, Damien. What's your plan?'

'I'm with Reid,' Damien answered. 'Money is for building, not spending. Sure, I'll spend a bit, but the rest I'm going to invest. The gangs in London are wide open right now. There's an opportunity for one man to take charge, impose his will, bring some order to the city. With the right amount of capital, that could be me.'

'The Godfather, right?' said Ivan gently.

Damien swigged back the remains of his beer and reached for another bottle. 'Somebody get me a horse and a large carving knife.'

'And you, Matt?' said Ivan. 'You've brought us all together here. What happens to your two million?'

Matt glanced towards Damien. 'I get married, that's what,' he said firmly. 'A new Porsche, my own yacht, a gorgeous babe hanging off my arm, and nothing to do all day but run and drink beer, and I'm happy.'

'We risk our lives to make all this money,' Ivan said,

'and when we get it, we do things we could have done with much less.'

'You're saying we don't need the money?' said Cooksley.

Ivan shook his head. 'I'm just saying maybe it's the pursuit we enjoy, not the possession of it.'

The night was drawing in, and the moon was already rising over the bay. Matt had just completed a five-mile run along the beach, picking his way through the tourists and the volleyball players, and the blood was pumping through his veins. He felt refreshed and relaxed. He had thought about it during the run, and his mind was made up. It was time to make the call.

He finished his shower, dried himself off, then picked up the hotel phone. It sat in his hand, a small, inert lump of plastic and copper wire. He put it down, walked once around the room, paused to look at the sun setting on the horizon, then picked the phone up again.

Christ, Matt. You killed at least two men last night. I can't believe you are frightened of calling a girl.

'Gill,' he said into the receiver as she picked up the phone. 'Is that you?'

There was a pause on the line. He could hear her breath, and he could imagine her expression, yet for several seconds she remained silent. 'Matt Browning,' she said eventually. 'The man who is too frightened to go through with his own wedding.'

The words stung more than Matt had imagined they would. He'd always known this was going to be a tough conversation, but he'd thought she might have softened in the weeks since they had last spoken. 'That's not fair, Gill,' he said firmly.

'Try telling all your girlfriends your wedding has been called off,' said Gill. 'You try taking your dress back to the shop, and calling up the cake-maker and the florist and all the rest of them, and telling them not to bother, your boyfriend can't be fagged to go through with it.' He could hear her choking back the sobs. 'That's bravery, Matt. Not clearing off and leaving me to clear up the mess.'

'I was in a jam, Gill,' said Matt. 'I could have been killed. So could you.'

'What kind of a jam?' she said. 'What's happened to you?'

'I can't tell you, Gill, it's against all the rules.'

'You're not back with the Regiment, are you? I thought you were finished with all of that.'

'No,' said Matt.

'And where's Damien gone? I haven't been able to get him on the phone for days. He's not involving you in a bit of crime, is he?'

Matt winced. 'No,' he replied. 'I can't talk about it, but it's almost over now. I just wanted to hear your voice and make sure you're OK. And to say, this will all be over in a week or so. I'll have my life back together.' He hesitated, allowing a moment for the words to sink in. 'When that happens, I want us to be together again.'

Matt held the receiver in his hands. He couldn't be sure how many miles separated Cyprus from Marbella.

They were at opposite ends of the Mediterranean. Yet, despite the distance, it was as if she were sitting right next to him. In his mind he could see her eyes and smell her hair. 'Gill,' he continued, 'would that be OK?'

'You think you can just break off the engagement, piss off on some stupid mission, then call me up and say, oh, I think its back on again – with one phone call?' Her tone was starting to harden.

'Two phone calls, then,' said Matt quickly. 'And a text message.'

She hesitated, then laughed.

First base, thought Matt.

'Twenty phone calls, and the biggest diamond you ever saw,' said Gill. 'And then I might just think about it.'

Well, at least that can be arranged.

The street market in the centre of Limassol was thronging with people. The sun was beating down and there was a sharp smell of citrus fruits hanging in the air. Matt walked slowly through the crowds, his eyes scanning the stalls. Most of it was just the usual tourist junk: T-shirts, ornamental daggers, salad bowls and poorly made leather handbags. He paused over a knife, argued briefly with the shopkeeper about the price, then went on to the next stall.

Somewhere around here there must be a piece of jewellery or something to wear that Gill would really appreciate.

'Find anything?' said Cooksley.

'Shopping for *girls*,' said Matt. 'Almost impossible.

No way to tell what they like and don't like.'

'Do you think Jane might like this?' Cooksley held up a brightly painted china salad bowl.

'For Christ's sake, no.'

The two men walked on in silence. Around them tourists were haggling, stallholders shouting, and a few locals out shopping. The sun was beating down, and as midday approached the temperature was starting to rise, but it was not yet uncomfortably hot. What's the rush? Matt thought. We've got a whole week to sit around Limassol buying presents. I might as well take my time. 'How about a beer down by the port?' he said. 'We can shop tomorrow or the next day.'

It was a ten-minute walk, through the main tourist districts, down to where the boats docked. Matt had been stationed in Cyprus for a couple of months of his Army stint, and the docks were the part of town he liked best. He could sit for hours drinking a beer and watching the ferries that worked the Aegean Sea, connecting the hundreds of tiny islands scattered between here, Turkey and Greece.

If I wasn't a soldier, I would have been quite happy to have been a ferryman. That's an honest, outdoor trade.

They stepped into the street. A few metres in front of them, a Mitsubishi Shogun suddenly swerved away from the kerb, its engine revving furiously. Matt pulled Cooksley back, tugging at the sleeve of his T-shirt, but it was too late – the car winged the side of his hip, sending him crashing on to the road, his body sprawled across the tarmac. The car stopped ten metres away as the driver slammed on the brakes. Matt started running towards it, shouting at the idiot at the wheel. Then he heard the sound of rubber screeching against tarmac and realised that the car was on the move again – in reverse.

The bastard was trying to drive back over Cooksley.

Matt dived on to the road, grabbed Cooksley by the neck and somehow managed to heave and roll his body across the road and into the gutter. He dived with him, and through the corner of his eye he saw the big, thick tyres of the Shogun crunching past him, missing them both by just a few inches. The driver slammed on the brakes again, the engine revved and roared as reverse was thrown into first gear, then the vehicle started moving forwards again. Matt had to use all his strength to roll a few more inches, drag both their bodies on to the pavement. Around him, he could hear people shouting and screaming. The Shogun's tyres slammed hard into the kerb and it bounced backwards. People started to crowd around them, but for a moment Matt could see the man sitting behind the wheel. Their eyes met for a fraction of a second, and Matt could feel the hatred pouring out of him.

Then the Shogun reversed, turned and disappeared up the street.

'What happened?' said Cooksley.

'Somebody just tried to kill you,' said Matt.

The mood around the table was sombre. They were sitting towards the back of the pool area, far enough away from the crowds that no one would hear what they were saying. Cooksley was wearing a bandage down the side of his face. He was bruised along his neck and arms, and there were plasters stuck on to three separate cuts. He would be OK, Matt had made sure of that. He had cleaned and dressed men with bullets through them, and a few cuts were not going to kill anyone. Certainly not a man of Cooksley's strength.

'You're sure somebody was trying to kill you?' said Damien.

'It was an attempted assassination, no question,' said Matt. 'We've all seen them close enough to know what they look like. This guy drove the car straight at Cooksley. Then he reverses, and tries to back over him. The first time could have been an accident. But the second time, no way.' He paused. 'Anyway, I saw his eyes. Looked like a rag-head.'

Reid shook his head, banging his fist on the table. 'I say we find him and we kill him.'

'Find him?' said Matt, shrugging. 'Where? He was driving a red Mitsubishi Shogun, I can tell you that. I didn't see the number plate – and anyway, I don't know how to trace cars in Cyprus.'

'The question,' said Ivan, 'is who would want to kill Cooksley?' He looked towards him. 'Well?'

Cooksley looked straight back. 'I don't know,' he answered. 'There isn't anybody, and anyway, nobody knows I'm here, except for us. Not even my wife.'

'Al-Qaeda,' said Damien. 'They're on to us already.'

'But how would they know it's us?' asked Cooksley. 'We killed all the buggers on the boat. Al-Qaeda have probably only just discovered it's missing. How the fuck could they find us?'

'Maybe it's someone after our money,' said Matt. 'Maybe someone saw us stashing the gear into the Land Rover and decided to take a bit of it for themselves.'

'What about your fence?' said Ivan to Damien. 'Does he know something?'

'That couldn't happen,' snapped Damien.

'He's a fucking gangster, isn't he?' said Reid. 'He knows we just nicked thirty million. He kills us off, and gets to pocket all of the loot for himself. Sounds like a good plan to me.'

'It's not just soldiers that have standards,' Damien replied angrily. 'Villains have them too. Our code is even stronger than yours. It's impossible for a fence to do something like that – he'd be cutting his own throat.' He paused. 'Anyway, like I said, he doesn't know who or where we are. I haven't told him. All he knows is a big shipment is coming in next week. From somewhere. Anyway, Matt said it was an Arab.'

There was silence around the table, as if they were all turning over different possibilities. Over by the pool, Matt could see a girl getting thrown into the water by a pair of boys. Suddenly he wished he could be somewhere else.

'Ivan spoke to someone,' Reid said, looking around the table. 'I saw him.'

Matt noticed four sets of eyes turn across the table and settle on Ivan. The rules had been made quite clear:

they would speak to no one until the mission was complete. Nobody must know where they were until the loot was fenced and the money banked.

I broke the rule myself when I spoke to Gill.

'Is it true?' said Cooksley. 'Did you speak to someone?'

Ivan raised his head. There was a look in his eyes Matt hadn't seen before: part fear, part embarrassment and part defiance. 'I had to call home,' he said. 'My wife and kids have been taken.'

'What?' said Matt.

'The organisation has taken them,' said Ivan. 'The one I used to work for.'

'Why?' said Matt. 'Has your cover been blown? Do they know you've been turned by Five?'

'I don't think so, but I took the Semtex we needed for this mission from one of their dumps,' Ivan answered. 'The IRA are meant to have decommissioned their weapons, but there is still plenty left. I guess they discovered I'd lifted some, put two and two together and decided it was for a private job. So they've taken Mary and the kids, and they want my share of the money. If I give it to them, they'll let her go.' He paused. 'The Provos like to keep a monopoly. Nobody is allowed to start freelancing.'

'You reckon they know you've been turned?' said Matt.

'Mary called me and told me all about it,' Ivan said. 'Said they knew I was doing a robbery, that's all, and they wanted the money.'

'I thought we'd agreed no contact,' said Damien. 'How did she know where to get hold of you?'

'She sent me a text message, then I called her back, simple as that.' He looked around the men at the table. 'Of course I left a way for her to get hold of me. I bet all of you have done the same.'

'Not me,' snapped Damien. 'I stick to my word.'

'And you guys?' said Ivan.

'I haven't spoken to Jane, but, yes, my mobile is switched on a couple of times a day,' said Cooksley. 'She could leave a message if there was an emergency.'

Reid nodded. 'Same here,' he said. 'You never know. Something might happen to the kids.'

Matt leant forwards on the table. 'If it's confession time – I called Gill,' he said. 'But I didn't tell her where I was.'

Ivan leant forwards, his elbows leaning on the table, the lines on his forehead creasing up. 'Let me get this straight, you spoke to your girlfriend?'

'I didn't tell her where we are,' Matt repeated.

'You owe a lot of money to a Russian gangster, Matt,' Ivan said. 'If he knew how much money you'd just taken, he'd be after you.' He paused, looking around the pool area. 'This is Cyprus. The place is crawling with Russian mafia, in case you hadn't noticed the accents in the bar. It's where they come for their winter holidays.'

'Let's get back to you, Ivan,' Reid said, his face reddening. 'If the PIRA know how much money we have, they'll be after the lot of us. Those guys would kill us for free, never mind thirty million. It's *you* that's the problem, you have been right from the start.'

'He's right,' chipped in Cooksley.

Ivan raised his hands into the air. 'I'm not defending myself,' he said. 'Nobody is more worried about this than me. But I fight my own battles. If there's a problem, I'll fix it.'

'Once a traitor, always a traitor,' said Reid, stubbing out a cigarette into an already bulging ashtray.

Ivan turned to look at Matt. 'Look, it was an Arab driving the car, you say?'

Matt nodded.

'Not an Irishman then. The Provos wouldn't go after Cooksley. They'd come after me.'

The first sign of trouble, and everyone starts turning on each other.

'So we have four possibilities,' Damien interrupted. 'It could be al-Qaeda, it could be a local gang, it could be the IRA, or it could be the Russian mafia. Either way, you know what that says to me?' He looked around the table, meeting the eyes of each man in turn. 'We get the hell out of here. Because whichever of those four it is, they already know where we are, and I don't want to be around when they catch up with us.'

Sallum parked the Lexus LS430 in the bay, next to the Fords, Vauxhalls and Rovers. A light drizzle was falling. Dark clouds had gathered in the sky, and even though it was only three-thirty in the afternoon, the night seemed to have started to draw in. He slammed the door shut, pocketed the keys, then walked swiftly towards the factory and the main office.

For Ibrahim bin Assaf himself to have asked to see him in person, he knew it had to be important. Field operatives rarely had any direct contact with their masters. That was not how the organisation worked.

Assaf Foods occupied a sprawling factory and warehouse on the outskirts of West Bromwich, close to Birmingham. It made Indian ready-meals for supermarkets, irradiated chicken tikka masala that sat in the microwave for five minutes. Assaf had started the business twenty years ago as a young Pakistani immigrant. Now he was one of the wealthiest, most respected figures in the British Muslim community.

If only they knew, thought Sallum as he strode across the factory floor. *The infidels wouldn't be so keen on their curries then.*

He sat for a moment in the waiting room, glancing out to the floor below. He could see the giant machines slicing the battery chickens, spitting out the bones and throwing the remnants into huge bins. Machine cutters were dicing vegetables, and conveyor belts dropped spices into huge vats of oil and grease. A small cloud of smoke hung over the factory, and the rich smell of raw curry powder infiltrated the building.

Disgusting. A nation that has forgotten how to cook for itself has also forgotten how to defend itself. That is why they are weak and we are strong.

'Sallum *alakim*,' said Assaf, standing up from his desk

and shaking Sallum warmly by the hand. 'You are well, my brother?'

Assaf was a short, compact man who looked younger than his fifty-three years. His hair was greying but still thick, and although there were lines around his forehead his skin was still smooth and velvety. His eyes were set deep into his head, and his long nose raked out from the centre of his face. He had bearing and presence, Sallum observed, and a natural sense of command. Yet at the same time, he was discreet: you wouldn't notice him until he meant to put you under his spell. That was probably what made him such a successful businessman.

'I am well, sir,' Sallum replied stiffly.

'The operation in Saudi Arabia, it went better than we could have expected,' said Assaf. 'You are to be congratulated.'

Sallum bowed his head. 'To serve the movement in any way is an honour.'

'Quite so,' answered Assaf. 'May it be just the first of many great victories.' He turned, walking back towards his desk. The office was decorated simply – a desk, a computer screen, and a couple of leather armchairs for visitors. A copy of the FT and a pair of trade magazines lay on a coffee table. There was a picture of his wife and children on the desk, and a modest portrait of the prophet on the wall. But otherwise there was nothing to suggest that Assaf was anything but the most respectable of businessmen.

'But any movement will experience setbacks as well as victories,' said Assaf.

Sallum moved closer to the desk. 'A setback?'

'Unfortunately so,' Assaf replied. 'A boat carrying gold and jewels belonging to the organisation has been attacked and sunk. All the goods on board have been stolen, and our men killed.'

Sallum could feel a bead of sweat forming on his brow. 'Nobody would dare,' he said. 'It is an outrage.'

'They have dared,' said Assaf. 'But they will regret it.' He laid out five photographs on his desk, each one depicting a different man. Sallum picked up the pictures one by one, holding them carefully between thumb and index finger. On the back of each picture was stencilled a different name in black ink: Matt Browning, Damien Walters, Ivan Rowe, Alan Reid and Joe Cooksley. 'Are these the men?'

'They are British,' replied Assaf. 'They took the boat, and stole our money.' He paused, turning towards the window and looking out at the drizzly suburbs of Birmingham. 'In the Koran, in the book of Abu Dawuud, it is written: "A thief was brought to the Prophet four times and his punishments were amputations of the right hand, the left foot, the left hand and then the right foot. On the fifth occasion the Prophet had him killed."' Assaf looked towards Sallum, meeting his eyes. 'I think we know what it is the Prophet would wish to be done.'

TWELVE

This is where it started, Matt thought, looking up at the drab brick façade of the Holiday Inn Express on Wandsworth roundabout. He walked briskly into the hotel, telling the receptionist that three rooms were booked in the name of Jim Arnold. Matt had pulled the name straight out of his head when he made the booking on the phone. 'This way, lads, second floor,' he said.

Cooksley, Reid, Damien and Ivan followed him up the stairs. They had flown back from Cyprus that morning on the first flight available. From Heathrow, they had made their way directly to the hotel. Matt had called Alison from the airport, saying they were back in Britain, and they needed a meeting. Urgently.

'When will she be here?' Reid asked.

Matt checked his watch. It was three-twenty now, and she had promised to be there by three-thirty. 'Another ten minutes,' he said flatly.

The decision had not been hard to make, and it had been taken jointly between all five of them. Regiment rules. They took decisions together.

Who had attacked Cooksley or why, they had no

195

way of knowing for sure. But it was obvious that someone was after them. They had talked about escaping, discussed lots of different places. They could have headed for Greece, maybe, or gone into Romania or the Balkans somewhere. There were lots of places a man could hide in that part of the world, and three of them knew Kosovo well. They could have crossed to Turkey or headed into north Africa. But it was Damien who had come up with the most practical solution. When you want to hide, go somewhere you know well. That meant going home.

Matt answered the door on the second knock. Alison was wearing a black trouser suit with a red cardigan underneath, a string of pearls slung across her neck. She glanced at him briefly, smiled, then looked across the room. There was something different about her today, Matt judged. She was colder, and a couple of lines seemed to have creased into her brow.

I'm not sure she's pleased to see us.

'The mission was a great success,' she said. 'You are all to be congratulated. You've achieved a significant blow against al-Qaeda. Without money, they are nothing.'

'Save us the speeches,' said Matt, turning to face her. 'What's going to happen to us?'

Alison stood with her back to the window, her face framed by the sunlight breaking through the clouds. 'You get to keep the money, pure and simple,' said Alison stiffly. 'So far as I know, there is no change of plan.'

'Somebody tried to kill me,' said Cooksley. 'In Cyprus.'

'Something's going on,' said Matt. 'And we want to know what it is.'

'Cyprus is a small place,' Alison answered, turning to face them, her tone harsh. 'Nasty little island full of cheap package tourists, Russian gangsters and a few half-drunk squaddies getting burnt in the sun. It's full of people who drink too much beer, and talk too much. So who knows what has happened? Maybe one of you shot your mouth off in a bar, started trying to impress one of the girls. Maybe the local villains tried to take it off you?' She paused, looking directly at Matt. 'How the hell am I supposed to know?'

'It wasn't like that,' snapped Matt. 'We were there, and you weren't.'

'Then how was it?'

'Nobody shot their mouth off,' said Matt. 'We stayed together at the hotel, and Ivan taught us how to play bridge.' He laughed. 'We were probably the most sober, best-behaved stag party in recorded history.'

Alison turned away again, reaching for her handbag. She pulled out a handheld Olympus tape recorder, and placed it on the table. 'Listen to this,' she said.

She pressed the play button. A stream of Arabic came out of the machine – one main voice, with a pair of less distinct voices in the background. Matt spoke a couple of words of Arabic, but not enough to make any sense of the words he was now hearing. But you didn't need to know any of the language to understand that the man speaking was afraid, very afraid. The fear was scratched into the tone of his voice.

'The voice you just listened to is the captain of the boat you hit,' said Alison. 'He's speaking over an Immarsat satellite mobile phone. He made the call just after you hit them. We've had it translated. He's telling his bosses that the boat has been hit, and that they need help. After the bomb went off, the line went dead. I guess the blast destroyed the transmitter.' She switched off the machine.

'How the hell did you get that?' said Matt, impressed.

'We and the Americans monitor the voice traffic right through the Mediterranean,' said Alison calmly. 'A satellite phone is not a secure line. The NSA taps all conversations.'

'Maybe they're hoping to get Osama on the line one day saying I'm having a birthday bash at my house,' said Cooksley.

Alison didn't laugh. 'They passed this on to us,' she said. 'If you guys had managed to shoot all of them straight away, then this wouldn't have happened.'

'We got them just the way we meant to,' Reid interrupted.

Alison shrugged. Rain was starting to hit the window, leaving a thin film of water on the glass. 'It's too late to do anything about that now,' she said. 'And I don't think it's that important. We've had the whole thing translated, and all it says is that some men are raiding the boat. Al-Qaeda were always going to get that anyway, when the boat didn't make it to its destination. It doesn't say who you are, what you look like, even what nationality you are.'

'But it does tell us that al-Qaeda might be on to us earlier than we thought,' said Matt.

'Either way, it's of no concern to MI5,' said Alison. 'The job is done – it was well done. Thank you very much, end of story.'

Matt raised his hands into the air. 'Hold on,' he said. 'You're washing your hands of us?'

'What did you expect?'

'Five have safe houses, don't they?' said Cooksley, interrupting. 'We've got a week until the gear arrives in Rotterdam. We need to stay out of harm's way until then.'

Alison laughed: a light, shrill sound that started at the back of her throat and cut right through Matt's nerves. 'You've been reading too much spy fiction,' she said. 'Five might have a couple of safe houses, but they are all occupied right now.'

'We risked our lives on this mission,' snapped Matt. 'We want some protection.'

Alison started walking towards the door. 'You seem to have forgotten something,' she said. 'This was never an official mission, and there can be no official protection.'

Matt put the round of five double-cheeseburger meals on the table. The McDonald's was right across the road from the hotel, next to the B&Q warehouse. None of them had eaten since breakfast, and Matt reckoned they should get some food in their stomachs before they made any decisions. He didn't want anyone flapping.

'Bitch,' said Reid, his teeth sinking into the burger. 'I never liked her from the moment I first laid eyes on her.'

'She's just using us,' said Damien 'Go get this boat, knock out al-Qaeda's money, then the minute something goes wrong we're on our own.'

'Sorry, boys, thanks for risking your lives, lah-de-bloody-lah,' said Reid. 'We'd love to help you but we're a bit busy right now.'

'I'll tell you something else as well,' Ivan chipped in. 'Five have plenty of safe houses. There are at least three I know about just in my patch over the water. I reckon there must be a couple of dozen in London. She could stash us away somewhere if she wanted to.'

'She doesn't want to,' said Cooksley. 'She's just a bloody Rupert in a skirt.'

I can't disagree, thought Matt. Better legs, and a softer smile – but she's a Rupert with blonde hair and perfume. And you can never trust a Rupert.

'I suppose she hasn't broken any promises,' he said, looking around the table. 'We weren't told we were getting any protection, just that we were getting paid. We always knew we'd have to look after ourselves.'

'We didn't know it was about to go wrong, did we?' Reid snapped, ignoring the no smoking sign and lighting up a cigarette.

'And we didn't know al-Qaeda would be phoning

details of the hit back to base, did we?' said Damien. 'She *says* there's nothing on the tape about who we are, but we don't know that.'

'Let's cool it,' said Matt. 'There's no point in going over this. She's said no safe house, and that's that. We have to look out for ourselves.'

Damien leant forwards on the table. 'We've got six days until the boat arrives in Rotterdam,' he said. 'After that, we're rich men – that makes life easier. Perhaps it was just some local Cyprus boys, whatever.' He paused, taking a swig on his Coke. 'If not, then we use our money to change our names, disappear. I know some boys down in Bermondsey who can come up with new passports, new credit cards, even a new face if you really want one.'

'Damien's right,' said Matt. 'We hold out for the next six days, we should be in the clear.'

'Until then, we stick together,' said Reid. 'We all look out for one another.'

'And we all meet the gear coming off the boat and take it to the fence,' said Ivan. 'Only then do we go our separate ways.'

'Agreed,' said Matt. 'For the next week, we should be on top of each other like a bunch of mosquitoes. Let's stay in this hotel until it's all over.'

Cooksley finished off the last of his chips. 'Except for me,' he said slowly. 'I'm going home.'

Matt looked at him closely, but his face was made of granite: you could no more read it than you could read a piece of stone. 'What's up?'

'The kids have taken a turn for the worse,' he said, his voice trailing away. 'I have to be there.'

'I know a house you can go to,' said Alison. 'I don't know if it's safe, though.'

Matt looked up from the window to the doorway. His hotel room door was unlocked, and she had opened it without knocking. He had a pint of lager in front of him he had ordered up from the bar, but he was drinking slowly. From the window he could just see the Thames, but most of it was obscured by an apartment block. There were a few salesmen, and a couple of stray tourists who can't have realised that Wandsworth isn't the glitziest part of London. This place is about as miserable as I feel, he thought to himself.

'I like you, Alison, but I don't think there's anything safe about you.'

Alison toyed with her necklace. 'Listen, sorry about what happened earlier. There wasn't anything else I could do.'

Matt looked hard into her eyes but could find no trace of pity there. 'You could have given us what we wanted,' he said. 'Five has plenty of safe houses in London. You know it, we know it, so there was no need to lie.'

Alison sat down on the chair next to him, close enough for Matt to smell the perfume on her neck. Fresh, he noted. She'd just put it on, as if she were heading out on a date. 'You don't understand the kind of pressure we're under,' she said. 'There's something big going off in the next couple of weeks. We don't know what it is, but the al-Qaeda networks we monitor are humming. Maybe Heathrow, maybe Parliament, maybe a bomb at Old Trafford on a Saturday afternoon. It could be anything.' She paused, taking a bottle of mineral water from the desk. 'We're all getting chewed up trying to break the network. We're really grateful for what you've done, and at a calmer time we'd be able to do something. Not now, though.'

'We're big boys, I suppose,' said Matt. 'We can look after ourselves.'

Her hand lingered against his knee, starting to crawl up the inside of his thigh. 'What are you going to do?'

'Cooksley's gone home to his family,' replied Matt. 'His kids are very ill, and he wants to be with them. The rest of us are going to stick together, lie low. We're staying here tonight, then we reckon we'll shift around some cheap hotels in London. I reckon it's the best place in the country to hide. Big, anonymous, nobody pays any attention to anyone. London is full of lost men; we'll just blend in with the crowd.'

'Let *me* know where you are,' said Alison. 'If there's any way I can help out, I will.'

'Thanks,' replied Matt.

She looked at him closely. 'My tape went missing,' she said. 'Did you take it?'

Matt took a sip on his beer. 'Me? No,' he said. 'Are you sure?'

'Quite sure,' said Alison. 'One of you must have taken it. Find out who, and get it back. We need it.'

Matt nodded. He didn't know what she was talking about and his mind was on other things. His hand was resting on her leg, his eyes tracking the curve of her legs, admiring the way her black stockings tapered into her black stiletto shoes. 'Look,' he said. 'I bought you a souvenir.'

'For me?' said Alison, her smile widening. 'How sweet!'

Matt fished through his pocket. The diamond was still wrapped in tissue paper. He placed it on the bar, letting her unwrap it. The diamond was cut to perfection, scattering tiny beads of light in every direction. 'My own al-Qaeda diamond!' Alison said. She looked up at Matt. 'I'll get it set in gold and make it a necklace. And every time I wear it, I'll think of you.'

THIRTEEN

Sallum sat alone behind the wheel of the Lexus LS430. The village of Pembridge was still fast asleep. Dawn had started to break twenty minutes ago, the sun gradually rising across the fields, sending shafts of bright orange light from the east. He had been here for two hours now, and the heat inside the car had gradually been dropping. Sallum could see his breath collecting on the windscreen, could feel the cold biting into the tips of his fingers.

He reflected for a moment on one of the hundreds of verses he had memorised from the Koran: 'Seek assistance through patience and prayer. Allah is with the patient.'

To sit, and wait and watch. That is the skill of the assassin.

Cooksley emerged abruptly from the front door. He glanced left and right, took a deep breath of air, then started walking. The collie bounced ahead of him, barking a couple of times, and dashing up the lane and towards the fields. Cooksley followed the dog at his own pace. He was walking slowly, his back stooped and his head bowed as if he was deep in thought.

Sallum glanced down at the photograph resting on

the passenger seat of the car, then up at the man walking down the lane. There could be no doubt. He was the target. He climbed out of the car, pulling the collar of his long, grey overcoat up around his neck. On his back he was wearing a small, black rucksack. He checked the Heckler & Koch P7 pistol was sitting snugly in his pocket, reassured by the feel of its metal against his fingertips. There was nothing like the barrel of a pistol to make a man feel more secure, he reflected. Or more powerful.

He walked slowly up the lane, his pace quickening to bring himself level with Cooksley. 'Excuse me,' he said softly, 'do you know the way to the church?'

Cooksley looked round, surprised. The accent was Middle Eastern, but American educated. Not the sort of voice you heard in Herefordshire very often. 'You're going the wrong way, mate,' he replied. 'Go back down the lane, past the Two Foxes, then you'll see it on the left. You can't miss it.'

'Is it far?' asked Sallum.

The collie had bounded back up to them and was bouncing enthusiastically around Cooksley's and Sallum's ankles. 'Not far, no,' said Cooksley. 'Ten minutes' walk.'

Sallum knelt down to pat the dog, rubbing it around the ears. The collie yapped, rubbing its jaw into his knees. From his pocket, Sallum pulled the P7. With his left hand he took the dog's two ears in a firm grip, holding its head absolutely still. With his right hand, he jabbed the pistol into the animal's fur, pressing it into the skin just between the ear and the eye. From there the bullet would smash straight through the dog's brain, killing it instantly.

He squeezed the trigger.

The dog whimpered momentarily and a trickle of saliva dripped from its open jaws. It collapsed on to the ground, blood spilling from the wound that had opened up in its head. Sallum jumped swiftly backwards, letting go of the dog's ears, and jabbed the barrel of the P7 hard into Cooksley's ribs. He could feel the metal pressing tightly into the skin. He twisted his wrist downwards, so the gun was pointing upwards. This man, he knew, was a trained soldier. He would know that the bullet from a gun fired at that angle would travel right through his ribcage and up through the bottom of his heart. He would die instantly.

'Don't say a word, don't even move,' muttered Sallum. His eyes looked into Cooksley's face. He could see no fear there. Just the ticking of a mind looking for some method of escape. 'Go back down towards the house,' said Sallum. 'Don't say anything, don't run.'

They walked slowly for the two hundred yards back to the house, Cooksley ahead, Sallum at his side, the pistol wedged into his ribs. Cooksley stopped outside the front door, opened it and held it ajar. Inside, Sallum could hear the sounds of children playing and their mother talking to them.

'Run, love, run!' Cooksley shouted as soon as the door was open. 'Grab the kids and run!'

'Shut up!' shouted Sallum. 'You'll only make it

worse for yourself.' He grabbed Cooksley's hair, yanking his head back hard. He forced the pistol into his throat, pushing him down the hallway. He could see the woman and the two children in the kitchen staring at him, their mouths open. Tears were starting to stream down the cheeks of the smaller of the two boys. 'Do exactly what I tell you, and you won't get hurt,' he shouted towards her.

'Don't do it, love!' Cooksley shouted. 'He's a lying bastard.'

Sallum pushed the man hard against the wall, which shook with the force of his weight, and a piece of ornamental china crashed from the shelf on to the floor. Sallum could hear the woman screaming. Cooksley lunged towards him, his fist raised and his muscles clenched, ready to smash into his face. Sallum swivelled and ducked, his movements elegant and delicate. Cooksley swung up at him with a boot aimed at the waist. Sallum turned again – like a ballerina, he could swivel perfectly on the balls of his feet. He caught the back of Cooksley's right wrist, slamming it against the wall. He pushed the P7 into the soft flesh of the palm, firing. The bullet hammered right through the hand, cracking open the bones and lodging into the wall behind. Cooksley doubled forward in pain, clutching his hand, trying desperately to staunch the flow of blood.

A man with a fresh wound through his right hand is effectively disabled.

Sallum moved in closer to Cooksley, slamming his

knee up into his jaw. Cooksley's head spun backwards and he lashed out, a line of blood from his hand streaking across Sallum's face. Sallum clenched his left hand into a ball and slammed the fist into the back of Cooksley's neck. The blow sent him crashing to the ground. Sallum delivered two swift kicks to the side of his head, leaving him limp and unconscious on the floor.

Sallum spun around, levelling the pistol directly at the woman's forehead. 'I'm a reasonable man,' he said. 'Stop screaming, do exactly what I say, and you won't get hurt.' With his left hand he threw a pair of plasti-cuffs down on the floor. The woman looked at her husband lying slumped next to them. Tears were streaming down her face. From the kitchen, the sound of the children's screams could be heard. 'Bind him,' barked Sallum. 'And shut those kids up.'

She shook her head.

Sallum kept the gun trained on her, moving backwards. He took the elder boy by the hand and led the child towards the front room. The toddler looked nervously at his mother, then down at his father, and wet himself. He stopped crying, biting his lip.

Sallum could feel the boy's hand shaking. He levelled the pistol with the top of the boy's skull, its muzzle resting in his black hair. He looked coldly towards the woman. 'Do exactly what I say,' he repeated. 'Tie him.'

The woman picked the plasti-cuffs from the ground. She fastened them around Cooksley's hands. She wiped away the sweat from his forehead, then leant forward to kiss him just between the eyes.

'Just bind him!' Sallum barked.

She snapped the cuffs into place. Callum ran towards his mother and threw himself into her side, gripping on to her legs. Danny ran out from the kitchen, looked edgily at Sallum, then hung on to his brother's legs, sucking furiously on his dummy.

'What do you want from us?' she said, her voice gradually regaining its strength.

'Be still,' answered Sallum. 'Don't say anything. Just watch.'

He shook the rucksack from his back, letting it land on the floor. From the bag he took out a Sony camcorder and a collapsible tripod. He walked towards the front of the room, glancing briefly out to the street, then put up the tripod. He placed the camcorder on top of the tripod, then pulled a black woollen mask over his face, with holes for the eyes, nose and mouth. He pulled on a pair of black surgical gloves, making sure not a trace of skin was visible, then switched on the camcorder. He could feel the eyes of the boys following him as he walked back towards their father, measuring each step across the floor, listening to each creak of the floorboard. As he worked, the woman remained completely still, her muscles frozen.

A religious man should never make a mother watch her children die.

Sallum knelt down before Cooksley, uncorked a small jar of smelling salts, and waved it under his nose.

With his thumb, he pulled up his right eyelid. 'I want you to watch,' he said.

Cooksley's eyes were bloodshot, his expression drained. Sallum could see the pupils moving cautiously from right to left, but he could tell nothing of what the man was thinking. He stood up, walking towards the centre of the room, making sure he was in direct view of the camcorder.

'Come here,' he snapped at the woman.

She looked at Cooksley, then back towards Sallum, shaking her head.

In her eyes, Sallum could detect a mood of defiance. 'Now!' he shouted.

She started to walk nervously the three yards across the floor. He levelled the P7 with her head, squeezing the trigger once. The bullet struck her in the windpipe, blowing a hole through her neck. Blood started to spit from her mouth, her knees buckled, and she dropped to the floor. Sallum walked one pace forwards, pushed the pistol down, firing another bullet. This time it struck her just above the eyes, crashing through her skull. Her body jerked once, then went still.

'It was quick, at least,' said Sallum, looking towards Cooksley.

The two boys were cowering beside the fireplace, clinging on to each other. Both of them fell silent. Sallum took two paces forwards, grabbed Danny by the hair and yanked him into the air. His mouth fell open into a scream. Sallum jabbed the gun into his open jaw and fired. The bullet went straight through his head, sending blood and skin against the wall behind him. The body wriggled, then died. Sallum released his grip on the hair, letting the body drop on the floor.

Sallum looked towards Cooksley. 'I'll let the other boy live if you'll do something for me.' He reached back inside his bag, pulling out a single piece of white card. Stepping back towards Cooksley, he knelt down in front of him. He could smell the sweat and blood on Cooksley's skin. 'Read this out for the camera,' he said.

'Fuck off!' Cooksley spat. 'You'll kill me anyway.'

Sallum nodded. 'Yes, but I don't have to kill the boy,' he said. 'I am a just man. So just read it.'

'Who are you?' said Cooksley, his voice dry and hoarse.

'I am your executioner,' said Sallum. 'You should know better than to steal, and you should certainly have known what the punishment would be. Now read.'

Cooksley glanced down at the piece of card resting on his lap. His lips were shaking as his eyes struggled to focus on the words written out in neat block capitals. 'Look up at the camera when you speak,' said Sallum.

Cooksley began to read. 'We shouldn't have stolen from al-Qaeda, boys,' he said, his tone dull and lifeless. 'I'm getting what I deserve, and you're about to get what you deserve. If you give back the money and turn yourself in, they'll just kill you and leave your families alone. Do it, boys, it's not worth it. You've seen what happened to me.'

Count to five. Let the man understand what has happened to his family before he dies. One, two, three, four, five.

Sallum lined up the barrel of the P7 with Cooksley's head. One bullet struck on the side of his chin, the second just below the ear. Cooksley's head slumped forwards, his leg twitched, and trails of blood started to seep from his wounds. Within seconds, the last breath had emptied itself from his lungs, and his body had fallen completely still.

Sallum stood back, taking a moment to compose himself. There were three bodies on the floor, and the blood and fresh wounds were starting to fill the room with the fresh aroma of a butcher's shop. He tucked the gun back into his pocket and walked back to the video camera, turning the off switch.

Next to the wall, the younger boy was crying. Sallum smiled down at him. 'Allah have mercy on you,' he said. He drew the P7 swiftly from his pocket. One shot was all that was needed. He fired straight at the boy's head, the bullet smashing into the side of the skull. The boy crumpled to the floor, blood seeping from the wound.

When the others see this, then they will learn to be truly awed by the pitilessness of our vengeance.

Sallum stepped out into the cold morning air and glanced up and down the lane. In the distance he could see a man walking his dog. He left the door open, making sure the bodies would be discovered quickly, and walked back towards the Lexus.

One limb severed. Four left. Just as the Prophet would command.

*

Alison was dressed in a hotel towel when she emerged from the shower. Her hair was wet, tied behind her neck, and droplets of water were still running down her smooth, tanned skin.

Matt caught a glimpse of the outline of her breast underneath the cloth, her nipples still stiff from the water. 'I ordered some breakfast,' he said.

'How sweet,' she replied, her lips breaking into a broad smile. 'A man who can slaughter a boat full of al-Qaeda, then provide breakfast. What more could a Five girl ask for?'

'Room service is about my limit,' said Matt. 'That and sausage sandwiches.'

'Pasta, surely,' said Alison. 'Guys can always rustle up a spag bol.'

Matt spread a thick layer of butter and jam on his toast and started eating. In the background he could hear Sky News talking about an explosion in Hamburg: al-Qaeda were the main suspects. 'They're getting closer, aren't they?' he said, looking up at Alison.

She nodded. 'There's going to be something in Britain soon, if we don't break them first.'

'It makes me want to rejoin the Regiment,' said Matt.

'You've done your bit,' said Alison. 'You can't save the world all by yourself.'

Matt threw the remains of his coffee down his throat. The blood of the men lying on the floor of the boat, and the severed limbs strewn across the hold after the Semtex had exploded were still vivid in his mind. This memory was still raw. And yet, as he listened to the details of the women and children killed in the Hamburg attack, he couldn't regret a single one of them.

They had it coming to them.

The mobile phone rang twice before Alison answered it. She had pulled on a pair of black tights and a blue silk blouse, but her skirt was still tossed over the back of her chair where Matt had undressed her last night. He found himself admiring the shape of her leg as she perched on the arm of the sofa, her head nodding briskly into the phone. 'Thanks,' she said briskly. 'I'll be there in twenty minutes.'

She put the phone down and looked directly at Matt. He could tell something was wrong. 'It's Cooksley,' she said. 'He's dead. And his family.'

Matt could feel his blood freezing. In the Regiment, you got used to dying. A couple of guys had gone down just on the induction course, and after that there'd been a regular two or three a year. One dark night, alone with a bottle of vodka, Matt had calculated that, of the twenty-five men in his intake, fourteen had already died. But each death struck you afresh, hitting you straight in the gut. Your mind suddenly filled with memories of all the times you had spent together, all the risks and dangers you had shared, and all the regimental reunions you wouldn't be sharing now that they were gone.

'What happened?' Matt asked.

Alison walked across the room and rested a hand on

his shoulder. 'Somebody broke into the house, shot all four of them.' She paused. 'Apparently there's a video.'

'A video?' said Matt. 'What the fuck . . .'

'The local police say there was a video left at the scene. They're getting a copy up to Five.'

Matt brushed her hand away from his shoulder. 'If you'd given us a safe house, this wouldn't have happened.'

'Don't give me that,' snapped Alison. 'You knew the deal.'

Matt stood up and walked to the window. He could feel the rage rising in his chest, his pulse was racing. 'My friend is dead!' he shouted, refusing to look at her.

The video had been sitting next to him all the way along the M4. Matt hadn't even wanted to look at it or touch it.

I have a strong stomach, and I have watched lots of men die. I've seen women who've been raped in Bosnia, and children garrotted in Chechnya. I know what pain and suffering look like.

He slammed the door shut on the Boxster and looked suspiciously across the car park. The Reading Travelodge was on the Basingstoke Road, a mile north of junction eleven of the M4. The Harvester Inn stood in front of it, facing the road, and the hotel was tucked just behind. Matt waited for a few minutes to make sure no one was following him, then walked inside. He had already booked a bedroom, checking it came with a video player.

He collected the keys from the receptionist, and walked down the corridor. He had spoken to Ivan, Damien and Reid right after Alison had told him of Cooksley's murder. It was too dangerous to stay at the hotel in Wandsworth: somebody was clearly on to them, and for all they knew they might be watching the place. Let's gather in Reading, at three in the afternoon, he'd told them. Alison had promised that the Herefordshire police could get a copy of the video up to London, and that she could give it to him by lunchtime. They'd met at the BP petrol station on Vauxhall Bridge Road, just across the river from Five's headquarters. Anyone looking at them would have thought they were just two people chatting as they filled up their tanks.

'Are you coming with us?' Matt had asked as he'd tucked the video into the pocket of his coat.

'No,' Alison had said, with a swift shake of her head. 'You're on your own.'

The words were still playing in Matt's ears as he swiped the card through the door and let himself into the room. We're on our own. Well, that's fine. That's how we fight best. As a small unit, following nobody's orders except our own.

He waited for ten minutes. The room was painted pale cream, with a double bed and a TV, a desk, and windows that looked out over the car park. Rain was starting to fall.

If there was one lesson Matt had learnt in combat, it was that once things started to go wrong, they kept going wrong.

A messed-up mission stays that way. The only thing you can do is get it over with as quickly as possible and hope to stay alive.

Ivan, Damien and Reid looked sombre as they walked into the room. They had taken a train up from London together, and caught a cab from the station. Their faces were drawn, their expressions shattered.

'We'd better watch this,' said Matt, slotting the video into the player. He picked up the remote and pressed play. The picture sprang to life on the screen. Matt braced himself, taking a deep breath.

The next few minutes are going to be among the most horrible of my life.

The film lasted only a few minutes. They watched in silence, none of them speaking, none of them moving. Matt was sitting on the edge of the bed, Damien on the chair, Ivan and Reid on the floor. The first shot showed the man in the mask, moving across the room. They watched as Sarah was killed, then the first of the children. Matt found it hard to concentrate on the screen, forcing his eyes back towards it as each murderous scene unfolded. He knew he had to watch if they were to have any chance of discovering who was after them, but his eyes kept closing. He could hear the man's voice, saying something to Cooksley. He looked back up at the screen and saw the face of his friend staring back at him – a face he had known through good times and bad, yet which he had never seen in such a state of total despair. Cooksley looked as though he knew it was all up for him, and he just wanted to get it over with as quickly as possible.

'We shouldn't have stolen from al-Qaeda, boys,' said the face on the screen, the voice as clear and loud as if the man was sitting in the room with them. 'I'm getting what I deserve, and you're about to get what you deserve. If you give back the money and turn yourself in, they'll just kill you and leave your families alone. Do it, boys, it's not worth it. You've seen what happened to me.'

Matt watched as the bullet went into Cooksley's face, and as the second child was murdered in cold, ruthless blood. He watched as the blood spilt on to the floor, and as the masked man stepped over the bodies and walked towards the camera. And then nothing. The screen went blank.

I have never been so determined to kill a man as I am resolved to kill him. Only his blood will satisfy me.

The room was completely silent. None of them moved, none of them spoke. To Matt it seemed as though the video had lasted for hours, but when he glanced at the clock he could see it had been just minutes.

He stood up, switching off the TV. 'That's it, then,' he said, his voice flat and lifeless.

'We'll get him,' Reid muttered through clenched teeth. 'The cheap, murdering scumbag bastard.'

'That's for sure,' said Matt.

Ivan cleared his throat. 'Unless he gets us first.'

Matt fell silent. 'Who the fuck is he then?' he asked.

'He's a professional,' said Damien. 'We know that

much. He's masked up, and he's wearing gloves so there's no way the police will get an ID on him. I'll bet any money you like he made sure nobody saw him go into the house, and nobody saw him go out again.'

'What's the video for, then?' said Matt.

'To frighten us, obviously,' said Damien 'He's al-Qaeda, that's what Cooksley says on the message. They want revenge, sure – but they also want us to give them their money back.'

'I'm not giving them any money,' shouted Reid. 'I'm going to find that bastard—'

Matt patted him on the shoulder. 'Yes. But the point is – who is he, and where do we find him?'

Across the room, Ivan was shaking his head. 'With due respect, that's not really the point,' he said.

Matt looked up at the Irishman. He was leaning against the wall, close to the window, his head bowed down in thought. He was speaking softly and clearly, and for a moment Matt found himself wondering why Ivan didn't seem more shocked by the scenes they had just witnessed. 'What *is* the point, then?'

'He found Cooksley so easily,' Ivan said, his voice slow and deliberate as if he were thinking over the issue to himself. 'First, Cooksley gets attacked in Cyprus. So we come back here. The rest of us stick together, he goes home – and within twenty-four hours he's dead. How can that possibly happen unless this guy knows exactly who he is and where to find him?'

Matt thought for a moment. Ivan was right.

How could he possibly know?

'Now,' Ivan continued, 'the most obvious explanation for that is that someone told him. One of us.'

'Don't be ridiculous,' Matt snapped. 'Why in hell would any of us do that?'

'I don't think you play enough bridge,' said Ivan. 'Think through the maths of this situation. We were going to be collecting ten million next week. Split five ways, that makes two million each. Now one of us is dead, I assume we split the money four ways. That makes two-and-a-half million each. I'm sad about Cooksley – but I'm also half a million richer. That sounds like a motive to me.'

Reid stood up, his face reddening. 'There's only one person who'd do that,' he shouted. 'And that's a lying, treacherous Irish Provo bastard like you! I knew we should never let you into the gang – you've been trouble since we started.'

Matt held Reid back. 'Bloody cool it, man. We're not going to start killing each other and doing al-Qaeda's work for them.'

Reid stepped back, his face sullen.

'I know you don't trust me – but if it was me, why would I raise the issue?' Ivan said. 'That would be pointing the finger at myself.'

'Well it's not one of *us*, is it?' barked Reid, his gesture including Matt. 'We're soldiers, not terrorists.'

'What about him?' Ivan nodded towards Damien. 'He's a gangster.'

Damien grabbed Ivan by the throat, snarling into his face. 'Say that again and I'll kill you. You *would* raise the issue to cover yourself. I'm not falling for your double-bluff.'

'Stop acting like bloody idiots!' Matt shouted. He looked towards Ivan. 'What the hell are you trying to do?'

Ivan shrugged. 'Think straight, that's all – and stay alive,' he said quickly. 'Somebody has to.'

Matt stood in the centre of the room. 'We all start fighting among ourselves, we're all going to get killed,' he snapped. 'Listen, we have to get one thing straight. We have to stick together. Regiment rules apply here, like I said right at the start. We all look out for each other, and everyone's voice counts for the same.'

I can say it. But I'm not sure I really believe it.

FOURTEEN

Matt swilled back the orange juice he had taken from the mini-bar and switched on the electric kettle for some coffee. The Travel Inn didn't run to breakfast in the room, and he certainly didn't want to go down to the restaurant.

'Can I trust Damien?' Reid said, shutting the door behind him.

Matt rubbed the sleep out of his eyes. After the argument he had managed to calm them down a bit. They had agreed that they should stay in Reading that night and figure out what they were going to do in the morning. There was a mood of mistrust and suspicion growing between them, and Matt wanted to give everyone a chance to rest and reflect before they made any decisions. He'd had three swift vodkas from the mini-bar before he went to bed, but it did nothing to help him sleep. Most of the night had been spent tossing and turning, thinking over what had happened to Cooksley and his family.

'You can trust Damien with your life,' Matt said firmly. 'I've known that guy since he was five. He's been like a brother to me. There's no way he'd betray

223

us, no way. There's nobody more loyal than a London villain.'

'What do you reckon, then?'

Matt poured hot water into his coffee cup. 'It's not me,' he said. 'And it's not you. Goes without saying you'd never have Cooksley killed, no matter how much money you might make. Not Damien either. That means it has to be Ivan – *if* someone is betraying us.'

'Just for the money?'

Matt shook his head. 'I don't know. He's a deep one,' he replied. 'He's always playing games. There's all kinds of links between the IRA and al-Qaeda going way back. I don't think we should have ever trusted him.'

'Maybe we should just beat the hell out of him, make him talk.'

'I don't think it would work,' Matt said. 'He's a Provo. They're trained not to talk under interrogation.'

'I'm worried about my family, Matt,' Reid said. 'I need to get them away from Hereford.'

'Where?'

'Up in Derbyshire – my uncle owns a small lodge in the Peak District. It's tucked away, quiet. I reckon we could stay there for a few days.'

'Could Damien go with you?'

Reid nodded. 'What about you?'

'You and Damien go and hide for a few days,' Matt said. 'I'll go off with Ivan. Damien and you can watch each other's backs, and as long as Ivan doesn't know where you are I reckon you'll be OK. Stick together at all times, and the assassin won't be able to touch you.

Damien is as good a man in a fight as anyone in the Regiment.'

'And you?'

'Like I said, I'll keep an eye on Ivan,' said Matt, 'watch him like a hawk.'

And I'm going to question him about that missing tape.

Matt glanced at his watch before punching the number into the payphone. It was just after ten in the morning, an hour later in southern Spain. The Dandelion playgroup should be on its mid-morning break.

Someone answered. 'Is Gill there?' Matt asked.

'Is that Matt?'

He recognised the voice: Sandy, one of Gill's colleagues. 'Yes,' he replied. 'Please get her for me, will you?' He looked out to the car park. Damien and Reid were climbing into a taxi, heading for the station. They were going to get the train back up to Herefordshire, collect Reid's car, then drive up to Derbyshire with Jane and the kids. They should be all right, Matt reflected. They're both good men, well able to look after themselves.

'Matt, is that you?' said Gill. 'Where are you?'

Matt cupped the receiver. It felt good to hear her voice: she was the only woman he had ever met who could make him feel better just by speaking. 'I can't say,' he replied. 'I just wanted to check in and see if you are OK.'

'What's happening to you, Matt?' she said, her voice full of anxiety. 'What are you doing?'

'Work, that's all,' Matt replied. 'Security stuff – but it's all gone a bit pear-shaped. I need a few more days to sort things out . . . I just wanted to check you were OK.'

There was a pause. Matt didn't need to be able to see her face to tell what Gill was thinking: anger and confusion were in her voice. 'Some men were hanging about watching us a couple of days ago,' she replied slowly. 'I was walking home with Sandy, and they gave us the jitters. They didn't whistle or jeer or anything, just watched.'

Christ, thought Matt. Kazanov's boys. Or worse. 'Anyone talks to you or approaches you in the next few days, stay out of their way.'

'What's happening, Matt?' she said quickly. 'No one's coming after me, are they?'

Matt hesitated. 'Let's just say the next few days are a bit tense for me,' he replied. 'Anything starts to happen, pack your bags and go away for a few days. Everything will be OK in a few days, I promise.' He paused, holding the phone closer to his mouth. 'Trust me, Gill. Everything will be all right.'

The Prince of Wales in Dalling Road, just off the Hammersmith Broadway, was a dark and gloomy pub. The yuppiefication of the 1980s and 1990s had passed it by. There were no stripped pine floors, no racks of Australian Chardonnay or South African Shiraz lining the walls. No ciabatta burgers chalked up on the wall. Just frayed and tatty red velvet chairs, a beer-soaked carpet and a barmaid who'd never see fifty again.

Matt could have used somewhere more cheerful. He needed something to lighten his mood. His nerves were still shaken and his head was aching from the lack of sleep. Still, Ivan had wanted to come here.

In moments of danger, we go back to the places we know.

'I'm worried,' said Ivan, pulling up a barstool.

'We're all fucking worried.'

They had taken the train down from Reading. Matt had left his car parked in a side street – he'd pick it up after all this was over, if some of the local villains hadn't nicked it. For the next five days – until the boat arrived in Rotterdam and they could unload their loot – none of them wanted to do anything that would reveal their locations. That meant not driving their own cars, not using their own houses, not using their own credit cards, and not phoning anyone on a mobile.

'I know.' Ivan took a sip on the pint in front of him. 'But I think the Provos might be after me.'

'The videotape said it was al-Qaeda that killed Cooksley,' said Matt. 'They wanted to frighten us – and they want their money back.'

'The other tape – the one from the boat – it went missing,' he continued. 'Alison reckons one of us took it.'

Ivan looked at him, a question playing in his eyes.

Either a great actor, or else he's surprised, Matt reckoned.

'Why would anyone do that?' Ivan asked.

Matt drummed his fingers on the table. 'Beats me,'

he said. He looked directly towards Ivan. 'Did you take it?'

'No,' Ivan said clearly. 'Why would I do that?'

Matt shrugged.

'It's a feint,' Ivan continued. 'Let me explain a concept from bridge.'

Matt rolled his eyes. 'For fuck's sake,' he muttered.

'You have some high diamonds, but you need to get rid of the other fellows' ace to win those tricks. You play a dummy card, misleading the other players, and try to force their card out of them.' He paused, glancing through the pub, making sure he couldn't be heard. 'I can't help feeling that Cooksley's murder was a dummy.'

'Provos posing as al-Qaeda? That's bloody ridiculous.'

'Not if they want to get at me, Matt. I think they suspect I've been turned. They know about a robbery – but how much do they know? After all, what would I be doing on a job with a bunch of SAS boys?'

'You're saying they took out Cooksley to flush you out. Why not just go straight to you?'

'I don't know. Perhaps they didn't know where I was, but they knew where Cooksley was,' Ivan replied. 'Then I'm next.'

'You're imagination is working overtime, Ivan.'

Ivan paused. 'There's a man near here who could tell us whether it's the Provos,' said Ivan. 'If you don't mind getting into a fight.'

'Fighting,' said Matt, smiling for the first time since

they had sat down. 'It's the only thing I've ever been any good at.'

They finished their drinks then walked slowly along the Dalling Road. It was about a mile, said Ivan – up towards Ravenscourt Park. Hammersmith and Acton had always been strong IRA areas in London. There were a lot of Irish there – always had been – but it was a lot less obvious than Kilburn and didn't have the same levels of Special Branch surveillance. There were several IRA safe houses in the area: places where men on missions in the capital could store themselves away for a few days. They were run by a man called Keith Whitson, an old Provo fighter who had moved to London in the late 1970s. If anyone was chasing after Ivan in Britain, he would know about it.

'But we'll have to beat the information out of him,' said Ivan.

'I thought the Provos never crack under torture,' said Matt.

'Whitson's not an active brigade man,' said Ivan. 'More of a housekeeper. He's tough, sure, but not as tough as the soldiers. I can't guarantee he'll talk – but it's the best chance we have of finding out what's going on.'

Unless it's a trap, thought Matt. Maybe he's leading me into a house full of his Provo mates to finish me off. *Just like they finished off Cooksley.*

They walked the rest of the way in silence. Matt had never liked this part of town: too many grey Victorian terraces, too much snarling traffic and not enough green spaces. If he had to be in London, he liked the centre, or the bits of Camberwell and Deptford where he had grown up. Nobody ever went on holiday to Camberwell, but at least it was home.

Some of the paint was scratched away from the surface of 16 Cedar Road. Whatever the Provos were up to these days, Matt noted, it wasn't DIY. The frames of the windows needed painting, and some of the brickwork was starting to flake away. Still, it was designed for safety, not for comfort.

'Let me talk,' said Ivan, and Matt stood silently behind him.

I'm not going inside until I'm certain it's not a trap.

The man who answered the door looked about fifty to fifty-five. His hair was greying and thinning, and deep lines were etched into the surface of his skin. Even though the years had ground away at him there was no fat on him, and his eyes were rock hard. 'Yes?' he said, holding the door ajar.

Matt noticed that his foot was barring the entrance, stopping anyone from rushing inside once the door was ajar. A professional.

'Ivan Rowe,' Ivan said quickly. 'A few years ago I was blowing some safes for the family.'

Whitson looked carefully at his face, scrutinising it as if he were looking at a forged bank note. 'Who's your friend?' he asked.

'I'll tell you inside,' said Ivan. 'I'm Portrush brigade. I need some help.'

The door opened slightly wider, and Matt and Ivan stepped into the dark hallway. A single light was shining in the kitchen towards the back of the house, but otherwise the building was shrouded in darkness. The walls were covered in faded paper, with one or two damp patches evident on the ceiling. The carpet was frayed and worn, and there was a stack of old papers and magazines filling the hall. A smell of old boiled potatoes filtered through from somewhere.

Matt hesitated before stepping inside – but the man had seemed so suspicious of Ivan, it looked unlikely to be a trap.

I'll take my chances.

'I won't be offering you a cup of tea because I don't think you'll be lingering,' said Whitson, revealing a set of grey and broken teeth. 'You can state your business and then be on your way.'

'I think there's a gang after me,' said Ivan bluntly. 'The family suspects I've been disloyal, and they've sent some cousins to sort me out. If there was a nutting squad over here, you'd know about it. I need to speak with them, tell them it's a mistake, sort the whole thing out.'

'And have you been disloyal?'

Ivan shook his head. 'I have not,' he replied.

'But you would say that, wouldn't you?' Whitson said slowly. 'After all, we know what the family thinks about cousins who want to leave.'

'If you just tell me where they are, I can speak to them,' said Ivan. 'If I convince them I'm OK, they can let me go. If not, they can kill me there and then. Either way, it saves them the trouble of finding me.'

Whitson leant towards him, his jaw open. Matt could

smell fried onions on his breath. 'Your name again, sonny?'

'I told you once,' said Ivan, 'I don't need to tell you again.'

'Ivan Rowe,' said Whitson, rolling the words over his tongue. 'I don't think I've heard anything about you. You can be on your way.'

Ivan's fist collided with the man's stomach, Matt, just like the victim, was surprised by the speed and force of the punch. Whitson doubled up in pain, clutching his stomach, gasping for breath. His eyes rolled up towards Ivan, and he tried to move away. Another fist collided with the back of his neck, sending him crashing to the floor, spluttering for breath. 'Tell me who's looking for me, and then I'll stop hitting you,' Ivan shouted.

'No one's looking for you, you idiot,' Whitson snarled, spitting on to the floor.

The side of Ivan's foot smashed into his ribcage. Matt could hear the sound of a bone snapping, and Whitson's face screwed up in pain. 'Tell me!' shouted Ivan.

'Fuck off! There's no one!' Whitson screamed.

'Hold him down,' said Ivan, glancing towards Matt.

Matt knelt, half his weight on Whitson's chest, pinning back both his arms. At his side, Ivan slapped the back of his hand hard against the man's face. Matt winced. He could smell the vomit rising in the man's throat. He's an old guy, he thought. There's not much punishment in him.

'Keep holding him,' Ivan said curtly.

Matt dug an elbow into Whitson's chest, crushing

the air from his lungs and pinning him to the floor. He moved his hand up across the neck, and used the back of his hand to force Whitson's mouth open. He could hear him struggling for air.

'Tell me where they are!' shouted Ivan.

Whitson coughed. 'There's nobody looking for you, I swear it.'

Ivan smashed his fist into Whitson's face. Matt could feel the force of the blow trembling through the old man's body.

If that doesn't make him talk, nothing will.

'There's no fucking hit squad after you,' croaked Whitson.

'Just tell me where they are, and I'll stop hitting you,' Ivan said coldly.

'There's no one, you have to believe me.'

'Hold the fucker harder,' said Ivan, looking towards Matt.

'There's nothing,' Whitson hissed, the voice gradually trailing away to a whimper. 'There's nothing.'

'I think he might be telling the truth,' said Matt, looking up at Ivan.

But Ivan slammed his fist into the man's face once again, cutting open the skin. Whitson wriggled, then Matt could feel him falling completely still. There was no sound at all. Matt put his hand up over the man's mouth, but could feel nothing.

'Christ,' he said, looking up at Ivan. 'He's dead.'

'Weak heart,' said Ivan matter-of-factly. 'Common with a man of that age, particularly when they eat too much fatty food. The pain builds up the blood pressure, and the heart cuts out. Happens all the time.'

Ivan's capacity for sudden, explosive violence was one side of the man's character Matt had not expected. 'As if we weren't in enough trouble already,' he said.

Ivan stepped away, into the darkness. 'But I think he *was* telling the truth,' he said. 'There's nobody looking for me.'

Matt stood up. 'You killed the man – just like that?' he said.

'Once we start questioning him, he knows we think someone is looking for us,' said Ivan, looking closely at Matt. 'That means we've definitely done something. If we let him live, someone will be looking for us.' He shrugged, walking back towards the kitchen. 'Anyway, he's a Provo, you're SAS. I thought you *liked* killing Irishmen.'

Just as we used to say in the Regiment – once a mission starts going wrong, it keeps going wrong.

Ivan was rummaging around in the cupboard. 'Stop getting in a flap,' he continued. 'We needed to find out whether the Provos were on to us, and we've done that. And we need somewhere safe to hole up for a few days.'

'You think we should stay here?'

Ivan flicked a switch on the kettle. 'You wanted a safe house,' he said. 'Well, now you've got one.'

FIFTEEN

Matt fished the mobile out of his pocket, glancing down at the display. It was Reid. He jabbed his thumb against the answer button. 'You OK?' he said quickly.

'A bit bruised, but still breathing,' said Reid.

'What happened?'

There was a pause on the line.

Right now, anything could happen.

'Your poofy pal, Damien,' said Reid, the words twisting on his lips. 'He's buggered off.'

'What?' Matt slumped back against the wall. He was sitting on the floor of the kitchen in Cedar Road. Ivan was brewing up a pot of tea. Ahead of him, Whitson's body was lying stretched out on the floor, waiting to be disposed of.

'Tell me about it,' he said.

The story took about ten minutes to tell, interrupted by some noises in the background from the children. The two men had driven together to Reid's house in Herefordshire, collected Jane and the kids, then driven across country towards the Peak District. In total, they had been driving for about six hours: three hours from London to Herefordshire, then another three hours by the time they arrived in Derbyshire. They stopped briefly in Derby, because Damien said he wanted to rent a car so he had his own transport – after that, he had followed them in a rented Peugeot 205. Reid had been exhausted by the time they got there. Jane had put the kids to bed, then rustled up some chicken and rice for supper. Reid had reckoned they would have a couple of beers to relax, then get some sleep. 'But Damien announces that he has to go out,' Reid continued.

'And you tried to stop him?'

'Of course, I bloody did. Cooksley's already dead, and someone is after us. You said we have to stick together.'

Matt sighed. He knew Damien well enough to know that he wasn't going to put up with Reid telling him what to do. Damien had always been a man who walked along his own path. He knew nothing about teams, or how to work with them.

'He lost it, right?'

'Like a rocket with the blue fuse lit,' Reid said. 'Started telling me I couldn't tell him what to do. I argued with him, said we had to stay together, that it was only one week until we collected the money. He seemed to accept that, calmed down for an hour or so. I was just ready to turn in, when out of the upstairs window I see him slipping out of the lodge, and heading for his car. I was about to run after him, but he'd locked the door to the bedroom and tossed away the key. By the time I got out he'd vanished.'

'No indication of where he was going?'

'Nothing,' Reid answered. 'I would have chased after him, but I didn't want to leave Jane and the kids by themselves.' He paused. 'I don't like it, Matt. I know he's a friend of yours, but that's no way for a man to behave. This is the guy who's meant to be fencing our money for us, and now it turns out we can't trust the bastard.'

'There's probably nothing to it,' said Matt.

'Fuck it, Matt – I don't like it one bit,' Reid snapped. 'I want to know where he is. And I want him back here where I can keep an eye on him. He could be buggering off to take all our money. Or he could be coming back in a black mask to kill us all.'

Matt glanced at the clock on the wall. It was ten past ten, and it had already been a long and tiring day. 'I've got his mobile numbers,' said Matt. 'I'll try to track him down. In the meantime there's nothing we can do. Try to get some sleep and we'll talk in the morning.'

'He better be bloody sorry,' said Reid, his tone starting to calm down. 'How are you, anyway?'

Matt glanced across at the body stretched out in the hallway. 'I've had better days,' he replied slowly. 'I'll be pleased when we've collected our money and put this whole thing behind us.'

Sallum looked down at the man at the door and handed across a ten pound note. The man was maybe twenty-five years old, with cropped dark hair, a black T-shirt and a single metal stud hanging from his left ear. He smiled upwards as he folded the money into the till. 'You're new here, aren't you?'

Sallum nodded.

'Down the stairs,' said the man. 'The showers and changing rooms are on the right. You'll find gowns and towels down there. Just grab one.' He looked closer at Sallum's face, as if he were examining him for something. 'Have fun.'

The Penthouse Sauna was on Tariff Street on the outskirts of Manchester. Sallum had followed the target from the moment he'd left the lodge, and was still waiting for the right moment to strike. He hadn't wanted to take him out on the road – car chases are fine for Hollywood films, but a professional assassin knows they are too dangerous and too unpredictable. Only an idiot would attack a man in a car.

He'd followed at a discreet distance from the Peugeot. It was dark, and that always made it harder for a driver to spot when he was being followed. Sallum had waited for ten minutes after Damien had pulled into the roadside and disappeared into the building. From the posters on its façade, he could tell that it was a gay club: there were pictures of men embracing, and of men dressed in leather and tight jeans.

There is no level of depravity that the infidel will not sink to.

Sallum walked down the stairs. It was dark and humid within the club. The temperature was turned up to eighty degrees, and soft, purple-tinted halogen lights kept the rooms in semi-darkness. He turned right into

the changing room, nodded to the man just emerging
from the showers, and started to strip off. He tucked his
clothes into the locker, and stepped into the shower,
turning the water on to hot.

I need something to cleanse my body already.

Wrapping the red gown around his body, he slipped
a four-inch double-bladed surgical knife from his
clothes locker into the pocket, and started to walk
through the building. The first room was a bar serving
beer and soft drinks, in which a huge plasma screen was
showing gay porn films. There could have been ten or
a dozen men in there, it was hard for Sallum to tell in
the near darkness.

He walked on. There was a steam sauna and a
fifteen-foot Jacuzzi, but both were empty. He saw a pair
of men disappearing upstairs, and followed them. There
was a series of doors on the landing, and from inside the
rooms Sallum could hear the sounds of men having sex.
Towards the back of the landing there was a fire door.
He snapped open the metal lock, shoved the door aside,
and a blast of cold night air hit him in the face. He
looked outside. A small, dark alleyway – illuminated
only by the distant neon sign of a Kentucky Fried
Chicken bar – led out on to the main street.

My escape route.

Downstairs, Sallum counted nine men in the bar. He
asked for a Diet Coke, and took a seat on one of the
couches lining the wall. He could see the victim just
across the room, sitting back, a beer in his hand,
watching the television. Sallum waited until the man

caught his eye, then smiled in his direction. The man smiled back, then nodded. He stood up, walking towards the staircase, glancing backwards. Sallum stood up, following in his footsteps, watching as he started to climb the stairs.

Inside the pocket of his gown, he ran his finger along the edge of the blade.

The sound of a man dying is not so different to the sound of a man having sex. No one will suspect a thing.

It was dark in the corridor. 'Wait,' said Damien, his hand reaching out and ruffling through Sallum's hair. 'I just need to wash.'

Sallum paused. Two men brushed past him, then another man, by himself this time. 'Here,' said a voice from the third bedroom. Sallum walked in to the darkness. The man reached out a hand and pulled him inwards. He could feel his gown being unwrapped and a pair of hands running through the hairs on his chest. He took the blade from the pocket, holding it squarely in his right hand, and jabbed it forwards – stabbing it straight into the heart, and pulling the blade roughly upwards to make sure the main arteries in the heart were severed. The victim gasped twice, then fell forwards into Sallum's arms.

Sallum held his left hand tight over the man's mouth, stifling the scream that was about to erupt from his lips. With his right hand he twisted the blade, and he could feel the life ebbing away. He paused, counting to twenty, making sure his victim was dead, then laid him out on the bed. Using the knife he cut into the bone and flesh, sawing away at the man's right wrist until the hand was free from the body. He removed the locker key from the stump, and walked out into the corridor. In the next room, he could hear the sounds of three men having sex together, and was grateful for the covering noise.

Sallum walked to the back of the corridor, opened the fire door, and dropped the severed hand into the alleyway. Turning back into the sauna, Sallum walked back down to the changing rooms, which were mercifully still empty. There was still some blood on his hands, but it washed away easily. One of the best things about blood, Sallum reflected. It never stains. He used the key he had just ripped from the man's wrist to open the locker, and, reaching inside, he took the wallet from the inside pocket of his jacket. Then, opening his own locker, he retrieved his clothes and dressed.

He combed his hair, checked himself in the mirror, then walked back up to the entrance. The man at the desk nodded towards him, asked him if he'd had a good time, but Sallum just smiled and walked on without replying.

He walked a few yards, and turned the corner into the alleyway. The hand was where he had left it. He picked it up, held it underneath his coat, and headed back towards the car. He swung open the car door, deposited the hand on the passenger seat, and fired up the engine.

Another perfect kill. The honour of the Prophet is satisfied.

*

Matt dialled the number impatiently. He held the phone to his ear, listening to the ringing tone. Nothing. Damien wasn't answering.

He jabbed the off button, then pressed redial. The mobile took a few seconds to locate the number, then started to ring again. Matt waited, counting ten rings. 'Welcome to the T-Mobile answering service,' started up the mechanised voice on the line. 'The person you are calling is not available.'

'Damn him,' muttered Matt, putting the phone down.

'Where's he gone?' Ivan handed down a cup of coffee.

'I haven't a clue,' Matt snapped angrily.

'I don't like it,' said Ivan thoughtfully. 'Your team is coming apart at the seams.'

Matt looked up at the window, and stared into the darkness.

Damien, where the hell are you?

It was now four in the morning, and Sallum wanted his work to be completed by sunrise. Assassins are like owls, he reflected to himself. We are night creatures.

He looked down at the hand, nodding his head and whispering as if in prayer. 'In the book of Sunan Abu Dawud, it is written: a thief was brought to the Apostle of Allah – may peace be upon him – and his hand was cut off. Thereafter he commanded for it, and it was hung on his neck.'

Sallum smiled to himself, drawing quiet, professional satisfaction from the way the execution had gone. An assassin, he reflected, should always act within the commandments laid down by the Prophet. A hand has many uses. Even a dead one.

From his coat, he pulled out the wallet he had taken from the locker. Two credit cards, one bank card, and three different types of reward card. All in the name of Damien Walters.

It's close to dawn. I must act quickly.

He turned the ignition on the car and pulled out of the lay-by on to the open road, turning the heat up high to fight back the cold. He hated winters, and at moments like this longed to be back in Saudi. As a boy he had grown up in a small village in the Ar Rub' al Khali Desert, the vast, desolate space that dominates the centre of the country and stretches down to the coast of Oman. Translated, 'Khali' means the empty quarter – and that was the way he remembered it: he could travel for days with his father and not encounter a single living soul or even a blade of grass. It was completely pure.

Just as soon as my work is done I will be back there.

The lodge from which he had seen the target emerge this morning was five miles away. He drove slowly, careful not to draw any attention from the few cars on the road. As he saw the rough, low-built building on the horizon, he pulled in to the side of the road.

From the glove compartment he took a pad of paper and a pen, ripping free one page. 'THIS IS THE SECOND

SEVERED LIMB, THREE MORE TO GO,' he marked out in neat, block letters. 'GIVE US OUR MONEY BACK, OR I WILL KILL ALL YOUR FAMILIES AS WELL.'

Sallum wrapped the paper into a neat square, then got out of the car, taking the severed hand with him. He prised open the fingers – for a man who had only been dead for an hour, the joints were surprisingly stiff. Sallum pulled hard, forcing the hand open. He placed the note inside it, plus one of the credit cards he had taken out of the wallet, then snapped the fingers shut, making sure they were holding on tight.

Stepping towards a stone wall, he selected a small rock, just bigger than his fist. Taking some gardening twine from the boot of the Lexus, he held the hand against the rock and wrapped the twine around them both until they were secured together.

He started walking towards the lodge. The ground was soft under his feet. Rain had fallen during the night, turning parts of the field into mud. Sallum walked slowly, making sure he kept to the contours of the ground, checking that nobody could see him. Looking up, he saw the lights were still out in the lodge. Everybody was asleep.

He judged the weight of the rock in his hand. Accurately, he could probably throw it fifty feet and be certain of hitting his target. He walked closer, edging forward until he judged he was about forty feet from the house. Standing upright, he swung the rock behind his head, putting the full force of his shoulder muscles into the shot. The rock spun away from his hand, and a second later he could hear glass splintering. The target had been hit.

Sallum turned and started running, his feet bouncing over the ground. By the time they heard the crash and looked out of the window, he guessed he should have made it to the car. The most they would see was a Lexus pulling away and disappearing down the road.

Now they will know what it is like to incur the wrath of the Prophet.

Matt had seen Reid in some tense situations. There was a time in Bosnia when they had been pinned down in a farmhouse, with a sniper hiding in the trees right next to the building: they'd had to survive without food for three days until the man showed himself and they could kill him. But Matt had never seen Reid as shaken as he saw him now: his voice was fractured, and there was fear in his eyes.

'Do you want to see it?' he said.

Matt nodded. No man wants to see the dead flesh of a close friend, but he knew he had no choice. 'I'd better.'

The assassin is getting to us. That's part of his plan.

Matt and Ivan had driven straight up to Derbyshire after getting the call from Reid early that morning. A hand tied to a rock had been slung through the window, he said. It had Damien's credit card attached to it, and a note telling them to give the money back. You didn't have to spend long figuring out where it might have come from. Or what had happened to Damien.

Does that mean it's not Ivan? Matt wondered to himself. I was with Ivan when Damien was killed. *Maybe Reid killed both Cooksley and Damien . . .*

'It's outside,' said Reid. 'I didn't want Jane or the kids to see it.'

The lodge was a simple wooden structure. It had two bedrooms, a wood-burning stove that doubled up as a cooker, and a shower room. The two children, Jack and Emily, had already filled the main room with toys and drawings: Jack was busy doing a picture of his little sister while Jane busied herself packing. She nodded at Matt, smiling but remaining silent. She knows something is up, Matt thought. She can see it in our eyes.

A woman always knows when her husband is not telling the truth.

'Over here,' said Reid, stepping out of the lodge and crossing into the field.

It was a desolate spot, high on the side of a hill, with a vicious wind whipping in from the east. A flock of sheep was grazing in the next field, and the road was just visible at the bottom of the valley, but otherwise the lodge was completely isolated. Whoever had put the hand through the window would not have been seen, reflected Matt. They could be certain of that.

He's a professional. He's not about to help us out by making a stupid mistake.

Reid stepped over a granite wall, and pointed to a pair of large stones. The hand was resting on top. The skin had started to change colour, turning to a grey-blue. Blood had stopped dripping from where it had been severed from the arm, and the fingers had been forced open when Reid took out the note.

He was my best friend, Matt thought. And it's my fault this has happened to him.

'It looks a few hours old,' said Ivan, kneeling down and examining the hand. 'I reckon he killed him first, then cut the hand off.'

Matt's mind was still full of memories of Damien: images of them running the same streets together, bunking off school, kicking footballs across the park.

Ivan stood up, unfolding the note Reid had passed to him. He looked at Matt and Reid, his eyes narrowing. 'There were five of us, and now there are three.'

Matt turned away, looking down to the valley stretching out below. 'How the hell did this man know where Damien was?' he said.

All three of them fell silent.

I can ask the question, reflected Matt. But I can't supply the answers.

'I don't like to admit it, boys, but I'm scared,' said Reid, breaking the silence. 'This guy was just a few hundred feet from my children back there. He could have come in and taken us all out the way he took out Cooksley.' He paused. 'I signed up for this mission because I needed work, and I needed a fresh start in life. Maybe we should give them the money back like they ask. I tell you, I don't care about it any more. I just want out.'

'Don't be stupid,' said Ivan, a rough edge to his voice. 'They won't take any apologies. Give the money back or don't give the money back, they'll kill you just the same.'

'It says it right here,' Reid jabbed at the piece of paper. 'Give us our money back now. If that's what they want I reckon we should just give it to them.'

'To who, exactly?' Matt said. 'It doesn't say who or what, just give it back. Christ, we don't even have the money yet.'

'It doesn't matter,' said Reid, his voice growing more and more distraught. 'Just give it back, that's all.' He stepped angrily towards Matt. 'We're going to be next if we don't do something about it.'

'You're being stupid,' Ivan interrupted. 'I used to be a terrorist, as you are so keen on pointing out. I know how these people's minds work. They want the money, but they want you dead as well. He's just saying that to try and unsettle you. You're letting them get to you.'

'The only stupid thing I've done was get mixed up in a mission with you,' said Reid.

'I've had to take enough nonsense from you,' Ivan snapped. 'How do I know you didn't kill both Cooksley and Damien?'

Matt recognised the tone in the man's voice – it was the same cruel arrogance he had heard just before Whitson was killed. 'Break it up, boys,' he said, stepping between them. He looked to Ivan, then at Reid. 'We have to stick together, and fight them together,' he said. 'That's the only way. Otherwise they just pick us off one by one.'

★

Matt walked alone along the ridge of the hillside. He could feel the wind curling around his ears, but a few rays of sunshine were starting to struggle through the clouds. He had told the others he would check the back of the lodge and explore the hills behind to make sure no one was watching them from a distance. But, in truth, that had been an excuse. He needed to be alone for a few minutes.

He was wearing a grey overcoat, and black leather shoes – a man dressed for the town, not the country. He was still struggling to come to terms with Damien's death. In the Regiment you got used to your friends dying – it was part of the job, an occupational hazard. You knew the risks when you signed up, and nobody expected to life for ever. But this was different. This wasn't someone he'd worked with for a few years, this was the man he'd grown up with, whose life he had shared, whose sister he was planning to marry. If I'd had a brother, this is what it would have been like to lose him.

In the Regiment it was usually some Rupert's fault that a guy got killed. This time it's my fault.

'I'm sorry about your mate,' said Reid, walking up alongside him.

Matt had been so lost in his own thoughts that he hadn't noticed Reid at his side. They were about two hundred yards above the lodge, with a panoramic view of the whole valley. If anyone approached, they'd be able to see him.

'I'll miss him,' said Matt.

'It's Ivan, I tell you,' said Reid. 'How else could the assassin know we were here?'

Matt shrugged. 'I was with Ivan this morning down in Hammersmith. It couldn't have been him.'

'Not personally, no,' said Reid. 'But who says he hasn't got an accomplice? He finishes you and me off, then he and his mate collect all the money. Makes perfect sense to me.'

'He didn't know where you were going,' said Matt. 'Not unless he overheard you saying something to Damien. Or he had you followed.'

'We did our best,' said Reid. 'I kept my eye on the mirror through the journey. I tucked into a couple of lay-bys, took a couple of detours by some side-roads. That should have flushed out anyone on our tail. But like I said, I reckon it's Ivan. OK, you were with him – but he could have slipped away to make a call.'

Matt said nothing.

'I think that stuff about the IRA chasing him was just a stunt,' Reid continued. 'How do we even know he was in the IRA? No – he's got an accomplice, and they're working it together. As long as we have nothing to do with him, we're safe.'

'So what do you want to do then?'

Reid paused. 'Maybe we should finish him off now,' he said quietly. 'Out here on the hills, bury him somewhere. No one will ever find the body.'

Matt took a moment before answering. 'We're not murderers,' he said. 'And we've got no evidence.'

They stood in silence for a while. A light rain had started to fall. 'We can't stay here then,' said Reid. 'We've got to lose him.'

'There's a place in Spain. I'd have to clear it with the guy who owns it, but if he agrees it's perfect,' said Matt. 'The place is wired for maximum security – cameras, light sensors, tripwires, the works.'

'And what do we tell Ivan?'

'We don't want anything more to do with him, we tell him that. If he doesn't like it, we'll just kick the hell out of him. There's one of him, and two of us. What can he do?' Matt looked down at the lodge below them. 'And if it turns out he's responsible for Cooksley and Damien dying – then we kill him. He deserves it.'

Ivan's face was drawn, his eyes bloodshot and his shoulders sagging. Matt had known the man for only a few days, but Ivan had always seemed to be in control, always knew exactly what to say, everything mapped and planned. But not now. For the first time, control seemed to be slipping from his grasp.

'We're off,' Matt said, looking at him directly. 'I'm not saying we don't trust you, but right now Reid and I don't trust anyone. So we're disappearing for a few days, until the money is ready. We're not telling you where we're going, and we don't want you to start looking for us.'

Ivan was grinding his feet into the ground. 'Each time a man dies, the share to those left standing goes up,' he said. 'Now you kick me out, and that makes five million each for the two of you.'

Matt jumped forwards and grabbed Ivan by the shoulders. 'Don't say that,' he spat. 'Damien was my best friend, and now he's dead.'

A slow chuckle started to rise through Ivan's throat. 'You think it's me, don't you?'

'We're not saying that,' Reid said.

Ivan pulled up the collar of his coat. 'You're making a big mistake,' he said. 'Sure, information is swilling around somewhere, but it's not coming from me. I thought it might be coming from the Provos, but I don't think it's them any more.'

Matt leant into Ivan's face. 'So where's it from, then?'

Ivan shrugged. 'Dig your own graves if you want to, boys, it's no concern of mine,' he said. 'What's the proposal for cutting up the money? That's all that worries me right now.'

'You'll get your share,' Matt growled.

'I'm not letting that money out of my sight.'

'We'll collect it together,' Reid said, 'the way we always planned. We'll take our shares in Rotterdam – you know as well as we do when the cargo ship's coming in – then we'll go our separate ways.'

Ivan laughed. 'No. I'm sticking with you until I get my money.'

Matt jabbed a finger at his face. 'You heard what we said, you'll just have to accept it.'

Ivan waited for a few moments, then nodded. 'OK then – but if either of you double-cross me,

I'll kill you,' he said. 'Then I'll kill your families as well. If it's the last thing I do.'

He turned to walk away. The rain was heavier now, and water was dripping down the side of his face. 'If you make it, that is,' he said, 'because it's *not* me.'

'So long as we're away from you, we'll be OK,' said Reid.

Ivan shook his head as he set off. 'A couple of bone-stupid British squaddies. You haven't figured it out yet, have you? And the rate your brains work, you never will!'

The coffee bar at Luton Airport was full. The eight-twenty Easyjet flight to Malaga was not yet ready, and looked like being delayed by up to half an hour. Reid had taken Jane and the children to have something to eat. Matt was sitting by himself. He didn't feel like anything more than a snack.

It's going to be a while before I feel like eating again.

'I was sorry to hear about Damien,' Alison sat down opposite him.

Matt glanced upwards but remained seated. She was wearing a white coat, wrapped tight around her waist, and knee-high leather boots. She put her bottle of mineral water down on the table. 'He seemed like a good man.'

'He *was* a good man,' replied Matt.

'What do you think happened to him?'

'Why don't you tell me?' Matt snapped. 'You're the intelligence officer.'

'I wish I knew,' said Alison, a sympathetic smile on her lips.

'Right,' sneered Matt. 'The whole of Five can't find out anything about a pair of murders.'

Alison's hand reached across the table. 'As I said, I wish we knew more,' she said. 'But tell me what you think.'

Matt shook his head. 'I'm not sure,' he answered. 'Reid believes it's Ivan.' He looked up at her fiercely. 'He's been nothing but trouble.'

'Did you ask him about the missing tape?'

Matt nodded. 'He denies taking it,' he replied. 'He denies everything.'

'Maybe there's something on it that incriminates him.' Alison unscrewed the cap of her water bottle and put it to her lips. 'You really think he might be behind the killings?'

Matt nodded. 'That way he collects all the money for himself. It has to be him.' He looked closer at her, scrutinising every inch of her face. 'Why did you want him along?'

'I told you,' Alison said sharply, 'you needed a safe blown, we needed to get him out of Ulster.'

'And now two of my best friends are dead.'

'I didn't plan it that way, Matt,' Alison slammed her bottle on the table. 'I'm sorry, but it's not my fault. You were all grown men and you knew what you were getting into.'

'If you want to play softball, go to the park – right?'

Alison leant across the table. 'I know this hurts for

you,' she said. 'Everyone in this business has lost people they care about. It hurts, always. But we fight on. MI5 is doing everything it can to track down the killer.'

'I thought you said Five didn't care what happened to us. That's why we couldn't have a safe house.'

'Five doesn't have feelings,' said Alison, leaning back in her chair. 'It's not that sort of organisation. We want to catch al-Qaeda though.'

'What do you have, then?' Matt snapped. 'If you get any leads, you have to share them with me. It's my life on the line here.'

'OK,' she said. 'I should level with you about something.' Alison glanced around the café as if she was worried someone might hear her. 'It's about Ivan. He told you his family were being held by the IRA. That was a lie. We checked it out. They are currently living in a rented villa in Chile. On the coast just up from Santiago.'

'The bastard.' Matt slammed his fist on the table. 'I knew it was him.'

Alison looked at him carefully. 'It might be, it might not be,' she said. 'Don't jump to conclusions.'

'Why would he lie?'

'Tell me where you are going to be, and we'll do what we can to protect you.'

'Puerto Banus,' said Matt. 'Kazanov's place. It's about the most heavily fortified building on the Spanish coast, so if we aren't safe there, we aren't safe anywhere. We hole up there until we collect the money in Rotterdam in three days. Then, I don't know. New faces, new identities, the works. We disappear, and put all this behind us.'

Alison reached out and brushed a finger along Matt's hand. He kept still, not responding.

'You see, Matt, if we work together, we can get through this.'

SIXTEEN

The house sat high above the sea, perched above a tiny, sandy cove. The noise of the waves echoed up from the rocks, and spray flew about their jagged edges. A side road from the main highway twisted down to the building, and two huge black iron gates guarded the entrance to the main drive. A series of twenty tiny digital cameras were studded into the gateposts, relaying images back to the security room. An assailant could take out one or two cameras, but not twenty without being spotted.

You can't see the security, Matt noticed. Like a spider's web, you only notice once you are inside the trap. That's what makes it so effective.

The white Mercedes limousine drew to a halt outside the main doors, and Matt clambered out. It was two in the morning, and both Reid's children were asleep on the back seat. The flight from London had taken two-and-a-half hours, touching down at Malaga airport at just after midnight local time. Both the children had been excited to fly on a plane, and had spent most of the journey demanding to play with Matt. By the time they'd collected their bags and found the car Kazanov had sent for them, another hour had passed. Now Matt was exhausted. It seemed like three days since he had slept, and he needed to get his head down.

Sleep isn't easy when you know you might die in the next few days.

'You're a lucky boy, Matt Browning,' said Harry Pointer, walking towards the door, 'getting to stay in a place like this after all the trouble you've caused. Mr Kazanov is a nice man. A much nicer man than he should be.'

After the hard bargain Kazanov had driven, Matt reckoned he didn't have any grounds for complaining. The Russian had said he wanted his money back by the end of the month, and had added an extra fifty per cent on to the interest he was charging. Matt hadn't bothered to argue. Either way it made little difference. If he was alive at the end of the month, it was worth spending the extra money; if he was dead, Kazanov wasn't going to get paid anyway.

'He's getting his half-million back, plus a tidy wedge of interest,' Matt said sharply. 'He's a businessman. He knows that sometimes you have to protect an asset. Right now that's me.'

Pointer rang the bell, and they waited while a guard walked to the door. The man looked at them through a spyhole, then started unlocking the heavy bolts.

Matt heaved the bags on to his shoulders and stepped inside. Reid carried Emily, Jane was holding Jack in her arms. Matt had only been here once before, for a party Kazanov had held one New Year's Eve, back when he still counted as part of the nouveau riche set on the Marbella coastline. A plane load of Natashas and Ivanas seemed to have been flown in for the event: if Matt had ever before seen so many stunning girls gathered in one place, it could only have been in a dream. What they were like to talk to, he'd never discovered. Gill had hung on to his arm all evening, and the only people he'd got to speak to all night were some local property developers and some oil prospectors from the Caspian Sea.

'Nice place,' Jane whispered, stepping across the black and white marble floor of the hallway. 'It's a big improvement on that lodge in Derbyshire.'

Reid hadn't told her what was happening. For all Jane knew, they were simply staying there a few days while Matt and Reid sorted out some business, and Damien had gone to collect some money. Better to keep it that way. If Jane had any idea what had been happening, chances where she'd lose it completely.

'I'll show you to your rooms,' said Pointer.

Reid and Jane started walking up the stairs, the two sleeping children still in their arms. Matt took their bags in his arms and followed. His limbs were aching with tiredness, and he needed to get some rest.

About ten hours' sleep, some breakfast and a five-mile jog. Then I can start thinking straight again.

'A drink!' boomed a voice from the bottom of the stairs. 'I can't let you go to bed without at least one vodka.'

Matt turned round to see Kazanov standing in the

hallway, waving him down. Even at two in the morning he was still wearing a suit and tie. He was a man who took his grooming seriously. He was never seen looking anything less than immaculate. Say what you like about the KGB, Matt reflected, but it certainly taught its operatives how to present themselves.

Matt followed him through to the front of the house. A huge log fire was burning in the fireplace, its light filling the room. A long window stretched across one wall, overlooking the Mediterranean. The moon was almost full now, casting deep shadows across the bay.

Last time I saw a moon like that, I was using its light to kill six men.

'Say hello, Irina,' said Kazanov. 'This is my friend Matt.'

The girl was draped over the sofa. She was about six feet tall, with a perfect figure and long brown hair, and the high, wide cheekbones common among Slavic women. She was wearing a tiny black dress, a pair of diamond earrings, and a single black stiletto. The other shoe had fallen off.

'Hello,' she said, glancing up from a magazine.

'Thanks for letting me stay,' Matt said.

'You're paying me in four days,' said Kazanov. 'Personally I don't care if you live or die – but I know I'm not going to collect my money from a dead man. What was it Lenin once said? The debts of the Tsar died with the Tsar.' He laughed, a huge booming racket that filled the room.

Matt took the glass of vodka Kazanov was offering him.

'A couple of weeks ago you were flat broke,' said Kazanov. 'Now you say you can pay me back half a million in a few days' time. Yet you also want somewhere to hide.' He paused, taking a sip of his drink. 'I don't know what you've done, but it must be very bad. I'm interested.'

Matt took a hit of vodka, throwing it against the back of his throat. He had avoided a drink on the plane, but he needed one now. Maybe it's him, he thought, his blood suddenly chilling. Maybe it's Kazanov who's been after us all along, just as I first suspected.

And I've walked right into a trap.

'I took some money.'

'You – a thief? Surely not,' Kazanov said. 'I always thought you were one of us. A soldier, an honourable man.'

'My conscience is clear.'

Kazanov nodded. 'But now they want it back?'

'Somebody wants it,' said Matt.

'I've been on both sides of the law, Matt,' Kazanov said. 'I've been KGB, and what in Russia we call a businessman. It's not so different, just buying and selling. People and secrets or oil and aluminium, there is always a trade in every kind of commodity.' He paused, walking forwards and resting a hand on Matt's shoulder. 'Remember this – trust no one. *Absolutely no one.*'

★

Matt wiped the sweat from his brow with a towel and walked back into the house. A run makes a man feel better, he reflected. It washes all the poison out of your system. Today it wasn't working, though. He felt just as bad as when he'd started.

Matt had risen just after eight. Jane and the children were already awake – he'd found her fiddling with the satellite box, trying to find some cartoon channels in English, but finally settling on Bob the Builder in German. It seemed to keep the kids happy.

Matt had taken himself off for a run while Jane fixed some breakfast, and spent the time attempting to put the events of the past few days into perspective. The moment he dreaded most was telling Gill her brother had been killed.

In the house he showered, then located Reid, who was to assist him with a review of the security. They'd have the house to themselves for the next four days, and nobody would disturb them. There was enough food to last them a week or more. That was the way Matt wanted it. They could trust nobody, and they would rely on nobody but themselves.

A perimeter fence stretched around the borders of the estate. The wire rose to seven feet, supported by thick concrete and metal pillars. The fence was electrified, and fitted with sensors that would trigger an alarm in the house should anyone try to cut it. Matt and Reid walked the length of the fence, making sure there were no breaks and no weak points. It had been well designed, Matt judged. Even the trees surrounding the estate had been cut down so no one could use them to vault their way in. And the ground around it had been fitted with sensors as well, so tunnelling in would be impossible.

'Could you get past that?' said Matt.

Reid shook his head. 'I think you'd have to blast your way through then storm the place,' he replied. 'Or else drop in by parachute or helicopter. But there's no way you could sneak in undetected. It's too well protected.'

They walked up towards the main gate. They both knew that no matter how well guarded a property was, the way in was the most vulnerable point. That's why burglars use the front door, Reid pointed out as they walked up the driveway.

'Not this one,' said Matt.

They were standing next to the two black metal doors that were the entrance to the compound. Each was made of eight-inch-thick steel reinforced with tungsten. It was, Matt noted, the same material tanks are made from, and, like an armoured military vehicle, the gate was designed to withstand a rocket attack. There was an electronic keypad with a four digit code for opening the entrance: make one mistake in entering the code and a pair of heavy steel bolts shot across the doors, which remained shut for three hours. 'Short of heavy, sustained shelling, there's no way anyone is getting through this gate,' Matt said.

They walked back to the house. To the side of the building, past the kitchen, was a security control room.

In total, there were fifty cameras slotted around the perimeter of the estate, and another fifty throughout the house. A hundred monitors were permanently active within the control room. Just about every square inch of the place was recorded twenty-four hours a day. Infra-red sensors laced the property at night, meaning that the guard on duty would be alerted to any sudden move-ments. During the day, computers were programmed to monitor any suspicious movements: anybody running suddenly, or crawling across the ground, would immediately set off an alarm.

'Fancy set-up,' said Reid, surveying the screens and computer equipment.

'Kazanov is a rich man, and a lot of people would like to take a slice of his cake,' said Matt. 'Without this lot he'd probably have been dead a long time ago.'

The two men walked downstairs. From the control room, a single metal staircase led down into a concrete bunker. Matt punched in the four-digit code Pointer had given him for the door, which slid open, and they stepped inside. Matt flicked a switch. 'The armoury,' he said, glancing across at Reid.

It was an impressive display. Across one wall there was a rack of single- and double-barrelled shotguns. Next to it were stored ten high-precision rifles, twenty semi-automatic sub-machine guns, five full machine-guns, twenty-five boxes of ammunition, five crates of hand grenades, five crates of mortar shells, ten crates of explosives, twenty-five landmines, a selection of knives, ropes and flares, and two flame throwers.

'Christ,' said Reid. 'He's better stocked than the Regiment.'

Matt took one of the rifles from the wall, a Russian-made Kalashnikov – not the familiar AK47, but the more modern AK74M, built for the Russian infantry. Matt weighed up the weapon in his arms: the AK74M was made from a glass-filled polyamide material, making it much stronger and lighter than the older AK47 with its polished wooden furniture. But it's not really the quality of the weapons that matters, Matt knew. It's the quality of the man trying to kill you.

He tried to put that thought out of his mind. 'You could defend yourself against an infantry division with this lot,' he said.

'More likely to be one or two men, not a division,' said Reid. 'Whatever it is that comes after us, we won't be expecting it.'

Matt looked across at Reid. Maybe it is you, he considered. A Regiment man who's gone bad, over-whelmed by greed, driven mad by the thought of too much easy money. After all, a couple of weeks ago you were dossing down in a farm because you were too frightened to admit to your wife you weren't earning anything. Maybe all that alcohol you've been putting in your bloodstream has started chewing into your brain. How well do I know you?

Maybe it's you.

It was in the tone of her voice. He could tell she was not going to forgive him. The words stuck in the back of her throat, as if she was reluctant to let them emerge from her lips. 'Say it isn't true,' she muttered into the phone.

'I can't,' answered Matt. 'Nobody wishes that more than me – but it is true.'

There had been no choice but to tell her, and no simple way of breaking the news. Every instinct within him had told him that he should take the risk, get out of the house and go tell her in person. To tell the woman you loved over the phone that her brother was dead was monstrous. News as grave as that deserved to be delivered eyeball to eyeball. But it was too risky. Get Gill to come to the house, and she could easily be followed. All of them would be slaughtered. For him to go outside would be too dangerous as well. If Gill was being watched – and he had to assume that she was – that would be the opportunity for the assassin to move in and make his strike. The first rule of hiding was don't reveal your position to anyone, ever. No matter how desperate the situation.

He had used a rented mobile phone he'd picked up at the airport, since he wanted to make sure nobody could trace the call. He'd just make the one call, then destroy it. It was Saturday, and he knew he would find her at home. There was no point in small talk. One lesson he had learnt from officers in the Regiment was that, when you had to deliver bad news, it was best done quick and straight. There was nothing to be gained by trying to soften the blow. Damien was dead, he told her, his tone flat, drained of emotion.

'I'm so sorry,' Matt continued. 'If I could have done anything to prevent it, I would have done.'

'What happened to him?' said Gill, her voice cold and distant.

Matt had dealt with bereavement before. He had been to see the wives and sisters and parents of men in the Regiment who had died in action alongside him. He knew that when you lost someone precious you always wanted to know the precise circumstances of the death. Some people were angry, some disbelieving, some suspicious.

I'll tell her the truth. That's the least she deserves.

'He was on a mission for the government, with me and some other guys,' said Matt softly. 'It was MI5 sponsored, but off the books. We hit an al-Qaeda boat for a lot of money and we get to keep it. Damien joined because he wanted the money, and we needed someone to fence the stuff.' He hesitated. 'It's gone wrong. I think one of the gang is betraying us one by one. First a guy called Cooksley's got killed, then Damien. Reid or I could be next.'

'His body,' said Gill. 'What's happened to his body?' She sniffed, wiping a tear away from her eyes. 'I'll have to organise a funeral.'

'I don't know,' said Matt. He hesitated before continuing: there was only so much truth you should subject a woman to, even one you loved. 'I think the police will recover it soon.'

Gill paused. Even though he couldn't see her, Matt could imagine that the tears were starting to flow. 'I'm going to hang up now,' she said. 'It's over, Matt. I don't want to see you again.'

Matt could hear something different in her voice now. Not the rage and anger he was used to with Gill, but the quiet determination of a woman who has made her decision, and plans to stick with it.

She's leaving me.

'Stop,' he said. 'We can . . . . I need you Gill.'

Gill choked, her voice full of anger. 'It's too late, you idiot,' she said, spitting the words out of her mouth. 'I've had enough of your soldier games. It was bad enough when you ran around the world trying to get yourself killed. Now it's my brother as well.' She hesitated, fighting back the sobs. 'You couldn't even come and see me. You had to tell me on the phone. I'm through with it. I don't want to be around when you get yourself killed on some stupid job. I don't want to be the widow weeping at some stupid graveside. That's not a life, and I'm not going to take it any more.'

'This is the last one, trust me,' Matt said, his voice starting to crack. 'This was about making enough money to get out of the game for ever. So we could be with each other. It was about us.'

'About *us*?' said Gill, her voice rising. 'It's never about *us*, it's always about you. There's always another job, another mission, another war. You don't get it, do you? I don't need you to be a hero or a millionaire, or any of the rest of it.' She took a deep breath. 'All I wanted was for you to be an ordinary guy who cared about me.'

The line went dead. Matt stood in the room, staring out across the sea, the phone still hanging in his hand. He put it down, and put his face in his hands. He had wanted to speak, but the words were choked in his throat. Gill had been angry with him before – they had shouted at each other hundreds of times. But this time felt different. She had just said goodbye.

Joe Reiss looked like a typical Five agent, decided Matt, as he opened the door. He was just under six feet tall, well built, with a rugby player's upper torso. About thirty, with thick black hair, and wearing chinos and a tweed jacket, he had minor public school written all over him.

Nothing like Alison. Nothing like as smart.

'Headquarters suggested I swing by,' Reiss said breezily at the door, 'to help with the security.'

Matt showed him around. Reiss said he was stationed in Malaga – he had been posted in Madrid, but MI5 already had a man on the southern Spanish coast, and Reiss had been sent down to join him. The area was swarming with drug dealers, gun runners, gangsters and terrorists. 'So they figured it was worth having their own man on the spot, getting plugged into the local network, seeing what he could pick up,' Reiss added. 'That's me.'

I can't imagine a twit like you getting plugged into anything but the toaster.

The tour took fifteen minutes – around the perimeter defences, into the control room, and down into the armoury. Matt could tell that Reiss was surprised by the extent and sophistication of the weapons and surveillance systems on display. Whatever piece of ground he'd been keeping his ear to, Matt decided, it obviously hadn't told him that Kazanov was a man with this sort of money and munitions at his disposal. 'So, you see, we're pretty well defended,' said Matt.

'Five wanted to put in a couple of extra tweaks,' said Reiss, 'if that's OK.'

'A couple of battalions of Gurkhas would be good,' replied Matt.

Reiss grinned. 'I was thinking more of a video link,' he said. 'We can just fix up the electronics so that all the video surveillance gets beamed straight back to headquarters. Anything starts happening, we can send some guys to help you out.'

'The cavalry?'

'That's the thing,' Reiss nodded enthusiastically.

'You'll be able to help clear up the bodies, then,' said Matt. 'Always good to have somebody to wash away the blood.'

Reiss looked hurt. 'We're just trying to help, Mr Browning. It's rare for MI5 to do this for anyone.'

'It's rare that Five does *anything* for anyone,' said Matt. He turned to walk away. 'Fix up your wires. We'll use all the help we can get.'

Reid was sitting upstairs, drinking a beer on the balcony. A sniper could get you from there easily thought Matt. You don't look nearly as frightened of dying as you should be. Matt walked slowly towards him, listening intently as he crossed the stone floor. Over the past couple of days he had grown used to watching every shadow, every nerve in his body switched to full alert, ready for an assault. He had also learnt the first lesson any target learns: when an attack comes, you may not see it, you may not feel it, but you will always *hear* it. It's like fighting in the jungle, Matt thought, where the thick trees and leaves stop you from seeing more than a few feet in any direction. A tiger's ears are its greatest weapon – they are ours too.

'The man from Five,' he said. 'He's connecting the video cameras to base. So they can send reinforcements if anyone comes to get us. Kazanov is going to go crazy. We'll have to get rid of it all before we leave.'

Reid took a swig from his beer bottle. 'And where are they going to come from? London?'

'They probably won't come at all,' said Matt, sitting down next to him.

'It's not about helping us,' said Reid. 'It's about watching us.'

Matt picked up the mobile phone and walked back into the kitchen. Jane was upstairs, struggling to get the children off to sleep. Some paella was cooking on top of the stove, Reid stirring it occasionally, and a jazz channel was playing on the radio. A bottle of rosé wine was uncorked on the table. Just a nice English family on holiday in Spain, thought Matt. Except someone is trying to kill us.

'Yes,' Matt said into the phone.

'Anton Heuhle here.'

Matt snapped to attention: this was the fence Damien had been using. 'The deal's on,' he said flatly. 'We'll meet you as arranged.'

There was a pause on the line. 'Has something gone wrong?' said Heuhle.

He must have heard something in my voice.

'Nothing's wrong,' said Matt firmly. 'The gear's worth thirty million, and we're selling it to you for ten. That's all you need to know. But it will be me making the pick-up, not Damien.'

Matt cut the call. He walked across the room to where Reid was standing. 'That was Anton Heuhle,' said Matt. 'He's the fence that Damien was going to use.'

'How did he know how to find you?'

'Damien gave him my mobile number, told him to get in touch with me if he didn't hear anything. He sent me a text message, and I texted him back with the new number.'

'Anyone with surveillance could have picked all that up.'

'I know,' said Matt. 'But we have to get on with getting the money.'

'Maybe they'll wait until we make the collection,' said Reid, 'take us then.'

Matt sighed. Reid was right, there was nothing safe about this mission. 'If we want the cash, we'll have to take our chances.' He paused. 'You and me, tomorrow night. You coming?'

'Who says we need to go and pick up the money?' said Reid. 'Why not get the fence to stash it away for us, wait until we've smoked out this assassin, then go get it?'

Matt shook his head. 'That's crazy,' he replied crisply. 'We have to be there when the boat gets in. I'm going, whether you come or not.'

Reid walked out towards the balcony. A wind was starting to blow in from the sea, whistling up through the rocks. 'I can't leave Jane and the kids, not at a moment like this. And I can't take them with me. It's too dangerous.'

'Then I go,' said Matt. 'I collect the money from Heuhle. I'll take the money to the cache we agreed back in Bideford. Once we decide it's OK for the family to travel, you come over and we split up the money.'

'And Ivan?'

'I reckon he'll be waiting for me,' said Matt. 'I'll be there to collect the money, and maybe he'll be there to finish me off, and take the money for himself.'

'And what'll you do then?'

'I'll kill him.' He turned around, looking at Reid. 'You OK with that?'

As he posed the question, he could see Reid's eyes start to change shape. 'You're bloody keen to get us all killed, aren't you. Maybe it's you,' Reid said, drawing out the words. 'Maybe it's you, Matt.'

Matt stood perfectly still, as if he had been frozen in a block of ice. The words rattled through his brain. 'What do you mean?'

Reid moved a step back. 'It all seems to be working

out very neatly, doesn't it?' he said, his voice edged with menace. 'Too neatly. You set up the mission with five guys, you're in charge. You're the one person who organises everything, who pulls all the strings. Cooksley's dead, Damien's dead, and you're about to kill Ivan. I'm left alone in the house of your friend.'

The back of Matt's hand collided with Reid's cheek, sending him reeling sideways. Reid staggered backwards, holding his hand to his face where the blow had struck. 'Don't accuse me of that!' Matt shouted, his voice raw with anger. 'Those men were my friends.'

Reid charged forward, his fist ramming into Matt's stomach. Matt doubled up in pain, choking on his own breath. Pulling himself upright, Matt swung his fist backwards. He clenched his knuckles, ready to strike, watching as Reid backed away.

'Stop it!' shouted Jane, appearing from the doorway to the balcony. 'Stop it, you idiots! What are you fighting about?'

Matt looked at Reid. 'Take it back.'

'Prove it isn't true. You weren't in the hotel when Cooksley got killed. You weren't with me when Damien got killed. Looks bloody obvious to me.'

'Don't be bloody ridiculous,' Matt snapped. 'If I was going to kill you I'd have done it by now.'

Reid took a step forward. 'I don't care,' he said, putting his arm around Jane. 'You and me stay here together,' he said to her. 'I'm not letting you out of my sight.' A sullen grin started to play on his lips. 'But I tell you, Matt Browning, I'll be watching your every move.

And if you try to get away or double-cross me, that precious nursery teacher of yours is dead flesh.' He ran his finger across his neck, mimicking the movement of a knife. 'She goes straight to the slaughterhouse. You understand me?'

SEVENTEEN

The train twisted slowly through the Dutch countryside. Matt sat by himself, in a smoking carriage towards the back of the train. He was sipping slowly on a cup of stale coffee, a biscuit lying half eaten at its side. He watched the flat fields stretch out into the distance, reflecting on how far he had travelled in the past two weeks, and how far he still had to go.

When a team starts breaking up, it stays broke. It's part of the iron law of screw-ups.

The KLM plane had left Malaga at ten past eight that morning, touching down at Amsterdam's Schipol airport just before eleven local time. He'd paid cash for the ticket, which had caused some consternation among the girls at the check-in desk. Not using a credit card marked you out as some kind of criminal these days, Matt realised. Only men with something to hide used old-fashioned paper money, everyone else used plastic.

I've moved on to the other side of the law now. And I might never come back.

There was a direct train from Schipol to the Rotterdam Central station, stopping at Leiden and Den Haag. The journey was only three-quarters of an hour, but Matt was grateful for the time and space to himself. He needed to sort out his thoughts. And decide what he was going to do next.

The money is like some kind of worm. It chews away at all of us.

Matt was still shocked by the way Reid had reacted the night before. They had never been the best of friends in the Regiment. But they had known each other for years; they were both Army men. Surely it couldn't be him . . .

He peered out of the window, watching the countryside rush by. Whatever else, he felt certain he had been right to slip away last night after Reid had finally gone to sleep. The man was cracking. There was no other choice.

I don't know. Maybe it's Reid. He could have killed Damien when they were up in the lodge together. He could have slipped out to kill Cooksley – he would certainly have known where he was. Maybe Reid is a complete psycho.

He took a hit of the coffee and finished off the biscuit. A taste of food reminded him that it was hours since he'd had anything proper to eat. His stomach was empty, and his head was aching from hunger.

Stop it, Matt – you're going mad yourself. Just collect the money, stay alive, and get this thing over with.

The boy couldn't have been more than sixteen or seventeen. He was tall and thin, strong in the way that teenagers are, with eyes that bulged from their sockets, and a shy manner. Sallum inspected him the way he might inspect a goat in the market: as a piece of meat for cooking, not as a living creature.

'Your name?' he said.

'Rami Shamil, sir,' he answered.

Sallum nodded, a smile exposing his gleaming white teeth. 'Rami. The marksman. It is appropriate.'

'I chose it, sir, when I joined our movement.' He sat down next to Sallum. The café was situated in the hills behind the main road running east from Puerto Banus. There were no views from here, and it wasn't on a road towards any tourist site. It was entirely Spanish, serving great plates of pork and beans to the truckers. Just as well, reflected Sallum. If we talk in English no one will understand us.

The boy had been supplied by the organisation. Sallum had contacted Assaf to say that he needed someone expendable, and the boy had been dispatched. Rami was Algerian, and had joined al-Qaeda three years before. He'd been in Afghanistan before the war for basic training, then moved to Qatar after the fall of Kabul. He was not an expert fighter, just a mule: a boy used as muscle. But he was devout and fearless, and ready to lay down his life for the cause. Even though he had no particular talents, his willingness made him a useful tool of the organisation. Perfect for Sallum's purposes tonight.

'You are familiar with the Koran?'

'Yes, sir.'

Sallum ordered two cups of weak peppermint tea from the waitress. 'Then tell me the story of Husayn.'

'The grandson of the prophet Mohammed, and the third Imman,' answered Rami. 'He and his band of followers were killed by the Caliph Yazid in 680. He was the first of the great martyrs of the faith, and the shrine to him at Karbala in Iraq is one of the holiest places in all Islam.'

Sallum nodded. 'You are a good student,' he said.

Rami took a sip of his tea, looking up towards Sallum, his expression calm and impassive. 'Am I to become a martyr, sir?'

'Not at all,' said Sallum, shaking his head, a benevolent smile playing on his lips. 'But, you know, those of us who fight for the faith must always be prepared to be martyrs one day. It is that knowledge, that we would lay down our lives at any time, that makes us strong and the infidels weak.'

Matt walked towards the parking lot, clutching the car keys. The blue Ford Focus was one of seven identical cars parked in a row in the Avis lot. He picked his from the number plate, climbed inside the vehicle and started driving.

He had used his own name and credit card to complete the rental forms. There was no way they would give him a car without showing his licence and some plastic, so he figured he had little choice. If anyone wanted to track him down, they could.

But they'll have to find me first. And if I keep moving that won't be so easy.

He checked his watch. It was twelve–twenty. He had

another forty minutes until he was scheduled to meet Heuhle, but first he had to find his way through the suburbs of Rotterdam. He pulled the car out of the lot and started heading east. He checked his mirror every few seconds to see if anyone was on his tail.

At this moment I could use a gun, he thought – but although there were plenty of Dutch gangsters who would have sold him one, he didn't have the time to find them.

He turned sharply right. According to the map on the passenger seat, this road would take him in towards the docks. The restaurant was an Italian place, Roos Marijn, a couple of streets from the main port. A local place, out of the way and discreet – Matt reckoned there was little chance anyone would see them.

He drove slowly through the neat suburban streets. His head was turning from right to left, making sure he read every street sign and tracking his position on the map. He was almost there. The next turning on the right, then the restaurant should be a couple of blocks along.

He glanced in the mirror. Nobody was following. He looked across the streets, checking for any cars with people in them. Nothing. He scanned the driveways of the houses, glanced at the street corners, then up into the trees.

If I was planning a hit here, where would I hide myself?

He could see the restaurant a block away: a two-storey building with a long glass front and a red neon sign on top. He pulled into the car park, switched off the ignition, and sat silent for a moment. There were two cars in the lot, both empty. In the mirror, he could see one man walking down the street. He waited for him to pass, tracking his movements, ready to respond. Only when he had disappeared from view did Matt climb out of the car.

OK, if Ivan's here, he's planning to make the hit after the money gets transferred.

Heuhle was sitting in a booth towards the back of the restaurant. Look for a man reading a copy of the *International Herald Tribune*, he had told Matt, but he needn't have bothered. The only other customers were a Dutch mother and daughter, and a man in his seventies by himself.

'Let's get one thing straight,' said Matt, sitting down in the booth. 'I've had a crap few days. People are getting killed all around me, and I'm probably next. I'm tired, and my nerves are edgy. So you fuck me around, I kill you. With my bare hands if I have to. We clear about that?'

'You should order the chicken soup,' said Heuhle. 'It might make you feel better. Calm you down.'

Heuhle was a thin man, in his early forties Matt judged, almost six feet tall, with light blond hair and a tan that suggested he took several holidays a year. He was wearing a black Boss suit and a dark grey shirt, with a couple of buttons undone at the neck. Fencing stolen jewels and gold looked like a trade that could earn a man a good living. That was to be expected. If he wasn't good enough to make money, Damien wouldn't have been using him.

'I'm sorry to hear about Damien,' said Heuhle.

'How well did you know him?'

Heuhle shrugged. 'In this trade, a man doesn't know anyone that well,' he replied. 'We have contacts, networks, references, but we're all freelancers. We work alone. I did three trades with him. London goods. Diamonds twice, some paintings once. He was reliable and sharp.'

Matt nodded. 'As you know, the *Ithaca* gets into the port this afternoon. About five, but it could be a couple of hours out either way. I suppose it depends how crowded the port is. But they should be unloading about six. I go in there, collect the gear, get past customs. Then we make the transfer at night. I give you the stuff. You give me the ten million. Agreed?"

'The money is ready.'

'Show me.'

Heuhle shook his head. 'It's in a safe place about five miles from the city. Once you get your stuff, we'll take it there and I'll give you the cash.'

Matt leant forwards, resting his arms on the table. 'How do I know I'm not just going to get my throat cut and my corpse tossed into some Dutch ditch?' he said sharply. 'You could easily have a bunch of guys waiting to finish me off.'

'I could, but I don't,' said Heuhle. 'Trust. That's the basis on which this business works.'

Rami held the TCI 89SR sniper rifle to his shoulder. Sallum had been amused by the choice of weapon: the

TCI was a gun manufactured for the Israeli Army, based on the American M14 SWS. A short, black metal rifle, the TCI was light, easily concealed, and had exceptional punch for a weapon of its size. That made it perfect for the tight, house-to-house fighting the Israeli Army specialised in.

The Jews might be among our greatest foes, but sometimes the devil has the best munitions. We'll use their guns if we need to.

'See if you can hit the fruit from that tree,' said Sallum.

They were standing in the hills behind the café, in the middle of a long stretch of waste and scrubland populated only by a few goats. In the distance there were two orange trees, struggling to grow in the barren, sun-baked earth. Rami found his target in the gun-sight, steadied his shoulder, and squeezed the trigger. The sound of the shot echoed around the hills.

The fruit didn't move.

'See if you can hit the tree, then,' said Sallum patiently.

Rami put the rifle back up to his shoulder. He spread his legs slightly wider apart, driving his heels into the sand to give himself a better balance. He took a deep breath, lined up the sight to his right eye, squinted to protect his vision from the bright afternoon sun, then squeezed softly on the trigger.

The tree remained undisturbed.

'Don't worry,' said Sallum, patting the boy on the

back, 'when we go in against our target you'll be much closer.'

This boy couldn't shoot himself in the foot.

The *Ithaca* inched its way carefully through the dock, its massive engines churning up water as the propellors screwed in reverse to slow the ship down. Along its side, sailors cast down ropes to their colleagues on the bay.

It's an ugly looking ship, though Matt. Twenty years of ploughing cargo through the Mediterranean, the Atlantic and the North Sea had battered its hull and scraped away whatever paintwork might have once decorated it.

But to me, it's the finest looking vessel I have ever seen.

Matt turned to Heuhle. 'Looks like my boat just came in.'

The two men walked closer to the side of the dock. It was five in the afternoon, and dusk was falling. A wind was whipping in from the north, and the spray from the sea was hitting Matt's face. A group of men were huddled around a makeshift wooden hut, filling in forms and collecting passes: most of them looked like Albanians, Kosovans or Kurds. *Temporary workers,* explained Heuhle, *signing on for the night shift. That's what the asylum seekers do while they are waiting to be sent home.*

Matt scoured the faces in front of them. *One of you could be the assassin,* he reflected. One man looked him in the eye, smiled, then looked away. *Maybe you,* wondered Matt. Another man stood next to him, lighting up a cigarette, looking down at the ground. Maybe you.

Until I get out of here I'm going to be looking at every shadow, wondering whether it's going to kill me.

He walked up closer to the *Ithaca*. The ship was bound to the dockside now, rolling only slightly with the swell of the water. Above, Matt could see the massive cargo cranes swinging into action. Huge steel beams swung out over the boat, lowering cables on to its deck, hauling containers up into the sky, then back down on to the dock.

I'm so close to my money I can almost smell it.

'Ticket number 219,' Matt said to the docks manager standing beside the ship, supervising its unloading. 'A couple of imported cars. How long?'

The man shrugged. 'An hour, maybe two,' he replied. 'It depends how deep down in the hold they stashed it.'

The waiting, thought Matt. That's always what gets to you. In the thick of the action you don't have the time to think or worry. When you are sitting around, that's all there is to do.

A small group of men was starting to gather, each of them, Matt supposed, here to make their own collections. Behind them, the car park was full of lorries and vans, all ready to take the stuff away.

Heuhle collected a truck from the car park and drove it up to the side of the dock, ready for the two containers to be loaded on top of it.

Matt counted three ships in this dock and two in the

next one, but the *Ithaca* was the only vessel being unloaded right now, and looked like the last of the day. Most of it was bulk cargo: fruit, and cheap manufactured goods, mostly clothes and furniture, that had been picked up in Turkey and Cyprus and was destined for the supermarkets of western Europe. Most of the truck drivers looked bored and uninterested. So would I be, thought Matt, if I just had to pick up a couple of these containers and drive them to Dusseldorf.

That, after all, is the point of all this. To save myself from an ordinary working life.

'Our number's up,' said Heuhle, standing at his side.

Matt snapped to attention and looked up. The crane had lifted a single steel container free of the boat. The metal screeched while the crane slowly turned, then the steel ropes started to winch the crate down.

Just a few more inches, thought Matt. Then it's back on dry land.

'Your ticket,' said the docks manager.

Matt took the receipt from his wallet and handed it across. The man inspected the piece of paper briefly, made a note on his pad, then nodded. 'OK,' he said tersely. 'It's yours.'

The container was lowered slowly on to the back of the truck. 'Take it away,' shouted the docks manager as soon as it was in place.

Matt hopped into the passenger seat and Heuhle drove the truck forward into the parking lot. From the corner of his eye, Matt could see the customs inspector approaching them. 'I'll do the talking,' said Heuhle. 'It'll be easier to speak Dutch.'

Matt could feel his stomach heaving as the two men spoke. He'd been told that about five per cent of the containers were searched by customs. The inspector nodded, looked at some paperwork, then cast his eyes over the container and stamped Heuhle's paper.

'We're clear,' Heuhle said, climbing back into the cabin.

Matt got out, lowered the back of the truck, fired up the rented Ford, and steered it on to the back of the lorry, tucking it behind the container.

'Can you drive this?' said Heuhle, looking towards Matt as he climbed back into the cabin.

'Of course,' answered Matt. 'If you can drive a tank, a truck is no problem.'

'Follow the red Audi,' said Heuhle, climbing down from the cabin. 'When I stop, that's where the money is.'

Matt turned the ignition, bringing the engine roaring to life. Pushing his foot on the accelerator, he gradually familiarised himself with the controls. Turning the wheel, he started to steer the truck out of the port and on to the main road. Up ahead, Heuhle's Audi was in view, driving cautiously in the slow lane. So far, so good, thought Matt. In another hour, the money will be safely stashed in the back of that rented Ford.

My money. Ten million, a third of it mine – and more if we finish Ivan.

★

The lights from the compound were only just visible over the ridge of the hill. Sallum looked over the cusp of the rock, surveying the panorama below. He could see the house, the drive leading up to it, and the high, wire fencing encircling the compound. Taking a pair of binoculars from his pocket, he looked down at the gates: black, thick, reinforced steel. The only way through was by cutting the wire – and that, he could be sure, was protected by a thousand different electronic sensors.

My sources were right. Only a man on a suicide mission would attempt to get inside there.

'How do we get inside, sir?' Rami asked, looking up towards Sallum.

'Wire cutters,' said Sallum.

From his backpack, he took out a pair of thick steel pliers. 'You cut the wire like this,' he said, crunching the pliers together. 'Snap a section of wire open, about one foot square. That will be enough for you to crawl through. Then wriggle along the ground, trying to keep low and out of sight. As you approach the house, get your gun ready. Go in through the main balcony window. As soon as you see anyone, shoot them on sight. Understood?'

Rami nodded. 'You don't think they'll see me coming in?'

'We wait until midnight, they should all be in bed,' said Sallum. 'It is just one man and his family. He can't stay up all night. So long as you are brave and quick, you'll be all right.'

'What have they done, sir?'

'They are infidels,' said Sallum gravely. 'They have stolen from the organisation to which we have pledged ourselves. The punishment they are about to receive is a just one.'

'Then may Allah be with me, as he was with Husayn,' said Rami, starting to pace down the side of the hill.

The boy has faith, reflected Sallum, if not much in the way of brains.

The Audi pulled up to a halt in a lay-by on the side of the road. Matt calculated that they were about six miles outside of Rotterdam, and at least two miles from the main highway. He could see Heuhle climbing out of the car, walking towards him. 'There's a right turning just ahead that leads to a copse of trees about a mile distant,' Heuhle told him. 'The stash is in there. You should be able to get the truck up the dirt track.'

Ivan must be following me, Matt decided. He must have some plan for taking me down just after I get the money. I just have to be ready for him.

Matt steered the truck out of the lay-by, back on to the road, then turned a sharp right on to the track. It led a mile between two fields towards the woods. The surface was rough, pitted with stones which were thrown up against the underside of the truck, but the ground seemed solid enough. The tyres were gripping, churning up mud but still pushing the machine forwards.

This is the point of maximum danger. If I were Ivan, I'd attack right here, right now.

Matt surveyed the scene ahead. The track opened up into a small clearing, surrounded by tall trees. It was pitch dark. The last farm Matt had seen was a couple of miles back, and this patch of wood was surrounded by nothing except empty fields. Plenty of places for a sniper up in those trees, thought Matt. If I was planning a hit, that's what I would do.

He brought the truck to halt, killing the engine. Heuhle had already parked the Audi a few yards ahead. Matt sat perfectly still, listening to the sound of the wind rustling the branches of the trees. He looked up, then right and left, searching for the points where thicker branches grew out from the tree trunks. It was in one of those niches a sniper would conceal himself.

Matt stepped down from the cabin. A branch creaked, and instinctively he ducked his head.

'A bit jumpy?' said Heuhle.

'Two men already died on this job. I don't plan to be the third.'

Heuhle looked at him closely. 'Where did you get this stuff?'

'Al-Qaeda.'

Heuhle whistled. 'You're a brave man.'

Matt shook his head. 'A desperate one,' he replied.

'Within twenty-four hours, it will have been split up and distributed among a hundred different dealers, and within a week it will be in a thousand different jewellery shops across Europe.'

That's the real beauty of gold and diamonds, thought Matt. Not the way they sparkled and glittered, but the fact that both commodities were completely untraceable. Nobody cared where they came from. They were money in its purest state.

'Let's move.'

Matt hopped on to the back of the truck. He was breathing more easily now. The shot hadn't come, and although he still had to be on his guard, he figured that any assassin hiding in the trees would have loosened off a few rounds by now. He had done some hits himself, and he knew the rules. When an opportunity for a clean shot at your target presents itself, you never pass on it. *You never know when it might come again.*

He unhooked the back of the container, stepping inside its dank steel hull. The smell of the sea was still hanging to it: a mixture of salt and brine and rust. He switched on the flashlight from the truck, the beam piercing through the darkness. The two Land Rovers were there, both strapped down to the floor of the container. It looked as if they had barely been disturbed during the voyage.

Matt stepped closer, Heuhle following him. He knelt down, his hand reaching underneath the first vehicle. He rummaged around until he found the catch and prised it loose with his thumb. Unlocked, the flat metal panel came free in his hand. Where you would expect to find the base of the car were a series of small wooden boxes, each one neatly stacked on top of each other. Matt pulled the first one free. He caught his breath as he slid the lid aside, flashing his torch on to its contents, and the diamonds sparkled back at him like the eyes of a child.

Slowly, he started unpacking the boxes from the two cars, stacking each one on top of the other.

At his side, Heuhle was opening each box, examining its contents, then placing it back on the stack. From his car he had brought a set of electronic scales. At random, he took a selection of diamonds and a selection of gold bars, measuring each one then weighing them. 'Once you know the right weights for a diamond of a certain size and a gold bar of a certain size, this is the quickest way of judging whether it's fake,' he explained to Matt. 'If the diamonds were made of glass, or if those gold bars had hollow shells, the weights would be all wrong.'

'And how are they?'

'Exactly as they should be.'

'Then I'll collect my money.'

The two men walked across the damp ground towards the wood. It was pitch dark, and Matt needed his torch to illuminate the path. The wind was picking up speed, rattling through the branches. He could hear creaking. A footstep? Or just a branch blown about in the gale?

If there's someone there, they'd better take me down with one shot. Otherwise they're dead.

'This way,' said Heuhle.

The oak tree was massive, its thick trunk towering into the sky, its branches reaching out imperiously across the rest of the wood. At least a hundred years old, judged Matt. At its base the roots curled up and out from the ground, creating dozens of tiny caves and crevices.

Useful for woodlice, rabbits and robbers.

Heuhle bent over, his arm reaching between a pair of roots. He tugged, pulling out a yellow canvas travel bag. He handed it across to Matt. 'Count it if you want to,' he said.

'How much in this one?'

'Two million dollars. One million in American money, half a million in euros, two hundred and fifty thousand in British pounds and the rest in Swiss francs.'

Matt pulled back the zipper. The notes were all there, folded into neat paper bundles. He could smell it. Not the fresh, inky scent of the newly printed note, but the familiar, grubby smell of the old, used note; the smell of cash tills, other people's hands and sweaty pockets.

My money. I'm a rich man again.

He watched as Heuhle pulled another bag from the tree, then another, until there were five bags in a row. Matt opened each one, checking the notes were all there, and that none of the bundles were stuffed with forgeries or blanks. That was all the checking he needed to do.

'Here,' said Matt, handing across the keys to the truck. 'It's all yours.'

He collected the bags, putting three over his shoulders and taking one in each hand. The money was lighter than he expected: ten million dollars was not such a big sum that a strong man couldn't comfortably carry it on his back. As he walked he scanned the trees, watching and listening.

'What happened to the other guys?' said Heuhle as they walked.

'Two died. The other . . . We decided we didn't like the smell of him.'

'You meet a lot of gangs in this trade,' said Heuhle. 'It's always the same. They are the best of friends until the job, but afterwards they all start arguing among themselves.'

'Arguing I can handle.'

'It's the money,' said Heuhle. 'It's always the money. It has the same effect on all of them. Within a few days, the oldest of friends are at each other's throats.' He paused, turning to look at Matt. 'You want my advice, you split that cash up, give a fair share to each man still standing, then get the hell out. Once the killing starts, it doesn't end until there's only one man left standing. And it won't necessarily be you.'

Matt swung the last of the bags into the boot of the Ford, which was still parked on the back of the truck. 'Thanks,' he said tersely. 'Always good to have some encouragement.'

Heuhle laughed. 'I just meant be careful,' he said. 'A man with ten million in unmarked notes in the boot of his car needs several sets of eyes. He'll have enemies he never even imagined.'

Matt turned the ignition on the car and carefully backed it down on to the dirt track. 'You look after yourself, too,' he said. 'A man with a truck full of gold and diamonds needs just as many eyes as a man with ten million in notes. Especially when it's jinxed.'

With a brief smile he wound up the window and started turning the car. The killing won't stop until only one man is left standing, reflected Matt – the advice Heuhle had just given him. He pressed his foot on the accelerator, looking out for the main road, and wondering how long it would be until he hit the turning for Calais.

Well then, I just have to make sure that man is me.

EIGHTEEN

Home, thought Matt, as he glanced up at the first of the familiar green-and-white British road signs.

It was pitch dark when he pulled out of the Eurotunnel. From Rotterdam he had driven due east, hitting the main road, and not stopping until he'd reached Calais. It was after midnight by then, and the terminal had been mostly deserted – truckers used the train at that time of the night to take advantage of the cheap rates, and a few frugal tourists, but there was plenty of space, and he had no trouble getting a ticket. He had drunk a couple of cups of machine coffee as he'd waited for his number to be called: it tasted like powdered sawdust, but he'd needed something to keep himself awake through the next few hours. As the caffeine kicked in, he'd steered the car into the carriage. For the twenty-minute journey he had sat alone in the car, composing himself and arranging his thoughts.

There was still no sign of Ivan, nor any word from him. The man was planning a hit later on. Perhaps when they split up the money. Or else he was completely innocent, and was just waiting for his share. It was impossible to tell, realised Matt.

But my life may still depend on getting the answer right.

Matt's heart had been thumping as he'd steered the car out of the train and back on to dry land. His hands were sweaty, and his throat dry. He'd glanced nervously at the customs office as he'd driven into a nothing-to-declare lane. He'd slowed the car down, keeping his eyes rooted to the black tarmac of the road, trying to act as casually as he could.

A few officers had been on duty, but they had seemed to be more on the lookout for asylum seekers and cigarette smugglers. Not men with five bags of used notes in their boot.

Strictly speaking, Matt decided, there is probably nothing technically illegal about carrying ten million across the border in cash. But you could be sure that if they found it, they would know you were guilty of something.

Matt glanced in the mirror. The customs post was now safely in the distance, and there was no sign of anyone running after him. He switched the headlights on to high beam and tapped the accelerator, taking the car up to seventy as he hit the M20. He didn't want to risk being stopped for speeding, not with ten million in his boot.

A few minutes' drive, and then I'll be there.

At junction ten he turned on to the A28, heading south towards Tenterden. Two miles along that road he turned sharply to the right. He drove for another mile up a B road, then turned left along a stretch of farming track that led across three fields to a small meadow abutted by woodland. Even in the darkness, as Matt struggled to find his way along the lane in the pitch blackness, this was a place full of strong memories. Damien and he had spent a holiday near here when they were about seven, when both of their fathers were still alive. For several days they'd camped, built fires and constructed dams across streams. They were days that Matt still kept among the happiest of his memories. They had been back here a few times together since, in their teens and twenties, when Matt was back on leave from the Regiment. It was their own personal hiding place, somewhere they could come together and get away from their day-to-day life. A place where they could drink beer and just be boys again.

Maybe that was why Matt had chosen to stash some gear here. Sentimental perhaps – but it was as good a spot as any.

And a man never knows when he might need some weapons.

The wood was just as he remembered it. It was hidden away from the road, and although in the distance you could just see the lights of Ashford, it wasn't overlooked by any houses. The nearest farm building was at least three miles away. Safe, secret, and hidden away. Perfect.

A gust of wind lashed his face as he stepped out of the car. He collected a spade from the boot and walked silently across the ground, counting out the trees. It was the fourth one along from the fence that he wanted. He stepped behind it, kicking his shoe in the mud. It had been churned up by some rain during the day. He knelt, digging his hands into the ground, starting to scratch away at the surface. Nothing had been disturbed. It would be just as they had left it.

It was hard not to think of Damien as he dug. He could see the face and hear the words of his friend as he worked. He had only ever been here with him, and the wood was fresh and alive with his friend's memories. If Damien had a ghost, it would be these woods he would haunt.

The box was just where they had left it: a four-foot green metal ammunition box they had picked up in an army surplus store in Ashford. Matt pulled it free of the trench. From his wallet, he pulled out a tiny padlock key and slid it into the lock. The padlock came away smoothly in his hand. He lifted the open case, glancing inside. The gear was all there – a Beretta 92FS pistol and a Browning 9mm, complete with ten magazines of ammunition each, plus ten sticks of dynamite, a pair of sticks of C4 explosive, complete with detonators. It was material Damien had acquired, and decided to put it in a safe place in case they ever needed it.

Matt picked the Beretta up, feeling its weight in his hand. It had seemed a bit of a joke at the time they had stashed this stuff away: Damien might have expected to be on the run one day, but Matt had been still a loyal soldier in Her Majesty's Armed Forces, and never expected to be doing anything illegal. Still, he had figured there was no harm in stashing a weapon away: everyone in the Regiment knew that old retired soldiers went into the security game, and a gun might come in handy in that business. 'You were right,' said Matt, muttering the words out loud to his dead friend. 'A man never knows when he needs a pistol and a few rounds of ammo.'

He stuffed the gun into the pocket of his jacket, took the spade and walked back to the car. He collected the bags from the car, walked into the woods a few yards, and started digging. The trench, he reckoned, needed to be three to four feet deep: far enough underground that some stray dog wouldn't start sniffing it, but not so far down that it might be impossible to retrieve later.

The money would be hidden for just two days.

Until I have dealt with Ivan, and until Reid can collect his share. Until the day we agreed we'd meet up and share out the spoils of our war.

He pitched his spade into the earth, slamming it down to break open the mud. Shovelling was hard, heavy work, even in the cold of night. After a few spadefuls Matt cast aside his coat, sweat forming on his brow as he dug. After twenty minutes, the hole was complete: a neat trench, four feet long and three feet deep. Well, thought Matt, looking down into the pit, this is the spot. In Bideford we said we'd put the money here if anything went wrong, and I'm sticking to that plan.

Time to bury the treasure.

Sallum trained his binoculars on to the edge of the fence. It was dark, but there was just enough light in the sky for him to see what was going on. Rami was crouching down low, the pliers in his hand, cutting his way swiftly through the wire mesh. The boy gripped a handful of steel and tore at it as if it were a piece of paper. Smart, thought Sallum, a wry smile playing across his lips. If you want to make absolutely sure you trigger the alarms, that's the way to do it.

He could see the boy push himself through the hole he'd made, making his body small, and wriggle across the dry earth. His shirt snagged on the wire and he had to turn to rip the cloth free. Then he stood, looking towards the house forty yards away. The land between was covered in immaculate lawn and flowerbeds, with two fountains closer to the building. It had been designed carefully, Sallum observed from his perch high on the hill. Between the fence and the house there was no cover a man could use. Any obstacles that would restrict the line of sight of the guards had been stripped away. All Rami could do was crawl slowly along the ground, keep his head down, and hope for the best.

He has faith, Sallum reflected. That will give him the courage.

He watched as Rami started to crawl forwards. The rifle was still slung over his back, and his hands were moving swiftly across the ground. Up ahead, at the side entrance to the house, Sallum could see the door swinging open. He switched his binoculars up an inch, focusing on the man emerging from the house. About six feet tall, he was dressed in jeans and sweatshirt, with black body armour strapped around his chest and a pistol in one hand, a rifle hung across his shoulders and a knife tucked into the buckle of his belt. He was twenty yards from where Rami was crawling forwards, ignorant of his presence.

You can protect yourself against most forms of attack, Sallum thought, watching as Reid approached the boy – but you can't protect yourself against a man who is committing suicide. The ultimate price will always claim the ultimate victory.

Sallum checked both his P7 pistols were secured to his body and fully loaded. He unclasped a knife from his belt, holding it in his hand, then started moving swiftly down the side of the hill.

Time to sever another limb.

There were only a few customers at the Road Chef service station on the M20. Matt sat down at a plastic table, ordered himself a full English breakfast with extra toast and coffee, and glanced through the restaurant. A few truckers, stopping off after bringing their trucks off the ferries, a few stray German and Dutch tourists, and one young family who, from the noise the kids were making, were on their way to Disneyland Paris.

He checked his watch – just after five-twenty in the morning. He scanned the restaurant to check no one was watching him. It was still impossible to say whether Ivan had put a trail on him or not.

After burying the loot, Matt had climbed back into the car and started driving. He had called Reid briefly to let him know the transfer had gone smoothly, and that the money was safely stashed away in the location they'd agreed upon down in Bideford. He'd given him precise co-ordinates of the location and directions of how to find it; if anything happened to him in the next few hours, the money belonged to Reid and his family.

Reid had been furious with him for slipping away, bursting into a rage and hurling a thousand insults at him, but eventually calming down when he realised that the money was safe – and that Matt wouldn't be calling if he'd been planning to steal it. Still, Matt had been grateful to hear he was still alive, and as he talked to him he'd become more certain that Ivan must be the traitor among them. If it was Reid, he wouldn't have been so desperate to protect his family – there would be nothing to protect them from. And there had been no more hits on the gang since they'd told the Irishman to get lost.

The food arrived at the table: a steaming plate of sausages, bacon, eggs and fried potatoes. Matt took a gulp of coffee and stuffed down a couple of mouthfuls of bacon, then he pushed the plate away. The more he thought about it, the more likely it seemed that Ivan or his accomplice was about to hit him.

When you feel certain someone might be about to try and kill you, it's funny how your appetite abandons you.

Matt checked his watch again. Five twenty-eight. He watched the faces of the people in the restaurant. A pair of truckers had just walked in, one glancing through a copy of the *Express*, the other talking on his mobile. No sign of Ivan. I suppose he might not come himself, he thought. He'll send his accomplice, whoever that might be: some psychotic kicked out of the IRA for excessive cruelty. It could be any of these people here, just sitting, eating their breakfast, silently preparing the bullet that will kill me or polishing the blade that will slit my throat.

Five-thirty. Matt reached for a slice of toast and started chewing on it. His throat felt dry and it was difficult to swallow. Fights he could handle – it was the waiting he hated, the moments of silence and reflection before the inevitable conflict.

He tried Gill on the mobile. He knew it was early in the morning in Spain, but he wanted to hear from her: not to ask her to take him back – he was starting to give up hope on that – but just to make sure she was OK. He needed to hear the sound of her voice.

Why isn't she answering? he asked himself as he hung up on the twentieth ring.

Five thirty-four. One of the truckers was glancing up in Matt's direction. Is it you? he asked himself. His eyes flickered towards one of the tourists. You? Or that family – maybe the kids are just cover, maybe you're planning to knife me in the car park.

In his jacket pocket, Matt was fingering the cold, steel case of the Beretta. Come out of the shadows, Ivan, he muttered to himself. Let's get this done.

He tried another piece of toast but found himself incapable of swallowing anything and spat the food out. Walking across to the payphone, he slipped some coins into the box then punched the number into the keypad. He listened to the slow, insistent ringing of the phone. In his mind, he could see the dark corridor in Hammersmith of the IRA safe house, Whitson's body rotting somewhere and Ivan pacing around or playing another stupid game of bridge on the computer. Answer the phone, man, Matt repeated to himself. I know you're there.

He hung up the phone on the twentieth ring, pressing re-dial instantly. The ringing tone again. Still no reply. Then he punched in the mobile number for Ivan, waited for the connection, and hung up when he heard the familiar voicemail message kick in.

Okay, Ivan, he thought to himself, we'll play it your way. If you won't come and get me, I'll just have to come and get you.

Sallum moved closer to the perimeter of the fence, making little sound as he walked. He kept his eyes trained on Rami, still crouching on the ground, still unaware of the man from the house walking towards him. Their confrontation could only be a few seconds away. This was the moment to strike.

A shot rang out, the sound piercing the still of the dawn. Sallum glanced up. Rami had fired, but missed. A mistake.

In any gun battle, the man who shoots first is almost always the loser.

Sallum ducked silently through the hole Rami had cut in the fence. He swerved to the right, intending to approach the house from the back while Rami was still distracting the man at the front of the house. He was dressed completely in black, no more visible in the darkness than a shadow flickering across the ground. Looking up towards the house, he realised that it occupied maybe five thousand square feet: a massive building, and he would have only a few minutes inside to find and kill the family while the man was distracted by Rami.

He could hear another shot. He couldn't see, but he knew it meant either Rami was protecting his position, or he had lost the initiative. It could only be a matter of moments before he was killed.

No matter. His work was done, and his sacrifice worthwhile.

The door from which the man had exited the house had been left ajar, just as Sallum had expected it to be. A man who sees an assailant on his way to kill him and his family doesn't have time to fish around for keys or shut doors behind him; he wants to leave a quick way back for himself should he need it.

Sallum heard the sound of another shot, then a scream. Rami had been hit but not killed. Over the years, Sallum had learnt to distinguish the screams of a wounded man and a dying man. The boy was young and strong, and could take a couple more bullets – *there was time left*.

Sallum slipped inside the building. He moved through the kitchen towards the main living room. Nobody there. He ran upstairs – that was where the family would be sleeping. He checked two bedrooms, both empty. In the third, the woman was sitting up in bed, a sheet raised to cover her body. The two children were lying at her side, both of them asleep. Her blue eyes moved up, meeting his. He could see the fear, but also confusion, terror. Silently, without moving her lips, she was pleading for mercy – but she already knew she would be rejected.

Sallum smiled, raised the silenced P7 and aimed. He knew the noise might alert the man downstairs to what was happening, but it would be too late for him to do anything about it.

He could see the woman moving instinctively to protect not herself but her children; she seemed to want to lie across them like a warm, smothering blanket.

The gun jumped in Sallum's hand as he fired first once, then twice.

The first bullet hit her just above the left eye, sending her head spinning and a splash of blood colliding with the back wall. The second bullet hit her on the left breast, smashing into her heart. Blood started to seep from the open wound as she slumped forward.

Both the children woke up. They instinctively clung to their mother, breathless and confused, unable to comprehend what had just happened. Sallum stepped towards the bed.

They are small. One bullet will be enough for each of them.

He stood next to the bed, pointed the gun, fired once, then twice. Both children were killed instantly. Their bodies slumped across the bed, still clasped to their mother. The boy was still holding a toy, and the girl had a dummy in her mouth. Neither seemed to have had any idea what was happening.

Sallum spent a moment admiring the delicate, soft purity of their skins.

For infidel robbers there can be no mercy. Not even for their children.

He walked to the window and looked towards the lawn. He could see Rami's body lying out on the grass, the man leaning over him, checking he was dead.

Sallum crept into the space behind the door, waiting. After a few seconds he heard the sound of the door slamming, then a man's footsteps on the staircase.

'Jane?' the voice rang out from the hallway. 'Jane? Are you OK?'

The man came through the door. He looked towards the bed, his eyes darting from body to body. Blood was by now dripping from the sheets, running some of the way towards the bathroom.

The man froze.

Sallum emerged silently and his hand circled the man's neck. Both men were the same height, but Sallum was slightly heavier and had more strength in his shoulders. He jabbed the silenced P7 tight into the man's neck. 'Their death is the first part of your punishment,' he said. 'The second part will follow – but I will allow you a few moments to reflect on what has happened to your wife and children before you die.'

Sallum squeezed tighter on Reid's neck, choking off the flow of air to his lungs. Reid was struggling to free himself, but Sallum's grip was tight, and without oxygen it was impossible to summon the strength to break free.

'Repeat these words,' said Sallum. '*Allahummagh fir-lee warr hamnee wah-dini warr zug-ni.*'

'Fuck off.'

'Would you like me to translate for you?'

'Fuck off you murdering Arab pig.'

'O Allah, forgive me, have mercy on me, guide me aright and grant me sustenance,' said Sallum, his voice touched with laughter. 'It is the dua that is always taught to a new Muslim. I thought you might like to convert, seeing as you're about to meet Allah. For he is a merciful God, and is always ready to greet a sinner who repents. Even scum like you.'

The man roared in anger, jabbing his elbow backwards and catching Sallum in the chest. Sallum's hand fell free from the neck and the man started to spin on his heels, his arm swinging out to grab Sallum's hand. Sallum rocked momentarily backwards on his heels before regaining his balance. He squeezed the trigger on the P7, blowing a hole through the man's neck. Blood and skin splashed on to the floor. Sallum pulled the trigger again, hitting his enemy just below the mouth. The lower part of the jaw was blown away, the bone splintering in different directions.

The man's legs buckled and he dropped to the floor.

Sallum tucked the pistol back into his pocket, stepping away from the body. From another pocket he took out a thin painter's brush. He dipped it into the pool of blood on the floor, and started writing on the wall.

Another limb severed. Two more to go. Then my work will be done.

NINETEEN

Matt walked alone through Regent's Park. It was just after ten in the morning, and apart from a couple of mums out for a walk with their children the place was empty. Heavy clouds were hanging in the sky and some light drizzle was falling into his face as he marched along the pathway.

He had driven straight back up to London after leaving the Road Chef on the M20. He didn't want to go to his flat, and he didn't want to be seen anywhere he might be recognised. So he'd dumped the car at an Avis office, grabbed a coffee, and come for a walk.

Maybe I should just go and take the money for myself. Clear off somewhere, change my name, fix my face and start a new life. After all, it isn't as if I have Gill to worry about any more.

Matt found his thoughts returning to the past. During his six-month selection for the Regiment, after a brutal two weeks of training, he had decided he'd had enough, that he couldn't take any more. For days he had been hiking across mountains, getting shot at, sleeping in open countryside with nothing to consume apart from a few biscuits and some spring water. He went home for the weekend, and decided not to go back. It was Damien and Gill who had persuaded him to return, telling him that he had no choice but to persevere, that he would never forgive himself if he didn't.

They aren't here for me any more.

Another time, during his first tour of duty in Northern Ireland, he'd suffered from a bad bout of what the shrinks would call post-traumatic stress, and the guys in the Regiment would call an attack of the shakes. Three of them had been out on patrol in border country, when they were ambushed by a Provo hit squad. They had been pinned down for ten minutes, coming under sustained fire, before one of them volunteered to break out by rushing their attacker. Matt had been more terrified than he could have imagined possible: his guts had been heaving, he'd thrown up three times, and his fingers wouldn't stop shaking for long enough for him to load his gun.

Those had been bad, low moments. But this was worse. This time he was alone.

Sallum collected his case from the carousel and walked swiftly towards customs. The flight from Malaga to Manchester had taken two hours, fifteen minutes, and there was not much time to lose. Assaf wanted to see him before lunch. It was eleven now. If he picked up a rental car in the next few minutes, he should be there in time.

The morning had gone well. Better than he expected.

But there is still some killing time left in the day. A truly holy man can never rest.

He walked slowly through the green customs lane towards passport control. Experience had taught him to walk slightly nervously through customs: exaggerated self-confidence was one of the signs the customs men looked out for in picking out their victims for random searches. Even then, he had little to fear. He never carried any kind of weapon on a plane – he had dumped the P7 into the Mediterranean, and always bought fresh weapons for each hit – and his false Saudi passport was perfectly in order.

The successful assassin keeps risks to an absolute minimum. That way you stay alive.

'Can we see your bag, sir?'

Sallum stopped and looked at the customs officer. His pulse skipped a beat, but he felt certain that the reaction was not visible on his face, his expression remaining calm and impassive. 'Of course,' he replied.

He put his bag down on the counter. It was a simple, black leather case with a combination lock. Sallum put the numbers in place and opened the clasp. The officer opened the bag, taking out its contents one by one: two spare shirts, a pair of Gap chinos and a pair of blue Levis, a black polo jumper, some socks, underpants, a shaving kit, and a copy of the Koran. 'Okay?' said Sallum, replacing the items in the bag.

'You'll have to follow me, sir,' said the officer.

Sallum paused. 'Can you tell me what the problem is?'

The officer looked at him. He was a man of about forty, with thick, black hair and hard, determined eyes. 'Just follow me.'

A set of screens divided the customs area from the back office. Sallum followed the officer – there was, he decided, no choice. Ever since the glorious victory in New York on 11 September 2001 – a day that would surely go down as one of the greatest in human history – every airport in the world had been teeming with armed police, and sometimes special forces soldiers. If he tried to make a break for it, he'd have half a battalion on him within five seconds. There was no other option but to do what he was told.

The officer pointed to a bank of six small rooms, each with a small, high window. From one, Sallum could hear the sound of a woman crying as she was searched. From another, the violent, rough sound of a man resisting arrest. The officer opened a door, and pointed inside. 'Just wait there, sir,' he said quietly. 'Someone will be along to see you in a minute.'

'Why am I being held?' asked Sallum, his voice more insistent this time.

'Just wait there.'

The room measured six feet by four, with grey wallpaper and a neon strip light. There was a simple wooden table and three black plastic chairs. On the table there was a jug of water and a stack of paper cups. Sallum took a sip of water and listened. The woman was still crying, the man overwhelmed and subdued. Somewhere in the distance he could hear men talking, but could catch nothing of what they were saying. He didn't need to. He knew they were talking about him, and what they should do with him next.

Sallum took his mobile from his pocket and considered making a call. No, he told himself. Too dangerous. *They are certain to be listening to every word I say.*

The mobile rang four times in Matt's pocket before he answered it. He sat down on a bench and put the phone to his ear.

'That you?'

Matt recognised the voice instantly – Harry Pointer, Kazanov's sidekick back in Spain. Probably the last person he wanted to hear from. 'Yes,' he replied tersely. 'Everything OK?'

There was a pause. Matt knew what that pause meant, and he steeled himself for the answer. He had heard officers calling the wives and mothers of men who had been killed in action. They always asked if everything was OK, and they always hesitated before delivering the blow. They knew they shouldn't – the rulebook said that if you have bad news, it's always kinder to deliver it quickly – but they couldn't help themselves. Inwardly, they recoiled from the task, and wanted to postpone it as long as possible.

'Bloody hell, Matt, it's like a sodding butcher's shop in here.'

Matt remained silent. Across the park he could see a toddler hassling his mum for some sweets.

'He's dead, isn't he?'

'Of course he's bloody dead,' Pointer snorted. 'The whole bloody family is dead. The wife, the kids – there's blood all over the bedroom, and all the way down the stairs. And there's all these bloody slogans written on the walls. In blood, Matt. Written in blood.'

'What do they say?'

'It says, "A thief was brought to the Prophet four times and his punishments were amputations of the right hand, the left foot, the left hand and then the right foot. On the fifth occasion the Prophet had him killed",' Pointer said, reciting the words written on the bedroom wall. 'Fuck it, Matt. These are complete sodding nutcases.'

'Al-Qaeda,' said Matt. 'Or someone dressing their actions up to look like al-Qaeda.'

Another pause. Matt glanced across the path again. The toddler appeared to have won and was sucking on a new packet of chews.

'I can't believe you're messing with those nutcases,' Pointer continued angrily. 'Mr Kazanov is not going to be pleased, Matt. Not pleased one little bit. We thought you were just hiding away from some local gangster. Not sodding al-Qaeda.'

'We're all ex-SAS, Harry,' said Matt.

'So what?' Pointer snarled, his voice rising with anger. 'Mr Kasanov is not going to be pleased, Matt. Bringing al-Qaeda into his house. He doesn't need that kind of enemy.'

'Frankly, there are so many people trying to kill me right now, you'll have to form a queue.'

'You might think it's funny, Matt, but Kazanov won't.'

'How the fuck did they get in, Harry?' Matt asked.

'Looks like a decoy,' said Pointer. 'There's a hole in the fence, and a young guy dead on the lawn.'

'Listen, just do one thing for me,' he said.

Matt could hear Pointer laughing. 'The favour jar is empty,' he said. 'Don't even ask.'

'Whoever did this, I want to catch them, and finish them,' said Matt. 'So do you.'

Pointer snorted. 'You're not winning me round.'

'Come on,' said Matt, his voice quickening. 'I just want to catch these guys and deal with them for you. Your video cameras should have recorded the whole thing. Just get me the tape of what happened.'

'What will you do with it?'

'Just get me the tape, Harry,' said Matt, his voice growing more insistent. 'I'll identify whoever is on it, then I'll kill him. And Kazanov can have his half-million back. The money's all there, so long as I can stay alive long enough to deliver it.'

'One tape, Matt, that's it,' said Harry. 'Call me back in a couple of hours.'

'Thanks, Harry.'

'Oh, and Matt, one more thing,' Pointer said. 'Give me an address for your funeral. I'd like to send a wreath.'

Matt disconnected the call and slipped the phone back into his pocket. The rain was falling more heavily now, the water dripping off his hair and down the back of his neck. The first lesson he had learned in the

Regiment, and maybe the most valuable one, was to curb and control his anger. To channel it in the right direction. To make sure that vengeance, when it came, was deadly, accurate and precise.

There will be time for grieving for Reid and his family later. After their killer has been dealt with.

Matt stood up from the bench and started walking. There had been five of them to start with, and now three of them were dead. In the next couple of hours he could take that down to one. It was time for some payback.

Sallum tapped his fingers against the table. The woman in the next room had been released and the row of interview cubicles had fallen silent. It was quarter past twelve according to the clock on the wall. They had kept him waiting for an hour already. There was no way he was going to make it to see Assaf before lunchtime now.

Of all the virtues the Prophet has taught his children, patience in the face of adversity is the greatest of them all.

Sallum looked up as the door opened. The man who came into the room was in his mid-thirties, with cropped blond hair and a tie loosened around his neck. His name was Ben Harper, according to the plastic name-tag slung around his neck. Without introducing himself, he sat down at the table opposite Sallum, a sheaf of papers in front of him.

'What's your name?' he asked, looking directly at Sallum.

'With respect, you know my name,' replied Sallum. 'Otherwise I wouldn't be here.'

'Nasir bin Sallum,' said Harper. 'Thirty-two, Saudi citizen, a businessman.'

This is just the warm-up act, observed Sallum. They'll send the comedian later.

'Why are you in Manchester?'

'Working.'

'What kind of work?'

'Like it says on the papers, I'm a businessman,' replied Sallum. 'Business work.'

'What business?' said Harper impatiently.

'I import football shirts to Saudi Arabia,' said Sallum. 'Manchester United, Liverpool, Newcastle. There are even some Bolton supporters in Saudi. I'm here to see some of the suppliers.'

'And in Spain?'

'Same thing,' said Sallum with a shrug. 'English football shirts. Spanish. We sell some German and French ones as well. European football is very popular in my country.'

Harper leant forward. 'It sounds like a good cover.'

'Really?' Sallum answered casually. 'To me it sounds like a good, solid business.'

Harper stood up. 'You wait here,' he said. 'A colleague will be along to question you some more later.'

'What's the charge?'

'No charges, just questioning,' said Harper.

'Then why are you holding me?'

Harper stood by the door. 'Prevention of Terrorism Act,' he said. 'We can hold you for three days, no charges. So shut up and get used to it.'

Matt walked from Hammersmith tube out into the Broadway. Traffic was flying around the roundabout and a thick layer of dark clouds had settled across the sky. He crossed the roundabout, dodging the cars, then started walking along King Street. The place was full of morning shoppers, but Matt kept his head down, ignoring everyone. This was not a moment to allow himself any distractions.

Before getting on the tube he had tried Gill again, but there was no answer at her flat. He'd called the school and spoken to Sandy, but she said Gill wasn't there, hadn't been in for a couple of days, and she didn't know where she was or what she might be doing. Maybe getting over the bastard who broke her heart by cancelling the wedding, she'd added acidly before hanging up the phone.

Women, reflected Matt. Now there's a Regiment that really knows how to fight for one another.

Cross one, and you take on the whole damned army.

Next he'd tried Janey at the Last Trumpet. Everyone at the bar was fine, she told him. Business was OK for the time of year: they were between the Christmas and Easter rushes, so it was quiet but no more than she would expect. Some men had been in looking for him. Any sign of Gill? Matt had asked, cutting through the small talk. No, answered Janey.

Hadn't been in, and no mention of her. Can you look? asked Matt. Ask the regulars in the bar, check with the local police, try anything you can. What's up? Janey had asked. Nothing, said Matt. Just trying to track her.

He could tell she didn't believe him.

It's not like Gill, Matt thought, turning up one of the side streets towards Ravenscourt Park. She wouldn't just take off like that. She wouldn't stop going into school without telling Sandy where she was and why. He could feel his heart sinking as he ran the calculations through his mind. They'd got to everyone else. Why not Gill as well?

Number sixteen Cedar Road looked no different from the last time he had seen it. The same peeling paintwork on the door, the same overflowing rubbish bins in the scruffy front garden. Matt pressed hard on the doorbell, then hammered at the door with the knocker. He knew exactly what he was going to say. It was time to get this finished.

'Christ, no need to wake up the whole bloody neighbourhood,' said Ivan, holding the door open.

Ivan was never a good-looking man. His eyes sloped away from his forehead, and his skin was blotchy and pale. But he looked worse now, Matt noticed. Like he hadn't been out for days, like he hadn't eaten – like he'd been cooped up with only a dead body for company. 'You look terrible,' said Matt. 'And in about five minutes you're going to look a lot worse.'

'Remind me to blackball you from the bridge club,'

said Ivan. 'We'll wait until you polish up your social skills.'

'Don't smart-talk me,' Matt snapped, and stepped inside. The hallway had the same musty, decayed smell he recognised from the last time he'd been here. Underneath the floorboards, Keith Whitson's body was probably starting to rot from the bones, filling the rooms with the sickly perfume of death.

'I want some answers and I want them now,' Matt said. 'No fooling around, no double talk.' He took the Beretta from his pocket, holding it in his fist. 'You mess with me any more, I kill you.'

Ivan looked into his eyes, his expression switching between sympathy and contempt. He raised one hand, then walked through to the kitchen. Next to the sink, Matt could see a pile of unwashed plates, saucepans and coffee cups. On the table, the remains of some breakfast cereal were still lying in a bowl. Next to it a laptop was open, a bridge game displayed on its screen. Ivan leant over, thought for a second, then pressed a key, making the cards move. A smile flickered across his face. 'You know what?' he said, looking up. 'A good bridge player always keeps one trump card up his sleeve.'

He walked away from the table and stood directly in front of Matt. 'Reid is dead, isn't he?' he said flatly. 'I'm sorry. He might have been SAS but he seemed like a straight enough sort of guy.'

Matt's fist hammered straight into Ivan's stomach. He doubled over in pain, coughing, then pulled himself up, his expression indifferent. 'One of these days a little light is going to go off in your head, Matt,' he said calmly.

Matt delivered a swift uppercut, his knuckles knocking into the stubble of Ivan's jaw. The man reeled backwards under the force of the blow, wobbling on his feet, his arms flailing outwards to regain his balance. He took two steps back, rubbing his jaw with his hand: his lip had opened up and a trickle of blood had started to dribble down his chin.

'I told you, no clever talk,' Matt shouted. 'Just the truth.'

'OK,' said Ivan with a shrug. 'The truth is I've been here for the last five days, ever since Whitson died. I'm just lying low until you tell me our money is ready to collect. I haven't been out, and I haven't spoken to anyone. I don't know where you or Reid went. I didn't have anything to do with his death. That's the truth, plain and simple. You can take it or leave it.'

'Then how did you know he was dead just now?' Matt snarled.

Ivan tapped the side of his head. 'I have a brain in here somewhere, despite your best efforts to punch it out of me. I can still add two and two together and get the right answer. If Reid wasn't dead, you wouldn't be here.'

'You told me your family had been picked up by the Provos, but that was a lie,' said Matt. 'You've lied about everything right from the start.'

'Who told you that?' said Ivan cautiously.

'Alison.'

'Interesting,' answered Ivan.

'There were five us when we started, now there are two,' Matt continued angrily. 'Only the two of us knew who was in the gang, and where we all were. It's not me, so it has to be you.'

'I didn't even know where you and Reid were,' Ivan answered, his tone turning patronising. 'You already decided it was me days ago. Two more men have died since then. I even knew when and where the money was being fenced, and I didn't move out of this house. When are you going to realise, you and I are on the same side now?'

Matt held the Beretta up, pointing it directly at Ivan. 'If not you, then who?' he said. 'If you can't answer that question, I'm going to kill you right now.'

'Like I just said, a trump card,' said Ivan, smiling. He held up a micro-cassette. 'This is mine. It will tell you who's responsible for Cooksley's, Damien's and Reid's death, and who will probably be responsible for your death and mine before the week is out.' He paused, dangling the tape in front of Matt's eyes. 'Want to listen to it?'

Sallum first saw the woman through the tiny window of the cubicle. He had been waiting for three hours, sitting alone, with nothing to look at but four grey walls. The minutes had ticked slowly by, each one allowing him to make a calculation. Whoever they were sending to see him, she probably came from London. The local police wouldn't take this long to get here. That meant MI5.

I'm in more trouble than I thought.

He examined the woman as she stepped through the door. Like many European females, he observed, there was hardly an ounce of womanly flesh on her. She was tall and thin, with blonde hair that tumbled down the back of her neck. Her face was painted with lipstick and mascara, but the femininity of her appearance was all just decoration, Sallum judged: beneath the perfume and the lipstick, she would be made from metal as tough as any man's.

Only the sickest, most decadent of societies would turn a woman into a warrior. That is a man's work.

Harper stood behind her, remaining silent. 'Good afternoon,' the woman said, sitting down at the desk, looking coldly across at Sallum. 'My name is Alison Hammond.'

Sallum nodded. He could disapprove of a working woman, but he would not underestimate her. 'Why am I being held?'

'Prevention of Terrorism Act,' said Alison curtly. 'I think you have already been told that.'

'I am not a terrorist.'

'That's for you to prove, and me to judge,' answered Alison. 'Why are you in Manchester?'

'On business.'

'What business?'

'I've been through that with your colleague,' Sallum snapped. 'Why don't you ask him?'

'I like the sound of your voice,' said Alison. 'So you tell me, please.'

'Import, export,' answered Sallum. 'All perfectly legitimate. You can look at the records if you like. The Saudi embassy will be happy to help you.'

Alison unfolded the pad on the desk, then took out a photograph from a plain brown envelope and pushed it across the desk. It was a shot of Cooksley, taken when he was still in the Regiment, but showing only his head, and dressed in civilian clothes. 'Recognise this man?'

Sallum glanced downwards. He blinked. Then he realised that he'd been caught with his guard down – he had paused, and that had been a mistake. He looked back up at Alison, meeting her eyes with a stare of pure stone. 'No.'

Alison pushed another picture across the desk: Reid, in Regimental uniform. 'How about him?'

This time, Sallum didn't pause. 'No.'

'I don't think you looked at it properly,' Alison replied.

Sallum picked the photograph up with his fingers, holding it to the light, his eyes squinting. 'No.'

'Or these men?' Alison pushed across pictures of Damien, Ivan and Matt. Sallum scrutinised each one in turn, shaking his head. 'I'm sorry,' he said slowly. 'I'd like to help you, but I have never seen any of these men in my life.'

Alison nodded. Her eyes moved up to meet his, and he could tell she was scrutinising him, trying to break through the impassive exterior to find out what was happening within. But his mind was encased within walls of steel, and she would never break through.

You can't read me, infidel, any more than you could read ancient Egyptian hieroglyphics. I'm not from your world, and you know nothing about me.

'Let him go,' said Alison, looking up towards Harper. She glanced towards Sallum, her expression somewhere between a smile and a frown. 'We're sorry to have detained you, Mr bin Sallum. Have a good day.'

TWENTY

Matt held the tape in his hand, a tiny piece of plastic, weighing less than a box of matches. 'OK,' he said, looking across at Ivan, 'play it.'

From the sideboard Ivan picked up a dictaphone and slotted the tape into position. He pressed play. Matt could hear a voice talking, and the unidentifiable sound of some machines in the background. The voice was speaking Arabic, he could tell that much, but his knowledge of the language was so limited he couldn't pick up the meaning of a single word.

'Recognise it?' asked Ivan.

Matt nodded. 'It's the tape Alison played to us in the hotel room, the one she's been looking for,' he answered. 'The al-Qaeda boys in the boat phoning home. Where the hell did you get it?'

'She left it on the table and I slipped it into my pocket when she wasn't looking,' said Ivan. 'You never know when these things might come in useful. It's the one thing I haven't been honest with you about.'

'It was unprofessional of her to leave it out,' said Matt.

'Exactly,' said Ivan. 'That's what I thought. She just

left the tape on the table, like she wasn't bothered what happened to it. You don't speak Arabic do you?'

Matt shook his head. 'Do you?'

'No,' said Ivan. 'But she knew that when she played us the tape. None of us would understand what it said. So I had it translated.' He handed another tape to Matt. 'Want to listen to it?'

Matt took the tape and slotted it into the machine. A voice started up: a slight Arab accent, but speaking English with a London accent. It was the kind of voice you would hear in any kebab shop in Acton. 'I would like to order two tickets to Cairo. I want to book return flights, business class, going out early in the morning on the tenth, then coming back on the eighteenth. I'm going to need a car rental at the airport and a hotel in the city.'

Ivan walked across the room and pressed his finger on the tape machine. The voice stopped. 'It's just some guy booking tickets to Egypt at one of the Arab travel shops along the Edgware Road.'

Matt lifted the Beretta, levelling it directly at Ivan's forehead. He released the safety catch. 'You're lying.'

Ivan stepped forward, bringing his forehead into contact with the barrel of the gun. 'Listen you bloody fool, it's Alison,' he said, spitting the words out of his mouth. 'She's been setting us up all along.'

Sallum slammed the door of the rented Golf. He stepped out into the car park, looking around him. He believed he hadn't been followed, but it never hurt to check once again. The mark of a great assassin is his attention to detail.

Assaf was standing twenty yards away, outside a phone box. Sallum walked slowly towards him, his eyes darting from right to left. As far as he could tell, the man was alone. 'Sorry for the delay,' he said, looking into the eyes of his master. 'I was taken in for questioning at the airport.'

'I know,' said Assaf. 'Are you certain you weren't followed?'

Sallum nodded. After being released from the airport, he had taken a taxi into Manchester, a bus up to Preston, then hired a car and driven down towards Birmingham. At each stage of the journey he had carefully checked his trail, watching for anyone who might be following him. He had doubled back and twisted around on himself – usually that revealed a tracker. He had bought a ticket for Coventry, then hopped on the Preston bus: that should confuse anyone following him by computer. He had checked into a hotel for an hour, showered, then checked into a branch of Next to buy himself a completely new set of clothes and luggage: he wanted to make sure they hadn't planted any electronic devices on him. If he was being followed, he had surely lost them.

'I have taken every precaution I could think of,' Sallum answered.

Assaf was a commanding man, with a natural sense of authority. His voice was deep and balanced, each vowel perfectly pitched for the desired impact. 'Did they know who you were?'

Before driving down to Birmingham Sallum had phoned Assaf, leaving a message with his secretary that they should meet in the car park of the Toby Inn, on the A518, just off the M5 between Birmingham and Manchester. He'd made the call from a phone box: if he was being followed, a mobile call could easily be tracked. It was now just before eight. It was dark, a light rain was falling, and the only witnesses to their meeting were a few people parking their cars and heading into the pub. Nobody was likely to overhear them.

'I think so. She showed me pictures of the five men – the three who are dead and the two who are still alive.' He looked up at Assaf, scrutinising his face. 'Something isn't right. How could they possibly know it was me? And if they know, why would they let me go?'

Assaf shrugged. 'Maybe they are just fishing around, stopping Arabs at random and showing them the pictures in the hope of shaking something loose. Ever since the glorious events of September the eleventh they have been persecuting Saudis.'

'Yes, but maybe they do know something,' persisted Sallum. 'How did we get that list of men? It was only a day or two after the robbery, and we already knew exactly who was responsible.'

'Out of the network,' said Assaf. 'A man in the mosque in Solihull. A low-level sympathiser. British intelligence think they turned him, he informed on us and collected a couple of hundred a week for his trouble. Actually, he's double-crossing them. We know he's an informer, and we use him to feed them false information. Let them spend their time arresting news-agents in Hendon! *He* told us their names.'

'Do you think he's a triple, then?'

Assaf shrugged. 'It had occurred to me,' he said. 'But they let you go, didn't they?'

Sallum turned around, speaking with his back to Assaf. In the service of a cause as great as this, there were many sacrifices that had to be made. Sometimes including your own honour, your dignity, even your life.

The task of a true servant of the Prophet is to accept all without question.

'Let me get this straight,' he said. 'You're saying MI5 organised the hit on our boat. Then they give the information to this agent in Solihull, who they know is double-crossing them. So he tells you, and then you go and send me to assassinate the men. They are watching all the time, and that leads them to me.' He paused, his eyes scanning the car park with new vigour. 'And I lead them to you.'

'Clever, you have to admit that,' said Assaf.

Sallum turned to look at him. 'I care nothing for myself, you know that,' he said. 'If it is necessary to lay down my life for the cause, I make no complaint about that. But to let me lead them to you . . . Without you, the whole network in this country would fall apart.'

Assaf smiled. 'You are a good man, but you worry too much,' he said. 'I was aware of what their plan might be. Of course I was. But as the information was offered, I had no choice but to act upon it. Men cannot be allowed to steal from al-Qaeda and live. That would be intolerable. I had no choice but to send you after them.' He paused, resting a hand on Sallum's shoulder. 'But I trusted your abilities enough to know you were unlikely to lead them to me. I have faith in you, as you should have faith in me, and as we should all have faith in the Prophet to lead us through difficulties.'

Sallum smiled.

The wisdom of the master is what I should surrender myself to.

'What should I do now?'

'They think they can outwit us with their double and triple crosses,' said Assaf. 'But we can out-think all of them, because we have faith and purpose, and they, for all their strength, have nothing but themselves.' He turned and started walking towards his parked car. 'Come with me. The moment of a famous victory is close.'

Acton Lane was thick with rush-hour traffic. Cars snaked and crawled along the road, the sound of the engines turning into one collective groan. Matt walked swiftly along the street, his head turning from side to side. A kebab shop, a mini-cab firm – they were looking for anywhere they might find an Arab who wanted to earn fifty quid without working for it.

'Here,' he said to Ivan.

The two men stepped inside the Paradise Kebab House. A poorly chosen name, Matt reflected as the smell of the place hit him. Some greasy looking meat was turning on a hot skewer and spitting fat. Ranged along the counter there was a selection of cut onions and gherkins, and some stale pitta bread. A couple of likely looking guys were standing at the bar, smoking. Another stood behind the counter. 'Anyone here speak Arabic?' said Matt. 'And want to earn fifty quid for five minutes' work?'

The two men looked at him suspiciously then shuffled out to the street. 'I don't mind, boss,' said the boy at the counter, 'so long as it doesn't get me into trouble with the law.'

Matt shook his head. 'Just listen to this tape and tell me what it says.'

He took the dictaphone from his pocket and placed it on the counter. The voice started up, droning on in Arabic. Matt was starting to find the sounds familiar even though he had no idea what they meant. 'OK,' he said, pressing pause. 'What's he saying?'

'Where's my cash?'

Matt peeled two twenties and a ten from his wallet and pushed them into the boy's hand. 'Well?'

'The guy is booking some travel tickets,' said the boy. 'He's flying to Egypt, and taking an internal flight from there, and he needs some hotel rooms reserved as well. Sounds like he's talking to a travel agent. If you want it word for word then you'll have to play it to me again.'

Matt shook his head. 'That's OK,' he said softly. 'I've heard enough. Give me a doner kebab, and one for my mate as well.'

He turned towards Ivan. The man had remained expressionless throughout the conversation, but somewhere behind his eyes Matt had detected a hint of satisfaction. Matt took a kebab from the boy. The rich, fatty smell of the meat drifted to his nostrils. 'You were right. It's her.'

Assaf pulled the case from the boot of his car and passed it carefully to Sallum. It was a standard black Samsonite attaché case: you could see hundreds of them on any commuter train into the City every morning.

Sallum held it in his hands. It felt heavy – much heavier than he would have expected for a case of its size. 'What's in it?' he asked, looking up at Assaf.

'Plutonium,' said Assaf. 'Not a nuclear device, but three pounds of radioactive plutonium next to a conventional Semtex bomb. The blast will create a radioactive, contaminated area that will be unusable for at least five years.'

Sallum's grip on the case remained firm. 'Am I to deliver it?'

'You are my best man,' Assaf answered. 'The one person I trust absolutely. You know how hard it is for us to obtain any plutonium. I cannot waste it on idiots. Other men will clear the way for you, but you will plant the device, and trigger the detonation.'

It is for moments such as this that we devote ourselves to the cause. Truly, Allah has blessed me with this most noble of tasks.

'What is the target?'

Assaf looked towards the pub, then back at Sallum. A pair of men were walking past ten yards away, and he waited until they were safely out of earshot before replying. 'We plan our targets with great care,' he said. 'We strike rarely, but with maximum force, so as to spread terror and confusion among the enemy. Yet we also operate by stealth – we come at them where they least expect us to strike. This bomb is to be placed at Clapham Junction. It's the biggest railway junction in Europe, and the busiest. It's the one crucial hub for all the people and freight coming into London. After this bomb goes off, nothing will be able to move through the area for at least a year, until the contamination dies down. Radiation will seep into the underground network and down into the water pipes. London will grind to a halt.'

Sallum permitted himself a brief, thin smile. 'That will teach them to underestimate our power.'

'The moment to strike is three nights from now,' said Assaf. 'I will give you a map. Other agents are working in London, and they will clear the way for you. There are twelve security guards protecting the station. Each will be killed at the same moment, five o'clock in the dead of night. Twelve of our agents have been assigned to that task. You will sneak undetected across the tracks and bury the case beneath the track. The bomb will have a thirty-minute timer on it, enough for you to get away from the area, but not enough time for it to be found.'

'I am honoured to be chosen.'

'But first we must deal with the last two of our

thieves,' said Assaf. 'Honour demands that they must die. As soon as I have it from our source, you shall be given the address of their hiding place, and you will go and kill them. Then you will deliver the bomb.'

Sallum looked to the sky. 'In the book of Surah it is written: "Muhammad is God's apostle. Those who follow him are ruthless to the unbelievers." Those are indeed wise words.'

'Your devotion to the way of the faith is an inspiration to us all,' said Assaf. 'May Allah stand at your side through the days ahead of you.'

Sallum nodded, holding the attaché case tightly in his hand, and walked back towards his car.

Of all the missions fate has chosen out for me, this is surely the greatest. Each man reaches his own moment of destiny, and this is mine.

Matt put the phone down, then slammed his fist against the wall. A section of plaster shook loose, sending a cloud of dust into the air. 'The bitch!' he snarled. 'The two-timing, double-crossing bitch.'

'What did she say?' asked Ivan.

The two men had walked back in silence, both of them chewing on their kebabs. Matt had hardly eaten all day, but the food failed to make him feel any better. The anger was growing inside him all the time. It was not just that she was responsible for the deaths of two of his Regimental comrades and his oldest and closest friend. It was that she had turned all that responsibility on to him. Were it not for him, none of them would have been on the mission – and all the time she had been setting them up for assassination.

As soon as they'd got back to the safe house Matt had put a call through to Pointer. He needed the answer to the question he had put to the man earlier: what happened to the video link Alison's MI5 stooge had put into Kazanov's house?

'Shot out,' Matt said, looking back up towards Ivan, 'according to Pointer – and he's got no reason to lie to me. The guy who killed Reid went into the video room and shot the whole place to pieces. He's obviously enough of a professional to know everything would be taped, and he didn't want to leave any evidence behind him.'

Ivan put down the coffee he had just finished brewing. 'Before or after he shot Reid – that's the question,' he said. 'I reckon it has to be afterwards. Think about it. You go inside the house, knowing that Reid has been distracted, and you have a few minutes to kill the wife and kids before killing him. You don't have time to worry about the video cameras.'

Matt poured himself some coffee. 'Right – you deal with it after the killing is done. So long as none of the tape survives, you know it doesn't matter. Would it occur to you that the whole lot was being transmitted back to London?'

'So that's what the Five man was there for,' said Ivan. 'You should have seen that at the time. It was nothing to do with helping you. Alison knew all along the assassin was going to come and get Reid. She just wanted to make sure they had film of him, so they could identify him later. It all fits together.'

'Like a game of bridge.'

'Right. She gets us to hit al-Qaeda,' Ivan said carefully. 'She knows they are going to send their best man after us. She finds some way of leaking who and where we are, knowing their man will go after us. Meanwhile Five are watching, waiting for one slip – then they have him. She didn't care about the robbery, not for a moment. It's the assassin she's after.'

'Christ, I'll tell you why as well,' said Matt. 'She's under a lot of pressure to catch the guy who killed the government minister in Saudi. And she reckons there's a big al-Qaeda spectacular coming up soon in Britain. Five are desperate for some kind of lead.'

'How do you know what she thinks?'

'I slept with her,' said Matt. 'Pillow talk.'

'Not just you, me as well,' said Ivan.

Matt paused. With all that he'd learned in the past few minutes this revelation shouldn't have surprised him – yet he couldn't help but see it as yet another betrayal. It hadn't been serious with Alison, but he hadn't expected her to be both trying to get him killed *and* sleeping with the rest of the gang.

'And I'll tell you what then, pal,' Ivan said, a hoarse laugh rising from his lips, 'it wasn't either of us that screwed her. It was the other way around!'

'Alison here.'

'It's Matt.'

She paused for only a fraction of a second. 'Are you OK?' she said quickly. 'I was really worried about you.'

She's good, thought Matt. The tone, the pause, the small catch in her throat. You could almost believe she really was worried about me.

Like a whore, she knows how to fake any emotion the moment requires.

'You heard about Reid?'

'Yes. I'm really sorry. He was a good guy.'

Matt held the phone tightly. He was sitting in the hallway of the Hammersmith house, his back to the wall. Only one light bulb was on shining in the kitchen, otherwise the house was in darkness. 'The Five man who put in the video link – did you get anything?'

Another pause. 'No,' she replied. 'The first thing the assassin must have done is shot it out.'

Matt nodded into the phone. 'Nothing at all? Not even a few shots of him coming into the compound?'

'No. I'm sorry, Matt. Nothing.'

'OK,' said Matt. 'I was just hoping it might have given us some kind of lead.'

'Whoever he is, he's too good to make a mistake like that,' she said. 'Did you get the money?'

'That's all taken care of,' said Matt. 'We'll be making the split just like we discussed in Bideford.'

'Is there anything I can do to help?'

'Listen, I'm hiding up with Ivan now. I think you should know where I am staying, just in case anything happens to me.'

'Don't talk like that, Matt – you'll be OK.'

'No, I have to be sensible. Three of the gang are dead, and I might be next. If anything happens to me, I'd like you to make sure the money is picked up and goes to my heirs. The Regiment will tell you who the money should go to. We all have to give details of who we want to leave our stuff to, and I haven't changed mine.' He paused, looking across at Ivan and smiling. 'I'm going to send you a text with all the details.'

'All right,' she said softly. 'You look after yourself, Matt. If there's anything we can do to help, just let me know.'

'We're big strong boys,' said Matt. 'We can look after our corner of the playground.'

He cut the call, walked to the kitchen to retrieve his mobile, and started tapping in the details of his address. He pressed send and waited until he knew the text had been sent. 'Well, now she knows where we are,' he said, looking across at Ivan. 'And where we are going as well.'

Ivan smiled. 'I remember when I was still a teenager,' he said, 'when I first signed up with the Provos there was an old guy called Mickey Royle who took me under his wing and showed me some of the ropes. He taught me lots of lessons about survival – but the first one he taught me was this: let the enemy come to you.' He rocked back on his chair, a casual smile on his lips. 'When you go to them, you make yourself vulnerable. You move about, you expose yourself. Much better just to let the opponent come to you. That way you fight on your own territory.'

'I know,' Matt said, smiling. 'I've been one of those targets, remember.'

Sallum stared at the ceiling of the hotel room. In his mind he was reciting verses from the Koran, playing them over and over, drawing strength from the majesty and power of the words of the prophet.

The moment when my soul can be joined with his in heaven. That is what I am working for.

There are many moments of solitude in the professional life of the assassin, and Sallum had grown used to them over the years. When he was by himself, as he was for most of the time, he liked to pray and to study the Koran, cleansing his spirit and his mind afresh for each kill. At night, when he lay the holy book aside, he found himself thinking of his childhood, back in the Saudi wilderness. He was one of twenty children by his father's eight different wives. Although his father had so many different children he could scarcely keep count of them, his mother Saja had not been very fertile, and Nasir had been her only son. His father had quickly lost interest in her – in the hierarchy of his harem she had ranked right at the bottom. He'd showed little interest in Nasir as well, but to his mother he was the only pleasure in an otherwise harsh and disappointing life. She had always been at his side, his constant companion through all his adolescent years, and he still prayed for her and spoke to her every day. It was only after she had died that he had joined the movement. Allah had been the only person he could imagine who could fill his mother's place in his life.

If father could see me now, he would be proud of me. He would know that I am doing his work. He would not ignore me and insult my mother, the way he always did in the past.

The phone rang twice before Sallum answered it. 'Hammersmith, west London – that's where you'll find the last two thieves,' said Assaf. 'Do you know it?'

'What address?'

'Cedar Road,' said Assaf. 'Number sixteen.'

'Allah shall guide us at all times,' said Sallum.

For a moment he thought about the woman who had interviewed him at Manchester airport. Maybe she had realised who he was. Maybe she was trailing him. Maybe this was all a set-up: the next two victims could be planning an ambush. He pushed the thoughts out of his mind. Not helpful, he told himself.

I will do my duty, no matter what the risks to myself.

He rested his head against the pillow. His eyes were starting to shut, and he could feel a sense of calm and peace washing over him as he drifted off to sleep. The cares and anxieties of the day had vanished into the air, and he was able to relax.

It is so much easier for a man to sleep properly at night when he knows who he is going to kill in the morning.

TWENTY-ONE

Observation – the first and most important skill the assassin learns. Unless you have surveyed every inch of the ground you are going to attack, all your weapons and your tactics are useless.

I look, I study, and only then do I strike.

Sallum had walked twice down Cedar Road now. He moved swiftly, with his head down, and changed his overcoat in the car before returning: if anyone was watching, he wanted to make sure he didn't draw any attention to himself. He glanced at number sixteen through the corner of his eye, using the few seconds available to memorise every inch of the building. It was a typical Victorian terraced house, built on two floors, probably with a cellar, and another room in the loft. There was no entry at the sides, and although the front door would come away easily enough under sustained gunfire, it was likely to be well defended.

They are trained soldiers, and they are expecting me. They won't die without a struggle.

Sallum walked on. Dusk was falling, and there were only a few people on the streets. Ash Road ran parallel to Cedar, another row of Victorian terraces, most of them bought up and modernised over the past few years – they all had expensive looking cars outside, and flash new kitchens inside. He walked along the street, counting out each house. Number twenty-two, unless he had made a mistake in his calculations, backed directly on to number sixteen. Unlucky, thought Sallum surveying the ordinary-looking house. But your number is up.

Sallum walked on, allowing himself one more glance over the house. If there were three or four men in there, he had a problem. He headed back towards the car, got in, and pulled out the laptop he kept under the back seat. Hooking up the computer to the mobile phone, he fired up a web connection, then logged on to the electoral roll site used by junk mail companies to compile their mailshots. You needed a password to get in, but Sallum had already signed up for a subscription using a false password.

He tapped the Ash Road house's details into the computer. The information was transmitted down the line, and the answer took almost a minute to appear on the screen. Mrs Westhoff, plus a Celia Westhoff, described as a minor. A mother and a daughter – maybe a divorcee.

She will offer little resistance.

Sallum snapped the computer shut and walked briskly down the road. There was one other person walking along the street, and he waited for them to pass before making his move. He rang once on the doorbell, fingering the P7 in the palm of his hand.

The woman who answered the door looked to be in her early forties, with brown hair tied up behind her head, a loose looking dress, and no shoes. 'Electricity meter,' said Sallum sharply, taking a pace inside the hallway, half-closing the door behind him.

People judge you by your appearance, Sallum reminded himself. So long as you wear new, clean clothes, are clean shaven and smell of soap, they usually trust you. She was wary, but not so wary as to slam the door in his face. 'Your card?' she said, looking at him suspiciously.

He took another pace into the hallway, and dug into his pocket as if searching for his wallet. Then he swung the P7 up and jabbed the barrel of the gun into her forehead. He squeezed the trigger twice, the two bullets smashing through her skull. She dropped to the floor, her knees buckling beneath her. A trickle of blood seeped from the back of her head, draining into the blue carpet that stretched from the hall to the kitchen at the back.

Sallum slammed the door shut, then held the gun up, ready for anybody who might be coming down the stairs to see what had happened. He counted to twenty, then tucked the gun back into his pocket.

At least she was alone, he thought to himself as he stepped over the body. He had executed several children already this week, and he was starting to tire of it. They whimpered and screamed and wriggled. They didn't know what death was.

Throwing two bolts across the front door, Sallum

checked first the kitchen, then the first floor. The master bedroom gave the best view of the houses behind. The neatly trimmed lawn of this house backed on to a wooden fence, then the gardens of Cedar Road. Number sixteen's was a tangled mess of weeds, a few metres of scruffy lawn, a rusted swing, and a huge pile of black plastic rubbish bags.

I imagine the woman I have just killed despaired of the way the neighbours behind keep their garden.

From the kit bag slung over his back, Sallum took out a Hensoldt 6 × 42 sniper rifle sight. The German-manufactured sight, as well as being one of the most expensive telescopic sights in the world, was the only one that fitted the Heckler & Koch PSG-1 sniper rifle that Sallum preferred for shooting at distance. He held the Hensoldt to his right eye. At up to six hundred metres it gave perfect vision; it was less than fifty metres to the house opposite, and he could see straight in. One light was burning in what he took to be the kitchen, and another was visible on the first floor. Scanning the other windows, he couldn't make out any sign of movement.

Never mind, he told himself. They will be there soon.

The smell rose from the body as if it were an open sewer: a harsh, putrid stench of decaying flesh, sweaty clothes and unwashed hair. The skin had started to turn grey, and the limbs were showing signs of softening.

He had seen enough of them in his time, but Matt had never grown used to the scent of a corpse.

'Let's get him upstairs,' said Ivan.

A clump of hair came off in Matt's hand as he grabbed Whitson's head. He cast it aside, lifted the corpse by the shoulders from under the floorboards, and started climbing the stairs. Ivan took the legs and lifted the body clear of the ground. They stopped on the first floor landing, propping Whitson up against the wall. His head slumped forward and one of his eyes fell open. 'The trick is to make him look alive,' said Ivan. 'Back home we used to pull this one regularly on the Army. Get a corpse, make him look like a live one, let the soldiers think they've shot him, and when they come over to inspect the body, you blow them up.' Ivan chuckled. 'Worked like a dream.'

Matt glanced down at Whitson's corpse: he looked like a stiff, and a badly decaying one at that. 'Christ, even when he was alive this bloke looked half-dead.'

'Wash him up, and put some powder on his cheeks, that will freshen him,' said Ivan. 'At a distance, he'll look alive. When you're about to shoot a man, you don't spend a lot of time checking how well he's looking.'

The barrel of the Heckler & Koch PSG-1 would have been just visible at the first floor window: an inch of black metal emerging from a circular hole cut into the glass. The rifle was mounted on a black metal frame that held it perfectly still. Behind it, Sallum stood completely motionless, the lights all switched off around him, his eye level with the Hensoldt sight.

Sallum had played out the sequence of events a hundred times in his head: his preparation was always immaculate, and it was only through constant mental and physical training that he felt certain he could always claim victory over the odds. He would wait here until one of the two men in the house revealed themselves at the window, then he would shoot him with the rifle. When he was dead, he would rush through the garden, scale the fence and start his assault on the building. One man he felt certain he could defeat. That was why it was vital he shot the other one before he went inside.

He glanced down at his watch. It was eleven-fifteen at night, and he had been in position for three hours. His shoulder was starting to ache where the butt of the rifle was jabbing into the muscle, and the skin around his right eye was sore from being pressed against the sight. The waiting, he reflected to himself. That is when our strength is tested.

He glanced up to the sky. A moon was shining down and the stars were burning brightly. Somewhere in the distance he could hear a police car rushing towards Hammersmith Broadway, and down on King Street he could hear some boys getting into a closing-time punch-up. Soon I will be back in the Empty Quarter, in my homeland, he thought to himself. As soon as the railway bomb was delivered, he would leave the country and hide in the Saudi wilderness for a year or more. He longed for the cleanliness and purity of the desert.

A movement – a glimpse of a man's head moving

across the first-floor window. Sallum pressed his eye closer to the sight, keeping his finger poised on the rifle's trigger. A man, definitely – he had vanished from view, but he had looked as if he was heading to the bathroom. That meant he would be back in a minute or two. Sallum composed himself. The moment of attack was approaching.

His mind drifted to thoughts of his friend Atta, who had led the attacks on the Great Satan with such spectacular success on 11 September 2001. A fine, upstanding man, Sallum still regarded him as the noblest individual he had ever met, and envied his martyr's death. He looked forward to being reunited with him and the other fallen comrades in the kingdom of Allah. Just before the attacks, Atta had given each one of the martyrs a notebook to inspire them, and he had given one to Sallum as well. He had memorised it by heart, and one passage leapt into his mind now as he waited for the target to re-emerge.

'Completely forget something called "this life". The time for play is over and the serious time is upon us,' Atta had written. He'd told them to consult the sura of the Koran called al Anfa, or the Spoils of War. Under his breath, Sallum recited the lines Atta had instructed them to commit to memory: '*Remember how they said: "O Allah! If this is indeed the truth from Thee, rain down on us a shower of stones from the sky, or send us a grievous Penalty."* '

Another movement. Even at a distance of fifty metres Sallum could make out a flash of hair, and beneath it the skin of a man's forehead. He steadied his arm, lining up the sights with the man's head, checked that it was perfectly aimed, then softly squeezed the trigger. The bullet exploded from the barrel of the gun, smashing through the window of the house opposite. Glass shattered and Sallum could see the bullet colliding with the head of the man. Through the telescopic sights, he could see fragments of skull splintered against the wall, and body dropping to the ground.

Sallum paused, waiting to see if the target stood up. Nothing. The victory was his, he decided, a smile of professional satisfaction on his face. He unhooked the PSG-1 from its stand, holding it in his right hand, and ran down to the kitchen and out into the garden. He scaled the back fence in one swift movement, landing just next to the rusty swing. The moment for the assault was here.

Four of the thieves are dead, and the fifth man is about to die. The anger of the Prophet will be satiated.

TWENTY-TWO

Alison walked alone through the woods. The trees were swaying in a wind that was picking up speed and force as it blew in through the English Channel and swept across the open Kent countryside. Dark clouds were drifting in from the west, and somewhere in the distance she could hear the rattle of a thunderstorm.

She paused, looking up at the sky. The collar of her green Barbour jacket was hoisted up around her neck, and her throat was protected by a red silk Hermès scarf. Her green wellington boots were almost new, and the mud was sticking to the soles as she trampled across the wet ground. In her hand she was holding a single sheet of paper and a compass. As she walked, she was measuring her paces, as if she was counting them out. She was searching for something.

The mobile rang twice in her pocket. She fished it out and held it to her ear. 'Hi,' she said. 'It's me.'

Her head nodded twice as she listened to the voice on the line. 'We have to be certain they are dead,' she said. 'We have to be certain it was them.' She paused, listening to the reply. 'That's great news. And what about bin Assaf – has he been picked up?' Another pause.

'Great. Without him, the whole network is going to fall apart. If we rough him up enough, we might even get him to tell us who all their people are across Europe. Particularly now he has finished off Matt and Ivan for us, all we need to do is alert every port and airport and border and make sure we pick him up as soon as we can.'

She walked on through the woodland, still holding the phone to her ear, still talking. 'Oh, I'm just collecting some extra funds. Five can always use some extra cash, especially if it's untraceable.' She laughed into the phone. 'Well, yes,' she continued. 'Perhaps a couple of new frocks. After all, when a girl has just cracked the al-Qaeda network in Britain, found the man responsible for murdering a cabinet minister, and prevented a major terrorist incident, I think she's earned a new party dress or two.'

A smile was playing on her lips as she snapped the phone shut and put it back in her pocket. She was reaching a clearing in the woods now. The trees parted into a small semi-circle, with dense foliage covering it, blocking out most of the little sunlight that was managing to break through the clouds. Her pace was quickening, and her eyes were darting from side to side as she scanned the territory laid out in front of her. She looked at the map, then back at the compass, then down on to the ground.

Time to say hello, thought Matt, looking down at her from his vantage point in a tree fifteen yards away.

There aren't many consolations to being a dead man, but the ability to surprise people is one of them.

The mobile rang in Alison's pocket. She paused, put the spade to one side, then held the phone to her ear, pressing the green button as she did so. 'Yes,' she said, a trace of irritation in her voice. 'Who is it?'

'Stay perfectly still,' said Matt. 'You're standing right on top of two pounds of Semtex. If you move a single muscle, it's going to blow that pretty body of yours into a thousand pieces. People will be scraping bits of you off car windscreens all the way down in Brighton.'

Alison froze. It was as if every nerve in her body had been switched off. Her limbs were motionless, and even her eyelashes appeared to have stopped blinking. From her mouth, a few traces of breath could be seen in the cold air. 'Matt,' she said cautiously, straightening up as she spoke. 'Is that you?'

Matt swung down from the tree, hitting the ground gracefully. He had been up there for three hours, perched on a damp and sagging branch, and the cold and the wind had started cutting through his overcoat, biting into his skin. He rubbed his hands together to get the blood flowing through his veins again. Ivan landed at his side, his knees buckling beneath him as he hit the ground. He straightened himself up, glanced towards Matt and smiled. 'I think we've got her right where we want her,' he whispered.

Both men started walking the twenty yards towards where Alison was standing.

Matt looked into her sharp, blue eyes. He had been wondering how he might feel at this moment. He imagined he might be angry, furious, shouting at her and seeking explanations and revenge. But now that he was confronting her, all of those emotions had evaporated. As he looked at her, he felt only the indifference a soldier feels towards the enemy.

He stopped a few yards short of where she was standing. 'Your sources must have let you down.'

'I can see that,' answered Alison softly. She started to move forward.

'Don't move,' barked Matt.

'What the hell am I standing on?'

'Semtex, he already told you that,' said Ivan. 'Rigged up to a simple weight trigger. A set of electronic scales is attached to the bomb. When there is a weight of more than one hundred pounds on top of it, that sets off the Semtex.' He threw his hands wide open. 'Boom.'

'Will you turn if off then?'

Ivan shrugged.

'You're a professional,' she persisted. 'If you just wanted to kill me, you would have done it from up in the tree.'

Ivan glanced at Matt, then held up a small radio transmitter used for controlling a toy car. He had picked it up at a toy shop on the drive down, and adjusted it so that it switched the electronic scales on and off. 'One flick of this switch, that's all it takes,' he said. 'Until then don't move.'

'What happened to Sallum?'

'We killed him,' answered Matt, his tone completely calm. 'He made his attack on the house, just as we knew he would as soon as we told you where we were. He was a good soldier. He did what any of us would have done if those were the orders. He attacked. We lived, he died.'

'But two bodies were found in the house,' Alison persisted. 'Who were they?'

'Sallum was one, the other was a man called Keith Whitson, an IRA stooge in London,' said Ivan.

'Five have probably got a file on him somewhere. Nasty fellow, with bad breath and rotten teeth.'

'We burned the bodies up so no one would recognise them,' added Matt. 'The police will figure out who they are eventually, but it buys us a few hours.'

He noticed the diamond. It was set in a simple gold chain, and hung around her neck, but it was definitely the same rock he had given her a week ago. A beam of light breaking through the trees hit the jewel, set it sparkling.

'What do you want?' she asked.

'Three of our friends died,' said Matt. 'They were good men, and they deserved better. We want to know what happened to them and why.'

Ivan held up the trigger, cradling it in the palm of his hand. 'And it had better be the truth,' he said. 'We've been eating lies, deceit and deception for the past few weeks, and we don't like the taste.'

Alison looked first at Ivan, then across at Matt. She was scrutinising his expression. She is trying to find out what I am thinking, he decided. To see what buttons she can press and what levers she has to pull within me to make me change my mind. All men are just puppets to her: marionettes waiting to have their strings pulled by soft words and sweet perfumes. She's just searching around for the right string.

It's not going to work.

'But you already know what the mission was about,' she said. 'Otherwise you wouldn't be here.'

'We want it from your lips,' said Matt. 'We like the sound of your voice. It will be something to remember you by.'

'Let's go and sit down somewhere,' said Alison. 'Then we can talk through the whole thing.'

Ivan laughed. 'We like you where you are right now. An inch away from death, just like we have been for the past week.'

There was a pause. Matt found himself wondering how Alison would play the next few minutes. He had seen men pleading for their lives before: in Bosnia, he had seen Serbian solders captured by Kosovan partisans who wept and begged and cried for their skins even though they knew they were just humiliating themselves before enemies who would show them no mercy. In the Philippines he had seen communist guerrillas squat in dignified silence mouthing silent prayers moments before their throats were about to be cut; and in Namibia he had seen robbers drinking pure alcohol to calm themselves on the morning of their hanging. But they had all been men who had been certain they faced death within a few minutes. This was a woman, and a smart one, who believed she still had a chance of saving herself. If only she could find the right string to tug on.

357

She looked towards Ivan and then Matt, her eyes suddenly angry. Her lips were curling into a sneer and her fists were clenched tightly together. 'You men are soldiers,' she snapped. 'What did you expect? I'll tell you what this mission was about, and if you don't like it, go ahead and blow me up. You're nothing but a pair of cowards. You don't mind taking the money, but you don't want to take any risks. Well, you should be smarter than that. Everything comes with a price, and the one demanded from you was completely fair.'

She paused, taking a gulp of air. 'I'll give it to you straight,' she said. 'We needed to strike back at al-Qaeda. The assassination of David Landau in Jeddah was one of the worst setbacks the intelligence services have suffered in years. Worse, we knew that al-Qaeda was gearing up for a spectacular in Britain. It's a tight, impenetrable network. We have moles all over the place, we have sleepers working their way up the organisation, we have men we've turned – all the old tactics we used to use against Ivan's old friends across the water. None of it was working. We were getting nowhere. That's when we came up with the plan.'

She hesitated, looking down at the ground, as if she were searching for the precise location of the bomb. 'You know what it was, of course,' she continued, her voice gaining in strength. 'We decided to stage a robbery. They are terrorists, and also Arabs. Honour is important to them. They would have to take revenge, and that would mean sending their best man after the robbers. If we leaked information about who they were, then watched them like hawks, eventually we would find the assassin. Keep tabs on the assassin, and he would lead us to the main man, the person who was pulling the strings right across Britain.' She allowed a brief smile to flicker across her lips. 'As it happened, it all worked out rather well. We got the main man. We've broken them – a lot more than the CIA have achieved in the past year.'

'And we were the hares,' said Matt angrily, 'to get the dogs running.'

Alison looked at him closely, her eyebrows drawing together. 'Don't sound so bloody hard done by,' she snapped. 'Think back a couple of weeks. You were nothing, a nobody, a washed-up ex-SAS soldier, drowning in a sea of debt and self-pity. In another couple of weeks, Kazanov would have killed you, and probably that girlfriend of yours as well.' She looked towards Ivan. 'As for you, you were just a corpse, walking around waiting for the bullet that kills you. An IRA man turned Five informer, who wanted out because he couldn't take the heat any more. Well, surely you know there aren't any resignations from that line of work? The only leaving party is the one where everyone wears black. You needed money, a lot of money, to get out and start again, and this was your only chance of getting it.'

Alison paused, wiping a bead of sweat away from her brow. 'I gave you both a chance. Sure, there was a risk you'd get killed. Boo-bloody-hoo. Go and wipe your tears on your mum's apron. You are soldiers, for

Christ's sake, or at least you were when you still had some pride left in you. You risked your life for your country. It's what you do.'

She paused for breath. 'Anyway, I knew you were both good enough that Sallum would never be able to lay a finger on you.'

'Soldiers sign up for missions – they take the risks knowing what they are doing,' said Matt, feeling his face redden with anger. 'Nobody deceives them about the risks they are running.'

'They don't?' replied Alison archly, raising her eyebrows. 'Christ, if I wanted to talk to children I would have gone to Legoland. Didn't some Rupert ever mislead you, Matt? Didn't some brigade commander ever send you on a futile mission, Ivan? This is war. Deceit is the most important weapon in any arsenal.' Alison tightened her scarf around her neck. 'All of the men on the mission needed money for different reasons. I gave them the chance to make it. Each man was taking a greater risk than they knew, I accept that. But each man also had a chance to defend himself.'

A thought started to rattle through Matt's mind: what if she is right? What if we were paid a fair rate for risking our lives? Isn't that what we do for a living?

'You told al-Qaeda where we were,' snapped Ivan. 'You betrayed us, and put our lives at risk.'

'As I said, you knew your lives were at risk,' said Alison.

Matt listened to her closely. Her tone was changing, the colour of each vowel turning brighter. She was growing more confident, as if she sensed she was winning the argument.

'Think about it,' she said. 'Three men died, true, but the two of you have survived, and countless innocent women and children have been saved.' Alison paused, her eyes switching from Ivan to Matt. 'If that bomb had gone off, thousands of people could have been killed or maimed. The economy of London would have been brought grinding to a halt. You men stopped that. You should be proud of yourselves.' She raised a finger into the air, suddenly resembling a schoolmistress admonishing a particularly dim class of children. 'And you are still getting five million each for your work. So, you took a risk, you saved thousands of people, and you got well paid for your trouble. What are you complaining about?'

Maybe she has a point, thought Matt. The only difference between what I did in the Regiment and what I did in the last two countries, was that I got properly paid for risking my life for my country.

Why not take the cash and walk away? Right now, I'm a free, wealthy man. Press this trigger, and I'm a fugitive for the rest of my life.

He glanced across at Ivan, but could see only an intense anger in the man's eyes: it was as if a fuse had been lit within him. 'Saving one person doesn't justify sacrificing another one. Who are we to make that choice? Who are you?' he said.

'Then what were you doing in the IRA, Ivan?' Alison snapped back. 'They made those choices all the time. What were you doing in the SAS, Matt?' She fixed both of them with a hard stare. 'Both of you already made the decision when you were a lot younger that lives were sometimes worth sacrificing for a cause. It's too late to go back now.'

'I don't need a philosophy lecture, thank you,' said Ivan. The muscles in his neck were bulging as the blood pumped to his head. He looked towards Matt, a question playing in his eyes. 'Let's give it to her and get out of here.'

Alison looked towards Matt, the fear creeping back into her eyes. She held out the diamond that was slung around her neck. 'Look,' she said softly. 'I had it set, and wore it. I've been wearing it every day since you gave it to me.'

Ivan held the trigger in his hand, his thumb poised on the button. 'Cut the violins,' he snapped. 'Press the button and go.'

In the middle of combat, a soldier trusts his instinct and only his instinct.

When there is no time to think with your head, you act with your heart.

Matt raised a hand. 'I say we let her go,' he said slowly. 'She has a point – we're soldiers, we get paid. Let's collect the cash and clear out of here.'

Matt noticed a smile starting to spread across Alison's lips – but it wasn't a smile of gratitude or relief. She was pleased, not to have survived, but to have won the argument. 'I always knew you were a man who could listen to reason, Matt,' she said. 'That's why I chose you.'

'Wait.'

Ivan lowered his hand, looking directly at her.

'What about Cooksley's kids?' Matt continued. 'And Reid's kids? They were just children, but you put them in the line of fire as well. How do you justify that?'

Alison shrugged, her expression suggesting that she was losing interest in the debate: her triumph had been secured, and now she had better things to do with her time. 'They were collateral damage,' she said coldly. 'I may have said this before, but I'll say it again. If you want to play softball then go to the park.'

Sometimes people say the wrong thing, thought Matt. And it costs them their lives.

'Collateral damage?' he said. 'No. They were just an innocent group of children.' He looked towards Ivan. 'I was wrong. Let's blow the fuse, and get out of here. The world will be a safer place without her.'

'Hold it,' she snapped.

'No! Enough!' Matt roared. 'Sometimes it is worth sacrificing one life for the good of everybody. Well, this time it's yours. Press the button, Ivan. Press it.'

'Please!' Alison shouted, her voice turning ragged. 'You have both made many mistakes, but the greatest one is to think me a fool.'

The wind had picked up speed, curling itself around the trees. Somewhere behind him, Matt could hear branches creaking in the gale. It was a dark and miserable place in which to die. But then, few have the luxury of choosing the places in which they die. Certainly not when it's an execution.

'Press it!' Matt snapped, glancing at Ivan.

Why doesn't the man blow her away?

'Because,' she said, 'only a fool would come here alone.'

Matt froze. The moment the words had escaped her lips, he'd known exactly what she'd meant by it. Inwardly, he started cursing himself. Naturally she would have some protection with her. A woman such as Alison made every calculation and checked every angle before she made a single move. She didn't make mistakes. That was what made her such a formidable opponent.

For half a second he resisted looking towards Ivan. He already knew what he would see, but wanted to delay the moment of confirmation. He saw it first in Alison's expression. A smile of smug satisfaction had spread on to her lips. Slowly he turned his head to the right. Pinky was standing a yard behind Ivan, a pistol in his outstretched hand, the barrel of the gun resting gently on Ivan's ear. Matt looked behind him: Perky was standing two yards behind, a gun lodged into the palm of his hand, pointing directly at his head. From that distance, it would be impossible for him to miss.

You had to hand it to them, they were good.

'Be very careful,' said Pinky, his voice so low it was barely more than a whisper. 'And hand me that trigger.'

The look of anger on Ivan's face intensified: the flame within him had just been turned up. For a brief second Matt wondered whether Ivan was about to blow

Chris Ryan

them all away. His hand dropped away, but his grip on the trigger remained just as tight.

'Give us that trigger right away,' said Perky, his voice booming around the woods. 'Or both of you die. Instantly.'

'Do it!' barked Alison. 'Give him the trigger.'

It's in the tone of her voice, noticed Matt. It doesn't matter what we do. We've threatened to kill her, and that's our death warrant signed, sealed and delivered. She doesn't need us wandering around the world somewhere, with time to plot and plan our revenge. She'll finish us now. If I were her, I'd do the same thing.

'Don't do it, Ivan,' he said.

Matt was surprised by how calm his own voice sounded. Maybe I have reached the point where I don't care any more.

The noose is already wrapped around my neck – I may as well tug at the chord myself.

'She's going to kill us anyway, whether we drop the trigger or not,' he continued, his tone getting harder as the sentence unfolded. 'Hell, if we're about to die, we might as well take her and these two bastards with us.' He chuckled. 'I always wanted the smell of Semtex in the air at my funeral anyway.'

Alison raised both hands, her eyes concentrating on Ivan. 'He's wrong,' she said calmly. 'Put the trigger down, take your money, and go wherever in the world. All debts are paid on both sides. You are free, wealthy men.'

'Don't listen to her,' Matt snapped. 'I've heard a

thousand different stories from her lips, and they've all been lies.'

Ivan looked first at Matt, then at Alison. Matt could see he was starting to hesitate.

'The mission was a success,' said Alison. 'Now, let's all pack up and go home.'

We've lost.

TWENTY-THREE

The trigger was still sitting in the palm of Ivan's hand, but his thumb had moved away from the button. A single bead of sweat was dripping down his forehead, past his temple and across his cheek. His mouth was turned down and there was a blank, empty expression on his face: as if, decided Matt, he was all out of tricks.

'I put this down, you'll let us both go, and we'll collect our money and get out of here,' Ivan said, looking directly at Alison. 'That's the deal, right?'

Alison nodded. 'I understand the anger of both of you,' she said calmly. 'But I don't resent it. Like I said, our work is finished and it's time to call all debts paid in full.'

Matt could feel a few drops of rain on his face. He glanced up into the sky. The clouds had grown darker now, obscuring the sun. 'Death has been swallowed up in victory. Where, O death, is your victory? Where, O death, is your sting?' he said, pronouncing the words slowly and deliberately. 'That's from Corinthians – although I suppose a good Catholic boy would already know that.' He turned to look at Ivan directly. Rain was spitting down from the clouds, lining his face with a thin film of water. 'Funeral psalms. Yours is coming up pretty soon, mate, if you do what she asks. I just thought I'd see what you'd like read out at the service.'

'Don't listen to him,' Alison snapped. 'He's lost it.'

The words passed across Ivan as if he hadn't heard them. 'There were five men when we started this mission, Matt,' he said slowly. 'Now there are only two of us. There's been enough killing. It's got to stop somewhere.' He tossed the trigger into the mud at his feet. 'In a few minutes you and I will be dead as well,' he said. 'It's not an acceptable casualty rate.'

Matt could see Alison flinch as the trigger settled into the mud: it was as if a thousand volts had been shot through her, and every nerve in her body had suddenly jumped. She stepped quickly forwards, moving away from where the bomb was buried. Behind him, Matt could see that Pinky was still holding his gun level with his head.

Alison rushed towards him.

'Do it!'

As the words spat out of her mouth a shot rang out, the noise of the bullet leaving the barrel echoing off the tree trunks all around them. Instinctively, Matt threw himself into the mud, shielding his face with his hands. He waited, counted to three, then realised the bullet had not been aimed at him. He looked up. Five yards ahead of him, Ivan was lying face-down in the dirt, his body crumpled up in agony. The bullet from Perky's gun had impacted just over his left ear, splitting open a wound on the side of his face. Blood was pouring out of him.

You fool. I told you not to trust her.

Matt reached out to grab the trigger device. It was four feet away, lying next to Ivan's fallen body. Alison was six feet to his right. His hand shot through the mud, his fingers stretching to collect the tiny bundle of plastic and wire. Only one thought was racing through his mind: to get to the trigger and to blow the Semtex. Take them all to hell.

Right now, that's the only place I feel like going.

His hand fell five inches short of the trigger, stopping in the pool of blood that was seeping from Ivan's head. He could see Alison moving swiftly towards him. Kicking with his legs, Matt thrust himself quickly forward. Another two inches . . .

That's all I need to destroy her.

He smashed his hand down towards the trigger. In the corner of his eye he could see the pale plastic sole of Alison's boot swinging delicately through the air. It caught his index finger, twisting it backwards, sending a sharp jab of pain down his arm. Matt flinched. Alison stamped hard, her boot forcing down the back of Matt's hand. His fist was pressed down into the dirt.

Looking down at him, her expression calm, Alison twisted her heel against the bones in Matt's hand.

He flinched as she bent down and picked up the trigger. She held it in her hand like a rare jewel, examining it with exaggerated care. 'Now, what was it you were saying, Matt?' she said, glancing down at where he lay in the mud. 'Something about how you thought Ivan should just finish me off?'

'Get on with it then,' said Matt, looking up towards Alison. 'You're a busy woman.'

At his side, Pinky jabbed a pistol into his chest. A snub-nosed German-made Walther P22 – the gun was instantly recognisable from the insignia stamped on the tip of its matt black barrel. Five yards behind him, Perky was standing with another Walther, this one aimed at Matt's head.

'I want to know where the money is,' said Alison.

Matt recognised the look on her face. A mixture of desire, passion and, yes, contempt – he had last seen it when they were in bed together in Bideford. He had failed to recognise it then, but he could see it clearly now. 'Get lost,' he spat.

'Tell me where the money is, or we shoot you right now,' she said.

'Stop threatening me,' said Matt, steadying his voice. 'I know you'll kill me anyway, whatever I do or say. We're all played out, Alison.'

She twisted her ankle again, grinding the sole of her boot into Matt's hand. The pain jolted through his arm and down into his spine. He took a deep breath, aware that he could endure whatever pain she might inflict on him in the next few minutes.

I have survived much worse in the past, and in a few minutes I shall be dead. This will all be over soon.

Matt attempted a smile, aware that with the pain shooting down his arm it probably came out more as a twisted grimace. 'You never give up, do you?'

He could see Alison raising her right foot, holding it

momentarily in the air, then stamping it down hard on his hand.

'Go fuck yourself,' he spat. 'I'm not telling you anything.'

'This is useless,' said Pinky, jabbing the gun harder into Matt's chest. 'I know these Regiment boys. It takes a long time to break them under torture. We'd need electricity, tongs, wires – the works.'

Alison nodded, glancing down at Matt. 'You hold him, I'll retrieve the money,' she said. 'It's got to be around here somewhere. Once we've found it, we'll finish him off.' She glanced downwards, meeting Matt's eyes. 'Anyway, it'll be useful to have a couple of holes in the ground. These two will be needing them.'

Escape, thought Matt – the word rattled through his brain. It was another lesson he had learned in the Regiment – a soldier who is still alive is a soldier who still has a chance of survival.

He watched as Alison paced about the clearing in the wood. She'd picked up a small spade from the bag Perky was guarding, and her eyes were rooted to the ground, examining it the way a doctor examines a patient, searching for any scratches or wounds in the surface. She knelt, picked up a piece of wet earth, and tossed it aside. She walked on a few more yards, stopping again, digging her fingers into the mud, turning it over.

Not there, thought Matt. You're not even warm.

The rain had picked up force now, and was spitting down into Matt's face. He could feel the water clinging to his hair and getting inside his clothes, dampening his whole body. The blood was still seeping from Ivan's head, the wound not yet staunched, and it was mixing with the rain, flowing away from his body. Matt could see some of it starting to seep into his jeans, staining them from blue to crimson.

'I'm going to enjoy the next few minutes,' said Pinky, grinning down into Matt's face. 'I always thought you were a difficult bastard.'

Matt could see Alison changing direction. She was walking towards one of the big oaks – not the biggest tree surrounding the clearing, but still a mammoth towering a hundred feet above them. She paused, examining the ground. There was a pile of leaves. Some were oak leaves, others were ash, all mixed together. The look on her face told Matt that she had seen something. If the ash leaves had fallen naturally they wouldn't be here; they would be a dozen yards away, at least. They were here only because someone had moved them. To hide something.

She's cracked it, thought Matt.

I can start reciting those psalms for myself.

Alison started scratching away at the pile, pushing the leaves aside roughly. She threw her hand into the mud. Matt could see her leaning over, then saw the spade chucking out piles of mud.

'It's here!' she shouted, her voice carried on the wind. 'I've found it!'

Another shot shattered the peace of the clearing, a single bullet cutting through the air.

'Don't!' shouted Alison from across the wood. 'I want to fire the bullet that kills him.'

Blood smeared across Pinky's face. Saliva drooled from his lips. His eyes bulged from his skull, his knees wobbled, and for a few brief seconds he tried to regain his balance. Then he fell forwards, his body crashing into Matt's chest. The wind was knocked out of him and it took half a second for him to recover his breath and to open his eyes to see what had happened. Pinky was lying flat across him, blood jetting from the back of his head like water from a tap. A hole, about the size of a penny coin, had been opened up – and it looked as if the bullet had travelled right through his brain, emerging just below his left eye, blowing open a square inch of his cheek.

Matt's first thought was a strange one: Whoever the hell fired that was a heck of a fine shot.

Using his forearms and summoning all his strength, Matt heaved Pinky's body directly on top of him. In the next few minutes, if he was any judge, there was going to be a lot more shooting. Pinky wasn't the best raw material for a shield: but right now, he was all Matt had available, and he would have to do.

The body was warm and sticky on top of him, a few final breaths still spluttering from his mouth as the last remnants of life ebbed away from him. The blood poured from his wound on to Matt, running over his neck. Matt closed his mouth tightly shut to make sure he didn't swallow any. There was some resistance in Pinky's arms, but the damage done to his brain stopped him from co-ordinating his movements.

Matt swivelled his eyes beneath Pinky's body. Five yards ahead of him he could see that Perky had thrown himself behind a tree, taking cover from the gunfire. His head and the barrel of his gun were just peeking out from behind the trunk, the pistol pointed in Matt's direction.

What the hell is going on?

Matt looked up. Alison had dropped two of the yellow canvas bags, and was running towards where Perky was stationed behind a tree. 'What the hell happened?' she shouted.

'How in the name of Christ should I know?' Matt heard Perky snap, his voice raw and ragged.

'Finish Browning now!' Alison shouted. 'Finish him!'

Matt could just see Perky, twenty yards away, holding the pistol in two hands, steadying himself and squinting to take aim. He rolled backwards, splashing into the blood and the mud. Using all his strength he held Pinky tightly to his body, making sure he covered every inch.

Two shots rang out. Perky stepped back with the gun's recoil. Pinky's body jumped as the first bullet slammed into his torso, and as the second sliced through his right leg.

If he wasn't dead already, he is now.

The clearing fell silent, and for a moment all Matt could do was smell the smoke of the bullets and feel the rain washing against his face. His hand inched forward, picking up the Walther that had fallen from Pinky's hand. Matt held it tightly checking the magazine. There were six bullets still inside. If he needed to, he could shoot both Alison and Perky three times.

He peered up carefully. From the shadows playing on the ground he could tell that both Perky and Alison were still stationed behind the tree, about twenty-five yards from where he was lying. They were whispering to each other, but the rain made it impossible to hear a single word. He glanced behind him. Thirty yards back there was a ridge in the ground, where the woods hit the fields. It was from somewhere behind there that the shot that had taken Pinky down had come from.

With Pinky's body as a shield, he started inching backwards toward the ridge. Progress was painfully slow. He had to shuffle an inch at a time, mainly using the strength of his stomach muscles, all the time dragging the corpse.

But if I can get behind that ridge, my chances of survival are going to dramatically improve.

Another bullet slammed into Pinky's body, making it jerk. Then another one. Matt buried himself tighter into the mud, the corpse above him. He could see both Alison and Perky leaning out from the tree, firing into him. It was impossible to raise his own gun to get a clear shot back at them without exposing himself to murderous fire.

Nothing to do but dig, shuffle and pray.

Two more shots rang out, then two more. This volley of fire came from behind the ridge. Splinters of bark split away from the trunk of the oak that hid Alison and Perky, and they disappeared behind it.

They're giving me covering fire, thought Matt. *Whoever they are, they are good men.*

He inched further backwards, straining every muscle to move another yard towards the ridge. I've got to get back there, he realised. Alison's going to be calling up reinforcements on her mobile. Another twenty minutes and we'll have a battalion of marines descending on us.

He heard another shot and a bullet flew past him, hitting the mud a couple of feet from where he was lying. A different direction this time – Perky had moved, and was hiding behind a tree ten yards to his right.

He's going to get behind me, Matt realised. Then he's got a clean shot, straight into my back. If I don't move quickly, I'm buggered.

'Give me cover!' he roared.

He stood up, his arm gripped tightly around Perky's chest. The corpse was heavy, at least two hundred pounds, and the lead that was filling up inside it was making it bulkier still. Matt stumbled backwards, struggling to hold his balance. From behind the ridge, a volley of shots rang out. Matt held his pistol in his right hand, firing four shots towards both Perky and Alison. The sound of gunfire filled the air, the noise of each shot bouncing off the trees, the echoes giving the impression of a hundred different guns being fired at the same time.

Matt waited until he had stumbled back to within five yards of the ridge. Then he dropped Pinky. He turned and ran, the adrenaline pumping furiously into his heart as his legs drove him forwards. Throwing himself into the air, Matt hurled himself at the ridge. His shoulder caught the edge of the mud, knocking him sideways. With a crash he fell into a pile of leaves and roots, his head smashing into the wood, which tore a cut down the side of his face.

'Remember Miss Christina?' said Damien. 'That French bird who used to take ballet class back at our nursery school? She always said you had rubbish co-ordination. I reckon she was right.'

Damien. He was wearing a black leather trenchcoat, the collar turned up around his neck, and he was holding a Czech-made VZ–52 rifle: a particularly rare but high-prized armament he had taken a liking to after being introduced to it by eastern European gangsters in London.

Next to him, Gill was holding a rifle. She was wearing a blue waxed jacket, high leather boots, and the rain had washed through her hair and was dripping over her face. She looked magnificent.

'You're meant to be dead,' said Matt.

'Out of fashion, maybe, mate. But not dead,' said Damien.

'And still getting you out of scrapes,' said Gill.

A volley of bullets flew past the ridge, and they all ducked. 'Our money's just down there,' said Matt.

He paused, peering above the line of earth. The rain was hitting him in the eyes, blown into his face by the wind, making it difficult to see anything. Alison was behind the same oak tree, Perky had moved to another one five yards away. There was a good chance that reinforcements were about to move in on them anytime. Fortune, Matt, decided, was about to favour the brave. This was a moment for maximum speed, maximum aggression.

'You know how to use that thing?' he said, looking towards Gill.

'Try me,' she replied.

Matt grinned. 'OK,' he said. 'Just give us plenty of covering fire. Damien, you take Alison, I'll deal with Perky. Gill, you pump as much ammunition as you can into the air. It doesn't matter if you hit them, it's just to keep them pinned back.'

His heart was beating furiously and the blood was pumping through his veins. He peered over the ridge. Their position had not changed.

He felt a momentary twinge of fear. My friend has just come back to me, he thought. So has my fiancée. And now I'm about to risk losing them again.

'Go!' he roared to both of them, bellowing above the wind and the rain.

Gill took up position behind the ridge. The rifle was gripped tight to her shoulder, a fresh magazine slotted into place, and five spare cartridges lay at her side. She pointed the weapon in the direction of Alison's tree and started firing. Then she turned it towards Perky, loosening off another round of bullets.

Matt tightened his grip on the Walther. There were just two rounds left in the magazine, and he knew he would have to make them count. It was maybe twenty-five yards to where Perky was standing. There was some cover from the trees, but he would have to move about ten yards across open ground.

An armed moving target is always difficult to hit.

Let's hope he's not a good shot.

Matt started to run. His feet were beating against the ground as he threw himself across the open space. The sound of gunfire rattled through his ears, but through the rain he couldn't tell where it was coming from. Gill was firing off round after round, so were Alison and Damien. Matt pushed forwards, keeping his head bowed: if a bullet did strike, it would be better to keep it away from the head or the chest where it would do most damage. He could see Perky loosening off a round, swerved, and managed to survive. He pressed forward five yards. The man was running now, switching from one tree to another. Matt hurled himself behind a tree trunk ten yards in front of him. A piece of bark splintering off the tree hit him in the face just below the eye, colliding with the wound that had already opened up on his face. The pain stung him hard, blurring his vision.

He paused, trying to recapture his breath. There was a silence. Perky had stopped shooting. Alison was steadying herself behind the tree that was covering her: even from this distance Matt could see she was reloading her weapon. Matt peered around the side of the tree. Perky was reloading the magazine on the Walther. From experience with that gun, Matt knew it would take between five and six seconds depending on how good he was.

Enough time for a man to die.

Matt jumped away from the tree, exposing himself on open ground. He held his gun straight out in front of him, lining the sight up with his eye. Perky looked up at him, a grin suddenly lighting up his face as he clicked the Walther's magazine into place.

Matt squeezed the trigger once, then twice, and cast the empty gun to the ground.

The first bullet hit Perky on the right shoulder, just above the heart. It sent him staggering backwards, twisting his shoulder and knocking the gun out of his hand. The second hit him straight in the chest, just below the heart, knocking him to the ground.

Matt ran forward, diving for the gun that had fallen from his grip. He jammed it into Perky's ear and pulled the trigger. The bullet lodged into his skull, killing him instantly.

'He's dead!' Matt shouted. 'Gill, turn your fire on Alison.'

He looked up into the woods. He could see that Alison was emerging from a tree forty yards away. Behind, Damien was descending on her position. Gill was crawling across the muddy ground to Matt's left, the rain lashing against her face. The gun was sitting between her forearm and her shoulder, her finger still poised on the trigger. A triangle was slowly being formed around Alison from which escape would be impossible.

Matt took Perky's Walther and ran across the woodland. He looked up ahead. Alison was clutching her shoulder, blood dripping down the side of her arm. Damien was standing next to her, the barrel of the VZ-52 pointing directly at her heart. Matt could see her gun lying on the ground at her side. Damien had shot it out of her hand by firing straight at her shoulder.

'Aren't you full of surprises?' said Matt, looking towards Gill and smiling. 'I didn't realise how much danger I was in when I cancelled the wedding.'

'You grow up in my family, you learn something about handling firearms,' she replied.

Matt stopped five yards short of where Alison was standing. 'March her back towards the pit,' he said, pointing to where Alison had been digging, and where the Semtex was still buried.

Damien tapped her on the shoulder with the VZ-52. She winced in pain. More blood was flowing now, staining her jacket. Matt could see the colour start to drain away from her face as the loss of blood took its toll. Over the past few weeks he had learnt to respect her strength, if not her honesty. He knew she would hang on to life like a crab to a stone.

Now Alison stood silently in the ditch. Matt could see her glancing down, wondering which of the bags contained the Semtex. He took the explosive's trigger and held it up in the air. Bending down, he gripped Ivan's shoulder, dragged him twenty yards through the mud, and left the body behind a tree.

Walking swiftly back to where Alison was standing,

he held up the trigger in front of her. 'Now, where were we before we got interrupted?' he said. 'I remember. I was about to blow you away.'

Matt detected a trace of fear in Alison's face, but mostly her expression was one of regret.

She minds because she is about to die – but she minds getting beaten more.

'You idiot,' she said, casting her eyes towards Gill. 'You don't know what you're doing.'

Gill shrugged. 'I'm the one holding the gun,' she answered. 'And I'm the only woman walking out of this wood alive. That doesn't make me so stupid.'

Alison laughed. 'You risk your life to save this pathetic washed-up squaddie,' she said, 'when for the past few weeks he's been screwing me every chance he gets. He doesn't care about you. All he wants is the money.'

The rain lashed harder against Matt's face. His hand gripped tighter on his pistol. He looked up into Gill's face. Maybe that was a tear running down her cheek, maybe it was the rain. He couldn't tell. But he could be certain of one thing – if she listened to Alison, the next few minutes could turn very nasty. Gill could control most things, but her temper was not among them.

The tip of Gill's rifle turned slowly away from Alison and towards Matt. Her finger was on the trigger; he could see the nail vibrating with rage. 'Is that true?' she said softly.

'This was about you all along, Gill, you know that,'

said Matt. 'I only got involved with this mission so that I could make enough money to clear my debts. Then we could be together again.'

'You sad little fool,' Alison sneered. 'You're sitting at home grieving over him, and he's screwing everything that moves.'

It's working, thought Matt.

She'll push Gill over the edge if I don't stop her soon.

'You know that photograph of you, the one in the bedroom in Spain?' said Alison. 'Right next to the picture of his first day in the Regiment? He even put that away.'

Matt could see Gill's finger hovering on her trigger. 'That's not true, is it, Matt?'

Blood was seeping from the wound on his face, trickling down his cheek and smearing on the edge of his lips. He spat on the ground. 'She's just trying to save her miserable skin,' he replied. 'I'd rather sleep with a rattlesnake.'

'I'm a dead woman, I know that,' Alison snapped. 'Either she kills me out of jealousy or you kill me for revenge.' She looked towards Gill, her eyes suddenly full of sympathy. 'I just think you should know the truth.'

'The truth is, everything she's saying is lies,' Damien said, stepping forward. 'Complete lies.'

Gill looked towards her brother.

'I've been with this man all through the mission – the training, everything,' Damien said. 'I tell you, nothing happened between them.'

Matt watched as Gill took in what Damien had said. He had known these two people since they were all children. She would always believe her brother. He glanced up towards Alison. She knew the end was approaching, and suddenly she appeared afraid.

In the end, courage abandons even the bravest of us.

Matt trained his gun on her. 'Everybody walk back ten paces,' he commanded.

He walked backwards through the mud, waiting until Gill and Damien were also a safe distance from the ditch. Then he looked up into Alison's eyes. 'I hope they need intelligence officers in heaven,' he said. 'Otherwise, they aren't going to let you in.'

'Don't do it, Matt!' she yelled. 'Please!'

Her voice turned into a scream, carried by the wind high up into the trees. Matt slammed his finger down on the trigger, moving quickly back another couple of paces. The explosion lit up the wood, sending shafts of bright light hurtling in every direction. Mud and smoke churned into the air, and somewhere in the middle of the carnage he thought he heard a cry that lasted no more than a fraction of a second.

The shockwave from the explosion rolled over him and he could hear the branches of the trees creaking and shaking. Then, within three seconds, the noise subsided and the wind started to blow away the smoke.

Matt took a few steps forward. The Semtex had blown a hole several feet in the ground. Alison had been torn in a hundred different pieces; strips of flesh were draped on the branches like ribbons, and her blood was already being washed into the roots of the trees by the rain.

Matt looked back towards Gill and Damien. 'Let's get our money and get out of here.'

There was a feeling of emptiness inside as he walked away. It was a familiar emotion, one he knew from every battlefield he had ever been on: a sense of loneliness that overcame him after each mission. You fought with your squadron alongside you, but every kill was your own responsibility. Nobody could share that with you.

Three weeks ago, I had been grateful to her for giving me another chance. Now I'm just as grateful that it's her who got blown to pieces, not me.

'What happened?' he said. 'We were all convinced you were dead.'

'That was the point,' said Damien. 'It was obvious that someone was following us. I reckoned I had a chance of surviving if he thought I was dead. So when I got sight of Sallum on my tail I pulled a switch – in a sauna in Manchester. I noticed a guy in there, a gangster called David. A small-time hit man. The world would be better off without him, I reckoned. I went upstairs with Sallum, then slipped out, told David there was a guy waiting for him, a real babe. Off he went. It's pitch black in those rooms, so he wouldn't notice it wasn't me.'

'He had your credit cards, the works,' said Matt. 'One came with a hand, flying through the window.'

'That was the clever bit,' said Damien. 'As Dave went off, I checked the locker number on his key ring. Number twelve. I went downstairs to the bloke on the desk, told him I'd lost my key, slipped him a twenty-quid tip, and got the spare key from him. Downstairs, I switched my stuff into Dave's locker, dressed in his gear – which looked bloody terrible, by the way.'

'And you just took off?' said Matt.

'Right,' answered Damien. 'I've just been lying low for the last week. I contacted Gill a couple of days ago to let her know I was OK. And I came along today because I didn't know where you were and this was when we scheduled the collection. If I'd have known I was running into this kind of trouble I'd have come along mob handed.'

Matt looked towards Gill. 'Thanks for coming to get me. I was a dead man until you two showed up.'

Gill slipped her hand into his. 'A girl doesn't want to be left on the shelf, you know,' she replied, a smile spreading across her lips.

Matt collected two bags from where they were stashed, tucking them under his arm. Damien took another two, and Gill one. Ten yards away they heard a low moan, and Gill ran back to where they had dragged Ivan. 'He's alive,' she called out. 'He's coming around.' She tore a strip of her shirt to start bandaging up the wound on his head. 'We must get him to a hospital.'

'We were wrong about Ivan,' Matt said, looking across at Damien. 'We were wrong about a lot of things.'

Damien started to shovel some earth over Alison's scattered remains, each clump of mud starting to obscure a different part of her body. Matt took up his own spade, shovelling furiously: the sight of Alison's splintered body disturbed him, and he didn't want to have to look at it for a moment more than necessary. The cut on his face was stinging viciously, but the work felt good. Like taking a run: hard physical activity always soothed him.

'Reid and Cooksley died on this mission,' Matt said, looking up at Damien. 'Their families are all dead, so there's no one to give the money to. I think we should bury their money.'

'You're having a laugh, right?' Damien exclaimed. 'Toss four million quid into the ground? That bump on the head must be worse than it looks.'

'No,' said Matt. 'I'm serious.'

Damien paused. 'You really mean to toss the money away?'

'If there is one thing I've learnt in the past couple of weeks it's that greed does funny things to a man's head,' said Matt slowly. 'Within a few days it made monsters out of all of us. I don't want any more than my fair share.'

Damien picked up one bag and tossed it into the ditch, then another. 'We'll keep one for Ivan,' he said. 'If he pulls through, it's his. If not, we'll look for his family, and give it to them. If not . . . well, let's see.' He laughed, watching the second of the two bags hit the ground, then tossed another shovelful of dirt on top of it. 'Christ, one day I'm going to be broke, I know it. And I'm really going to regret doing this.'

Matt grinned. 'You've got two million, how quickly can you spend that?'

Damien wiped sweat from his brow and collected some leaves to pile on top of the freshly dug earth. 'Do you think that will be discovered?' said Damien.

'I reckon Five will think she ran off with the money herself,' said Matt. He hauled his bag on to his back and started walking into the wind and the rain. 'Some stray dog might come across it one day. But we'll be long gone by then. Leading a new life, and who knows, maybe even a better one.'

EPILOGUE

A mellow sunset was resting on the horizon, sending a pale orange light across the Mediterranean. Matt sat back on his chair, a bottle of San Miguel on the table. But it was the atmosphere and the view he was enjoying, not the beer. Somewhere in the distance, he could hear the sound of the early-evening crowd piling into the Last Trumpet. The usual mixture of villains, retired car dealers and stray tourists, the noise of their conversation swept across the verandah like the waves sweeping across the rocks in the bay below.

They were an odd bunch of people, with hardly a single redeeming feature between the whole pack of them. Still, they were Matt's customers.

I better get used to them.

He took a swig of beer, letting the alcohol relax him. It was six months since he'd bought Kazanov out of his share of the restaurant and become its sole owner. Gill was living with him here now, and the marriage was set for the new year. They were going to go back to London to do it at St Giles in Camberwell Church Street – bridesmaids, morning suits, Damien as the best man, the full works. Those were the only terms on which Gill had agreed to forgive him. That woman is a sad loss to the banking industry, he reflected. She knows how to make a man pay out on his debts. With interest.

'Look at this,' cried Gill.

She walked out of the back of the restaurant towards the private patio where they often had a drink together. Fifty yards towards the bay he could see the villa that was being built for them. It was taking a fair chunk out of the money he had made from the mission, but his debts were all paid, it had been a good summer for the restaurant, and property overlooking the sea was always a good investment.

We need somewhere to start our married life together, and it might as well be somewhere nice. It isn't as if I haven't got the scars to prove that I earned it.

'In the paper,' Gill said, leaning across the table and pointing.

Matt could smell the mixture of perfume and soap on her skin: a familiar scent that always reminded him of how much he loved her. He glanced down at the copy of the *Daily Telegraph*, two days old, and judging from the smell of beer and tobacco clinging to its pages, picked up from the bar. The story was on page four, below the fold. 'Mystery over buried millions,' ran the two-deck headline.

'The body of a woman together with several million pounds in used bank notes was discovered yesterday morning in woodlands near Ashford in Kent.

'The remains were found by a man walking his dog. The woman, who has not yet been identified by local police, had been killed by an explosion believed to have taken place some months ago.

'The bodies of two other men, also unidentified, were found buried within a few yards of the original discovery.

'Two bags were discovered buried with the woman. Each one contained in excess of one million pounds in used bank notes. Local police have not yet disclosed exactly how much money was found at the scene.

'Jack Turner, the local resident who discovered the body, said, "It was an amazing amount of cash. Dollars, pounds, and euros, and some others. I've never seen anything like it."

'The bodies are believed to have been buried for six to eight months.

'Police said they suspected the killings were the result of a gangland operation or money-laundering scheme that had gone wrong. A spokesman for the Kent police admitted it was highly unusual for money to be buried alongside the body of a murder victim. "We're a bit puzzled by that aspect of it," he said. "We are actively trying to trace the source of the money to see if it will give us any clues as to who these people were, and how the money got there."'

Matt laughed, looking up towards Gill. 'I tell you what, I don't think they'll be trying very hard to solve that case,' he said. 'Someone from Thames House has probably given them a call to tell them they have more important things to do with their time.'

'You don't think they'll come after you?'

'If they were going to do that they would have done it by now,' Matt answered. 'It was a black operation from start to finish. All off the books. If they brought me in it would create too many problems.'

'And Ivan never went after the money?' Gill asked.

Matt shook his head. 'Damien went to see him a few weeks ago. He's with his family, relaxing and recuperating. The wound to his head was a bad one, apparently. It took out a few slivers of brain, so the doctors said, but he had plenty to start with, so I don't suppose he'll miss it that much. Damien gave him his two million, and told him we'd buried the rest of it in the ground.'

Gill wrapped her arms around his shoulders, her lips playing with the back of his ear. 'We don't have to worry about that any more, and I'm grateful for that,' she said. 'We have a restaurant that's thriving, a new house that is nearly finished, and we're getting married in a few months' time. We have no worries in the world. I've never been happier.'

Matt paused. His eyes were dwelling on the City pages of the papers, some calculations running through his head. 'I don't know,' he said, his finger jabbing at a pair of different prices. 'I haven't checked for a few days – I didn't realise quite how terribly my portfolio was doing.'

He looked back towards Gill. 'Still, don't worry. I'm never going on another mission, no matter what happens. I'm staying right here with you.'

THE POWER OF READING

Visit the Random House website and get connected with information on all our books and authors

EXTRACTS from our recently published books and selected backlist titles

COMPETITIONS AND PRIZE DRAWS Win signed books, audiobooks and more

AUTHOR EVENTS Find out which of our authors are on tour and where you can meet them

LATEST NEWS on bestsellers, awards and new publications

MINISITES with exclusive special features dedicated to our authors and their titles

READING GROUPS Reading guides, special features and all the information you need for your reading group

LISTEN to extracts from the latest audiobook publications

WATCH video clips of interviews and readings with our authors

RANDOM HOUSE INFORMATION including advice for writers, job vacancies and all your general queries answered

Come home to Random House

www.rbooks.co.uk